Praise for *Too Hard Wrong Spot*

"Hysterical."
　　—Vic "Each Way" Rizzuto, professional punter

"Terrific debut."
　　—Dave Turner, musicologist

"I'm still laughing."
　　—Bobby Bombolone, bookmaker

"Surely, there will be a sequel."
　　—Art Deco, top bloke

"Gary Delaney is my kind of man."
　　—Anita Hardone, adult entertainer

The first in the Gary Delaney series

Too Hard Wrong Spot

Available by emailing Martymelbourne@gmail.com
or through Forty South Publishing at fortysouth.com.au

GREAT BARRIER GRIEF

GREAT BARRIER GRIEF

Marty Shevelove

Published by
Forty South Publishing Pty Ltd
Hobart, Tasmania
fortysouth.com.au

Printed by
IngramSpark

Cover images
Alamy Stock Vectors

About the author

Following the success of his debut novel, *Too Hard Wrong Spot*, former journalist Marty Shevelove followed through on his promise to leave Melbourne's cold winters and relocated to warm and sunny Far North Queensland where *Great Barrier Grief* was written. He hosts a radio show called Rock 'n Rant  on Cairns FM 89.1 two afternoons a week and spends his free time dodging crocodiles, curlews and wallabies, and yelling at neighbours with leaf blowers.

The author can be reached via email: Martymelbourne@gmail.com

1

"WHAT DO YOU MEAN THE PAPER IS SHUTTING DOWN? I just got here," Gary Delaney shouted at *Turf News* editor Bob Nicholls. Expecting a spray, Nicholls had closed the door to his office after Delaney arrived for the hastily called 10am Tuesday meeting.

"I've been here all of sixteen months for goodness sake. I've taken shits that have lasted longer."

"Let me explain Gary, please," Nicholls said. "Take a seat."

The racing paper's senior writer and sub-editor plopped his frame into one of the two leather chairs facing Nicholls' desk, took off his glasses, rubbed his brow and placed them back on his nose.

"You've got the floor Bob."

Nicholls, 54, was two years younger than Delaney but had aged about 10 years in the last six weeks. That's when the Crockett brothers, Walt and Forrest, the owners of *Turf News*, first told Nicholls about their money problems. Nicholls began to lose his hair, stopped eating and developed a rash which covered half his body. The $5 million Golden Slipper – the richest turf race for two-year-olds in the world – now lasted longer than one of his infrequent erections.

The twice-weekly racing paper/form guide was haemorrhaging money at an alarming rate. The Crocketts had a six-figure loan payment due at the end of February – two weeks away – and their shifty accountants – Rabinowitz, Rabinowitz and Glickstein – were busy going over the publication's books to find the money to cover the payment. The three wise men were not finding enough.

Money from the Crocketts' once lucrative breeding operation – which had kept *Turf News* afloat – had stopped coming in and Walt and Forrest were not about to mortgage their fancy Port Melbourne homes and take their kids out of private schools to keep the paper afloat.

"You know the stallion Appalachian Trail?" Nicholls asked. Delaney nodded.

"Our owners, the Crockett brothers, were getting $85,000 a pop every time he serviced a mare. Most seasons he would hump about 200 which put roughly $1.7 million into their coffers."

"The Crocketts own Schtup Farms?"

This time it was Nicholls who nodded.

"Shit," Delaney said.

Delaney had written the story about Appalachian Trail getting spooked by lightning in his paddock and running into a fence. His injuries were so bad, the 10-year-old money maker had to be put down the very next day. The valuable stallion was insured but the payment was not even close to what the Crocketts owed.

"Don't tell me Lifeboat is one of theirs too?"

Again, Nicholls nodded.

Delaney had subbed the story written by *Turf News* reporter Adam Swoboda and knew all about the stallion.

The six-year-old had won eight Group 1s in Australia – from 1400 metres up to a mile and a half – by the time he was retired to stud. The Crocketts were asking and getting $75,000 for each coupling.

However, not one mare he serviced in his first season came into foal. Lifeboat was sterile.

"How the fuck could he be sterile?" Delaney asked Swoboda when he read the yarn. "He's got a dick longer than my arm for fuck's sake."

So, with one stallion buried under a large gum tree and the other now basically a gelding, the Crocketts were fucked.

"They're losing their farm," Nicholls said in a sombre voice.

"And I'm losing my job. Fuck me. And the others?"

"Well, it is not all bad news Gary. The Crocketts want to keep our website up. Two reporters, Swoboda and Greg Grote, are staying, plus one photographer and two from the IT team. One of them will put together the form guide and the other will keep the site up and running. If we sell enough subscriptions to those who read the paper, we'll break even."

"And what sort of coin am I looking at Bob? What do I get as a redundancy payout?"

"The Crocketts have said they'll give you a quarter of your yearly salary Gary – $21,250. You've got to admit, it's a very generous offer. Add in your leave, sick pay and it will come close to $25,000. All tax free."

"It's fair," Delaney said. "But, I'm 56, nearly 57. My chances of getting another job in the business are slim and none, which are the same odds the TAB is offering on a Buttigieg presidency."

"Who?"

"Mayor Pete, the gay bloke running for president in the US. And don't ask me how to spell his name, he can't even spell it."

"I really am sorry Gary. We had a good thing going here."

"We sure did. How many more editions are we printing?"

"Five. The one this Friday and then the usual two the next two weeks after that."

"You get to keep your job Bob?"

"On half my wage. Like you, I've been a newspaperman my whole life. What else am I going to do? And Gary, not a word to anyone until I make a formal announcement later in the day. Okay?"

"Okay."

Delaney shook hands with Nicholls and slowly walked back to his desk. He slumped in his chair, turned it around so he faced the MCG and pondered his future. It was not looking bright.

2

WELL, IT'S A HELL OF A START TO THE NEW YEAR, Delaney thought on his way home on the crowded 5:24pm Frankston line train which surprisingly left Flinders St station in the heart of Melbourne's CBD on time. *First Michelle walks out, and now this.*

Michelle Harris, 53, Delaney's partner the past four years, moved out of the couple's rented Ormond apartment a week after a disastrous New Year's Eve party at an upscale three-bedroom, two-bathroom duplex on the banks of Yarra River owned by Big John McGraw, the head of City Winners Syndication and majority owner of Melbourne Cup placegetter Too Hard Wrong Spot. Delaney owned a five percent share in the six-year-old chestnut gelding and had more than quadrupled his $15,000 investment in the 14 months since joining McGraw's group.

The year before, much to the shock of everyone, Too Hard Wrong Spot was a late Cup scratching when he refused to be loaded into the Flemington starting gate.

The balcony of McGraw's luxury home was a prime viewing spot for Melbourne's multi-million-dollar midnight fireworks show. Fifteen minutes before the first shell was fired, Too Hard Wrong Spot's Melbourne Cup run seven weeks earlier was shown on a half-dozen big screen televisions scattered about the massive apartment.

The big crowd, almost all of whom were part of McGraw's large syndicate, let out a collective groan when Too Hard Wrong Spot was impeded in the final 200 metres by the second-place finisher which cost him the race.

Too Hard Wrong Spot was eventually placed second by the Flemington stewards, who disqualified Irish bred No Interest No Deposit and placed him fourth. City Winners Syndication received the second-placed prize of $1.1 million and not the $4.4 million winner's cheque, which went to the Hong Kong-based owners of Midnight Run.

Close to $45,000 was deposited into Delaney's bank account two weeks after the 3200m race which pissed off half the nation.

"The jockey didn't file an objection. The trainer didn't say a damn thing. How the fuck could the stewards object? Those fuckers cost me thousands," was the common thread.

Those on the other side of the fence, including professional punter Vic "Each Way" Rizzuto, had nothing but praise for the Flemington suits as he counted his winnings. "They saw something and did what they're supposed to do. Good on 'em. I love dem guys."

It wasn't the first time Too Hard Wrong Spot had run into trouble. Six months earlier in the Sydney Cup at Royal Randwick he was hampered by a loose horse which had thrown its jockey and kept running.

Too Hard's jockey, Damien Smithton, had to change course twice in the stretch to avoid the loose horse and once again finished second.

"I'm beginning to think we are jinxed," McGraw told his well-lubricated guests after the tapes of both cups were shown. "But, those two races put $1.5 million into our kitty and we're expecting a couple of wins from him in the autumn and again next spring."

Delaney treated Michelle to a Christmas holiday in Hawaii with his share of the Melbourne Cup prize money where they ran into Australian PM Morris Scott on Waikiki Beach.

"Shit, that's really him. Parts of New South Wales, SA, Victoria and Queensland are burning, and he takes a holiday? He should be back home," Michelle said. Delaney agreed. Both were amazed at the lack of security around the casually dressed PM and his wife, who were sipping coffees at an outdoor table.

"Do you think his security people would come out of wherever they're hiding and cuff us if we went up to him and told him what a shitty job he's doing?" Michelle asked.

"We? You're on your own hun. They'd take you in and by nightfall Hutton would ship you off to Christmas Island," Delaney quipped.

After six nights in Hawaii, Delaney and Michelle returned home in time for McGraw's New Year's Eve bash. There were additional fireworks well after midnight when Michelle caught Delaney fondling a young lovely's massive boobs.

His excuse of having one drink too many and being teased by the provocative filled-to-capacity, low-cut tops worn by many of the female guests did not go over well. Michelle stormed out of McGraw's apartment, took a cab home and tossed Delaney's pyjamas and pillow on the living room couch.

The young lovely in question, 22-year-old Jill Duggan, didn't mind having a man's hands on her full 36DD boobs, even if that man was more than thirty years her senior. If a forensics exam had been conducted on Miss Duggan's natural wonders an hour after midnight, Delaney's finger and palm prints would have been found on every square inch of them. Not to mention her barely covered arse which many chose to gaze at instead of the pyrotechnics.

"I'm serious Gary, don't come in," Michelle yelled when Delaney arrived home and opened their bedroom door at nearly 2am.

"Can't we talk about this honey?"

"Not tonight. Leave me alone, okay?"

He did as she asked and when they talked the next afternoon Michelle made it clear that their relationship was over.

"Don't I get a second chance? It was a one-off Michelle, I swear."

Michelle looked straight into Delaney's eyes.

"I want to believe you Gary, but I can't. I'm moving out next Saturday. For the next week you're sleeping on the couch."

"Don't make any hasty decisions Michelle. Take a few days to think it over."

"I don't need a few days. My mind is made up Gary. I can't trust you. There is nothing to think over. Let me put it in terms you'll understand. The result stands."

"Can I file an objection?"

"No. Correct weight has been called."

Over the next eight days, the two barely exchanged a word. Each went back to work, Delaney to *Turf News* and Michelle to her admin job at the National Gallery on St Kilda Rd. At night Michelle packed her things in the bedroom while Delaney sat in front of the TV which he never even turned on.

The following Saturday morning a muscle-bound friend of Michelle's, a much younger work colleague of hers named Jordan, showed up at their apartment. A rented moving van was parked out front. Jordan easily carried a dozen boxes, several flowerpots from the backyard, then the bed, the fridge, and lastly the couch Delaney had been sleeping on to the van.

Jordan waited outside while Delaney and Michelle exchanged a few words, embraced and said goodbye.

"I really am sorry Michelle."

"Me too Gary, me too. Take care of yourself."

Michelle didn't look back as she closed the front door behind her for the last time.

Delaney wiped a tear from his eye, walked to the window, parted the curtains and looked towards the street. Michelle was in the passenger seat of the rental truck, her head in her hands, crying. Jordan gave her a few tissues, hugged her – just a friendly sort of hug Delaney thought – started up the truck and drove off.

Delaney backed away from the window, looked at the near-empty apartment, sat down in his favourite chair and closed his eyes for a few moments.

"Looks like I've got some shopping to do," he said. "A bed, couch, fridge, linen." He tried to convince himself that things weren't as dire as they looked. "I've got some money in the bank, a job, friends, a damn good horse. I'll be alright."

He rang his mate Chris Simmons.

"How'd you like to come shopping with me? I could use the company."

"I thought you'd be at Caulfield today," Simmons said.

"Me too. But something has come up. I'll swing by in about 30 minutes."

There was a pause.

"Where are we going?

"To Fantastic Furniture and Harvey Norman. I'll explain on the way."

3

THE DAY AFTER THE FINAL PRINT EDITION OF *TURF News* rolled off the presses, a quiet afternoon gathering in its Southbank office marked its passing.

"We had a great run, nearly 50 years," Bob Nicholls told the staff. "May our online presence last just as long."

He reminded those who were leaving that they would get their full entitlements. Among those not asked to join the digital team was editorial assistant Wendy Seaver, who was so helpful to Delaney when he joined the staff 16 months ago. They reminisced over a glass of wine and nibbles and talked about their futures.

"I heard you and your girlfriend parted ways. Sorry to hear that Gary."

"Thanks Wendy. It's been a tough couple of months. Not that it matters but who told you?"

"Swoboda."

"One of these days his big mouth is going to get him into trouble. But guys like him always seem to land on their feet. He stays and we go. Fifty years of experience out the door."

"I'd like to say it's their loss, but we're the losers. I don't like the idea of starting over at the age of 45," Seaver said. "And the thought of applying for Newstart to tide me over is not something I am looking forward to."

"I hadn't even thought of Newstart," Delaney said. "I'll look into it. Eleven hundred plus dollars a month would help. I can't access my super until I am 60. Without Newstart it would be all one-way traffic out of my bank account."

"What do you say we get out of here Gary? I cannot stand being here another minute. It is just too damn depressing."

"I'm with you. Let's say our goodbyes, wish the few staying good luck, and go drown our sorrows."

The pair wound up at one of the many restaurant/bars lining the Yarra River which as usual was the colour of mud. It was barely 4pm, so they were able to snare an outside table. In an hour the place would be overrun with cashed-up twenty and thirtysomethings celebrating the end of another working week. A warm breeze gently tousled Wendy's shoulder-length blonde hair.

Delaney had rarely given Wendy a second look in the sixteen months he worked with her. And why would he have? He was in a happy, long-term relationship with Michelle. They sat on opposite sides of the newsroom, so their paths rarely crossed. And when they did their conversation always revolved around ad placements and the form guide. He didn't even know if she was married or if she had kids. There was a wedding ring on her finger but lots of single women wore wedding rings to keep from constantly being harassed by overeager men.

Now sitting across from her, he realised just how attractive she was. She wore little make-up, had a nice smile and her blue eyes sparkled in the late summer sunshine.

They split a bottle of red, talked about their lives outside of work – she was divorced with two high school-aged boys who were spending this weekend with their dad; an executive in the marketing department of Channel 8 and Triple A radio.

Delaney was not that big of a drinker and was glad he had a big lunch earlier in the afternoon. The last time he had half a bottle of wine on an empty stomach he tried to hijack an elevator and fly it to Cuba. "I want to see Fidel," he told the dozen people in the elevator. When a bloke mentioned that Fidel Castro had been dead for several years, Delaney vowed to start watching more of the ABC and less of Channel 78 (racing. com). Then he passed out.

Delaney ordered a soft drink to dilute some of the wine in his system and when Wendy excused herself to go to the ladies, he started to daydream about what it would be like to have Wendy sharing his relatively new bed. Two months of sleeping alone after four years of snuggling up to someone every night was beginning to wear thin.

"Penny for your thoughts Gary," she said on returning which snapped him back to reality.

"You might not want to know."

"Tell me. Let me be the judge," she said with a smile as she sat down.

"Well ... how can I put this?"

"Just say it Gary. We're both adults."

What's the worst that can happen? Delaney thought. *She stands up, says something like 'I thought you were different', storms off and leaves me with the bill.*

"I was thinking about how nice it would be to go to bed with you."

"Sorry Gary, I don't sleep with men who are unemployed and about to go on Newstart. I've got standards, you know."

Delaney was taken aback by her straightforwardness until he realised she was kidding.

"Buy me dinner and I just might. And, order us another bottle."

"Beer goggles?"

"Nah, you're not that bad," she said with a wink.

So, before you could say Benedict Cumberbatch, the newest additions to Australia's unemployment roll were in a taxi headed to Delaney's modest apartment.

"Were you robbed?" Wendy asked when Delaney opened the front door to the sparsely furnished one-bedroom rental.

"I guess you could say that. Michelle took most of the stuff. I'm slowly replacing everything."

"You have a bed, don't you? I'm not doing it on the floorboards."

Our charming host steered Wendy to the bedroom where a new double bed sat in the middle of the large room.

"How about a coffee?' Delaney asked. "We can sit on the couch. You'll be the first other than me to plant his butt on it.

"Aren't you the popular one," Michelle quipped.

Delaney laughed, made the coffees – instant was all he had – put them on a tray with some milk and sugar, and placed it on the new coffee table – $129 from Fantastic Furniture.

"Help yourself," he said.

Ten minutes later they were helping themselves to each other. In less time that it took to boil an egg, Delaney had run his race.

Wendy noted that if she had been putting together the comments for the form guide, it would read 'pulled up short of the winning post, needs a vet certificate before next start'.

"I've never been with anyone who couldn't finish Gary. You have any medical issues?"

"Not that I know of. I'm sorry Wendy. Damn, I guess I'm starting to show my age."

"We'll give it another go later if you're keen," Wendy said.

"Oh, I'm keen. Very keen."

Sometime in the middle of the night, Wendy climbed aboard her former colleague and rode him hands and heels to the line.

"Much, much better," Wendy said. She kissed him and he nodded off. *He needs to start taking afternoon naps, and do something about that snoring,* Wendy thought.

When Delaney woke the next morning, Wendy was gone. He checked his phone. There was a text message. *Thanks for a nice evening Gary. It was fun but just a one-off. Good luck at Centrelink.*

On the way to her taxi, Wendy nearly collided with Michelle on the pathway leading to Delaney's apartment. Michelle had a couple of coffees with her and a small bag from Bakers Delight. She had heard that *Turf News* had published its last issue and was popping by to see if her former partner was all right.

"Who are you?" she asked Wendy.

"Up until yesterday I used to work with Gary. And you are?"

"Michelle Harris, his former girlfriend. Did you spend the night here?"

"What's it to you? From what I hear, you broke up with him."

"After I caught him fucking around with some woman young enough to be his granddaughter. Were you fucking Gary when I was still living with him?"

"Relax hun, tonight was the first time."

Before Wendy could add "and the last", Michelle started banging on the front door of Delaney's apartment.

"Hold on, hold on. I'm coming."

Delaney opened the front door and was shocked to see Michelle standing in front of him. Wendy was at the curb getting into a cab.

"Were you fucking her when we were together?" Michelle screamed, pointing at Wendy.

"No. No. What are you doing here anyways?"

"I brought you a coffee and some breakfast you fucking arsehole."

Michelle took a cinnamon bun out of the Bakers Delight bag and squished it in Delaney's face.

Then she threw both coffees at him. Delaney ducked – much like George W Bush did that time in Iraq to avoid a pair of thrown shoes – and watched the coffees splatter on the living room floor.

"I hate you Gary, I hate you," she screamed.

The commotion brought a few of Delaney's neighbours to their front doors. "What's going on?" one of them asked.

"It's nothing really. Go back inside your homes. There's nothing to see here," he said waving his arms.

"Nothing? Nothing? I was the best thing that ever happened to you." She picked up that morning's rolled-up newspaper in front of Delaney's door and started to belt him with it. "Go to hell," Michelle screamed. She turned on her heels, walked to her car and sped off.

Shaken, Delaney closed his front door, locked it and slumped into his well-worn chair. "What in the wide, wide world of sports is going on? It's not even 9 o'clock."

Over the next few days, Delaney was half-expecting Jordan, or another of Michelle's friends, to stop by and pick up where she left off. He laid low for a while. He took early morning walks around the neighbourhood, wearing a different ballcap and sunnies each day to conceal his face, and made quick dashes to *Woolies* to pick up supplies. Even though he had the paper delivered each day, he bought the same one at Woolies and left the delivered ones outside. *If anyone comes by looking for me, they'll think I've gone away,* Delaney thought. *Maybe I should have gotten out of town for a while.*

Delaney stayed away from the local TAB and the race meetings at Caulfield, Flemington and Sandown for the next two weeks.

"I guess I'm in the clear," he said after the two weeks passed without a word from Michelle or any unannounced visits by Jordan.

4

LIKE AN OLD PENSIONER, DELANEY NEEDED TO SAVE every dollar he could. Unlike an old pensioner, he walked up to five kilometres each morning to keep fit and breathed a sigh of relief when his redundancy payment of $25,012 landed in his account.

If he budgeted just right, the $25k would get him through the rest of the year. His outgoings included rent, utilities, car insurance, rego, medication, private health insurance and about $175 a month to City Winners Syndicate for Too Hard Wrong Spot's upkeep.

Big John McCraw and trainer Jack McCarron had put Too Hard in cotton wool after his run in the Melbourne Cup and pencilled in the $4 million Queen Elizabeth over 2000m at Royal Randwick in April as his Autumn grand final. It was bit short of his best distance, but the race was worth far more than anything else that autumn. The Sydney Cup was run over the more suitable distance of two miles, but it was worth only $1.5 million. "We need to go after the big money," McGraw said in over-ruling McCarron, who preferred to have another crack at the Sydney Cup.

On the first Tuesday in March, Delaney went to his local Centrelink office to enquire about the Newstart allowance. *Better to speak to someone in person than waiting on the phone for an hour.*

"Your call is very important to us, please hold for the next available customer service representative."

"If my call is so fucking important to them why am I waiting an hour on the phone listening to some godawful music played on a fucking $50 Casio keyboard?" Delaney screamed the first time he called and waited and waited and waited.

When he arrived at Centrelink it took just 10 minutes until his name was called. He was ushered to a desk by a very pleasant middle-aged woman.

"You're wondering if you are eligible for Newstart. Is that correct Mr Delaney?" Valerie O'Donnell asked.

"It is."

Delaney told Mrs O'Donnell about his recent redundancy and how he had no income other than a five percent share of prize money won by a racehorse he partially owned.

"What's the horse's name?" Mrs O'Donnell asked.

"Too Hard Wrong Spot. He ran second in the Melbourne Cup a few months ago."

"Interesting name," she said.

"People don't forget it, that's for sure."

"You've brought your bank details with you?"

"Sure have." Delaney handed his statements over.

Mrs O'Donnell turned, put on her reading glasses, faced her computer and started typing away.

As she punched in Delaney's details – including the word zero in the line for monthly income – Delaney had a look around. Just about every bloke in the office waiting to be helped – and several women – were wearing trackie dacks.

Since when did trackie dacks become acceptable outdoor apparel? Delaney wondered. *For fuck's sake, put on a pair of trousers and a shirt with a collar. And what's with all the tattoos? Was there a massive jailbreak or is the sixth fleet in town?*

A lone unarmed rather non-threatening security guard stood off to the side and watched the riff-raff come and go. If trouble ever broke out, he'd need some help, a lot of help.

"Do you have a MyGov account?" Mrs O'Donnell asked.

Delaney nodded.

"Good. Go online and link Centrelink with your account. If you qualify for Newstart, and I can't see any reason why you would not, you'll need to meet several conditions before payments begin.

Mrs O'Donnell continued. "You'll either need to apply for five jobs a week – and show us that you have – or, you can do 15 hours of volunteer work each week."

"Like at an op shop?"

"That would be acceptable."

Delaney thanked Mrs O'Donnell for her help and nodded to the security guard on his way out.

Before he got back home, he knew what he was going to do.

Two weeks after filling out a stack of paperwork and getting a police check done, Delaney was cleared to start work at his local Vinnies on Mondays and Wednesdays.

"Six weeks ago, you were in an office overlooking the MCG, in the mounting yard at Flemington, and now you'll be working in an op shop? What the fuck Gary?" Chris Simmons asked when he and his pal met up for a coffee.

"It wasn't my idea Chris. If I want those Newstart payments, I need to do volunteer work or start sending out resumes. After six weeks of doing nothing it won't be so bad."

Two older women, women in their mid-70s, greeted Delaney when he reported to work on Monday morning.

Mae Howard and Mavis Hanson manned the front of the shop and handled the till. Before the doors opened at 9:30, the two widows, one of whom was a bit hard of hearing, introduced Delaney to an old-timer named Harrison Downs, who he would be working with in the back of the shop.

Their job was to sort out merchandise that had been "donated" over the weekend. Half of the donations belonged in a dumpster. Clothing which remained was sorted, cleaned, washed and priced before going out onto the shop floor. There wasn't one piece of clothing Delaney went through that first Monday he would have paid 50 cents for.

However, the now retired journo enjoyed going through the donations of books. He put a John Grisham and a Tim Winton book to the side for himself. Most of the books were old romance novels, copies of *Marley and Me* or anything written by the late Bryce Courtenay. There was always at least one copy of *The Da Vinci Code* and *Fifty Shades of Grey* among the donations.

It was boring and tedious work, but Downs, a retired attorney, was a good bloke to spend time with – he owned a few horses over the years – and it beat sending out letters for jobs he would never be able to get. Fifty-seven-year-old men were not an organisation's first choice, unless it was a university hospital looking for cadavers.

Delaney received 30 minutes for lunch – always at 12:30 – and went to a nearby sandwich shop where he watched people come and go and had a quick look at the daily *Consume and Devour* tabloid which was laying on every other table. A large photo of Prince Harry was on the front page. "Oy," he groaned, tossing it back onto the table he got it from.

He ate at an outside table, but as the weeks went by and the days grew cooler and shorter, he began to have his lunch inside.

"Shit. Do I really want to spend another winter in this freaking ice box of a city?" he asked himself at home one Friday night while watching the footy with a portable heater blowing away. "I mean, what's keeping me here? I never hear boo from my ex or Michelle. Chris is a busy bloke. It's too cold and windy to play golf or go to the races and I can work at an op shop anywhere."

On one of those Friday nights, Delaney decided to move to the warmer climes of Queensland.

He was still 10 years from retirement age and the start of the aged pension. After working or studying continuously since the age of twelve,

Delaney had been keen to retire at the age of sixty-seven, collect the pension and for once put himself first. His ouster from *Turf News* changed everything.

He was in decent enough health. He had all his teeth, thanks to twice-yearly visits to the dentist, most of his hair, needed glasses just for reading and at nearly 180cm tall looked about a decade younger than he was. With no chance of a reconciliation with Michelle, the decision to escape the cold and dreary Melbourne winters and its blazing summers was a no-brainer.

But where would he go? Delaney had vacationed in the warmer climes of Cairns and Noosa over the years and enjoyed his time in both spots. There was no way he could afford to live in Noosa, the Melbourne of the north, so he settled on Far North Queensland. Sure, there would be the tropical humidity to deal with in the summer months and the occasional cyclone, but it was better than sitting rugged up in a unit with a blanket covering his legs and a hot cup of tea by his side.

Delaney pictured himself sitting on a balcony overlooking a large sun-splashed pool wearing a pair of shorts and an opened short-sleeved shirt and cradling a bottle of cold beer while a warm breeze ruffled the pages of the day's newspaper.

Delaney routinely checked the real estate listings online and saw there were numerous apartments and units available for rent in the Cairns area for much, much less than they went for in Melbourne. Many were furnished and close to the centre of town. He could move in with just a toothbrush if he desired.

He rang several real estate agencies based in Cairns and explained what he was looking for. He got along well with Marge Sinclair of Suncoast Realty, who said she would take care of everything and have several units for him to look at, all in his price range, when he arrived at the beginning of May.

"Let me know the exact date you plan on arriving and I'll line up accommodation for you for a week. Mates' rates. That will be enough time for you to pick a place out."

Delaney thanked her effusively and told her he would ring as soon as he had an exact date.

"And don't forget, I'll pay three month's rent in advance."

That should be enough to put me over the top if there are other applicants, he thought.

Later that night, out of curiosity, he visited Suncoast Realty's website to see if there was a picture of Ms Sinclair. There were eight realtors in a group photo, three of them women, standing in the front of a cream-coloured two-storey building flanked by the greenest, healthiest looking palm trees he had ever seen. Ms Sinclair was sandwiched between two casually dressed men, who looked to be in their thirties. She was wearing a sleeveless beige top with a matching skirt and sported a massive rock on her left index finger which sparkled in the sunshine. Delaney guessed she was in her early fifties.

It sure would be nice to find a woman up there like that, he thought.

In the weeks after he made up his mind to go to Cairns, Delaney attempted to organise a farewell lunch with several mates including Chris, sportswriter Steve Symons from *Consume and Devour,* Swoboda, and his new op shop pal Harry Downs. It was to be a simple affair. They'd have burgers, chicken parmas, drink a few beers and have a few laughs at the local pub, O'Keefe's, which was rumoured to be changing hands in the next couple of months.

"A tapas bar? You're kidding me, aren't you?" Delaney said to a young bartender late one afternoon as he nursed a cold one on the way home from the driving range. "Is the TAB staying?"

"Not sure mate. But if it is you might find yourself betting on races from Madrid," the bartender joked as he fingered his dark beard.

The farewell lunch, a seemingly good idea on paper, never got off the ground. Bernie Harwell – a reformed punter – refused to go to O'Keefe's because it had a TAB. Another wasn't keen on the menu and a third didn't care for the people who frequented the establishment.

"They're lowlifes. Can't we go somewhere classier?" Hank Kapinsky asked. This coming from a sixty-two-year-old man who frequently wore a faded twenty-year-old Metallica T-shirt.

After a flurry of back and forth text messages which left his fingers numb, Delaney became so frustrated he just about cancelled the whole thing.

"I'll be at O'Keefe's next Saturday at 1pm for a burger and a beer. If anyone wants to come by please do," he said in a group text.

Regrettably, Steve had to cover a VFL game on the other end of town and couldn't make it. Even Chris was busy. He was umpiring an Under 18 game somewhere on the peninsula. Just one, Ted McMurtry, an accountant with a handicap of sixteen showed up. Also known as the Prince of Patterson Lakes, McMurtry drove a silver-coloured fuel-guzzling SUV the size of a tank and had a thing for women the same age as his youngest daughter.

After about seventy-five minutes, Delaney downed the last of his second beer, stood up and said, "I think we're done here."

He paid his cheque, shook hands with McMurtry and walked to the door. As it closed, he heard McMurtry ask the bartender for both receipts. "Tax purposes. It was a business lunch."

Delaney had a separate lunch with Chris. They had a few laughs, reminisced about the women who had come in and out of their lives – Chris was hopelessly single, but always looking – and like most men in Melbourne talked footy and racing.

The following Saturday was the final day of "The Championships" and brought the Autumn Carnival in Sydney to a close.

"How's Too Hard travelling?" Chris asked.

"From what McGraw and McCarron are telling me he is cherry ripe for the Queen Elizabeth after that run of his two weeks earlier over 1800m. If there is some speed in the race it should set up nice for him even though it might be a little short. He'll need every metre of the Randwick stretch to reel in the leaders."

Delaney was too busy packing and chucking things away for his move up north to travel to Sydney to watch his five percent share of Too Hard Wrong Spot run. And, he would save a small fortune too, when airfare, meals and accommodation were added to the mix. The money would be better spent on his trip north.

Delaney and Chris watched the race together on Channel 7 and were happy they kept their money in their pockets. Sent off the $2.20 favourite in a field of thirteen, Too Hard was flying at the end of the 2000m and came up a half-length short. It was his third straight second-placed finish.

"He's got seconditis," Chris quipped.

"Better second than second-last," countered Delaney.

Ten-dollar chance Tidal Wave took home the lion's share of the $4 million purse. Delaney and City Winner's Syndication collected $755,000.

After trainer McCarron (ten per cent) and jockey Smithton (five per cent) took their cuts, Delaney's share of the second-place prize was worth about $32,000.

"That's the end of my Newstart for several months," Delaney told Chris. "Any incoming is income according to Centrelink and they're right. Better the money goes to those who really need it."

5

JOHNNY PASTRAMI WAS TOWELLING HIMSELF OFF after his morning shower when he heard his phone start to ring and buzz. He tied his bath towel around his waist and grabbed the phone off his bedroom nightstand just before it went to voicemail.

It was his mate Frankie "Fingers" Tannenbaum. Two years earlier Pastrami and Tannenbaum won close to a million dollars when I Get No Respect won the Melbourne Cup. The scratching at the gate of Too Hard Wrong Spot sent Pastrami and Tannenbaum into raptures since they had targeted Too Hard as the main danger to the French mare I Get No Respect, who they had bet a bundle on.

All the late nights Pastrami spent watching races from the UK, France, Ireland and Germany paid off three and a half minutes later when I Get No Respect gave Pastrami and Tannenbaum the biggest win of their punting careers.

"You did it Johnny, you did it. We'll never have to work again, although we never really worked before," Tannenbaum yelled as he repeatedly hugged and high-fived his former cellmate.

The dapper Pastrami had recently served 16 months in the clink for his part in a real estate Ponzi scheme. The feds seized most of the proceeds from the scheme, but not all of it, which allowed Pastrami to live comfortably upon his release.

Tannenbaum, a low-level mobster, was sent to the same minimum-security prison, and received an 18-month sentence for his role in an elaborate bookmaking operation which took bets on any sporting event on the planet.

Tannenbaum even set a line on the Victorian Blow Carting Championships prior to his incarceration after reading about it in his local paper, which has since folded. Over $180,000 had already been wagered on the final on the Mornington Peninsula between Murrumbeena's Marcus Flavel and Red Hook's Fred Fielding.

"What the fuck is Blow Carting?" Tony "Breadsticks" Battaglia asked Tannenbaum when he saw the line go up on a massive chalkboard in the loft which housed their operation.

"Breadsticks" ran the show for the Battaglia crime family. The show never closed and delivered millions to Battaglia and his associates.

"You won't believe this Tony. I didn't until I saw it. Grown men put fucking sails on go carts and they race around a course set up in a parking lot. No wind, no race. But the bureau's forecast for Sunday is for gale force winds that might blow the both of them to Pisspot Creek in Tassie."

"And people are betting money on this shit?" Breadsticks asked.

"We're holding $180k and the race is still two days away. And ESPFuckingN is televising it."

"You're a fucking genius Frankie, a fucking genius. And a very stable one at that," Battaglia said while he chomped on a cigar the size of a city bus.

Tannenbaum was ringing Pastrami from his home in Airlie Beach which he paid for in cash with his Melbourne Cup winnings. Since their stay in the slammer both had gone legit, knowing a second discretion would put them away for a lot longer than 18 months.

"Sorry to ring so early," Tannenbaum said.

It was just before 9am.

"I'm up mate. Just got out of the shower. What's going on?"

"Would you be interested in a betting proposition?

"Always interested mate. You wouldn't believe what I'm paying in body corporate fees in this damn building I'm living in."

"There's an unraced two-year-old in work on a private property up near Kerang. He is putting up some incredible numbers."

"What kind of numbers?" Pastrami asked as he sat down at the edge of his bed.

"He broke 57 seconds over 1000 metres three mornings ago."

"Shit. On grass or one of those synthetic surfaces?"

"Grass. They did a penetrometer reading and the track was between a good four and a soft five."

"Who knows about it?" Pastrami asked.

"Just the trainer, the two owners and the hoop."

"Who trains him?"

"Vern Baker."

"Never heard of him," Pastrami said. "How many does he have in work?"

"Just four."

"Baker told you?"

"No. One of the owners Johnny. Let's just say he owes me one."

"Go on mate, I'm getting interested."

"To make it all look legit, the horse was entered in a couple of trials at Casterton. Both times, the trials were called off due to very heavy tracks. Anything over 1200m and the horse sits down. He won't go another 10 feet.

"Now, here's where things get interesting. Baker entered the horse this morning for a maiden race on Friday at Warracknabeal. The markets just opened and – are you sitting down Johnny?"

"I am."

"He's listed at $126."

"You're kidding me, aren't you Frankie?"

"Nope. $126. He's got no public trials, he's from a sire nobody has ever heard of – Broadway Joe – and Baker hasn't won a race in six years. It's time to put some serious coin on him, and fast."

"Easy Frankie, easy. I want to see this nag in the flesh before I put any money on him. Tell the owner and Baker not to put a cent on him until I run my eye over him. I'll leave here as soon as I can and head to Kerang. Text me the details on the property so I can find the bloody place."

"It's race three and he's drawn the six hole. Baker has a four-kilo apprentice on him. The kid has ridden him in every workout the horse has had. As long as he breaks well, it is a sit and steer job."

As Tannenbaum was talking, Pastrami looked up the fields for Warracknabeal.

"What the name of this horse mate?"

"Sun-Up."

"Found him. Race 2 1100 metres. A field of 12 which I like, with four emergencies so we'll have a full field. Hmmm. And the top two choices have drawn inside. Even better.

"You know why Baker picked Warracknabeal Frankie?"

"The short straight?"

"Bingo. Two hundred and twenty metres long. If he is as fast as you say, he can have three lengths on them when they turn for home. By the time those two favourites get out, the race could be over."

"Sit tight. I'll ring you when I get up there."

Pastrami nudged his girlfriend of three months awake as he got dressed. "Want to go for a drive up north hun? I'm heading off in 20 minutes to have a look at a horse. We'll get some grub on the way."

Anna Nimmity stirred, rubbed her eyes and looked at her phone. It was just after nine.

"I hate getting up early Johnny, but it will be nice to get out of Melbourne for the day."

Anna got out of bed, stretched, and wearing nothing more than what she came into the world with 25 years ago, walked straight to the bathroom. Ten minutes later her make-up was done, she was fully dressed and ready to go.

I don't know how the heck she does it day after day, but I am sure glad she's doing it here, Pastrami thought as he followed her shapely behind to the elevator on the sixth floor of the luxury Southbank apartment building he called home. For a moment he forgot where he was and where he was going.

"You said something about a horse Johnny. Are we going to the races?"

"Uhh, no hun. We are going to look at a horse."

Pastrami eased his Mercedes from the underground parking garage and inched his way towards the West Gate Bridge.

Pastrami turned off the car's heater when the warm autumn sun broke through the clouds.

"Make yourself comfortable. It's about a three-hour plus trip depending on the traffic.

Anna took her phone from her oversized bag, pulled out a pair of wireless ear buds and leaned back in her seat.

Pastrami flicked between Melbourne sports radio stations RSN and SEN. There was nothing said about any betting plunge on Sun-Up. If Sun-Up checked out all right, the betting plunge would begin later that afternoon.

FLUSH WITH CASH, DELANEY PASSED ON THE IDEA OF A garage sale. *I don't want to start haggling with people. I'll just put everything out on the nature strip. This way everything will go to good use,* he thought.

Ten days after his lunch with McMurtry, and on the morning of his departure, one of Delaney's neighbours, a young strapping footballer who played for one of Melbourne's top amateur clubs, helped him move all his new furniture – a double bed, chest of drawers, bookcase, couch, fridge and a nearly new washing machine – to the nature strip in front of their group of units. Delaney placed a sign on each item which had just one word written on it in bright red letters – FREE.

"Tell your mates," Delaney told Gary Austerman.

"I will. It will all be gone by this afternoon," Austerman said.

Delaney tried to hand Austerman a $50 bill for all his help, but the twenty-year-old turned it down.

"Glad to help out," he said.

Delaney knew plenty of people who would not only have taken the money but asked for more.

"Thanks again," Delaney said. "And good luck the rest of the season."

Delaney returned to his unit and made one last run-through. His light blue Honda CRV was packed tighter than a box from IKEA. The back door was locked, the lights and water were turned off. Getting the power turned off on the correct date though proved to be a nightmare.

Delaney had rung his local energy company a week earlier to inform it he was moving out of state and to turn off the power three days after his departure, on the 17th of the month. A pretty straightforward request, and one that occurs thousands of times a day across the country. Delaney had a difficult time understanding a Filipino woman's thick accent over a crackly phone line to Manila, but thought his request was all taken care when he hung up the phone.

However, two hours later when he sat down to watch the 6pm Channel 7 news, the TV flickered and shut itself off along with the lights and fridge. *What the fuck?* he wondered. Delaney got up and looked out the window to see if any of his neighbours had also lost power. None had.

"Those idiots," he yelled. "The seventeenth. Not the seventh."

He immediately jumped back on the phone and since it was after 6pm he was transferred to a different call centre in Manila. After twenty-five minutes on hold he finally spoke to a live human being. He explained what had happened but was told that power could not be restored until the next day.

"Let me speak to your goddamn manager – now," Delaney yelled.

A minute passed and then another. Then a voice speaking surprisingly clear English came on the line.

"This is Ferdinand. How can I help you, Mr Delaney?"

"You can turn my freaking lights back on, Ferdinand."

"I am sorry for what happened, sir. Obviously, there was a mistake on our end and for that we sincerely apologise."

"No kidding," Delaney interrupted.

"Unfortunately, the power has to be turned back on by someone in Melbourne and that won't be able to happen until the morning."

"So, I have to sit here in the dark all night because of your fuck-up? Even my goddamn oven is electric."

"Mr Delaney, sir, I would appreciate it if you talked to me without using profanities."

"Shit, I'm just getting warmed up."

"Mr Delaney. I have sent an email to the Melbourne office – marked urgent – and they will send someone over in the morning to reconnect your power."

"Going to charge me for the reconnect too?"

"Not in your case, Mr Delaney. Is there anything else I can help you with?"

"Yeah, you can send someone over here with an edible meal," he said before hanging up.

Delaney raised the blinds and opened the curtains to let in what little natural light remained. He went to the small ivy-covered shed in the backyard and found the battery-powered lantern he bought over the summer when he and Chris went camping.

"I hope this thing still works," he said out loud. He flicked it on and was bathed in its artificial light. "Thank goodness."

Since he didn't feel like going out for dinner, Delaney examined his options. There was just one. He took a carton of milk from the warming fridge, grabbed a box of Corn Flakes from the pantry, cut up a banana, filled a large bowl to the top and started shovelling its contents into his mouth.

I guess I shouldn't complain, he thought. *There are millions of people going hungry tonight.*

After returning the half-full carton of milk to the darkened fridge and sealing the packet of Corn Flakes with a plastic clothes pin to keep it fresh, he put the empty bowl in the sink and walked over to his favourite chair with the lantern. He checked the news from the ABC website on his smartphone and quickly turned it off to conserve its power.

Fifty-two percent. That should last me till the morning.

Delaney turned the lantern on, cracked open a book and fifteen minutes later fell asleep. He woke up just before 11pm with the book on his lap and a sore neck. He took two Panadol tablets and slowly made his way to his bedroom by feeling the walls around him. He lay down in his unmade bed, got under the covers and made a mental note to recharge the lantern when power was restored.

Ten days later Delaney locked the apartment's front door for the last time, took its keys off his keychain, chucked them into the mailbox where a real estate agent would later claim them, climbed into his gassed-up SUV and took off. He was hoping to make it well into New South Wales before stopping for the night.

7

SUN-UP WASN'T MUCH TO LOOK AT. HE HAD NO DIS-tinguishing marks and wasn't particularly big. He had a good rump on him, which was always the mark of a good sprinter. But his coat was a bit dull and his near side hind leg seemed a bit crooked. *This horse broke 57 for 1000 metres? How?* Pastrami wondered.

Sun-Up stood quietly picking grass in his paddock while Vern Baker told Pastrami all about his promising colt. Anna Nimmity leaned over the wooden fence as Baker and Pastrami talked and Sun-Up walked straight to her and bowed his head a bit. Anna gave him a good pat and fed him a couple of carrots Baker provided.

"You do have a way of attracting the boys, don't you hun?" Pastrami said.

Anna merely shrugged her shoulders and smiled. "I guess." Baker's mind was elsewhere. Women like Anna did not show up at his property every day, or ever. He was jolted back to reality by Pastrami.

"Sorry to ask mate, but I have to. You didn't treat this horse with anything before he broke 57, did you?"

"No sir," he said loudly. "All he's ever had in his life is his regular feed. Nothing more. I love these animals. I'd never do anything to hurt them."

Pastrami patted Baker on the shoulder. "Good."

"Now what about that near side hind leg of his? Is he sound?"

"As sound as my Toyota which has 300,000 ks on it. He's been in work for the past two months and he's never had one setback, not one. You can run your hand over that leg after a workout and it is as cool as a July morning."

Pastrami nodded.

"Are you a betting man Mr Baker?"

Baker adjusted his worn Akubra before he answered.

"I'll put a tenner on one of my horses if I think he is any sort of chance, but that's it. I've seen too many men go broke at the windows."

"What are you going to put on Sun-Up? Something tells me it will be more than a tenner. A few pineapples maybe?"

"Oh, it will be more than that Mr Pastrami. This is a once in a lifetime chance."

"You do know he is listed as a $126 chance for his debut?"

"That I do."

"And you believe he'll run well?"

"He'll win if that is what you are asking."

A smile appeared on Pastrami's face and he nodded.

"Let's talk about our betting strategy," Pastrami told Baker.

"Hey hun, keep Sun-Up company while Mr Baker and I talk business. Okay?"

"Sure Johnny. You thinking of buying him?" Anna asked.

"I don't think Mr Baker would ever consider selling him. Would you Vern?"

"Nope. I bred him. He's staying here. This is his home."

Baker walked Pastrami to a shed which served as his office.

"You don't want to buy him, do you Mr Pastrami?" Baker asked. "Cause he really is not for sale, no matter how he runs at Warracknabeal."

"I'm more of a wagering man Vern. I'll leave the ownership to you and the two fellows you're in the horse with."

"That would be Nick Marino and Dale Mullins. They own 50 percent of him. Me and my missus own the other 50 per cent."

"I take it Mr Marino and Mr Mullins like to have a punt every now and then?"

"They do."

"We've got to coordinate this because as soon as the money comes in for Sun-Up his odds are going to come way down and you'll be getting a few calls from the media."

"Nobody from the media has ever talked to me about any of my horses."

"Well Vern. There are not many sure things in racing, but I guarantee you, they'll be calling – before and after the race. And you might be hearing from the stewards too. You've never been in any sort of trouble, have you? Made any large bets?"

"Like I told you before, just a tenner here and there."

"And Marino and Mullins?"

"Two local businessmen. Marino owns the pub and Mullins runs the newsagency. Marino is friends with your mate Tannenbaum. That's as much as I know."

"They went to school together," Pastrami said. "Melbourne High. They played a bit of footy, were on the swim team. Frankie put together the financing when Marino bought the pub. He returned the favour by telling him about Sun-Up. Frankie told me and that's what brought me up here. I wanted to see this horse and talk to you before I put down any serious coin on him."

"How much are you going to put on him?" Baker asked.

Pastrami took his phone out of his pants pocket and checked the reception. Four bars. *Better than what I get in that apartment of mine,* he thought.

Pastrami pressed on his TAB app and brought up his account. He scrawled through a maze of race meetings before he found the card for Warracknabeal. Race two, 1100 metres for maidens. Number 8. Sun-Up. Trainer: V Baker. Barrier 6. Odds: $126 win, $31 place.

In the bet type window Pastrami typed in win and $5000. He also punched in $5000 for the horse to place and showed the phone to Baker.

"Holy shit. Five thousand fucking dollars? Are you serious?"

"Very serious Vern. Very serious. Now before I make the bet official, I'll ring Frankie."

Pastrami checked his Rolex. It was 1:10.

"Frankie. I'm up here with Vern and the horse. It all checks out mate. I'm putting 10 grand on Sun-Up; five to win and five to place. I'll place the bet at 2pm sharp. Make your wager at the same time and tell Marino and Mullins to place their bets not a minute before 2pm, okay?"

"Got it Johnny. You really think this horse is that good?"

"To be honest he's not much to look at, but any horse that can break 57 seconds on a cow paddock will run even better on that carpet they have at Warracknabeal. And the two he has to beat have drawn inside. If Sun-Up breaks well, he wins. It's as simple as that. Hold on mate."

"Vern. How is Sun-Up from the starting gate? Any issues?"

"Not one. He's never missed the start in all the times I've worked him."

"You hear that Frankie? He's good to go mate. Two pm. Just watch. He'll go from $126 into fours. The guys at racing.com will be pissing themselves. The plunge of the decade. Get on mate. Get on."

Pastrami put his phone back in his pocket. "The bets go on at 2pm. Your phone will be ringing within a half hour. When you are asked about the betting plunge, say something like 'it's not my money'.

"Nobody needs to know I was here. Okay? We're not doing anything illegal Vern. This sort of thing happens every day. We're just doing it on a larger scale. Put some money on him yourself while he is at $126. I'm going to grab a bite and head into town. How's the food at Marino's pub?"

Baker patted his bulging stomach. They both laughed and shook hands.

"Thanks Vern. Just get Sun-Up on that float to Warracknabeal in one piece. He'll do the rest."

Baker went into his office. Pastrami walked back to the paddock. He gave Sun-Up a pat on the head. "See you on Friday boy."

He took Anna's hand. "What do u say we get something to eat hun. Mr Baker said there's a pub in town which serves good meals. "You up for a parma?"

"Maybe half of one," Anna said, lifting her top to show her flat stomach.

"I've got to keep myself in shape, don't I?"

Pastrami smiled. "Yes you do."

AS PLANNED, DELANEY DECIDED TO TAKE THE SMALL town – albeit longer – route when he reached Seymour two hours into his trip.

Why put up with the traffic heading into Sydney, and all the traffic through northern New South Wales and the Gold Coast? He was in no rush.

I'll see some of the country, see what everyone misses when they're flying 35,000 feet overhead.

He passed through Shepparton, the large regional and farming centre in northern Victoria and crossed the mighty Murray at the small town of Tocumwal where he stopped for lunch.

As it was a weekday and well after the Easter holidays, the town was quiet except for a few locals and travellers like himself.

He had a chat with a young fellow manning the till of the local bakery, who turned out to be the owner, while one of the women working at the sandwich counter made him an oversized salad roll.

"How'd a young bloke like yourself come to own a bakery in a small town?" the always inquisitive Delaney asked. "Most people your age would be drawn to a place like Melbourne or Sydney."

"I prefer living in a small town. I went to Melbourne Uni and studied business, but it wasn't for me," Bob Gilmour said as he smoothed out his apron. "I used to come into this bakery when I was a lad. While I was in my last year at uni my parents rang me and told me that it was for sale. The owners, who I knew fairly well, wanted to be closer to their kids who live in Canberra. They have government jobs there.

I came up one weekend to look over their books and decided I could make a go of it. I took out a business loan, got a job as an apprentice baker at a Bakers Delight close to school and learned as much as I could over those twelve weeks. The rest, as they say, is history," he said with a smile.

"You're making a go of it?"

"We're doing all right. We make the bulk of our money over summer and on long weekends. Except for the early start – I'm here at 3:30 every morning – it's been good fun. Plus, I get to see my wife every day. She's making your salad roll."

Sally Gilmour, who must have been listening in, waved a gloved hand in the air. "Hope you enjoy this," she said as she handed the roll to her husband.

"I will, and while I'm at it let me have an apple cake too. They're my weakness."

"I baked them this morning," Bob Gilmour said. He placed a large apple cake into a small white bag.

Delaney grabbed a bottle of water from the large soft drink fridge, took a couple of extra serviettes from the counter and paid the Gilmours.

"Thanks for the chat. Hope the business continues to thrive."

"Thanks mate," Bob Gilmour said. "That SUV of yours out front is packed tighter than a tram on St Kilda Rd. Where are you headed?"

"Cairns. I've just retired and have lived through too many Melbourne winters," Delaney answered.

"Good on ya. I was there a couple of years ago on holiday and loved it. It's a long drive so take it easy."

"I will, thanks."

The pair shook hands.

"Thanks for stopping in," Gilmour said.

"My pleasure. I am going to enjoy this," he said pointing at the bag containing his lunch.

Delaney walked across the street to a near-empty park with bright thick green grass and numerous picnic tables. He took a seat in the shade to avoid the sun's warm rays and looked down the steep hill to the Murray. There was one old timer casting a line into the water from the shore. Apart from a few birds chirping, it was as quiet as a TAB outlet when a 100-1 shot gets up.

Delaney polished off the salad roll and ate half of the massive apple cake, deciding to save the rest for later in the afternoon.

"Sally knows how to make a sandwich," he said as he walked to a nearby bin to deposit the brown paper bag his roll came in.

He heard a woman's voice call out from behind him as he did.

"Hey mister."

Delaney turned around and saw a young woman dressed in jeans and boots with a large handbag slung over her right shoulder heading towards him.

What does she want? he wondered.

"Are you going north?" she asked. "I can use a ride. With all the stuff you got in your car it doesn't look like you're out for an afternoon drive."

"Planning on being a detective?" Delaney asked. "And by the way, shouldn't you be in school?"

"I'm curious, okay, and looking to get out of here. Can you help me? And for your information, I finished school a year ago. I'm nineteen. I look a little young for my age."

That she did. She had a face of a sixteen-year-old which was heavily made up to make her look older. She sported a nose ring through her left nostril, and she twirled her medium length dark hair like someone who was trying to get acquainted with a new haircut.

"What's your name?" Delaney asked.

"Is it important?"

Her voice sounded like an adult's and her eyes had a hard look to them.

"I'd like to know who I am going to be riding with, if I give you a lift that is."

"My name is Lori, Lori Brooks."

"Well, Lori, where are you headed?"

"I've got some friends in Dubbo. Are you going that way?"

"I am, actually. And that's all you have with you?" he asked, pointing to her handbag.

"I packed a small suitcase," she said nervously. "It's behind a bush not far from where you were sitting. Can I get it? Will you give me a lift, please?"

Delaney mulled the situation over for a few moments.

"If you don't mind me asking, Lori, what are you running away from?"

Lori looked down at the grass and pawed at it with her boots for a moment. When she looked up, her eyes were teary.

"My stepfather," she said looking around as if someone was watching her. "I've got to get out of here. Please mister."

"All right. Get your bag and let's hit the road."

"Thank you, thank you," she said, giving him a quick and unexpected hug.

Delaney walked across the street, unlocked his Honda and removed a map and a newspaper from the passenger seat.

He got into the driver's seat and backed out of his parking spot in front of the bakery. He moved the car to the river side of the street where Lori Brooks was standing with a dark blue suitcase.

Delaney made some room for her bag and then shoved it in the back of the Honda like some bloke trying to squeeze a large bag into a plane's overhead compartment.

After making sure he would still be able to see out of the rear-view mirror, he closed the back door.

"Hop in," he said.

9

LORI BROOKS OPENED THE PASSENGER SIDE DOOR AND
sat down. She pulled down the visor and looked at herself in the mirror,
dabbing at the dark mascara around her eyes with a tissue she took out
of her bag.

Delaney put the SUV in gear and pointed it towards the sign for A39
north, the Newell Highway which runs through country NSW up to
the Queensland border.

"Settle in Lori, Dubbo is about six hours away. If we make good time,
we'll get there about 8pm, okay?"

"That's fine by me. I am just so glad to get out of this place."

She smiled for the first time since Delaney laid eyes on her.

"I don't even know your name," she said.

"Gary," he said. "Have you eaten anything today, Lori?"

"Not really. I had a candy bar for breakfast."

Delaney looked at the rest of the apple cake he was saving for later.

"You're welcome to the rest of this," he said, passing a small bag and
its contents to her.

"Thank you."

She took a bite, reached into her bag and pulled out a bottle of water.

"Get this from the Gilmours?" she asked as she bit into it. "They make
the best apple cakes anywhere. That's about the only thing I'll miss about
this place," Lori added as Delaney steered his two-year-old, and recently
serviced SUV, onto the Newell Highway.

Neither said anything for a few minutes. Lori adjusted the passenger
seat and then broke the ice. "You sure have a lot of stuff in here," she said.

"All I own," Delaney replied. "Got rid of all my furniture back in Melbourne."

"What are you running away from?" she asked, putting added emphasis on the word you.

Good question, Delaney thought.

"I'm not really running away from anything. I've decided to spend my sooner than expected retirement in the warmer weather of Far North Queensland."

"Sooner than expected? What did you do for a crust?"

"I was a journalist my whole life and was just made redundant."

"Well, that sucks."

"Sure does, but now a new opportunity has come my way and I'm going to make the best of it."

"What about your family? You'll be so far away from home."

"There's not much of a family left anymore," Delaney explained. "I'm divorced and don't have any kids."

"What about your friends?"

"I have a couple of close ones and I'll miss them, but we'll meet up somewhere once or twice a year; play a little golf, go to the races, catch up and reminisce."

"Pretty gutsy going that far by yourself. Do you have any friends where you're going?"

"I guess one could look at it that way. The only person I can say I know is the realtor who is finding me an apartment."

"Wow, that is gutsy."

About 30ks out of Tocumwal, a batch of road work signs started to appear, warning drivers to slow to 80kph, then 60 and then 40. *Be prepared to stop* read the next which is what Delaney did when a green signal on a portable traffic light turned red.

A young worker, decked out in bright orange reflective clothing and holding a stop sign, stepped in front of Delaney's SUV. From what he and Lori could see, a good 400 metres or so of road ahead of them was being resurfaced. Slowly cars started backing up behind him. He'd be leading the charge when the go ahead was given.

Delaney lowered his window and asked the young chap if he knew how long the wait would be.

"Not more than five or six minutes."

Delaney decided to put the car in park and turn the engine off while he and Lori waited.

Several minutes later, traffic headed southbound towards Victoria slowly started to approach. With all the loose gravel on the road, they inched along. A large 18-wheeler led the procession. In the well-fitted out cab of the truck, Kirby Pearson took notice of Delaney and Lori and did a double take.

That sure looks like Lori Brooks, he thought. He slowed down a bit and looked back in his rear-view mirror. *Yup, that's her. But who's the old bloke?*

Kirby was hauling a load of cattle to the saleyards outside Shepparton and if he didn't have such a tight schedule to adhere to, he would have pulled over and done some investigating.

He tried raising Dave McKinley, Lori's stepfather, on his truck radio, but McKinley wasn't answering. He tried his mobile and Dave picked up on the first ring.

"You saw her where? And with who?

"Don't know who the guy was Dave. He looked to be about 50 or so, and they seemed pretty chummy. They're in a blue Honda CRV. I didn't get the rego number."

"I reckon that's why she took off, to be with him. Makes sense now. I wonder how long it's been going on. Shit. I'll wring both of their necks when I find them. Thanks for letting me know Kirby."

"You goin' after them?" Kirby asked.

"Sure am. They only got about a 40-minute head start. Lori always said she liked surprises. Well wait till she sees me."

McKinley threw on a pair of jeans and a T-shirt, took a couple of cold ones from the fridge and ran to his ute. McKinley was a big unit, about 6-foot-2 and 85 kg with a thatch of dark hair which had just started to turn grey. He hadn't shaved in several days and in his current state of rage was someone to steer well clear of. He got in his ute, started her up and hurriedly drove off, squealing the tyres. He didn't even stop to tell his third wife, Darlene – Lori's mother – who was in the backyard gardening, where he was going.

Once Delaney got through the road work, he kept to the 100/kph speed limit and stayed in the left lane as cars and a few trucks continuously whizzed passed him. He pulled over at a rest stop 10 minutes later to stretch his legs and go to the toilet and then got back on the road.

He and Lori were travelling at the same lazy 100kph when 90 minutes later, Delaney caught a glimpse of a white ute in his rear and side-view mirrors rapidly gaining ground on him.

"Shit, he must be doing about 140, maybe 150," Delaney said.

The driver of the ute stayed in the right lane, drew level with Delaney and started honking his horn.

A big middle-aged bloke with a mop of greying hair was screaming out his open passenger side window. Delaney lowered his window but with the sound of the air rushing by he couldn't quite make out what the guy was saying. *Do I have a flat? Did I drop something back there? Is he a copper?* Delaney wondered.

Lori quickly ducked down and tried to hide. She jabbed Delaney in his side. "That's my stepfather," she said.

"Your who?"

"My fucking stepfather."

"I PICK UP ONE HITCHHIKER IN TWENTY YEARS. SHIT!"

Delaney was no lip reader, but he now was easily able to make out what Lori's stepfather was yelling. "Pull the fuck over, pull the fuck over."

They were the only two cars on the road, nothing was in front of them or behind them for miles. Nor was there anyone heading southbound.

"There's an exit coming up in 500 metres," Lori said. "Take it."

"I'm a fucking journo, not Jamie Whincup."

"TAKE IT!"

Delaney sped up as did the ute. Delaney's SUV was a bit higher than the ute which blocked its driver from seeing the exit sign. With the exit just 50 metres away, Delaney quickly swung to his left and sped down the exit ramp. The ute tried to follow but McKinley lost control. It flipped over several times and came to rest on its side.

"Holy shit," Lori screamed.

Delaney slowed and came to a stop. He turned his head and surveyed the damage. Two of the ute's tyres were still spinning and steam was billowing from beneath the bonnet. The ute was totalled but its driver was crawling out of the passenger side window and seemed to be okay.

There wasn't another car to be seen in any direction. Lori and Delaney looked at each other.

"Let's get the fuck out of here," Delaney said. "We'll pick up the Newell further down the road."

Memo to self, Delaney thought. *Change this registration plate as soon as I get to Cairns.*

Neither Lori nor Delaney said a word until they were safely back on the Newell.

"Where is everybody? We haven't seen a car in any direction for 10 minutes."

"That's the country for you," Lori said. "You okay?"

"I'll let you know as soon I find my balls and put them back where they belong."

McKinley tried to stand up, but his knees wobbled, and he collapsed. Blood from a deep wound on his head stained the bitumen.

The first paramedics on the scene quickly sized up McKinley's injuries and radioed Canberra Hospital to arrange for him to be airlifted there. "He's breathing, but is unresponsive," Bob Cook told the senior nurse in the hospital's emergency room.

Senior Constable Len Danielson was the first officer to arrive at the site. "How bad?" he asked Cook.

"Bad. Severe head trauma. I just rang to get him airlifted to Canberra."

Sixty minutes later, McKinley was being worked on by a team of doctors and nurses in the ICU at Canberra Hospital. "He's fucked," neurosurgeon Peter Elliott told one of the nurses after he looked at scans of McKinley's noggin. "See if we can locate his family."

Constable Danielson found McKinley's phone in the wreckage of the ute. Unlike its owner, it didn't have a mark on it. Constable Danielson rang McKinley's wife – Lori's mother – but there was no answer. He left a message urging her to call him.

After looking through McKinley's phone, Danielson rang the last person McKinley had spoken too, a Kirby Pearson.

"He's where?" Pearson asked. "In Canberra? The ICU? What the heck happened?"

"He was involved in an accident on the Newell Highway. His ute rolled. He seemed to be okay but collapsed as emergency crews arrived. He's suffered a head injury," Constable Danielson said. "I'm sorry."

"Do you know why he was on the Newell Highway headed north? I rang the trucking company he works for in Cobram and they informed me his runs are primarily in northern Victoria."

Pearson thought for a second before answering. *Shit, I'm on probation. I can't afford to get mixed up in some police investigation.*

"I have no idea why he was in New South Wales constable. I was ringing to see if he wanted to have a beer after his shift."

"What did he say?"

"That he'd meet me at our usual spot in Cobram."

"That's it?"

"Yes. Can I go see him in Canberra?"

"You can, but he is unresponsive."

"Shit. He's really that bad?"

"I'm afraid so Mr Pearson. Do you have another number for his wife?"

"Just the one you probably have. She likes to tend her garden. Maybe she left her phone in the house."

"Maybe. We'll send a car over there. Thanks for your help Mr Pearson. I'll be in touch."

Pearson put his phone down and asked himself what Danielson meant when he said he would be in touch. *It's probably routine. As long as Ray didn't text or ring anyone after we spoke, I should be in the clear. But poor fucking Ray. He must have been doing 150 clicks trying to catch up to Lori and that bloke when he lost control of his ute. It wasn't in the best of shape anyways.*

Later that afternoon two constables pulled up to a run-down house in Tocumwal looking for Darlene Brooks. An old Holden was parked in the carport.

They knocked on the front door but there was no answer.

"Let's try around back," Junior Constable Tom Edwards told his partner.

He and Junior Constable Eric Roker walked to the back of the house, unlocked a gate and called out Darlene's name.

They found her asleep in a chair. Her left hand was wrapped around a glass of wine. Pruning shears dangled from her right hand. A lit cigarette was in an ashtray on a table next to her along with a nearly empty wine bottle.

"Mrs Brooks," Edwards said. "Wake up Mrs Brooks."

Edwards gently touched her shoulder to roust her.

Darlene Brooks came around and waited for her eyes to focus on the two officers standing in front of her.

"I ain't done nothin' wrong. Is it illegal to have a drink in my own backyard?"

"Not it isn't," Edwards said.

"I'm afraid we have some bad news for you."

"Something happen to Lori?"

Edwards looked at his partner, who shrugged his shoulders. Edwards knelt down. His face was even with that of Mrs Brooks.

"It's your husband, Mrs Brooks. He's been in an accident and he's in hospital."

"Cliff had an accident? Last I heard he had a desk job and wasn't down in the mines no more.

Edwards looked at Roker, hoping he had more information. He didn't.

"It's not Cliff. Ray McKinley has been in an accident. Isn't he your husband?"

"He is. Arsehole number two. He's useless. He's a one-inch cock."

Darlene Brooks put her half-empty glass of wine on the table next to her and straightened up.

"What's happened?"

"He lost control of his vehicle on the Newell Highway. It flipped over several times. He crawled out of it but then collapsed and was airlifted to hospital in Canberra. He's in the ICU with a severe head injury."

"Dear me. Did he have his seatbelt on? I always told the arsehole to buckle up."

"We're not sure at this time Mrs Brooks. Investigators are still at the scene," Junior Constable Roker said.

"What do you mean by a severe head injury?"

"From what the doctors treating him have told us, if he does pulls through, he'll likely be a vegetable."

"A vegetable? What, like a fucking eggplant?" a disbelieving Darlene Brooks said.

"I'm sorry. He'll need round the clock care if he makes it."

"We're sorry Mrs Brooks. We can take you to Canberra to see him if you like."

"I don't think so. He's totally worthless to me now."

Roker and Edwards looked at each other in disbelief. "Are you sure mam?" Roker asked.

"I'm sure. Either of you two single? I like having a man around the house."

"Err, we are both married Mrs Brooks," Roker said.

"Then you're both useless too. Now get on outta here."

Roker handed Mrs Brooks a card. "If you want to talk to someone Mrs Brooks, you can call this number."

She glanced at it, crumbled it up and tossed it away.

"I'd rather talk to my sweet potatoes."

Edwards glanced at his watch. "Well, we're going to get going. We're sorry about what's happened to your husband."

"I ain't."

10

"WELL, THAT WAS CERTAINLY INTERESTING, DON'T YOU think?" Delaney asked. His passenger merely shrugged her shoulders.

Delaney and Lori drove on in silence. There was hardly any traffic. The fields on both sides of the Newell were a yellowish brown due to the lack of rainfall in the western part of NSW. While the coast was getting its share of rain, the western part of the state hardly got a drop. The dams were barely full and the creeks they drove over were bone dry.

He changed the subject.

"Those friends of yours in Dubbo who are taking you in, have you known them for long?"

Lori fidgeted in her seat before answering.

"Wendy Tindal has been my best friend for ages. I'm going to stay with her and her boyfriend until I get things sorted out. They have an extra room and they're not going to charge me anything for staying with them."

"That's a plus. Do you think you'll stay there for a while?"

"I'm not sure," Lori said softly. "I've only been to Dubbo once, when I visited Wendy about a year ago. She went up there to live with her parents when her dad got a job at the open range zoo. He got her a job there too, nothing glamorous though. She met this guy up there. He's a bit older than she is. Her parents weren't keen on the idea, so she moved in with Steve, that's the bloke's name. Wendy still sees her dad most days at work. They get along okay. Her mum barely talks to her."

"That would be hard for her," Delaney said.

"Yeah," Lori said.

Delaney left it at that.

Several minutes later he looked over at Lori. She was fast asleep, her head on her handbag which was placed up against the side window.

Delaney checked the clock on the dashboard. It was coming up to 4pm. He turned the radio on, keeping the volume low, and found an ABC station to get the latest headlines. Maybe there would be something about the incident with Lori's stepfather.

There wasn't anything – yet.

Topping the bulletin was news of Trump threatening all-out war with North Korea unless the rogue state gave up its missile program while the Aussie Prime Minister was announcing yet another energy scheme designed to keep the declining coal industry afloat.

Great, Delaney thought. *The world could come to an end before I even get to Cairns and I'll be stuck in Parkes spending my last moments on Earth with a fucking Elvis impersonator.*

Lori's snoring picked up as they approached Narrandera. He decided to keep going and take a toilet break in West Wyalong, 140km away.

The late autumn sun was beginning to cast long shadows on the road. The empty fields were dotted with dead trees, many struck by lightning, their bare branches reaching out in every direction. Sundown was about an hour or so away, just about the time Delaney and Lori would be pulling into West Wyalong.

The loud horn from a passing truck woke Lori about half an hour later. She rubbed the sleep out of her eyes and glanced over at Delaney, who nodded. For a few seconds it seemed she had no idea where she was. Then it hit her: *the old guy giving me a ride.*

Delaney smiled at her.

"How long have I been asleep for?" she asked.

"About two hours."

"Have I really? Well I didn't get much sleep last night. My stepfather was after me again."

"After you?"

"Yeah, every time he drinks, which is nearly every night, he tells me how pretty I am and asks me to come sit with him."

"And your mother?"

"He waits till she's asleep."

"Have you ever told her?"

"I did once and she told me I was making it up, that no husband of hers would never do something like that."

"Typical."

"Do you think I'm crazy for running away?"

"Not at all Lori. The best thing for you is to get to a more stable environment."

A few minutes of silence followed before Lori continued.

"He came after me last night."

Tears filled her eyes.

Delaney reached over and with his left hand opened the glovebox where there was a packet of tissues. He handed them to her.

"Thank you," Lori said. She wiped her eyes and blew her nose.

"He had a few drinks. I locked myself in my room, grabbed what I could and tossed everything into my bag and suitcase. I put a chair under the door – like I've seen them do on TV – to keep him out and climbed out the window."

"You spent the night in the park?"

"Yeah. My mum kept calling and texting this morning, but I couldn't deal with it and didn't answer."

"Maybe you can send her a text message just to let her know that you are okay. She'll be worried about you. Tell her you took a bus to Sydney. Don't tell her you are going to Dubbo. You're nineteen-years-old. You're free to go wherever you want and do whatever you want."

"I should have left right after high school. I thought things would change. I was so foolish."

"No, you weren't. It took a lot of courage to stand up to him like you did and more to walk away. You did the right thing."

"Thank you. It feels so much better to have got that all out. You'd have made a good dad."

"Your real dad Lori? Where is he?"

"He left about 10 years ago to take a mining job out west. The last I heard he was in Port Hedland."

"Do you ever hear from him?"

"I used to. He sent me a card and a graduation gift when I left high school. I haven't heard from him since."

"I'm sorry, Lori."

"Yeah, me too."

Lori looked out the window, and occasionally rubbed her red eyes. A few homes started appearing up ahead. West Wyalong was not too far away.

"Have you thought about going to uni?" Delaney asked.

"I have. Charles Sturt University is in Dubbo. I'm thinking about going there. I'd like to make something out of my life instead of working as a waitress as I was doing."

"Were you able to save any money?" Delaney asked.

"Not much. My mum made me give her money for room and board."

"You're kidding?"

"Nope."

"Want to have something to eat in West Wyalong? My treat."

"That would be nice, thank you."

Delaney and Lori Brooks arrived in West Wyalong around 5pm. They drove into town, bypassing the usual fast-food outlets and slowly made their way down its winding and narrow main street. Delaney spotted several cafes and restaurants and pulled into a parking space in front of the newsagency. Working the stiffness out of their legs, Delaney led the way.

They looked at the menu on the window of the first restaurant they stopped at, nodded in agreement and went inside.

Four of the approximately twenty tables were occupied. They waited at the front of the restaurant until a waitress approached. Delaney guessed she was about 40.

"Table for two?" she asked.

"Yes, please," Delaney answered. "Something by the window."

The waitress directed them to a table, handed them each a menu and said she'd be back in a tick with a jug of water.

Delaney spent more time looking outside than he did the menu even though the incident with Lori's stepfather was more than 200ks back. He was half-expecting a copper to pull up behind his SUV, walk into the restaurant and ask if anyone owned the vehicle parked out front. A copper never showed. Even though he looked to be in the clear, Delaney kept his eyes peeled out front.

After a good feed, Delaney peeked at his watch. It was nearly 6pm. The sun had just gone down, and it was starting to get dark.

"We better get on the road if we want to get to Dubbo tonight," he said. "We've got a three-hour drive ahead of us."

Delaney got the waitress's attention and scratched at the air with an imaginary pen, giving her the universal sign for the bringing of the cheque.

"You take care of the bill while I visit the gents'," Delaney joked as he got up and walked to the toilets in the back of the restaurant.

"Anything else?" the waitress asked Lori as she placed the bill on the table.

"No thank you. We've got to get back on the road."

"Where you headed?"

"My friend is dropping me off in Dubbo."

"You and the old-timer an item?"

"No, no. He's just giving me a lift."

"Be careful, okay? An old guy like that sees a young pretty girl like you and next thing you know he's pulling into a motel somewhere."

"It's nothing like that," Lori snapped.

Delaney returned to the table, picked up the cheque and took it to the front of the restaurant where he paid the bill by card.

"Looking for your friend?" the waitress asked.

Delaney nodded.

"She's waiting for you outside."

Delaney walked outside but there was no sign of Lori.

She probably went back inside to use the toilet, he thought.

After five minutes passed Delaney walked back into the restaurant.

"Excuse me," he said to the waitress who served them. "The young woman I was with, did she come back inside to use the toilet?"

"Nope. The last I saw of her she was talking to some bloke outside. Maybe she took off with him."

"Why in hell would she do that?" Delaney said.

He went back outside, walked twenty or thirty metres in each direction and stood there dumbfounded.

"I have her suitcase in the boot. Or do I?"

Delaney scampered back to his Honda. Her suitcase was gone. He went through all his stuff to make sure nothing was taken. Everything seemed to be intact.

"How the fuck did she open the back door and get it out of there?" he asked himself. "I know I locked the car, or did I?"

He had one last look around before he got into his Honda.

I guess she got a better offer.

Delaney shook his head, started up the car and got back on the road.

He turned on the radio and kept his eyes on the unlit road, watching for kangaroos.

With few cars on the road he whizzed through Forbes and later Parkes, the home of the massive radio telescope which relayed the pictures of the Apollo 11 moon landing and moon walk back to Earth in 1969.

Dubbo was more than an hour away.

When he finally arrived he headed into town and stopped at the first decent-looking motel he saw. He paid $105 for a basic room and parked in front of room 26. He took his overnight bag out of the car, turned the key to the room and opened the door. He searched for the light switch, flicked it on and looked around. *I've stayed in worse*, he thought, opening the sliding window by the door to let some fresh air into the musty smelling room. He also opened the window in the bathroom, letting the cool evening breeze inside to get some cross ventilation.

Delaney put his bag on the queen-sized bed and tested the mattress. Not as soft as one might have expected. He got undressed, walked into the bathroom with a bar of soap he brought from home – motel and hotel soaps he found were generally awful – and washed the dirt and grime of the long day from his face. He reached for a towel, but then remembered the towels were on the end of the bed. Dripping a little water onto the carpet, he grabbed a face towel and dried himself off.

Delaney took an apple and a bottle of water from his bag, sat down in a wooden chair and leafed through a booklet on the motel and town that was sitting on a rickety table. He peeled the apple with a sharp knife he brought inside with him. Apart from the open range zoo, university and racecourse, it was a typical bush town, and it was so far away from Melbourne and Sydney that a house could be bought for about a third of what they were going for back home.

He turned on the large TV, a brand he had never heard of and flicked through the channels as he did at home. Since it was the middle of the week there was not even a game on to watch. He moved up and down the thirty channels on offer. He spent sixty seconds on a CNN report of another Ebola outbreak in Africa, and 10 more watching Fox News – a new record. SBS was airing yet another documentary on the

Nazis and since the last thing he wanted to see before he turned off the TV was Hitler, he kept clicking until he landed on WIN News. There was footage of a ute being loaded onto a flat-bed truck.

"A Tocumwal man is lucky to be alive after a single-vehicle crash on the Newell Highway this afternoon," a female reporter said. "Police say he apparently lost control as he tried to exit the road at high speed. The driver was airlifted to Canberra Hospital where he is listed in serious condition in the ICU."

"Holy shit," Delaney said. "Holy shit."

He turned the TV off, set the alarm on his phone for 7:30, plugged the charger in, turned out the lights and replayed the events of the day over in his mind. It was well past midnight before he fell asleep.

11

THE NEXT MORNING DELANEY SHOWERED AND
checked out of the motel.

He topped up his SUV's fuel tank, bought a cup of coffee and a
muffin at the same service station and checked his twitter feed before he
got back on the Newell Highway.

He nearly choked on the blueberry muffin when he read a report
on turfnews.com of a massive betting plunge on that day's races at
Warracknabeal.

"One hundred and 26 dollars into fours? On a maiden race at
Warracknabeal in late April? What the heck is going on there?"

He called up the entries for race two. "Vern Baker? Leonard Hawley?
Who are these guys," Delaney wondered when he saw who was training
and riding Sun-Up. "I'll give Swoboda a ring and see if he knows
anything about it."

After finishing his coffee and muffin, Delaney rang his former
colleague. The new father of a couple of months had managed to keep
his job and was churning out yarns for the *Turf News* website, which
Delaney had to admit was looking sharp.

It ought to be for the $10 a month it was charging readers.

"Adam? Gary. Changing diapers or doing the form?"

"On diaper duty mate."

It was the first time the two had spoken since Delaney was given his
marching orders several months ago.

"I heard you're leaving us, heading north. Is that true?"

"It is mate. I'm actually on the road now. In Dubbo."

"Taking the long way?"

"Just wanted to dodge all the Sydney and Brisbane traffic. Adam, the reason I'm calling is this massive plunge on a maiden race in Warracknabeal today. Have you heard about it?"

"I've had a couple of messages this morning. He's $4.20 and money is still coming in for him. I thought I knew every trainer in the state, but Vern Baker is a new one to me. And the horse's sire? Broadway Joe? The only winners he's ever had were at the picnics."

"Someone knows something," Delaney said.

"There was a bet of $5000 to win and $5000 to place on the horse two days ago. Now everyone is jumping all over him. The two favourites are out to $6 and $7."

"Ten thousand bucks on a $126-1 chance? That's bloody insane," Delaney said.

"It is. I don't know what to think. But I'll be tuned to the TV at 1pm."

"You having a wager on one of those early favourites?"

"I'm sitting this one out Gary. My money is tied up in diapers and baby food."

Delaney laughed. "Good luck with the bub."

"And you enjoy the nice weather up there. Send us something on the Cairns Cup. There's always a couple of Victorian runners or jockeys in it. Late August I think it is run."

"Will do."

Delaney hung up, placed his phone in the car's middle console, put on his seatbelt and took off. The sun was shining.

"Let's have a quieter one today," he said. "And no hitch-hikers."

He turned east at Gilgandra and continued through the country towns of Coonabarbran, Narrabi and Moree before arriving in Goondiwindi.

The second at Warracknabeal was thirty minutes away.

He kept fiddling with the radio as local stations drifted in and out. A buy, swap and sell show featuring farm equipment and livestock gave him a few chuckles. "I just had someone on the line earlier selling a tractor just like the one you want. Did you get the number?" the male host asked the caller.

"Didn't hear it, I just tuned in," the old-timer said.

Delaney pictured a fellow sitting in his favourite chair calling on a landline with his dog by his side.

"Hold the line and my producer will get you the number," the host said. "With luck, the two of you can work out a deal. It's that easy. We've got lines open and we'll be on 'til the top of the hour, so give us a ring."

The ABC had the strongest signal and he listened to its newscast at the top of the hour whenever he was on the road. There was something reassuring about hearing the musical fanfare introducing the bulletin. No matter where you were, in Delaney's case far west NSW heading east, the ABC made you feel like you were home.

Delaney switched stations a few minutes before 1pm and easily found the station which aired the day's races.

"Sun-Up got as low as $3.60 but is now a big drifter as the money continues to come in for Make Me Smile and High Hat," the announcer said. "Make Me Smile is into $3.40 and High Hat is at $4.00. Sun-Up is out to $8. Let's go up to Warracknabeal and our race caller Ben Dover.

Also at Warracknabeal were Pastrami and Tannenbaum, who had flown down from far north Queensland, and Sun-Up's two other owners, Nick Marino and Dale Mullins. Professional punter Vic "Each Way" Rizzuto had also rocked up.

If it wasn't for good signage along the way and Google maps none of them would have made it to the track on time. The small town in northwest Victoria came alive only on race day which was just once every six weeks.

It was Marino who had given Tannenbaum the heads-up on Sun-Up. The two never made eye contact before, during or after the race.

Trainer Baker was interviewed before the race and gave nothing away. Due to the betting plunge, Racing Victoria stewards and vets gave Sun-Up a thorough examination when the horse arrived on course. He was given the all-clear.

Blood and urine samples were taken and would again be taken again after the race – whether he won or lost. Any illegal substances in the horse's system would easily be detected, and if found, any purse money won would be surrendered. Baker would be suspended and sent for a long vacation. But Baker had never given any of his horses anything illegal and wasn't about to start with Sun-Up.

"I have no idea why he's been backed the way he has," Baker told a local reporter when he saddled up the two-year-old. "I think he'll run alright, but all I have is a fiver on him."

He took the ticket out of his shirt pocket to show the reporter. "See. Five bucks." Baker didn't show the reporter the tickets stashed in his wallet.

Baker gave Hawley a leg up in the mounting yard and Sun-Up galloped onto the track for his debut.

"There's not much of him and he's not much to look at. I cannot recommend Sun-Up. High Hat is the pick of the yard for me," racing. com on-course reporter Dirk Anderson told the station's viewers.

As the horses warmed up on their way to the starting gate on the backstretch, Pastrami focused his high-powered binoculars on Sun-Up. "That action of his is a bit weird Frankie. But, if Baker says there's nothing to worry about ..."

The more conservative of the two when it came to gambling and lifestyle, Tannenbaum had $1000 each way on Sun-Up at $61 and $17. "I'm glad we don't do this every day Johnny, I don't have the stomach for it." Tannenbaum popped a couple of Gaviscon tablets into his mouth as the horses reached the starting gate.

"The red light is on and we're racing in the second at Warracknabeal," race caller Ben Dover said.

Sun-Up broke with the field and after 200 metres was fourth on the outside. The two favourites, Make Me Smile and High Hat, had no early speed and settled towards the back of the field.

As the leaders began to tire near the 500-metre mark, Hawley eased Sun-Up into the three path and under very little urging, reached the front. "I hope he hasn't moved too soon," Pastrami said.

As the field rounded the turn and reached the top of the stretch, Sun-Up led by two widening lengths. Make Me Smile and High Hat finally got into the clear with 100 metres to go but by then Sun-Up was five lengths in front. He got a little tired in the final 50 metres but won by four lengths.

Pastrami and Tannenbaum high-fived each other. Marino and Mullins simply nodded.

"I knew he was good, but I didn't think he was that good," Baker told a handful of reporters as Hawley brought the horse back to the mounting yard.

"Where are you going to take him next?" a reporter asked.

"We'll see how he pulls up and make a decision in a couple of days," Baker said.

Back in Melbourne, Adam Swoboda was kicking himself. "I should have had something on him. He bolted in."

Somewhere in New South Wales, Delaney pounded the dash. "What a great story. Shit. I wish I was writing it."

12

DELANEY MADE IT TO TOOWOOMBA LATE IN THE AFTER-noon and continued east towards Brisbane and the Sunshine Coast. He wasn't even halfway through his journey but was happy with his progress.

Spurred on by an Allman Brothers CD, Delaney was determined to make it to Gympie before he called it a day. Finally, after nearly eleven hours on the road, a road weary Delaney pulled into Gympie and checked into a motel for the night.

Under brilliant sunny skies, Delaney set off the next morning with the goal of reaching MacKay – about halfway between Brisbane and Cairns – by dusk.

He stopped at Rockhampton for lunch and fuel. Delaney plonked himself down at a lone wooden picnic table at a nearby reserve and just as he was polishing off his salad roll, a baseball rolled to a stop in front of his feet.

Delaney got up and tossed it to the lad who had hit it. He was wearing cleats and baseball pants. Tufts of dark hair sprouted out of both sides of his New York Yankees cap.

"Thanks," he said, catching the waist-high throw barehanded like a cricketer.

"Practising your hitting?" Delaney asked the youngster, who looked to be about fourteen.

"Yeah," he said. "All of my mates are still in school so I'm just hitting a few balls off a tee from the cricket nets."

Delaney had a look where the lad was pointing. The nets were about a hundred metres away.

"Got a glove with you?" he asked.

"I do. It's at the cage. I have a portable screen that I use for fielding practice. I throw the balls into it and it bounces back. You never know where they're going to go so it's a good drill."

Delaney finished his soft drink which had gotten quite warm despite being in the shade.

"Mind if I toss a few to you? I used to play a little ball back in Melbourne."

"You played?" the lad said with a great deal of scepticism. "No offence, but how long ago was that?"

"About thirty years ago. I played in the thirds for Cheltenham. I was never much of a cricketer and always liked baseball, so one night about half a dozen of us rocked up to training and signed up to play. We played for the fun of it. If we happened to win it was a bonus," Delaney said as he and the lad approached the nets.

"You play for one of the local sides here?"

"Yeah, the Under 14 Hammers. I play in the outfield and bat fifth most days."

Delaney picked up the lad's mitt and a couple of balls and walked approximately sixty feet, the distance from the pitching mound to home plate. He forced his left hand into the tight-fitting glove. The sun was at his back. The lad, who batted right-handed, adjusted his cap and dug in at the plate.

"Take it easy on me, okay? I'm just going to lob these first few in."

Delaney's first throw landed six feet in front of the plate. "Just warming up," he shouted.

His next delivery sailed over the lad's head. "Are you sure you played ball?"

Delaney shook his head in the affirmative and sent his next pitch right across the imaginary plate. The lad swung and missed. "That better?" Delaney shouted.

Delaney picked up the last of the four baseballs at his feet. The lad planted his feet, took a couple of practice swings and waited with a determined look on his face. Delaney again threw the ball right down the middle but this time the kid made solid contact, the wooden bat sending a line drive high over his head. It came to rest in the grass about two-hundred-and-fifty metres away.

"That's a heck of a swing you got there," Delaney said as he took off the lad's glove and tossed it back to him. "I've got to get back on the road. What's your name? If you make it to the big leagues, I'll have a story to tell."

"Jake McCoy."

"Now that, is the name of a baseball player. Keep swinging," Delaney said, giving Jake a pat on the shoulder.

Delaney flexed his fifty-seven-year-old right arm a few times as he walked back to his car. *Four pitches and I'm sore. Shit.*

In the next couple of days, he passed through Mackay, Prosperine and Bowen.

The farther Delaney drove, the warmer it got. Instead of turning on the air conditioning he opened the car's windows and breathed in the warm, tropical air.

The last leg of the long journey was from Townsville to Cairns and took less than a day.

13

SIX DAYS AFTER SUN-UP RETURNED TO HIS KERANG paddock, the results of the colt's pre and post-race urine and blood samples were relayed to Racing Victoria stewards.

They were clean.

"Thank goodness. The last thing we needed was a scandal," head steward Dean Ayres told his colleagues at their end-of-the-week meeting. "We might have a star on our hands too. He ran the quickest 1100 on the day and that trainer of his ... what's his name's again?"

"Baker, Vern Baker," Racing Victoria communications director Tom Andrews said.

"Yeah, Baker. He's quite a character. Hasn't trained a winner in years, has his own property in Kerang. He even drove the float to Warracknabeal and back. Let's send a crew up there, do a piece on him."

"We're on it Dean."

"And gentlemen, out of all the tests we conducted in the past week, we did not have one positive. Our crackdown is working.

"Back to that race at Warracknabeal with Sun-Up, our integrity team had a good look at the betting patterns and has given it the all clear. There was one massive each way bet placed on him three days prior to the race by a TAB customer who has a history of making big bets and collecting too. Everyone else just piled on. A lot of big bets were made but I don't have to tell you that turnover is what drives our business.

"Alright. We've got a meeting at Mornington this afternoon and five meetings this weekend. Everyone have their assignments?"

There were nods around the table and an audible yes.

On the same morning four thousand kilometres north of Melbourne, Marge Sinclair showed Gary Delaney a vacant one-bedroom furnished unit at Coral Reef Apartments in the northern suburb of Hollaways Beach, a few kilometres north of the Cairns CBD and just two blocks from the beach.

Delaney had a quick look around the complex before Sinclair showed up. He liked what he saw. The complex's footpaths were surrounded by lush green gardens and palm trees and featured a massive swimming pool, a nicely laid out barbecue area with picnic tables, a tennis court and a putting green which Delaney planned to use regularly. He'd have a view of it all from his balcony.

Marge Sinclair arrived 10 minutes later and showed Delaney the unit. It was clean, well looked after and just the right size. Sinclair did not have to use any of her charm to get Delaney to sign the lease. He signed the year-long lease on the kitchen counter and added his bank details. Suncoast Realty would automatically deduct the monthly rent of $1252 on the first of every month.

"I told you I'd find you something suitable," Sinclair said.

"That you did. Thank you."

The two shook hands.

Three days later Delaney left his hotel room in the Cairns CBD and moved into his new home.

Barbara Stevenson said hello to Delaney from her balcony on the morning he moved in and welcomed him to the complex of 55 units. She was happy to see someone who didn't use a walker, and a man seemingly on his own. Delaney was carrying a heavy box and if he had put it down to chat, he'd have a hard time picking it back up. So, he slowed down just enough to say hi and safely made it up a flight of stairs to his second storey unit. The door wasn't locked, so Delaney gave it a slight nudge with his knee to open it. He dropped the box onto the floor and took a deep breath. He wiped the sweat off his forehead and stuck his head under the kitchen tap to cool down.

An elevator would sure be handy, he reasoned as he walked down the stairs to continue unpacking.

"Let me give you a hand," Barbara said as she introduced herself at the bottom of the stairs.

"Thanks. That's very nice of you. I can use the help. Gary Delaney," he said extending his hand.

"Nice to meet you Gary. You'll like it here. Going to be staying awhile?"

"I sure hope so. I signed a one-year lease," he said, grabbing a large black suitcase from the back of his Honda.

The flat was owned by a young couple who bought it as an investment property. Delaney was their first tenant and since he took such good care of the flat and always paid his rent on time, the owners had decided to never raise his rent. Phil and Maggie Garvey didn't need the extra $100 a month they could have received by upping the rent. They bought the flat purely for the tax breaks which negative gearing delivered.

Barbara, 58, lived four doors down from him in a one-bedroom flat she owned.

Delaney looked around, basking in the afternoon sunshine.

"I could get used to this," he said.

"Where are you from originally?" Delaney asked his neighbour, who was dressed in blue shorts, a light-coloured top and sandals.

"I'm a native Queenslander, originally from Brisbane. Been up here for about 10 years," she said adjusting her sunnies.

"Geez, that sun is strong," he said as he emptied more of his belongings from his car.

Delaney retrieved his favourite, but somewhat battered, fishing hat from the passenger seat and plonked it on his head.

It took five trips up and down the stairs to lug everything to his unit.

They placed the lot on the living room of the unit which featured a large flat-screen TV atop a well-polished black entertainment centre. A light blue couch and matching recliner faced the sizeable screen which would be perfect for watching the footy.

Delaney turned on the ceiling fan and opened a window and the sliding door leading to the balcony. Both had strong screens to keep the mosquitoes and bugs outside where they belonged.

"I hope water is okay; that's all I've got – for now," Delaney said. He found two clean glasses in the cupboard, filled them both from the tap and walked onto the balcony. Four chairs surrounded a small glass table. "Have a seat, Barbara. Thanks for the hand. I needed one."

"You're welcome, Gary. To your new home," she said, raising her glass and clinking it with his.

"And to helpful neighbours."

He took a long look around as he drank.

"I'll enjoy sitting up here," he said as he put his feet up on one of the two empty chairs.

He bombarded Barbara with questions about the complex for the next thirty minutes, mostly about the sort of people who lived there. The last thing he wanted was noisy neighbours. Nosey neighbours he could deal with. Marge Sinclair had told him the complex was a quiet one, but he wanted to hear it from someone who lived there.

"I'd say most of the people who live here are like us; they're retirees, some from Melbourne and even from Tassie. There are a few families on the other side of the pool, but you never hear a peep out of them. And the body corporate is very serious about its No Pets rule," Barbara said, which was music to Delaney's ears.

He later found out that the only noise would be from planes coming into land at the city's international airport which was only about five kilometres away. Most arrived in the afternoon and early evening, and depending on the time of year, brought tens of thousands of tourists to the sun-drenched north each week.

The two spent the next hour telling each other about their former occupations – Stevenson had been an accountant – past relationships and children.

"Sorry for being a little forward, but you wouldn't have dinner plans, would you?" Stevenson asked.

"Not yet. I was going to go over to Woolies or Coles in town later to pick up a few things. I saw plenty of places on the drive over here to grab a bite. Can you recommend one?"

"The RSL in town on the Esplanade has a two-for-one special for locals tonight. The food is pretty good. We can sit outside, and we won't even spend $20 between us."

"You're the numbers lady and it is hard to argue with a number like that."

Delaney spent a few hours that afternoon unpacking. There was plenty of closet space for his things, and when the last box was finally emptied, he flattened them all for recycling, tucked them under his arm, walked downstairs to the parking lot and tossed them in one of the complex's large recycling bins.

Delaney drove the fifteen minutes to the RSL. He found a nearby car park and quickly grabbed the last unoccupied outside table for himself and Barbara. Tourists were out in force on the warm night and the two locals had a few laughs at their expense as they walked by. They were easy to spot with their Cairns baseball caps and Great Barrier Reef T-shirts. So many were licking ice cream cones that Delaney wondered if there was some short of shortage overseas.

Ever the gentleman, Delaney paid for the meals.

Stevenson bought the drinks.

Just as they tucked into their mains, the heavens opened without warning, sending the tourists scattering for cover to escape the deluge. The diners were sheltered from the downpour which was so intense that the statue of a soldier on top of the massive cenotaph across the street took out a large umbrella. Delaney and his new neighbour had coffees in the lounge and dodged a few puddles left by the rain on their way to Delaney's car which was parked around the corner. By then the rain had tailed off to a drizzle.

"Just wait until the rainy season begins. It buckets down then. This was just a passing shower," Stevenson said.

14

BACK IN MELBOURNE, PASTRAMI PICKED UP HIS PHONE, tapped on his NAB bank app and once again looked at his bank balance.

"Holy shit."

Forty-eight hours after Sun-Up's win, at his direction, over $1.5 million had been deposited into his savings account by the TAB.

There was nearly $2.25 million sitting in his account. The next day he went to his local NAB branch, sat down with the assistant bank manager, and put $1.75 million into two separate term deposits. Locked in, the interest alone would bring him more than $35,000 a year. He kept the other $500,000 in his everyday account.

"That's my walking around money," he told Tannenbaum while they went for a walk on Airlie Beach one early May morning. It was 25 degrees, or 15 degrees higher than the temperature at Tullamarine where Pastrami and Anna Nimmity had departed the day before.

"You sure picked a fantastic spot to live Frankie, and a wonderful gal to share this all with. Jacquie is absolutely lovely."

"Sometimes I can't believe it myself," Tannenbaum said getting a bit emotional. "If I hadn't met you in the joint who knows where I'd be or what I'd be doing. We are even talking about having kids. Children. Me and her."

"You deserve it all mate, all of it."

Back at Tannenbaum's fully paid for beach house, Jacquie Sutton and Anna Nimmity were busy preparing a seafood platter for lunch.

"This was all caught last night, amazing isn't it?" Sutton asked.

"I guess," Anna said.

Anna preferred her fish dipped in batter with a side of chips. How she never gained a kilo was a marvel of medical science. The leggy model/spokesperson/presenter never weighed in at more than 54 kilos. She was in such demand due to her natural good looks that she had to hire an agent to sift through all the offers that came her way.

Under Bernie Russo's guidance and steady hand, Anna had graduated from catalogue work for Myer and K-Mart to being the pin-up girl for every country cup carnival in Victoria and New South Wales. She even presented the weekend weather a couple of times on Channel 11.

"She pointed to Perth and said Sydney was due for some rain and then confused Hobart and Darwin," news director Sammy Jorgenson told Russo the day after her latest fiasco. "Look she's bloody gorgeous and all. I get a hard on just thinking about her. But I can't put her on the air again until she has a few geography lessons."

"I'll take care of it. Put her down for the weekend of the 27th and 28th okay? It gives me three weeks to work with her."

"I don't know Bernie. She's too green."

"She told you about Sun-Up, didn't she? How much did you win because of her, eh? Twenty? Thirty thousand? The 27th and the 28th Sammy. By then she'll be able to find Kakadu blindfolded."

Russo spent so much time with Anna that Pastrami wondered if Russo was cutting his lunch. Russo was tempted, who wouldn't be? But after meeting Pastrami just once, he had enough sense not to push his luck. *I must be the only agent in the country not sleeping with his client.*

Anna however did introduce Russo to one of her model girlfriends, a 24-year-old dark-haired stunner named Dixie Moore.

When Miss Moore learned that it was Russo who lined up Anna's television appearances, she dumped her tradie boyfriend and all but moved into Russo's Docklands apartment.

The 45-year-old Russo had been around the block a few times, but never had he come across a woman as insatiable as the rather buxom

Dixie Moore. After a week of continuous humping he was as sore as a 35-year-old footballer.

"Easy Dixie, easy," he told her after their latest sexual encounter. When Russo recovered, he noticed that his bed had moved about 10 feet from the wall and the bed's headboard had come loose. *I don't know which is going to break first, the bed or my pecker, he wondered.*

"I'll be gentler Bernie, but sometimes I just can't help myself. You turn me on so much."

"I do?"

"You sure do." She proved it by giving him a long kiss.

"Can you get me on TV like you did for Anna?" she whispered in his ear while rubbing his crotch.

Russo broke from her embrace, got out of bed, put on his undies and rearranged his merchandise. "So that's what this is all about? You're fucking me so I can get you on TV?" he hollered.

"No, no Bernie. I am sleeping with you because I really like you."

Well there is only one way to find out, Bernie thought. Dixie was sitting up in bed, her 36D breasts were on fully display.

"Dixie," Bernie quietly said. "Number one, I am not your agent."

"Then take me on," she said.

"Let me be blunt Dixie. You're gorgeous and fantastic in bed."

Dixie smiled.

"But," Bernie continued and then lost his train of thought. "I'll see what I can do," he said after a long pause.

"Thank you," Dixie gushed. "Now come here and let me show you what I can do."

Three weeks later over Easter weekend, Dixie Moore got her chance on Channel 11's six o'clock news. With most of the news team away enjoying the long weekend, Sammy Jorgenson was down to his team of second stringers. He was down yet another reporter when Linda Reinke sent Jorgenson a text message on Easter Sunday morning saying she was ill and would not be able to come in the next two days. "Sick my arse, she's probably on some goddamn Easter egg hunt."

Jorgenson had agreed to work over the long weekend in exchange for the following weekend off. He and his wife Sarah had booked a few days at a Phillip Island bed and breakfast. Their two kids and dog would be looked after by Sarah's mum.

Jorgenson gazed at the large white board on the wall in his office which listed that day's assignments. Story, reporter and cameraman. He erased Reinke's name and reluctantly replaced it with the name of Dixie Moore. "Even a high school reporter with her own YouTube channel couldn't fuck this up."

Moore had been spending her free time over the past few weeks practicing at Russo's place. She set up her iPhone to record herself and holding a note pad started to speak into a hairbrush which served as her microphone.

"Police are investigating a home invasion which took place in the early hours this morning in Cranbourne in Melbourne's east. Police say that four armed men of African appearance broke into a home on Anderson Crescent and held a family of four at knifepoint while they ransacked the home apparently looking for drugs and cash. Finding none, the men took the phones from their victims, ripped out the cord of the landline phone from the wall, demanded the keys to the family's two cars and drove off. No one was injured. Police are examining security camera footage."

Dixie "interviewed" Sr Constable Cynthia Parker who remained at the scene and then looked straight into the camera and said "From Cranbourne, Dixie Moore, Channel 11 news."

Moore had been recording the Channel 11 newscast each evening and repeating what the reporters said in their stand-ups.

"That's not too bad," Moore said to herself as she replayed her phony report on the home invasion on her iPhone. "I can do this."

Jorgenson walked into the half empty newsroom. Dixie was chatting to cameraman Greg Vickers. "Dixie," Jorgenson said, "Linda has called in sick. You're doing her yarns. You and Vickers head down to St Patrick's and do a report on Easter Mass and then go over to the MCG, mention the big weekend of footy and that Geelong and Hawthorn close out Round 6 in front of an expected 85,000 fans tomorrow.

Moore scribbled as much as she could on her note pad.

"Did you get all that?" Moore asked Vickers after Jorgenson returned to his office. "Yup. A pretty easy day if you ask me."

Producer Craig Oliver spent over an hour with Dixie in the editing room after she returned to the newsroom. He made a few cuts, had her add a few extra words as the camera scanned St Patrick's and leaned back in his chair. "Alright. It's ready to go on air."

"Did I do okay?" Moore asked.

"For your first time? Yes. But Jorgenson is the one who will decide if you get another assignment," Oliver said.

"How did it go?" Anna Nimmity asked Dixie when she came back to the newsroom. Anna was back for her fourth stint doing the weather. She had been practicing with Russo over the past couple of weeks for her grand final.

"I'm not sure. I think I did alright. But."

Moore sent Russo a text, telling him that she would be doing her first on-air reports on the 6pm news.

Dixie watched from the newsroom as her report went to air at 6:07pm.

Sitting at home that night, Russo turned on Channel 11 at 6pm to watch the television debut of his girlfriend. "Please don't let this be a train wreck," he said.

"That wasn't too bad," Russo said with a sigh of relief after Dixie's report aired. "She wasn't that nervous and looked comfortable in front of the camera, but I'll advise her to keep doing her modelling. It's a better earn although she is getting close to her 26th birthday, nearly retirement age for some models."

Despite reporting from the studio, Anna had the tougher job of the two aspiring presenters. Anna's weather report aired live. At 6:55, anchor Lawrence Stone introduced her.

"We had a beautiful Easter in the city with the high reaching 18 degrees at 2:30 this afternoon after a low of 9 this morning. It is currently 14 with a light breeze from the southwest"

"So far so good Anna," Russo said. "Keep going hun."

Watching a few kilometres away, Pastrami hadn't been this nervous since last year's Melbourne Cup. "Stay calm. We rehearsed this a hundred times Anna."

"Around the nation," Anna continued as the screen behind her brought up the national weather map. "Perth is looking at a soggy Easter Monday with a high of 22, Sydney is expecting sunny skies and a high of 24 while in Melbourne tomorrow we're looking at a high of 17 under cloudy skies for the Geelong-Hawthorn clash at the MCG. A few showers are expected to come through at night, well after the game ends."

Anna threw it back to Stone, who wrapped up the telecast. "And that's the latest from the 11 newsroom. Thank you for watching, we'll see you again tomorrow at 6."

"And ... we're clear," stage manager Richie Garcia called out.

"Thank fucking Christ," Jorgenson said in his office where he watched the telecast. "No major gaffes. But Anna and her friend need a few runs in the twos before they're senior side material."

Jorgenson rang Russo the next morning. "I was surprised to tell you the truth Bernie. I thought one of them would fuck up, but they were okay. We're even for the tip on Sun-Up. Agreed?"

"Yes, Russo said.

"Now, talking as a news director to an agent. I'm gonna be blunt. Anna and Dixie have potential, but they have got to learn the business just like anyone else. And that means time in the twos."

"Where are you going to send them?"

"Cairns. There's a good general assignment reporter at our affiliate there who deserves a chance in the big time and the weather girl is ready for a step up as well. If they're interested, they'll have to be in Cairns and ready to start in three weeks."

Cairns? Russo said to himself. Hmm. *That's not a bad idea. I'll miss Dixie, and the sex but I'm not getting any younger. She'll find some young bloke up there and forget all about me.*

"I'll have a word with them both Sammy and let you know right away."

Later that afternoon Russo met with Anna and Dixie at Pastrami's Southbank apartment. At first Jorgenson's proposal did not go down well.

"Way the fuck up there? Cyclones, crocs. And it is so fucking hot," Dixie said.

"Not this time of year. It's 27, 28 every day and the humidity is down," Russo said.

"What do you think Johnny?" Anna asked her boyfriend of nearly four months.

"It's a good opportunity Anna. There are kids spending four years at Uni studying journalism who would do anything for an on-air job. If you're serious about television I would take it."

To be truthful, Pastrami had been tiring of Anna. He was a bit jealous of Frankie who had a winner in Jacquie Sutton.

It's time to settle down with someone more refined, more mature, Pastrami thought. *Someone who doesn't act like she is still in high school.*

"Why don't you two talk it over in private," Russo told Dixie and Anna. "Johnny and I are going to run downstairs and pick up some dinner."

"Thai sound alright girls?"

"Yeah, whatever," they replied in unison.

"What do you think Anna? Should we move to Cairns?" Dixie asked as soon as the front door closed.

"I'm not sure I want to give up modelling and all those country cup appearances. It's a good earn."

"We'll make less, but we can share an apartment, meet some guys, guys our age," Dixie said.

"I thought you liked Bernie."

"I do. But he is 45 years old. My dad is 54 for goodness sake."

Dixie's outspokenness caused Anna to think about her relationship with Johnny. *Sure he is 15 years older, but he treats me nice, he has tons of money, this nice apartment. But is he the one? I don't know.*

"Do you really think we should leave Melbourne?" Anna asked.

"I think so. We only have a few more years left modelling. Seventeen and eighteen-year-olds will start to push us out soon. Then what do we do?"

Anna took a deep breath. "Alright. We'll give it a go."

"Fantastic," Dixie said embracing her BFF.

"Can you tell them when they get back? I don't think I can," Anna said.

15

TWO WEEKS AFTER THEY MET, DELANEY AND BARBARA spent their first night together.

Delaney had not slept with anyone in several months. Stevenson's last fling had been more than two years ago.

"I'm afraid I've put on a few kilos over the years," she said as she patted her stomach. "And gravity is starting to take its toll," she added, looking down at her sagging breasts which were encased in a lacy black bra.

"You look fine," Delaney reassured her. "Look at me, I've got grey hair everywhere, and I mean everywhere, and I'm about to say a prayer to whomever is in charge of erections."

Barbara laughed. "Even so, can you turn the lamp off? Please? Maybe after I'm more comfortable ..."

"Sure," Delaney said. "It's fine, really. It doesn't matter."

Since they lived just a few doors down from each other, Barbara Stevenson and Gary Delaney saw each other every day and spent several afternoons a week together.

They took walks on a nicely laid out bicycle/walking path adjacent to the nearby beach where signs warned those fancying a dip of stingers and crocodiles, and instructed swimmers or waders what to do in case of a stinger attack. Vinegar was used to treat the sting and bottles of it were placed every couple of hundred metres along the path.

What kind of a fucking place is this? Delaney wondered. *Crocs, stingers.* He had even read of pythons – small ones – falling out of trees.

If a fucking python falls out of a tree and lands on me, I am on the first flight out of here.

With the ocean temperature at a delightful 27 degrees, Delaney decided one afternoon to have a dip in the Coral Sea. However, he wasn't tempting fate. He walked to a large netted area patrolled by a lifeguard and with no danger of encountering a stinger or croc, enjoyed the warm water crashing over him for several minutes.

Two kids knee-deep in the water then started screaming at the top of their lungs. They were simply enjoying themselves, but their piercing screams drowned out the sound of the surf and drove Delaney out of the water. He towelled off, gathered his few belongings, and walked back home.

One morning Delaney and Barbara shared a bucket of balls at a nearby driving range. It was the first time Barbara had ever hit a golf ball. After a few misses and a bit of instruction she managed to send a few balls past the 100-metre marker.

They advanced to a nine-hole course with mixed results, took a day trip to Green Island and went to the races at nearby Cannon Park Racecourse one Saturday where he told her about his involvement with Too Hard Wrong Spot and how his winnings were tiding him over. He still hadn't hung any pictures of his money maker in his unit.

"The Melbourne Cup? Wow," Barbara bubbled.

She was surprised when Delaney told her how much he had banked as part-owner. "Sure beats working, doesn't it?"

"It sure does. Now all he needs to do is win the big one. He's developing a habit of coming in second."

"What's wrong with second?"

"The big money goes to the one who finishes first," he said and explained how the winner of the cup gets nearly $3 million more in prize money than the horse who comes in second.

"That's more money than I'll ever see," Barbara quipped.

In the third race of the sunny and warm afternoon Barbara placed a bet with her three favourite numbers and hit the trifecta for $256.

"I've never won this much money before, never," she bubbled as she counted her winnings.

"Just don't spend it all in one place," Delaney quipped.

"Why not? That's where I won it. Dinner is on me tonight."

Unfamiliar with the local horses, jockeys and trainers, Delaney struggled to back a winner or even find a placegetter. He thought he was on to a good thing late in the day; a horse who liked to lead was breaking from an outside gate over 1200m and was wearing blinkers for the first time. He was a $22 chance, so Delaney put $10 each way on him. There was a delay as the horses reached the starting gate and then an announcement by the race caller came over the speakers.

"The blinkers on number seven, Ocean Stinger have broken. The horse will now race without blinkers."

"What do you mean no blinkers? That's why I backed him," Delaney loudly said to no one in particular.

The gates crashed back. Ocean Stinger jumped in the second half of the 12-horse field and beat two horses home.

"They don't have a spare pair of blinkers at the gate that can be put on horses in a situation like this? The horse should have been scratched," Delaney said.

"What are blinkers?" Barbara asked.

"Well," a rather heated Delaney started to say. "I'll tell you over dinner."

16

DELANEY AND STEVENSON GAVE SOME THOUGHT TO moving in together several months later.

Much of the reasoning on setting up house together was based purely on the economics of having one set of bills instead of two. There would more money for an overseas trip, more money for a nicer and larger unit in a more upscale development and less worry about the bills which landed in each of their post boxes with frightening regularity. Each preferred paper bills rather than electronic ones.

They had three divorces between them. Stevenson's second husband, a boat captain who ran tourists out to the dying Great Barrier Reef five times a week, died of a stroke a year after their divorce became final. Stevenson had two children from a first marriage, both of whom were so consumed with their own mortgage-sucking lives in Sydney that they barely checked in to see how their mother was doing.

Stevenson and Delaney enjoyed their time together and thought the same way politically, which was important to them both. Delaney couldn't see himself spending more than an evening with a right-winger and they were generally in agreement over what to watch on television each evening – nothing.

The stumbling block was Delaney's snoring. It kept Barbara up at night. She didn't want to rock the boat and say something, but one night when Delaney got up to pee, which often was three times a night, she wasn't sleeping next to him.

What the ...? Where is she? he wondered.

Delaney checked the bathroom first – empty. He then walked into the living room and found her fast asleep on the couch. Her head was resting on a throw pillow with her robe draped over her.

He decided to let her sleep. They'd talk about it in the morning.

"It's your snoring Gary," Barbara said as they ate breakfast. "I couldn't get to sleep so I decided to sleep on the couch. You're not mad, are you?"

"No. not at all. I wish you'd have woken me. I would have slept on the couch."

"I'm not going to kick you out of your own bed Gary. I slept alright on the couch, really."

"How bad is my snoring? Bad, bad or just bad?"

"Well," Barbara said, choosing her words very carefully. "The painting hanging over the bed? It shakes when you snore."

"It shakes? You're joking, aren't you?"

"I am, but we have to do something."

They tried a humidifier – a top-of-the-line $199 model – which helped a bit. The painting of the calming seascape over Delaney's bed now just rattled. Two days later Delaney spoke to a local pharmacist who suggested that he clear his nasal passages with a medicated spray each night before turning in. That night he gave each nostril two spritzes. Barbara gave him the result in the morning.

Amazingly, the nasal spray worked.

"Phew, what a relief. I guess we can count sleep apnea out."

"For now," Barbara said. "But we better keep an eye on it."

"Agreed," Delaney said.

Delaney had seen sleep apnea machines at the chemist and did not like the looks of them. *A mask over the mouth? Tubes from the nose connected to a $2000 machine. No thank you. I couldn't wear one of those* *fucking things. As long as the spray – $12.50 – for a month's worth works, I'm sticking with it.*

Delaney had another health scare just a few weeks later when he noticed some blood in the toilet after laying some cable. "Holy shit," he yelled – no pun intended. "I better see Dr Lawson."

Three mornings later, Delaney and Barbara were seated in Dr Ernest Lawson's waiting room. After a short wait he was called in.

"What can I do for you today Gary?" his GP of a few months asked.

"Well, I went to the toilet a couple of days ago and how can I put this? There was some blood – from my errr, back passage – mixed in with my poo."

"Is there any family history of bowel cancer?" Lawson asked.

"Bowel cancer? I remember my dad had some polyps removed years ago, but it turned out to be nothing."

"Have you had a colonoscopy before?"

"I haven't."

"Well, let's have a look."

"A look at what?"

"Drop 'em and bend over Gary."

"This is embarrassing doctor."

"It has to be done and it will take just a few seconds."

Dr Ernest Lawson, aged 55, pushed his stylish glasses back on his nose, took out a plastic glove, slid it over his right hand and went where no man – or woman – had gone before.

"Looks like you just have a haemorrhoid. But, since your father had polyps, I suggest having a colonoscopy just to be sure. You're over 50 anyways and everyone over 50 should have a colonoscopy."

"Okay," Delaney said.

Lawson took the glove off his hand and disposed of it in a specially marked bin.

"You have private health insurance, so we'll have it done at a private hospital. I'll give you a referral to a very good gastroenterologist, Murray Bridge. His office is in Edmonton, just south of here. Hopefully we can get it done in two or three weeks.

Delaney laughed. "Murray Bridge? Like the town in SA?"

"Yup. I have sent hundreds of patients to him over the years. Not one has given me a bad report. Come back and see me after the colonoscopy and we'll go over the results."

"Now let's take your blood pressure and see if it has come down a bit."

As Dr Lawson put the cuff around Delaney's upper left arm and pumped it up, Delaney tried to relax by looking at several winners' photos on the wall that were taken at Cannon Park Racecourse.

Dr Lawson had been a part owner in several horses a few years back. All had saluted at one time in their careers and Lawson often told his friends that being part owner of a winner, even at a country course like Cairns, gave him a thrill like no other despite never having made a cent from the venture. These days Lawson's money was tied up in his wife and kids and a hefty mortgage. However, he still liked having a modest punt on the bigger races in Sydney and Melbourne and over the Brisbane winter carnival.

Lawson listened as the cuff of the monitor eased and gazed at the machine's screen. "One thirty-five over ninety-five. A little high, Gary, but I'm guessing it is because you're a bit anxious and nervous over what we've been talking about. I'll keep an eye on it. If it remains high, we might have to change the dosage of your blood pressure medication."

"Geez Doc, I'm falling to pieces and I've just got up here."

Lawson laughed. "You'll be here for many years to come Gary. Don't worry about it. This is strictly routine."

Delaney took the referral, shook Lawson's hand, the same hand which entered his butt, and walked back to the reception area. He waved at Barbara and approached one of three women seated behind a U-shaped table.

"I have a referral here for Dr Murray Bridge," Delaney told her.

"I'll fax this over to Dr Bridge's rooms for you right now," a beaming Rhonda Cook said. Cook got up from her chair, walked to a massive combination copier/printer/fax machine/coffee maker, pressed a few buttons and off it went.

"Dr Lawson has bulk billed you for today's visit."

"Really," Delaney said. "That was nice of him. Oh, I'll need to make a follow-up appointment. Maybe in four to six weeks?"

Cook sorted out a date and time, handed him a card and told him to ring Dr Bridge's rooms right away. "He gets very busy. Hopefully he can get you in soon."

"Me too."

Delaney used the hand sanitiser at the counter – just a precaution – and walked over to where Barbara was seated.

"And?" she asked.

"I tell you outside."

Delaney filled her in on the examination and told her that Dr Lawson suggested a colonoscopy.

"That's not too bad. It's probably nothing," Barbara said taking his hand in hers as they walked to Delaney's car.

17

THE NEXT STOP ON THE COLONOSCOPY TRAIN TOOK
Gary Delaney to the southern suburb of Edmonton which is where
a couple of college backpackers from the US state of New Jersey
inadvertently ended up a year earlier complete with their snow skiing gear
after mistaking Edmonton in Queensland, Australia, for Edmonton in
Alberta, Canada when they booked their overseas trip online. However,
Junior McGee and Fred Dillon's stupidity, lack of common sense and
limited knowledge of geography paid off when they wound up on TV
news bulletins worldwide and were handed million-dollar contracts by
MTV to host a new travel show.

"These guys are so stupid they are fucking hilarious," network junior
producer Lefty Cohen said when he pitched the idea to Jacob Gotlieb,
the head of programming. "They'll be bigger than that bunch of arseholes
we locked in that beach house last summer on the Jersey shore."

Gotlieb and senior producer Reginald McKenzie agreed and gave
Cohen the green light, a budget of $2.15 million and half a year to get
six episodes ready to air. McGee and Dillon wound up on the cover of
People magazine under the heading *The Future of America* while Cohen
found himself in hot water for knocking up a script writer at a wild wrap
party following the filming of the sixth and last episode.

Dude, first dibs on the kid if it's a chick but only if she's hot, McGee
informed Cohen in a text message.

The office of Dr Murray Bridge was up a long and narrow flight of stairs
in an older building in the upscale and growing suburb of Edmonton

about 10 kilometres south of the Cairns CBD.

Delaney took a breath after reaching the top of the stairs and found himself in the waiting room.

There should be a fucking Sherpa here to guide patients to the top, he thought.

Delaney spent fifteen minutes with Dr Bridge. He was on the ball, going over his entire medical history. He questioned Delaney about his late father's polyps, his own eating habits and then told him he was booking him in for a colonoscopy in two weeks at a private hospital a block away.

"It's just routine, don't worry about it."

Bridge's receptionist billed him $200 for the consultation, $80 which he got back from Medicare.

Before Delaney left, he was given a pamphlet by the receptionist which had all the details of the colonoscopy prep he was to begin the afternoon prior to his admittance.

"You can pick up the sachets at any chemist," she added.

Delaney had asked Dr Google what was involved and was not pleased with what he had discovered.

"Are those sachets really that bad?" he asked the receptionist.

"They're better than they were. There's less to drink than there was five years ago, but I'll be honest with you, it's not a pleasant experience.

"We have never had a patient who couldn't drink the mix. You'll get through it," she said.

With my luck I'll be the first, he thought as he gripped the handrail and climbed down the steep flight of stairs. It was raining when Delaney stepped outside, not a steady rain and he could see patches of blue sky in the distance. Choosing not to get wet, he waited a few minutes for the rain to pass, got to his car and then went to grab some lunch. He started to read the pamphlet while he ate but got nauseous and put it away.

18

IT MAY BE THE MOST VILE, REVOLTING AND DISGUSTING concoction ever designed for human consumption and Gary Delaney had to drink not one, not two, but three tall glasses of the powdery mixture over the next six hours.

The cleansing of the bowels on the night before his colonoscopy was about to begin. Delaney opened one of the sachets, took a brief sniff and quickly pulled it away. *Just three glasses*, he told himself. *Three glasses*.

With the deadline for the first glass rapidly approaching, Delaney plunked the powder into a glass, filled it with cold water, stirred it several times and gazed at it. Getting it down without his breakfast coming up was the first challenge.

Standing over the kitchen sink just in case his breakfast reappeared, he took the first sip of the orange-flavoured mixture and shuddered.

"THIS IS FUCKING HORRIBLE," he shouted. After taking a deep breath, he took a longer drink of the putrid liquid and then polished off the rest of it, slamming the glass down on the kitchen table when it was finally empty.

"One down, two more to go," he said loudly.

At least four glasses of water or some other approved drink to combat dehydration was next on the menu. Now ordinarily, a cool glass of water would be easy to down. Anyone can do it. Even his elderly uncle, Robert, who these days had to ingest everything through a straw. A fucking straw. But four straight glasses of water? It was a chore. Bloated and exhausted after downing the last of the four, Delaney took a seat on the sofa.

He repeated the entire exercise three hours later, and again around 9pm and waited for the anal fireworks to begin.

His colonoscopy was scheduled at 11:10 the following morning and he was hopeful that the flushing of his toilet would cease by midnight.

Barbara had told him of her brother Thomas, who two years ago flushed his toilet 36 times and went through a roll-and-a-half of three-ply toilet paper prior to his colonoscopy.

"Poor Thomas thought by the last flush the bloody toilet handle would come off from overuse."

Thirty-six times was nearly a record according to *The Guinness Book of World Records*. Yes, the good book even has a record for most flushes in one night and it is held by a somewhat portly fellow named Louis Childress, who won last year's Independence Day (July 4) hot dog-eating contest at Coney Island in Brooklyn in the US.

Not content with eating just the dogs, the fuckwit had put mustard and sauerkraut on every one of them. He won the contest and a year's supply of hot dogs but did not leave his bathroom until the afternoon of July 8 and passed away the following morning.

An overdose of sauerkraut was the official cause of death according to Brooklyn coroner Clay Mitchell, who was immediately relieved of his duties by the New York City Health Department and placed on paid leave.

Mitchell celebrated his unplanned paid holiday by taking his family to Coney Island. "Is this a great country or what?" he boasted to his wife and two young children before boarding *The Cyclone* without them.

At its uppermost point, Mitchell lifted the safety bar, attempted to take a selfie and fell to his death from the historic wooden roller coaster which opened on June 26, 1927.

He became its fourth victim. The obese middle-aged woman he landed on – one would think she would have broken his fall – was wearing a Keep America Great T-shirt with Donald Trump's picture plastered on the front and back. She became victim number five. As the remaining passengers were safely taken off *The Cyclone* by Coney Island staff and emergency personnel, it became clear to Clay's wife, Courtney, that he was the one who had been ejected from the ride.

Sobbing uncontrollably and holding her two kids by their hands, Courtney was escorted to the area where her husband and the Trump supporter were mashed together and covered by a green tarpaulin. Courtney took a quick look as the tarpaulin was lifted by a police officer and let out a massive scream.

After her crying subsided, she lifted her head from the chest of the police officer who was consoling her and asked, "Will I get any of his paid leave money?"

"You'll get plenty more than that with a good lawyer," the copper said.

At the sound of those promising words, Courtney Mitchell's tears and sobbing were replaced by a wide smile.

It was just before midnight when Delaney made his last disposal of the evening. He trudged off to bed, his sore and raw arse aching – sent a couple of spritzes of his nose spray into each nostril – and was asleep within five minutes.

He was up 90 minutes later and another two hours after that to finish the evacuation job which was into its 14th hour.

Remembering not to eat or drink anything when he awoke, Delaney showered, got dressed, had a look at the morning paper and waited for Barbara to drive him to Edmonton Private Hospital.

He arrived at 10:45 am for his 11:10 appointment, kissed Barbara goodbye and went into the modern three-storey building.

"I'll see you in a few hours," Barbara said. "Don't worry."

Not even 10 minutes after arriving, he heard his name called out and took a seat alongside a nurse who asked him a laundry list of questions.

"Do you have any metal objects in you? Do you have a pacemaker? Are you an intravenous drug user? Have you been out of the country in the last few weeks?"

"No. No. No, no."

"Is it true your partner is leaving you just as soon as she recovers her eyesight?

"Huh?" Delaney said with a puzzled look on his face. Once he realised she was joking around, he let out a nervous laugh.

"Just checking if you were paying attention," the nurse said.

She was pleasant enough, in her early 30s he guessed. She was a bit rough around the edges, a bit overweight and had tattoos up and down one arm.

She rolled up his sleeve to check his blood pressure and much to his surprise it was a perfect 122 over 78.

She then took his temperature with some new device that barely touched his forehead. Again, near perfect: 36.7. His weight was an even 79kg, which counted his shoes and clothing.

"Now follow me," the nurse said. They walked down a long corridor to a bunch of cubicles. She opened the door to one and told Delaney to take off all his clothes – everything – and then to put on a gown which she handed him. "Make sure the opening is at the back," she reminded him.

A white robe and disposable cloth slippers finished off the ensemble.

"When you are done," she continued, "put all your things in this basket and take it with you to the waiting room. The anaesthetist will call you when it is your turn. She flashed a smile. "Good luck," she said.

Delaney shut the door and got undressed, put the paper blue gown on – with the opening at the back – and then the white robe which resembled something one would get at a classy hotel or an upmarket massage parlour. He put on the cloth slippers and with his things packed into a small basket, he extended its handles, picked it up and walked to the waiting room where four men and one woman were seated. They all had on the same blue gown, white robe and cloth slippers.

"Looks like we all shop at the same store," Delaney said as he took a seat.

One of the men smiled and another adjusted his merchandise to keep it out of sight. The other two couldn't be bothered from looking up from their phones. The woman let out an uncomfortable laugh. She was the next one called. A nurse took her basket and escorted her into the operating theatre.

Delaney picked up a golf magazine with a picture of someone who looked like Lee Trevino on it. *How old is this magazine anyways? Only 18 years. Par for a waiting room*, Delaney thought.

"Golf is a good walk spoiled," Mark Twain once wrote. Perhaps, but when you send a tee shot 250 metres down the centre of a fairway or hit an iron to within two feet of the cup, or sink a putt from 20 metres, there is not a better feeling on Earth; unless it's your divorce attorney ringing to tell you your ex doesn't want anything.

Delaney lifted his head when he heard his name called by the anaesthetist. Holding a clipboard, he motioned for Delaney to follow him into a small office. "Leave the basket," he said. The anaesthetist looked to be in his 50s. He was tall with dark hair and not overly enthused. He had probably put 15 or 20 people under since his first patient at 7am.

"Allergies?" he asked.

"Penicillin," Delaney answered although he couldn't be 100 per cent sure. It was one of those things your mother told you when you finally left home for good. But better to be safe than sorry so he always answered penicillin when asked.

After his request to have the IV inserted into his arm instead of the top of his hand, which hurt like a motherfucker and left a nasty mark, was refused, Delaney walked back to the waiting room to wait. And wait some more. Two more had gone into surgery during his brief absence leaving a cosy group of four. Delaney had overheard a lot of weird phone conversations over the years but the next was about to make its way to the top of the list. The phone of the bloke sitting next to him started to ring. He pulled it out. From where, Delaney did not want to know.

"That's alright mate." Silence followed and then came the corker. "Listen, I am about to have a colonoscopy. Yeah, a colonoscopy. So, I'll get back to you."

Delaney's name was called next. He knew the drill; hand the basket to the nurse and walk into theatre. He was greeted by the anaesthetist.

"Lay down on your left side please with your right arm extended and relax," he was told. He felt the doctor's hand looking for a vein. "Now you'll feel a little prick."

With the needle firmly in place and his hand throbbing, Dr Murray Bridge, resplendent in his surgical garb, sauntered over and took a seat on a stool facing him. A tall, distinguished, good-looking man with a full head of hair and a pair of trendy glasses, Dr Bridge had a good bedside manner. He uttered a friendly hello, looked at his clipboard and then Delaney.

"You're looking well Gary," he said.

Well? Delaney said to himself. *Hardly. I haven't eaten a full meal in about 36 hours and spent the better part of the previous evening in the crapper. I'm also half-asleep laying on an operating table in a paper gown with my raw and red arse fully exposed.*

The last words he heard came from the anaesthetist. "Count backwards from one hundred please."

Delaney woke up less than an hour later in a reclining chair, the IV still firmly stuck in his hand and farting like he was an extra in the campfire scene from *Blazing Saddles*.

He wondered how he got from the operating table into the recliner but drew a blank. *Maybe it's better not to know,* he thought.

The curtains on both sides of his recliner then opened revealing a nurse carrying sandwiches and juice.

He picked up a sandwich, and unsure of what it was, examined it and sniffed it.

"CHOPPED LIVER IN A CATHOLIC HOSPITAL? Is this some sort of a joke?" he asked the nurse.

"Well, it was either that or Gefilte fish, but the chopped liver goes down easier," the nurse said.

"Gefilte fish? That's even worse than the crap I drank yesterday. Do you have any hot dogs?" Delaney asked. "Oh, and if you do, hold the sauerkraut, okay?"

Dr Bridge came around soon after and told Delaney that everything had gone well and didn't believe there was anything to worry about. Just a haemorrhoid.

"I took a few samples anyway and they'll be sent to pathology. Have a follow-up with your GP, but I expect everything to come back fine."

Barbara was waiting for Delaney in the reception area when he was released forty-five minutes later. Still a bit groggy from the anaesthetic, she drove them straight back to Coral Reef Apartments. He went straight to bed and woke up around dinner time. Barbara came by a bit after six with a massive container of lasagne. She heated up some garlic bread and the feast began. Not having eaten since the previous day, Delaney had two big portions and after Barbara returned to her apartment he sat on his balcony and enjoyed the warm breeze coming off the Coral Sea.

The next morning Delaney took the best shit of his life. Remnants of the previous night's meal slid out of him like an exuberant kid going down a water slide.

Delaney wondered how he ever got anything done when he was working five days a week. It seemed every appointment he now had was with a doctor or specialist.

A somewhat nervous Delaney saw Dr Lawson two weeks later to get the results of the biopsies which as expected came back negative. Delaney let out a big sigh of relief and then another when Dr Lawson told him he didn't need another colonoscopy for three or four years.

"Just to be on the safe side," he said.

"Good, maybe those sachets will taste a bit better by then. They were brutal."

"I wouldn't count on it," Dr Lawson said.

19

DELANEY GOT A COLD BOTTLE OF WATER OUT OF THE fridge when he returned home and drank it slowly while sitting on his balcony. Not seeing anyone on the putting green, Delaney grabbed his putter from his golf bag, grabbed his hat, a couple of golf balls and walked downstairs.

On his way to the putting green Delaney crossed paths with a barefooted woman wearing pyjamas. It was a little past 4pm. Delaney said hello but the woman, who appeared to be about thirty-five years old, continued walking without even acknowledging his greeting. Her mouth was open as wide as a Murray River carp and her eyes looked straight ahead.

She has got to be on something, Delaney thought, *but what?*

Delaney had noticed her once or twice before. She lived on the other side of the complex with a much older man who did odd jobs around town and kept to himself. He never saw the stocky man – or the woman – in the pool or using any of the complex's facilities.

Could the woman be his daughter? Nah, she didn't bear any resemblance to him. She was taller and looked nothing like him in the face. She had shoulder length blonde hair while his hair was brown and turning grey. His girlfriend? Not with an age difference like that.

Delaney opened the gate to the putting green and tossed three scuffed balls onto the green. He knocked the ball closest to the pin into the cup and then two and three-putted the other two.

He'd bent down to take the balls out of the cup when he spotted the pyjama-clad woman approaching a downstairs unit. She stood in front of the door for a minute and then banged on it loudly. It opened. The same stocky man appeared. Clad only in a pair of shorts, he let her in, had a quick look around and slammed the door shut. He did not notice Delaney, who witnessed the whole episode.

What the hell is going on in there? Delaney wondered. *Could he be holding her against her will?* He vowed to get to the bottom of it.

Delaney stayed on the putting green for another thirty minutes or so and made a detour on the way to his unit. He quietly walked past the flat occupied by the old-timer and the woman. He tried to have a peek inside, but the curtains were tightly drawn shut. The only noise coming out of the unit was from a radio tuned to a station broadcasting the day's racing.

Delaney sauntered over to the parking lot behind the units opposite his and had a look at the guy's ute. There were some empty paint buckets, rollers and brushes in the back. He peered into the windows. Cigarette butts littered the floor along with some beer bottles and fast food wrappings. There was a bit of tomato sauce – or maybe even blood – on the passenger seat. A long piece of chain was on the floormat of the passenger seat. He looked closer, shielding his eyes from the sun and then felt a tap on his shoulder.

"Looking for something, mate?"

Delaney jumped at the unexpected sound of a man's voice. One of the golf balls he was holding fell out of his hand and rolled away. He turned around and came face-to-face with the ute's owner.

"What the hell are you doing?" Lawrence Adderley asked.

"Well, I need some work done to my unit, saw the paint in the back of your ute and wondered what other sort of work you do."

Adderley looked Delaney in the eye, turned and spat on the ground. His tanned belly hung over his shorts. He reeked of cigarette smoke and beer.

"I don't do no work around this here place. Now get the fuck away from my ute and keep out of my business, you understand?"

"Sorry to bother you, mate. I'll find another painter," Delaney said.

He retrieved his golf ball and slowly walked away, taking the long way back to his unit. He did not want the bloke to see which unit was his although he knew he could find out if he wanted to.

Adderley made sure his ute was locked and angrily dashed back to his unit.

"Don't be walking around outside unless I give you the okay," Adderley yelled when he got inside. He fastened a chain to Megan Beale's ankle and anchored it to the wall. He tossed her on the couch, pulled her pyjama bottoms down and yanked her top off. He sucked on her large breasts, pulled his shorts off, climbed onto her and stuck his small dick inside her. Megan Beale never made a sound. She looked straight ahead, focused on a small hole in a wall where a picture once hung as he finished.

Satisfied with himself, Lawrence Adderley stuffed his limp dick into his shorts and walked over to the sink. He poured a glass of water and reached for a bottle of tablets he kept on a shelf above the stove. He took one and handed it to his flatmate. "Take this," he barked at her. "It's good for ya."

Megan Beale did as she was told and washed the pill down with a few sips of water.

Adderley asked Beale to open her mouth to make sure she had swallowed the pill and when he found no evidence of it, gave her a pat on the head like a dog. "That's my girl," he said.

That night over dinner at Barbara's place, Delaney told her what happened that afternoon.

"Do you really believe she's being held against her will?" Barbara asked.

"If I was a betting man I would say yes. She seems to be drugged to the eyeballs and that guy – whose name I now know is Lawrence Adderley – looks to be nothing but trouble."

"How'd you find out his name?"

"I went through his letterbox."

"Aren't they all locked?"

"I jimmied it open with a paper clip."

"You did what?"

"Relax, it's hardly a big crime," Delaney said. "Once I had a look, I put everything back in and relocked it. Nobody will know."

"Are you sure you want to get involved in all this?"

"Well, it wasn't my idea to become some private investigator, but if that woman is being held captive in that apartment, I can't just ignore it."

"You're right," Barbara said. "Are you going to get in contact with the police?"

"Not yet. First I want to see exactly what is going on in there."

"And how are you going to find that out?"

"That's where you come in." Delaney smiled.

"Uh oh, I don't like the sound of that."

"Nothing will happen to you. Here's what I am thinking. I overheard two tenants talking as I was getting my mail and they mentioned that the local water company will be here in the morning to fix a leaking pipe. Apparently, it's affecting several units on the other side of the complex.

"With luck, Adderley will leave in his truck before they get here. Once he's gone, I'll give you the all-clear and then you go to his unit. I've got you a reflective vest, work pants and shirt, a hat, work boots, clipboard, an ID card to hang around your neck. You say you are with the water company and you're there to check the water pressure due to the broken pipe in the complex. If you're let in, turn on the taps in the kitchen and bathroom, flush the toilet, have a good look around and then say something like 'it hasn't affected your unit, so there is no need to turn off your water while repairs are being made'. Then you simply walk out."

"Hmmmm, that could work."

"It will. That woman's never seen you before and she'll never be able to identify you. She's so drugged up she probably doesn't even know who she is. So, you'll do it?" Delaney asked.

"Just let me know if that Adderley fellow comes back early. I don't want to be in there if he does."

"You won't be," Delaney assured her. "I'll be waiting down the street. If I see his ute approach, I'll ring and tell you to get the hell out of there. He'll notice the water department's truck and the work going on when he leaves, so he won't think anything of it if the girl tells him that someone knocked on the door. But she won't do that. If anything, she'll tell you to help get her out of there."

"You seem to have every angle covered."

"In this business you have to," Delaney quipped in between bites of the apple pie Barbara baked that afternoon.

"Fantastic pie, Barbara. You sure know how to treat a fellow."

"It has been said that the best way to a man's heart is through his stomach. Am I in your heart?" she asked.

"You are. But aren't you forgetting something?" Delaney asked.

Barbara had a quick look around. "I don't think so."

"The ice cream, the ice cream," Delaney jokingly cried. "Don't get up, I'll get it," he added.

"We need to be in uniform and ready to go by 0700 hours, Colonel Stevenson. Is that clear?" Delaney said on his return to the kitchen table.

"Yes sir," Stevenson answered, firing off a salute.

She waited a few moments.

"Permission to speak, sir?"

"Granted."

"Are you planning some sort of pre-emptive strike this evening, General?"

"Now that you mention it, I might be. Will the target be safe to approach?"

"As far as I can tell the target will be unguarded."

"So, there should be no resistance?"

"None."

The co-conspirators were up at 6am, giving them plenty of time to prepare for their morning mission. Delaney made the coffee and prepared a light breakfast of toast while Stevenson showered and got dressed.

She looked rather convincing as a water department employee as she sat down at the kitchen table. Delaney had on the same clothes he wore the previous day.

"When you go out, take off the vest, hat and ID card. And put a light sweater over your work shirt. We don't want anyone seeing a water department employee coming out of this unit. Otherwise, we are right to go. To the success of our mission," Delaney said, raising his mug of coffee.

"To success," Barbara said, clinking her mug with his.

"Oh, and can you call me General one more time? I kind of liked that."

Delaney left Barbara's unit and went the few doors down to his place just as the sun was coming up. He picked up his copy of the *Cairns Examiner* lying by his door and had a look across the complex. There was a light on in Adderley's unit; a good sign that he would be going out.

Delaney texted Stevenson to tell her and went to his car with the paper and the binoculars he usually took to the races. He put on a hat and sunglasses, drove down the block and pulled into a driveway of a house under construction. He was out of sight but had a good view of the entrance to the apartment complex.

It was just after 7am.

With his binoculars at the ready it took less than five minutes for Delaney to notice Adderley's truck leaving the complex. He took his binoculars out and looked at the truck. He was alone. Megan Beale was in the unit by herself. All was going according to plan.

Delaney sent Stevenson a text to give her the news.

When the water works crew arrived, he'd text her again with the all-clear to get moving.

As if on cue, a water works truck drove past Delaney just as he put down the phone.

It's your time to move colonel. The coast is clear. I'll stay where I am and call you if I see Adderley coming back. Good luck!

Barbara ducked out of her unit and had a look around. There was no one about. An hour later kids would be heading off to school while their parents went to work.

Barbara carried her vest, hat, clipboard and ID badge in a grocery bag to her car. She drove to the other side of the complex and put on her disguise.

The water company workers did not see her walk to the front of the units and knock on the door of Adderley's unit.

There was no answer, so Barbara knocked again, this time using the clipboard to make a bit more noise. She pressed her ear to the door and heard what sounded like a chain being dragged across the floor.

Geez. Could Gary be right? she asked herself.

"Water department," Barbara said, again knocking on the door.

The door gradually opened.

"Hi, I'm with the water department," Barbara said, pushing her ID badge inside the door.

"We're doing some work outside and I need to check the water pressure in the unit. Can I come in for just a moment?"

There was no answer from the other side of the door, but it slowly opened to let Barbara inside.

A woman was on her knees. Clamped on her right ankle was a chain which was fastened to a hook on the wall in the kitchen. It was pulled taut, obviously having been measured to keep her from going outside but allowing her access to the toilet. She was wearing a soiled white top and grey pyjama bottoms. Her feet were filthy, and her hair was matted on both sides. She had a vacant look in her eyes.

Barbara walked to the sink which was full of dirty dishes and glasses. She turned on the tap and a strong stream of water poured out of it.

"I'm just going to check the water in the bathroom," Barbara told the woman who sat on the kitchen floor.

The bathroom was a complete mess.

They're not going to be getting their bond back, Barbara thought. She flushed the toilet which looked as if it hadn't been cleaned in months, turned the basin's tap on and walked back into the living area after having a peek at the bedroom.

Barbara walked over to the woman. "Are you okay?" she softly asked.

There was no reply.

"It doesn't look like this unit will be affected by the outage. I'll let myself out. Thank you."

She turned, took her phone out and snapped a quick photo, closing the door behind her.

My, God, how can that man treat her like that? she asked herself, taking a breath of clean air.

Stevenson walked back to her car the same way she came. Nobody noticed her, not even the three guys from the water department some hundred metres away who were using a jackhammer to tear up a piece of pavement to reach a leaky pipe.

Her phone rang just as she got in the driver's seat.

"Adderley is coming back. Get out of there, quick," Delaney said.

"I'm out. You were right. The woman is chained up. It's horrible."

"Did she say anything?"

"Not a word. I'm going back to my place. I want to be safely inside before he shows up."

Barbara took off her vest, cap, badge and work boots and stuffed them back into the grocery bag she had left on the front seat. She drove back to her side of the complex, parked in her spot and ran upstairs to her unit.

Delaney watched Adderley drive by and lost sight of him as he turned into the complex's parking lot.

Adderley heard the three fellows from the water department before he noticed them. He parked and waited for the pounding of the jackhammer to stop before he walked over. He peered into a deep hole which was full of water. "Leaky pipe. We're replacing it," a worker in a hard hat hollered.

Adderley nodded, walked back to his ute, and pulled two bags of groceries from it.

He looked around as he neared his unit, stuck his key in the door and quickly slammed it shut.

Megan Beale cowered in the corner when he opened the door and walked in.

"You been a good girl? I've got us some food for later. A couple of pizzas we'll heat up."

Adderley tossed the frozen pizzas into the fridge along with some beer. He lit a cigarette, sat down on the couch and turned on the TV, settling on a show where people pawn their belongings for fast cash at a massive shop on the Las Vegas strip.

"Hey sweetheart," he called out. "Come over here and keep Daddy company."

Megan Beale did as she was asked.

"You know what I like," he said nodding to his crotch.

Stevenson rang Delaney when she got back to her apartment. "Where are you? We have got to talk about this."

"I'm at the beach, at the picnic table where we have a sit during our walks."

"Stay there. I'm coming over," Stevenson said.

Barbara Stevenson put on her favourite pair of runners, a pair of white shorts and a navy-blue top, took her hat and sunnies off the coffee table and quickly walked to the beach.

"Mission accomplished?" he asked as Barbara took a seat.

She took out her phone and showed Delaney the photo she took of Adderley's apartment.

He had a long look. "My God, we have got to get her out of there; today."

"Off to the cop shop?" Stevenson asked.

"Yeah, but we can't show them the photo. They might not be too happy with your impersonation of a city employee. I'll tell them how I saw her walking around the complex in her pyjamas and about the guy's ute. It'll be a simple welfare check."

The two amateur detectives walked to Delaney's car and drove through the morning traffic to Cairns District Police Headquarters on Sheridan St. Delaney found a place to park in front of the two-storey building. They followed two uniformed officers inside and headed for the main desk.

"Morning folks, what can we do for you?" asked a senior constable who looked as if he was on leave from his rugby league club.

Delaney did the talking. "We live in a complex on Palm Drive and have a strong feeling that one of our neighbours is keeping a woman there against her will."

"Would that be the Coral Reef Apartments?"

"It is. How did you know?"

"We sent a couple of cars over there about twenty minutes ago. A water department employee heard a woman crying and screaming but took nearly an hour to ring us. People just don't want to get involved. I guess his conscience eventually got to him. Hold on a sec."

The constable moved closer to a police radio which crackled behind him. A senior sergeant was giving permission to break down the front door of Adderley's unit.

"The officers on the scene asked the man inside to open the door but he refused so we're about to break in there."

"Geez," Stevenson said. "Looks as if we were right."

"I'm going to need a statement from both of you," the senior constable said. "The more information we have the easier it will be to press charges against him, if in fact he has done anything wrong."

Stevenson and Delaney nodded in unison.

"O'Reilly," the senior constable shouted. "Come here, would you?"

Tom O'Reilly walked over to the main desk.

"O'Reilly, these people have some information on that situation unfolding at Palm Drive. Can you take their details and get statements from them please? They live at the complex."

Constable O'Reilly introduced himself to Delaney and Stevenson and asked them to accompany him to his desk which had a picture of a pretty brunette with a young child perched on her knee placed prominently to the left of his computer screen.

"Can I get you two anything?" he asked. "A coffee?"

"I'm okay; how about you, Barbara?"

"Nothing for me either, thanks."

A chair short, O'Reilly grabbed one from a nearby desk and asked Stevenson and Delaney to sit down. They faced the constable, who looked to be in his late twenties. He adjusted his glasses and pushed a stray strand of hair off his forehead.

"So, what exactly did you see?" he asked, holding a pen in his right hand.

As Delaney told O'Reilly the story of seeing the apparently drug-affected woman walking through the complex the day before, four police officers knocked down the door to Adderley's unit and barged in with guns drawn.

Adderley had taken the chain off Megan Beale's ankle and moved her into the bedroom when the cops first arrived. He moved a large dresser against the bedroom door and pondered his dwindling options. When he heard the cops break in, he grabbed Megan and put a kitchen knife to her throat.

The cops secured the kitchen and living area and checked the bathroom.

"Let the woman go," Senior Sergeant Arthur Sheehy yelled through the bedroom door.

There was no response.

"Open the door and let her go," Sheehy screamed.

Again, there was no response.

"We can do this the easy way or the hard way. It is up to you, Adderley."

Sheehy backed away from the door and took out his radio.

"Are you in position?" he softly asked the officers stationed outside the bedroom window.

"We are," was the response.

"Proceed as planned," Sheehy said.

Ten seconds later a stun grenade was fired through the bedroom window. The loud blast rattled the walls of the unit. Two officers jumped inside and quickly subdued Adderley, who was temporarily blinded by the grenade's flash.

"We've got him," one of the officers yelled. "The woman is unharmed."

Two other officers climbed through the window, moved the dresser away from the door and opened it. Sheehy and Senior Constable Sarah Sloan entered the room.

"Look after her," Sheehy told Sloan, who wrapped a blanket around the stunned woman and took her out of the unit.

Adderley was handcuffed and placed under arrest. "You are in a shitload of trouble," Sheehy told Adderley. "Illegal imprisonment, abuse, rape." After noticing a kitchen knife on the bedroom carpet, he added the word assault.

He motioned to one of the constables to grab the knife as evidence. It was placed in a sealed plastic bag.

Adderley was dragged out of the unit, placed in the back of a divvy van and driven away just as a television news truck arrived.

Megan Beale was given some water by Senior Constable Sarah Sloan, who hugged her. "It's over. You're going to be okay."

Beale lifted her head, looked at Sloan and burst into tears.

"Don't you dare use that footage," Sheehy barked at a cameraman who was filming it all. "The woman has suffered enough. She doesn't need this plastered all over the TV for goodness sake."

Nick Hamilton stopped filming and put down his camera. He had the footage he needed. A producer would decide if it went to air.

Stevenson and Delaney watched the drama on television that night, which included the footage of Senior Constable Sloan comforting Megan Beale, whose tear-stained face was pixelated.

20

THE RESCUE OF MEGAN BEALE AND THE ARREST OF Lawrence Adderley took up most of the front page of the next day's *Cairns Examiner*.

There were also several pages on the inside devoted to the drama. Since it had unfolded mid-morning, it gave the newspaper's reporters all day to flush out the story. And flush it out they did. They found old photos of both Adderley and Beale, talked to the water department worker who blew the whistle and to several neighbours.

The neighbours, even those who lived next door to the now cordoned off unit, all said Adderley was a quiet type who kept to himself and never caused any trouble.

"He used to say good morning and all when I saw him," Gordon Newman said. "I never had any idea he was keeping that woman a prisoner. If I knew I would have done something."

Stevenson and Delaney decided to steer well clear of the newspaper and television reporters who descended on the quiet complex and watched the events from Stevenson's balcony.

"Let Adderley think it was someone else who went to the coppers," Delaney said. "We got lucky with that water pipe bursting. It got us off the hook."

A couple of newcomers to the Channel 12 newsroom, Dixie Moore and Anna Nimmity, spent much of their day trying to figure out how Beale had ended up with Adderley.

A few flirtatious phone calls and in-person interviews yielded a stack of information as tall as the weathered statue of Captain Cook which looked out over the highway to Port Douglas and bared his name.

They fed all the information to Channel 12 reporter Tegan Winterbottom, the star of the station's 6pm news team, who was at the Coral Reef Apartment complex.

"You sure about all this?" Winterbottom asked the two novices thirty minutes before she went on air.

"We are. It was like putting together a jigsaw puzzle. The pieces fit," Moore said.

"You girls better be right. It's my arse if it isn't."

"Beale apparently had been living on the streets of Cairns for several months after losing her job as a medical receptionist and getting booted from her apartment for non-payment of rent when she was befriended by Adderley six weeks ago," Winterbottom said. "Police confirm they found the date rape drug Rohypnol inside the apartment which may have been used to keep Beale in a semi-conscious state."

Ch 12 showed footage taken inside Adderley's filthy unit and of Beale being walked out of what Winterbottom called "the torture chamber".

"Reporting live from Holloways Beach, Tegan Winterbottom, Twelve news."

"Damn she is good," Moore said to Anna in the newsroom where they watched the broadcast. "We can learn a lot from her. She knows her stuff."

When Winterbottom and her camera crew left the complex around 6:30pm, life finally returned to normal although neighbours talked about Adderley's imprisonment of Beale for weeks. The police tape around Adderley's unit and the boarded-up bedroom window and front door remained for several weeks while police finished their investigation.

Adderley, 64, had been renting the unit for the past five years. The real estate company he dealt with – FNQ Realty – said he had never been late with the rent. As for the yearly inspections of the unit that were supposed to have taken place, the head of FNQ Realty, Cameron Eldridge, admitted that the unit had not been inspected for two years. "We find that tenants who pay their rent early or on time generally keep the units in good shape. Obviously, we'll re-think that. We might have dropped the ball on this one but how could we have known he was keeping a woman prisoner in there?" he said. "We're just as shocked as anyone, as is the owner."

The unit's owner, 58-year-old Homer Tarkenton, came by the unit two days after Beale's rescue to have a look at the damage. "Shit, this is going to cost me," he told Gordon Newman, the fellow who lived next door. "New window, a new front door, carpeting, cleaning. Damn."

"Don't worry about it," Newman said. "There will always be some arsehole wanting to rent it due to the notoriety that will go with living there. You'll even be able to raise the rent," the retired sugar cane factory worker said.

"You're right. The first thing they'll do is put it up on Facebook with photos. 'Look where we are living'." Tarkenton laughed at the thought.

It turned out Adderley had worked as a tradie since moving to Cairns about twenty years ago. According to several of his bosses contacted by the *Cairns Examiner*, he was an okay worker who always showed up on time.

"He was a little sloppy with his bricklaying at times, but he was never late to a job, not like these kids today," Barnaby Fogel said. "Never asked him about his personal life and he never said a word about it. I figured he was divorced and angry about it too."

Apparently, he was a better housepainter than bricklayer. Tucker Boozer, whose lips never touched a drop despite his surname, remembered hiring Adderley as a casual for Coral Sea Painting. "He answered one of our ads," Boozer said as he painted the kitchen of a home in Trinity Beach. "He did as he was told and did good work, I never had a problem with him. In fact, he was still doing the occasional job for us. With him going away for a while I'm going to have to hire someone else. We've got three jobs this week and we're nearly booked out for the rest of the month," he told Emerson Snell, a young reporter for the *Cairns Examiner*. "What do you say you put down that pen and notebook and come work for me? We probably pay more than you're making at the paper."

"Just out of curiosity, how much do you pay your workers?" Snell asked.

"The average is about $32 an hour," Boozer said. "How much you on?"

"Six dollars an hour less," Snell said dropping his head.

"Take my card, kid," Boozer said. "Now get going. I need to finish this room by today. A pissed-off customer is bad for business."

After questioning both Adderley and Beale, police released more information about Beale's imprisonment to a hungry media pack which was looking for a new angle every day. The shocking story had been picked up by every news organisation in the country.

Delaney and Stevenson had an inkling that a book would be on the shelves in the next few months followed by a television movie.

Beale was reunited with her estranged family on the Central Coast of New South Wales. It was filmed by a Channel 12 camera crew rumoured to have forked over $200,000 for the exclusive rights.

Five years earlier Beale had left the home she shared with Brian Collins after finding her husband to be, a highly regarded plumber, checking more than the pipes of her best friend Mandy Ellinson. Humiliated and distraught, Beale left her job at Central Coast Medical Centre, emptied the joint savings account she shared with Collins, packed her things and headed north in her Toyota sedan.

Her mother and father, now in their early seventies, told Twelve News they expected Megan would be back in a few weeks after things had quieted down.

"I guess it affected her more than we thought," Earl Beale said as his wife Marjorie sat by his side wiping away a constant flow of tears. "We rang her and sent her text messages. We heard from her about a week later, saying that she was fine and needed time away. We never knew she was up in Cairns and mixed up with some sicko like that Adderley fella."

"My baby, my baby," Marjorie Beale wailed, much to the delight of the Channel 12 producers and camera crew.

"We'll use that in the promos, ought to be good for another 100,000 viewers," producer Janet Childs whispered to her assistant, Emily Maxwell.

Childs and Maxwell managed to track down Megan Beale's ex and his wife. Brian and Mandy Collins lived in the same small town and had three children – twin girls and a boy. He was still a plumber and apparently one in high demand judging from the Mercedes and new ute in the driveway.

Childs and Maxwell knocked on the front door of the family's split-level home two days later. Collins glanced out the front window, noticed the Channel 12 car parked in the street and didn't answer.

"We'll pay plenty for an interview," Childs yelled.

"Call the camera crew, Emily, and have them come over here. We'll get some footage of the house, fly a drone over it. Maybe get some video of the kids playing in the yard. That'll teach them to fuck with us," Childs said as she and Maxwell walked back to their car.

It took Beale nearly two weeks to come to grips with what had happened. She could not believe that six weeks of her life had all but disappeared and she had been drugged and held captive in chains.

Senior Constable Sarah Sloan was at her side every day. She was the only person Beale trusted.

Beale stayed at Cairns Base Hospital for several weeks. She met with a women psychiatrist every other day and after close to a dozen sessions, Dr Helen Birmingham, who had never come across a case like Beale's in her twenty years of practice, told Senior Constable Sloan that Beale had made an excellent recovery and was able to go home. Sloan agreed.

But where was home?

Birmingham and Sloan agreed that it was best for Beale to leave Cairns and return to her family on the central coast of New South Wales. Sloan accompanied Beale back home. They left before sunrise one morning through an underground exit to dodge the press who were still camped outside the hospital. They flew to Newcastle first class, with Sloan wearing civilian clothes and Beale a wig. Sloan rented a car and drove Beale home. The press had ended their stakeout of the Beale family home, but to keep Beale out of view Sloan parked the rental car in the garage and quickly closed the garage door.

Beale's parents wept with joy when they saw her. They were a bit shocked by her gaunt appearance and more than surprised by her lack of emotion.

"You have to consider what she went through," Senior Constable Sloan told Brad and Sheila Beale. "But her psychiatrist and I believe the emotional support from the both of you and your extended family will make a huge difference. She's been on anti-depressant medication since she was rescued and if all goes well, eventually she'll be able to be weaned off it."

Her parents nodded in agreement.

"And," Senior Constable Sloan added, "don't ask her to talk about what happened to her in Cairns. When she's ready to talk about it with you she will."

Sloan stayed with Beale and her family for several days before flying back home, and noticed that Beale was slowly beginning to emerge from the protective shell she had placed herself in.

On her way back to the airport though, a Channel 12 news truck flew past her in the opposite direction. "Shit. I hope the Beales tell them to fuck off," she said.

21

"ISN'T THAT WHERE YOU'RE LIVING GARY? CORAL REEF Apartments?" asked Chris Simmons, Delaney's mate from Melbourne, when he rang a couple of days after Adderley's arrest. "What is going on up there? It's all over the news and in the papers down here."

Delaney told Chris that it was a one-off event and it just happened to take place at the complex where he was living.

"It's actually pretty quiet up here. From what I can tell there's very little crime but I'm usually at home most nights. Maybe the heat and humidity sap the energy out of people. But I'm enjoying it so far."

Delaney didn't mention his involvement in the Adderley arrest. As far as he was concerned it was over and done with although he wondered if Megan Beale would ever be able to recover from her ordeal. *She'll need months of counselling to get her life back together again,* he thought.

"You still keeping company with that woman you told me about?"

"I am and it's going alright. Barbara looks after me, cooks for me and is good company but you should see the women up here Chris. They are incredible. Young, old, the locals, the tourists; they're all gorgeous. And with the heat they barely wear a thing. I've had to sew the fly on my shorts shut."

Chris laughed. "You lucky bastard. I knew you'd like it up there. Hey, I've got news. I'm seeing Alison again."

"The schoolteacher?"

"Yup. I ran into her at the Sunday market in Bentleigh a couple of weeks ago. I'm taking it very slowly this time, very slowly."

When they first started seeing each other several months back Chris dove into the relationship head-first and it came back to bite him in the arse. This time he was going to approach it the way an old man gets into a swimming pool – a step at a time.

"Good idea. Maybe down the road the two of you can come up and visit."

"We couldn't get away until after the Christmas holidays, sometime in early January. I'll mention it to Alison, see what she says.

"Hey, before I forget," Chris continued, "what's the latest with that nag of yours?"

"Too Hard is spelling over the summer. He's being set for the Queen Elizabeth again. He'll have one or two runs before the big one.

"Is he sound?"

"Not a thing wrong with him. He's on holiday and from what (Big John) McGraw is telling the syndicate members, he's looking better than ever. He's really matured and settled down."

"How much ahead are you, after expenses and all?"

"About $130,000 after those placings in the spring. And I'll tell you, without a weekly paycheque, the extra money has come in handy. I'm thinking about volunteering a couple of days a week at Vinnies, like I did in Melbourne. That would get me back on Newstart."

"Good on you. You're keeping busy. Between footy and basketball coaching and my counselling work the only free day I have is Sunday."

"And your golf game?" Chris asked. "Taken a few strokes off your handicap?"

"Not a one and I've yet to break ninety. But, it's good fun. There's a group of us and we go out once or twice a week. They're a good bunch of blokes. A little older, all retired – but you'd fit right in. I'll introduce you to them if you come up here."

After he and Chris said their goodbyes, Delaney realised just how much he missed his long-time pal. *I've got acquaintances here, not real friends. But, you never know what's around the corner.*

22

AS THE INCREASING HEAT AND HUMIDITY USHERED IN the start of the rainy season, Delaney's first in the tropics, the complex's large putting green became so soggy from the daily showers that it was unplayable most afternoons.

His favourite golf course, Saltwater Lakes, became a no-go zone due to the numerous crocodiles that roamed the course over the summer looking for food or a female to mate with, which meant they had the same thing on their minds as majority of the course's golfers.

Any woman, no matter what age, who showed up at the Saltwater clubhouse for a round of golf, a drink or a meal was immediately leered at by groups of men wearing white pants, loud flowery shirts, worn out golf shoes and hearing aids. Married, partnered up or single, they looked at the women the same way crocs eyed a raw chicken held over the side of a boatload of tourists.

They were harmless though, and rarely approached any of the women, who ranged in age from thirty to eighty. They were all fit, even the eighty-year-olds, due to their preference for walking eighteen holes instead of driving around in a motorised golf cart.

Over a few beers the boys made wisecracks about so and so's breasts, a tall one's long legs or someone's shapely arse. The leader of the bunch, a wide body named Al Whitlow, who couldn't walk the first nine holes of a miniature golf course if his life depended on it, constantly made the same "wonder what par her hole is" comment, always digging an elbow into the ribs of the bloke seated next to him. His drinking buddies kept the laughter coming since Whitlow, who had made a fortune building homes in western Sydney, always picked up the bar tab.

In the lead-up to Christmas, the back nine at Saltwater Lakes became more dangerous since that's where most of its small lakes and ponds were situated. Delaney decided to leave his well-worn clubs at home and forgo his twice-weekly golf games until the end of the rainy season to avoid a potential run-in with one of the prehistoric beasts. However, he went to the clubhouse one or two days a week for a beer and occasionally hit a small bucket of balls at the practice range.

"Don't you want to go find your ball, mate? It's brand new."

"Not at all. I'll take the two-shot penalty and play my next shot from right here."

That was the sort of conversation golfers had while playing Saltwater Lakes during the rainy season.

The warning signs for crocs, and there were many, even at the pristine beach at beautiful Palm Cove, about twenty kilometres north, were a reminder of just how dangerous life in Far North Queensland could be.

Every now and then there was a story of someone finding a python in their home which to Delaney was only slightly more nerve-racking than the middle-of-the-night home invasions which were becoming all too common in Melbourne. Imagine being fast asleep and waking up at 3am to find a gang of crazed teenagers armed with pipes and baseball bats in your living room demanding the keys to your car, your wallet and your phone. Although, if a python was ever found in his unit, Delaney would have been out of there quicker than shit through a goose.

Delaney got a scare one morning as he prepared to shave. On the windowsill next to the sink was a black bug so disgusting and so big that it had its own number plate. He jumped back a few steps and waited for his heart rate to return to normal.

Delaney stepped a bit closer and examined the creature which had not moved. With no time to Google what it was, Delaney surmised it was some sort of giant cockroach. If nuclear weapons ever rained down on the earth, a strong possibility with Kim Jong-Unfuckable reigning over North Korea, Delaney was convinced that the bug he was looking at would be one of the survivors. What to do next? How would he kill it?

He had the answer in his hand – shaving cream. He gave the can a good shake and sent a steady stream of blue-coloured foam onto the creature which toppled off the windowsill and fell onto the tiled floor. Delaney then buried it in even more shaving cream much the way a fire crew sprays foam on the wreckage of a small plane. The creature was covered in several inches of Gillette's finest. Delaney stood over it and pumped his fists. His celebration turned out to be a bit premature. As Delaney wondered how to get rid of the remains, it sprang to life. It wiggled its way out of the foam and shook it off much the way a dog shakes the water from his coat after a dip in the ocean.

The bug eyeballed Delaney. "Is that all ya got motherfucker? Huh? That all ya got?"

"Oh, I got more, you son-of-a-bitch."

Delaney grabbed a shoe from the bedroom, one with a smooth bottom, and bashed the fucker over and over until he was sure it was dead. There was foam on the floor and walls, but this time he had prevailed.

Delaney scooped the mess up with a circular that was dropped in his mailbox the day before and tossed it into a plastic bag. He tied the bag into a knot, put it into another plastic bag and made sure it was tied tighter than a socialite's botoxed face. He carried the mess downstairs and tossed it in a bin. To be on the safe side he put two bricks on the lid. When Delaney returned upstairs, he grabbed the can of shaving cream and made a thorough search of the entire unit in case the deceased had not wandered in alone. He found nothing but stayed on guard for the next couple of days.

"There are bugs in Melbourne, but I have never seen anything like that," he told Barbara later that night.

"Welcome to the tropics," she said.

Delaney spent a few afternoons a week at the Cairns Public Library where the air conditioning kept the heat and humidity at bay and he was able to read the out-of-town newspapers, especially *The Age* from Melbourne, for free instead of shelling out $5 a copy at the local newsagent and more than $6 on Saturday.

"I'm on the pension," he snapped at anyone who asked why he didn't just go and buy a copy every day.

Right smack in the CBD, the library occupied a stately looking cream-coloured building. In its past it might have housed the local council or served as the city's courthouse.

I'll look into that, Delaney thought. These days though the most pressing business involved patrons digging into their pockets for loose change to pay fines for their overdue books, magazines, DVDs and CDs.

The library had many new books, but the shelves of books took up just a small portion of the library's floor space. The children's section in the front of the library was a popular spot for parents and toddlers, especially in the mornings where there are special events – including singalongs and book readings – scheduled just for them. It took just one verse of *Row, Row, Row Your Boat* for Delaney to gather his things and merrily get the hell out of there before *Old MacDonald* and his mates on the farm made an appearance.

At least three-quarters of the library was set aside for those typing away on their laptops. People of all ages sat in comfortable chairs at long tables going about their business; students doing their assignments, and businessmen and women working on reports and spreadsheets. There was barely an empty seat most afternoons and people were so into what they were doing, many with earbuds securely in place, that hardly a word was exchanged between anyone.

One overcast afternoon Delaney took a copy of that day's *Age* from the newspaper rack and sat down in what he had found to be the library's most comfortable chair. A diehard St Kilda fan, he was reading the latest AFL footy news and enjoying the peace and quiet when a tall bloke about fifty with a full head of dark hair and a large ring in his left ear appeared. He looked at the numerous seating options but decided to sit in the chair next to Delaney, who nodded and said hello. Dressed in jeans and a polo shirt and carrying a backpack, the bloke put his belongings on the wooden table in front of them and then proceeded to narrate each task as he carried it out.

"All right. Let's get settled," he said out loud. "We'll put the water over here, the phone here. Can't believe the water is still cold," he said after taking a sip. "Now, where's that pen? I know I took it with me. Ahh, here it is. It must be blue ink, never black. Glad I printed out these emails. Let's give them a good look. Nah mate, ain't going to happen. Much too expensive. Bring down the price and maybe we can do business."

It went on and on and on. Delaney gazed over at the fellow and, deciding not to make a scene, got up from his chair with the newspaper and walked away. Wanting to get as far away from the talker as possible, Delaney went out the back door and found a dry and clean bench to sit on in the large garden behind the handsome building. Several massive fig trees blocked out the overcast sky. The trees were home to a large population of flying foxes, and they made less noise with their constant screeching than the bloke he left back inside. But their shit covered everything – footpaths, benches, and at times, the odd pedestrian. The side of the building closest to the colony was streaked in bat shit. It was not a good look.

After he finished reading, Delaney walked back inside and put the newspaper back where he borrowed it from.

The narrator with the earring was still carrying on. "What should I have for tea? Chicken? Nah. Not two nights in a row. Pizza? Yes, that's it. Pizza. Domino's has a special. I've got the coupon for it. That's what I'll do."

The guy was still talking as Delaney dashed out the front door. Dark clouds coming in from the ocean were rapidly covering the city and, having left his umbrella at home, Delaney high-tailed it back to his car just before the late-afternoon deluge struck. He watched the rain bucket down from the front seat of his SUV. Fifteen minutes later the rain stopped. The storm had dropped the temperature a few degrees, taking it to an even thirty. Sticky? Yes, but infinitely better than a winter day in Melbourne with its thirteen-degree days and strong Antarctic winds.

Delaney soon discovered that some of the city's most interesting people could be found at the library. Students and businesspeople were always there, as were backpackers not used to the stifling summer heat.

Many afternoons Delaney saw an older man using a walker slowly cross the library floor towards the comfortable seats. He was so stooped over that his head was facing the ground. Somehow, he managed to see what was in front of him and was able to get around on his own. It took a lot of effort for him just to sit down and even more to get back up.

One afternoon he spotted the bearded and scruffily dressed old-timer, who Delaney reckoned was in his early seventies, making his way to his favourite chair. He had a massive book on the seat of the walker. Delaney looked at the title: *Quantum Physics*. The fellow sat down, placed the book on a table in front of him, opened it and slowly flicked through the pages, stopping midway through it. He then took out a yellow legal pad and started writing down notes.

Studying for his final exam? A former physicist? Or maybe someone who just likes physics. Delaney watched him. The old-timer never looked up as he filled several pages of his pad with notes. After more than an hour, he closed the book, put down his legal pad and pen and rubbed his eyes. He struggled to get to his feet, put the book back on the walker, tucked his pad and pen away and returned the book back to its place on the shelf. He walked out the front door without having uttered a word.

The former journo deduced that his behaviour was a bit unusual but not anything abnormal. Some people sit down with books on art or cricket or travel and can immerse themselves in them for hours. Being rather curious, Delaney could not help wondering how the fellow lived, if he had a family, what he once did for a living, and how his health was. Perhaps one day he would ask.

While listening to some guy yacking away on his mobile phone one afternoon, Delaney thought back to his school days when a library was quieter than a Gold Coast Suns crowd at Metricon Stadium. If someone did raise their voice, an angry librarian would quickly be on the scene asking the person in question to keep their voice down. Where was that librarian now? Where was the old spinster with her hair tied up in a bun and her glasses hanging from a lanyard around her neck who was as tough as a prison guard. She would have picked up any loud and inconsiderate bastard by the scruff of his or her neck, escorted them to the front door and booted them out, but not before cutting their library card to pieces. This noisy bloke, who Delaney figured was in his late forties, had his phone on speaker so everyone was able to hear both ends of his conversation with a woman from Telstra based in the Philippines. Delaney always put his phone on silent before entering the library so as not to annoy others if it rang. The call to the Manilla call centre was painful to listen to. But he wasn't done. He made another call, leaving a long-winded message with someone who might have been his wife about his conversation with Telstra before he got up and walked out. One young fellow in the immediate area applauded as the talker left. Delaney did the same.

Like many retirees, Delaney found himself with a lot of free time on his hands: okay too much free time on his hands. Unless one was Phil Mickelson, there was a limit to how much golf one man could play.

Delaney had just enough money to get by but needed something to do. There was always whittling, but he decided against it after realising what the absence of one or two digits would do to his short game. He didn't want to wind up sitting on his balcony waving to people passing by, so he gave some thought to doing some volunteer work one or two days a week to keep busy.

Working for Vinnies back in Melbourne wasn't all that bad and maybe here the volunteers would be a little younger and more active.

Option two was volunteering at a hospital. But the thought of watching old-timers lose their battles with cancer, dementia, heart disease and if they were lucky – old age – was one he couldn't stomach.

Delaney sent an email to Meals on Wheels to see if they needed any drivers to deliver hot meals to the elderly, who were unable to cook for themselves. But it had all the drivers it needed and offered to put him on a waiting list.

Two steamy afternoons later, wearing a dark sports jacket and pressed blue shirt, Delaney showed up at the head office of Vinnies in the CBD and made his way to the reception area. It was brightly lit with new carpeting and judging from the smell in the air seemed to have been newly painted.

"I have an appointment with Geoff Duckworth," Delaney told the receptionist.

"Right through this door," she said pointing to a door on her right.

"Yes, yes," Geoff Duckworth said, getting up from his chair. "Thanks for coming in," he said vigorously shaking Delaney's hand. "It's not often that someone with your sort of background wants to volunteer, and the fact that you have already worked for us in Melbourne sure helps."

Duckworth was an impressive looking man. Tall and fit with dark hair just starting to turn grey, Duckworth had strong, chiselled features and a face that belonged on Mt Rushmore, not in an office in Far North Queensland.

"Sit, sit," he said smiling like a politician on the campaign trail. "How are you liking Far North Queensland so far?"

"So far so good. I'm living in a nice apartment complex, met a woman on the day I moved in and my golf game keeps improving."

Duckworth laughed. "Not too hot for you? This time of the year can be brutal."

"Don't get me wrong. It's warm and can get uncomfortable, but it's much better than being in Melbourne during the winter. I burned my long underwear before I left."

Duckworth laughed.

"Tell me about the work."

Duckworth gave Delaney the rundown on working in one of the shops and the warehouse.

"All we would need is a police check and you can get started right away."

"Would one day a week be okay or two half-days?"

"Either. Go to the courthouse and they'll take care of the police check for you. It is strictly routine. Here's my card and number. Let me know when it's sorted, and you can start. We're a bit short-handed in the store and warehouse."

The two shook hands as if they had agreed to some monumental trade deal.

"I'll show myself out," Delaney said.

That night over dinner at Barbara's place, he filled her in on his meeting with Duckworth and his eagerness to have him join Vinnies.

"You'll be of more use there than on a golf course," Barbara noted.

As much as he enjoyed his golf, Delaney agreed with her.

He went down to the courthouse the next afternoon and underwent his police check, filling out several forms and forking out $42 for the privilege. The officer who took his money had a nervous tic or maybe the onset of Parkinson's disease. Every few seconds his head bobbed up and down like a pigeon. Delaney surmised that he had recently been moved to a desk job to accommodate his condition.

"You'll get something in the mail," he told Delaney.

Since the forms took fifteen days to be processed, Delaney emailed Duckworth, and told him he would be available in two weeks. "Put me down for the full day on Monday, the 24th, in one of the shops, not the warehouse. I'm getting too old to be lifting couches and mattresses."

23

DUCKWORTH GOT UP FROM HIS CHAIR AND GAZED
out the window which had a view of the mountains behind the city.

The late-afternoon sun was dipping from view, leaving long shadows
in the adjacent parking lot. It was coming up on 5pm, quitting time
for the masses who were thinking more about their weekend than the
projects on their desks.

Tradies were packing up their gear, mothers were on their way to pick
up their kids from day care. Sightseeing boats were coming back to the
marina from a long day out on the reef, fishermen were on their way out
to their favourite spots while the city's many restaurants were gearing up
for a big Friday night.

Meanwhile, just a few blocks away, a small group of teenagers was
causing a ruckus at the city's main bus stop.

Fuelled up on cheap booze, they were harassing commuters who
simply wanted to go home. The biggest of the three had a lit cigarette
in his mouth and another tucked behind his left ear. He knocked the
groceries out of a man's hand and helped himself to a bag of chips that
had fallen on the pavement. He washed them down with the contents
of a bottle hidden inside a brown paper bag. The other two, who could
not have been more than sixteen or seventeen, followed their mate's
lead. They took an older man's pizza, scarfed it down in a few bites
and tossed the empty box at his head. There was not a cop or a bus in
sight.

Two twenty-year-old lovelies dressed for a night out wisely decided
to wait until the punks left and took refuge in the nearby Woolies. The

other commuters, which numbered about a dozen, stayed until their buses arrived.

"What the fuck are you looking at? Yeah, you," the head troublemaker said to a middle-aged woman who had her belongings in a small two-wheeled shopping cart.

He hurriedly walked towards her.

"Don't you come near me," she screamed.

Just then a bus approached the terminal. When the main thug found himself being stared down by the bus driver he called out to his mates and the four took off. It was a good thing they did because the driver of the bus was a refrigerator of a man named Ernie Walters.

Walters was as wide as he was tall and had canned hams for biceps. After his passengers disembarked, Walters got off the bus to stretch his legs and was approached by several waiting commuters. With his muscles straining against his extra-large work shirt, he listened to Elma Watson and the others tell him about the hoodlums who took off when he arrived.

"It's a good thing they left, ma'am, otherwise I would have kicked their arses from here to Townsville. You're safe now. Hop aboard. Don't worry about the fare. I'll ring the coppers and they'll keep an eye out for the bastards. And if they try any of that shit when I'm around I'll break 'em in half and feed 'em to the crocs."

The bus passengers applauded.

24

AS THE SUN SET BEHIND THE MACALISTER RANGES, foot traffic on Abbott Street in the Cairns CBD picked up.

Having set foot again on dry land after their day trips to the reef, sunburned backpackers scurried in and out of Wollies, picking up supplies for the night ahead and breakfast the next morning. Unsurprisingly, half of their purchases were from the liquor department.

After being run off earlier, the four hoodlums had regathered and were again looking for trouble.

"Where ya been mate?" Big John Thornton asked, greeting Robert Fuller with a fist bump.

"It's my mum's birthday. We had dinner and cake."

"Cake? What are you, five years old? You blow out the candles for her too?"

"Funny," Robert said, glancing over at Tom "Hitman" Hearns, who for better or worse had the same moniker as the former US boxing champion. Thornton, who was the size of a small truck, had hung the name "Hitman" on him during Year 11.

Hearns had to Google the name Thomas Hearns to find out what he was going on about. One he realised he was named after a four-time world champion he preferred to be addressed as "Hitman" and he was.

Rounding out the foursome was Mitch Weller, a slight kid who could not have weighed more than sixty-five kilograms in his birthday suit.

The quartet went through high school together with Weller and Fuller doing the bookwork for all four of them. Thornton was such an important part of Far North Queensland High School, or FNQHS as it was called, that all he had to do was show up to be given a passing grade. At about 110 kilograms and 200cm tall and with the speed of a runaway motorbike, he was named to every schoolboy rugby league and FNQ state team. Agents followed him throughout Year 12, eager to get his signature on a contract which would set both player and agent up for life.

But a tackle late in the second half during an intrastate match against Central Queensland in Mackay ended Thornton's pro career before it even got started. With Far North Queensland ahead by thirty points, Thornton grabbed a clever no-look pass from fullback Cameron Crooke and sprinted down the sideline toward the goal line.

Just one man stood between Thornton and his fourth try of the afternoon – Mackay wingman Bob "Cannonball" Blake. With just 10 minutes left to play and the result a foregone conclusion, the Year 11 speedster could have attempted a half-hearted tackle. But he was not the only one aware of the many scouts and agents in the stands and gave chase. Thornton sidestepped Blake at the thirty-metre line and, thinking he was clear, slowed up just a bit. But Blake gave chase and grabbed a hold of Thornton's left foot at the 10-metre line like a dog latching on to a postie. He let go after Thornton fell to the turf screaming in agony. His left hip had come out of its socket. Blake got up and frantically waved for the trainers. The Central Queensland and FNQ trainers – six in all – each raced to the left-sideline where Thornton was writhing in pain.

The first trainer to reach him nearly keeled over himself when he had a look at Thornton's displaced hip. One of the FNQ trainers ran to the parked ambulance which was required to be on hand at all intrastate games. One paramedic raced to Thornton while the other slowly manoeuvred the ambulance onto the playing field. The paramedic on the field immediately set up an IV and gave Thornton a shot of morphine to ease the excruciating pain. Fifteen minutes after the tackle, Thornton was lifted into the ambulance and taken to hospital. Officials called the game. Blake was overcome by the guilt of ending Thornton's career and did not play again for a year. FNQ head coach Hugh Mulligan came under fire for leaving the state's best player on the field with the game already won and was given his walking papers once the school year came to an end.

"You fucked up," the superintendent told him.

A week after undergoing surgery for his dislocated hip and several fractures, Thornton was flown back to Cairns. The hip and fractures healed after 10 weeks but after a lengthy stint of rehabilitation he was told by his surgeons that the blood supply to the bone had been disrupted and despite their best efforts he would have to undergo hip replacement surgery. His rugby playing days were over.

The state paid for all of Thornton's medical bills and he received the biggest cheer of anyone on graduation night when he hobbled to the stage on crutches to collect his diploma.

The diploma meant little since Thornton had hardly done any schoolwork. Teachers covered for him while mates, who were happy to be a part of his growing entourage, willingly did his homework for him. Thornton, just eighteen, had no idea what to do with his life and with little guidance at home – his father and older brothers worked in the mines in Western Australia –he quickly fell in with the wrong crowd. He also became hooked on the powerful painkiller Oxycontin which he popped in his mouth like Tic Tacs and washed down with cans of Carlton Draught.

"Just one more script doc, the bloody pain is killing me."

He told the same thing to several different doctors. All were familiar with his injury and readily wrote him more scripts. What he didn't put into his mouth he sold for $10 each.

25

DRIVING HOME FROM THE WOOLIES IN THE NEARBY Smithfield Shopping Centre one morning, Delaney was patiently waiting to make a right-hand turn into the Coral Reef Apartment complex when his eyes were drawn to the tattered front fence surrounding both sides of its entrance. The waist-high, cream-coloured picket fence was missing a post on the left side and two on the right. Plus, it was in dire need of a paint job due to a combination of neglect and the harsh north Queensland sun.

A few weeks earlier, Barbara mentioned that the condition of the fence had been brought to the attention of the body corporate which turned down the request to fix it, citing the cost. The committee had recently shelled out a few thousand dollars on a new pump for the swimming pool and was in no hurry to spend any more money.

"When the damn thing tips over we'll look into it," committee chairman Keith Gibson said at the time. "Shit, between that pump and my rates I'm barely breaking even this quarter. I can't raise the rent on my tenants. There are too many units on the damn market," he said between puffs on a cigar that was as big as a log.

"All in favour of delaying the work on the fence raise your hands." Eight of the twelve hands in the small clubroom adjacent to the pool went up. "The motion to fix the fence is denied," Gibson said. "Anything else on the agenda madam secretary?" he asked, pointing his cigar in Barbara Stevenson's direction.

"Not unless anyone has anything to add," she said.

The 10 others looked at one another. A few shrugged their shoulders.

They were like young kids in a classroom too afraid to answer a teacher's question for fear of being wrong.

Betty Johnson wanted to bring up the issue of the complex's large bins not being put back into place quickly enough after the garbos came around but decided to wait until the next meeting in two months. In the meantime, she and next-door neighbour Hillary Miller would push the bins back where they belonged.

Gibson brought down his gavel and loudly banged it three times on the circular table everyone had gathered around.

"Meeting is adjourned." He stood up, shoved a bunch of papers and the gavel into a battered brown briefcase and bolted from the room after a few quick goodbyes.

As usual, Johnson was the last to leave the room. She gathered the empty coffee containers and soft drink cans, stepped outside and dropped them in the pool's recycling bin. Not in any hurry to join her husband of thirty-two years back at their unit, Betty turned out the room's lights, locked the door, closed it behind her and ventured to one of the lounge chairs by the pool where she stretched out and gazed at the night time sky.

Back at their second floor unit, Len Jackson opened his fourth beer of the night. Using his phone, he put a $5 bet on a greyhound named White Picket Fence at a meeting in country Victoria. Breaking from the inside box at odds of $4.50, the dog jumped straight to the front and was never headed. Betty heard him loudly cheering the dog home through their open balcony door.

"Stay there, stay there. Yes!" In a few moments the win was credited to his account and his new balance, now in triple figures, appeared on his phone.

The fence wouldn't be that hard to fix, Delaney thought. As he went over the figures in his mind his train of thought was broken by the toots of a horn from the car behind him. Delaney glanced in his rear-view mirror and saw a young woman flailing her arms about. With his window open Delaney heard her shouting, "Go arsehole, go!"

"Take it easy," Delaney said calmly through his open window.

"You old fuckers shouldn't have a licence," the woman screamed as she whizzed past him.

Delaney noticed the car's P plates as he eased into the parking lot. "Why doesn't that surprise me?" he asked.

He parked a few metres away from the fence under a large palm tree which provided just enough shade for his two bags of groceries on the back seat.

He walked to the fence and examined it. He gently ran his hands over the still sturdy structure to avoid getting a splinter.

Just needs some fresh paint, he thought. Behind the fence were the missing posts. They were a little tattered but otherwise intact. A couple of nails and they'll be back in line. Delaney peeled off a small layer of paint from the back of the fence to bring to Bunnings which he hoped had something similar in colour.

With nothing on that afternoon, Delaney visited the local Bunnings and headed straight for the paint section. After scanning the aisles, he found the colour he was looking for. He walked back to the front of the store, retrieved a trolley and put two four-litre cans of cream-coloured outdoor paint in it. Sandpaper was in the next aisle along with the paint scrapers, brushes and drop cloths. He had a hammer and nails and not much else in an old toolbox at home so, with his shopping expedition over, he wheeled the trolley to a register where a cheerful young woman in her regulation red and green apron ran a scanner over the barcodes of the items. "One hundred and thirty-nine dollars and seventy-five cents," she said.

Delaney handed her three fifty-dollar notes, collected his change and steered the trolley to his car which was baking in the afternoon sunshine. He put the paint in the back of his Honda, tossed the rest of the items onto the passenger seat and wheeled the trolley to one of the collection points in the massive parking lot.

An oversized trolley from a neighbouring Coles store was where it shouldn't have been so Delaney took the offending cart out of line, slotted his trolley into its proper place and trudged a hundred and fifty metres with the Coles cart to its proper collection point. With a strong shove he put it back where it belonged.

The next morning, Delaney put on a pair of shorts, an old long-sleeved shirt and a worn pair of sneakers. He slapped sunscreen on his face, plonked a white hat on his head, took a cold bottle of water from the fridge, grabbed his rusty toolbox from the hall closet and the sandpaper, scraper and drop cloth he had bought at Bunnings. The two cans of paint stayed in the car overnight. There was no point lugging the heavy suckers upstairs and then back down. When it was time to use them, he'd drive his car over to the fence and unload them.

He made his way over to the fence, first stopping at the pool area to grab a plastic chair. It was just after 9am and there wasn't a single cloud in the sky to block the sun's rays. A slight breeze offered little respite from the heat.

Delaney opened his toolbox and took out a pair of gardening gloves. He went to work sanding and scraping each fence post. Alternating between sitting and standing, he found the old paint came off the posts with the same regularity as the sweat from his brow. He stopped every five minutes or so to wipe the sweat from his eyes and to adjust his hat which was already as wet as his shirt.

The back of the fence was in better shape than the front which soaked up more of each day's sunshine.

A few tenants came and went as Delaney worked. He got a thumbs up from one fellow and barely a look from the others. When the posts were as smooth as tissue paper, Delaney hammered the missing posts back where they belonged, two nails for each post.

The noise caught the attention of Barbara who was having her morning coffee and a read of the morning paper which Delaney had dropped on her doorstep two hours earlier.

What in the world is that? she wondered. She walked onto her balcony, was unable to figure out where the noise was coming from and went downstairs to investigate.

As she got to the pool area, she found the source of the racket. A worker was hammering nails into the complex's front fence. Knowing that the fence had not been scheduled to be fixed she approached the worker only to find out it was Delaney.

"Gary? What in the world are you doing?"

Delaney looked up and smiled. "Hey Barb. Just fixing the fence."

"But the body corporate hasn't approved any repairs."

"It won't disapprove either once I finish. The paint goes on tomorrow."

Barbara took a moment to take it all in.

"I got tired of looking at the fence the way it was, Barb, and I'm using my own money. It won't cost anyone a cent. We'll talk about it later, over dinner, okay? My treat."

Delaney stood up and kissed Barbara on the cheek. "I'm going to get back to work. Another hour and I'll be done for the day.

"Okay, I guess. What if someone asks me what's going on?"

"Just tell them the fence is being repaired at no cost to anyone."

Barbara nodded. "Okay, see you later. Knock on my door and let me know what time you want to leave."

Delaney took a long drink of water, put his work gloves back on and got to work scraping and sanding the back of the fence. Seventy minutes later he was done. He got on his hands and knees to pick up the drop cloth which collected the cream-coloured shavings that had fallen from the posts and left the area looking cleaner than he had found it.

He returned the chair to the pool area, gathered his belongings and took a long look at the mended fence which was back in one piece and ready for a new coat of paint. "It's looking pretty, pretty, pretty good," he said, mimicking Larry David.

Delaney trudged upstairs to his unit, took off his sweat laden clothes – even his underwear was wet – and took a cool shower. He felt the effects of his work later that night after dinner and took a couple of Panadol for his aching arm and shoulder muscles before he went to bed.

He set the alarm for seven in a bid to get the painting done while it was relatively cool.

With thick, white clouds blotting out the early morning sun, Delaney drove his car to the fence and retrieved the two cans of paint. He parked the car in a visitors' spot, locked it and tucked a drop cloth, paint can opener and two paint brushes into the back pockets of his shorts. He again borrowed a chair from the pool area and set it down on the grass in front of the fence.

Delaney laid the drop cloth on the grass and pulled it under the inch or so gap between the bottom of the fence and the grass so that any spilled or stray paint would land on it. He put on his gloves, adjusted his cap, took a seat and pried open the first can. Needing something to stir the paint with, the newly-turned handyman found a thick, long stick by the side of the road. He peeled off the bark and put it to good use.

With the paint ready to be applied, Delaney dipped a thick brush into the can and slapped a brush full of the cream-coloured paint onto the post farthest away from the complex's entrance. A small bit of paint dropped onto the cloth as he worked from top to bottom. He used a smaller brush to do the sides of the posts and within an hour he had reached the last post on the left-hand side of the entrance. He got up and took a long look at his handiwork. "What a difference. It's a hundred percent better," he said.

After a water break and a few stretches to relieve the small amount of pain he was feeling in his back and legs, Delaney got started on the right-hand side of the entrance.

The paint went on nice and smooth and with half a can left to work with it looked as if the second can would not have to be opened until it was time to work on the back of the fence.

The early morning clouds had drifted to the west, so Delaney and the fence were bathed in sunshine; good weather for the paint to dry but not ideal for the fifty-seven-year-old man applying it.

With just four posts to go, Delaney was startled by the sound of a woman's voice to his left.

"Excuse me sir," she said taking off her sunnies. "You are doing a wonderful job with the fence."

Delaney pushed back his hat and got up from his chair. He was half a head taller than the smartly-dressed woman who looked to be about five years his junior.

"Thank you," he said. "I must say it is looking pretty good."

"I was driving by and saw you working on it. My fence needs painting and I was wondering if you or someone from your company would be able to paint it. I could never do it by myself."

"I'm not with any company," Delaney explained. "I live in this complex and just wanted to see a fresh coat of paint on the fence."

"Oh. And I thought you were a painter," the slim, dark-haired woman said, sounding slightly embarrassed.

"That your car over there?" Delaney asked, pointing to a white Toyota parked on the street.

"It is. I was on my way to do a little shopping. I have a doctor's appointment later and wanted to get it out of the way."

"Nothing serious, I hope."

"I hope not. Just a follow-up. You know how it is at our age. There's always something that needs looking after."

"Including fences, eh?"

The woman nodded.

Delaney stuck out his right hand and introduced himself. "Gary Delaney, retiree turned fence painter."

"Judy Seymour, financial advisor. Pleased to meet you."

The two shook hands. "The pleasure is mine," Delaney said, taking notice of her bright red nails and the barren ring finger on her left hand.

"I'll tell you what. How about I come around to your house later this afternoon and have a look at the fence? I'll see what needs to be done, how much paint might be required. That okay with you?"

"It is. I'm over on McKenzie St. 13 McKenzie St."

"Not too far at all, just a few blocks away," Delaney said. "Shall we say about 4pm?

"Yes, that would be perfect," Judy Seymour said as she put her sunnies back on. "See you then."

Judy Seymour walked to her car and turned around as she opened the driver's side door only to see Delaney staring at her.

"Mates' rates?" she asked.

"Always," Delaney replied.

Delaney backed away from the fence to have a better look at it.

"It's looking better than I thought," Delaney said to himself as Judy Seymour drove off. "How about that. A new career at my age. The guys at Saltwater Lakes will have a good laugh when I tell them about it."

Delaney finished slapping paint on the four remaining posts and then got started on the back of the fence. The work was easy enough but the constant bending down to reach the bottom of the posts was beginning to aggravate his back.

The energy-sapping heat wasn't helping. But Delaney persevered. He found working outside exhilarating after more than thirty years of sitting at a desk with his eyes glued to a computer screen.

Delaney was nearly halfway through with the back of the fence when he ran out of paint. He got up from his borrowed pool chair, stretched his back and fetched the other can. He opened it and gave it a good stir with the same cream-coloured stick he had used on the first. He put on his paint-covered gardening gloves, reached for the larger brush and got back to work.

Delaney didn't notice the lad who had got off his bike and laid it on the grass until he spoke.

"Painting the fence, eh?" he asked.

Delaney looked up. He figured the kid was about twelve.

"I sure am mate. Come to lend a hand?"

"In this heat? Nah. I'm heading home for the air conditioning."

"Fair enough. What made you stop?" Delaney asked.

"From a distance I thought you were my pa. He used to be a house painter and I used to tag along on his jobs when school was out. I haven't seen him for over a year."

Delaney put down his paint brush, took off his hat and wiped his brow.

"Sorry to hear that. If you don't mind me asking, what happened?"

Avoiding eye contact the lad said there had been a nasty argument between his dad and grandfather more than a year ago over an unpaid debt. As far as he knew the two hadn't spoken since, and his dad had told his pa to stay away from him.

"I haven't seen my pa in a long time, and I miss him. I thought that might have been him painting this here fence. He always wore a white hat when he worked."

"In this weather you have to. What's your name, son?" Delaney asked.

"Tim Lake, like the street in town."

"Nice to meet you Tim. Gary Delaney."

"Been painting for a long time? It's the only job my pa ever had."

Delaney chuckled.

"What's so funny?"

"I've been painting for all of two days, Tim. I live here and got tired of looking at this ragged-looking fence every day."

"Two days? And here I thought you were a painter."

"You've got a bit of knowhow. How do you think it's coming along?"

Tim Lake studied the front side of the fence and had a good look at the back. "Good job. It's going to need another coat."

"Thanks, mate. I'll be doing that tomorrow. I figure I've got just enough paint to get through it."

Tim peered into the can which was nearly full. "You'll make it."

"I'll be out here about 8am tomorrow if you want to help out," Delaney said.

"Not sure my dad would like that. He's always telling me not to talk to strangers."

"Well, he can bring you by himself if he likes and decide then if I am someone he can trust."

"Okay. Do you think my pa is mad at me?" Tim asked.

"Not at all. The argument is between him and your dad. Unfortunately, sometimes when there is a family disagreement, others suffer."

"Like me?"

"Their argument won't last forever, Tim, and when it is over you and your pa will be back spending time together just as you did before."

"I sure hope so."

Tim Lake picked his bike up off the grass and put on a white helmet which was a bit too snug for him. His light brown hair poked out the back and through its earholes.

"Take care, Tim. Maybe I'll see you tomorrow."

"Maybe," he said as he pedalled off.

26

THE RUMBLING COMING FROM HIS STOMACH SIGNALLED lunch time, so Delaney hid his painting gear behind the fence and covered it all with the drop cloth that had served its purpose well. Splashes of paint had stained parts of it but not one drop of paint had landed on the grass. His old sneakers had not been as lucky.

Delaney took off the pair of gloves he had been painting with only to find that there was plenty of cream-coloured paint on his hands and forearms. He filled up his water bottle at the water fountain by the pool, poured some of the cool water over his hands and arms and started scrubbing. Despite the lack of soap, the paint came off quite quickly. The paint staining his fingernails would be dealt with later.

Feeling refreshed after splashing some water on his face, Delaney walked three blocks to a corner café where he'd had lunch before. He and several others dodged the sunshine by walking on the shady side of the street. When he rocked up to the café, he saw a large sign hugging the footpath. It featured a caricature of an older fellow with a black moustache sipping a coffee with the words, "Today's Special: Hot Coffee", printed in bright red above it. Delaney chuckled as he looked it over.

Every other day the coffee is served cold, but today ...

Delaney walked through the cafe's open door and waited to be served. There were three women behind the counter, each wearing an apron with the cafe's name splashed on the front. One looked to be in charge of the coffee machine. The barista was likely on more coin than the others.

A cheerful young woman with caterpillars for eyelashes and talons for fingernails greeted Delaney and asked him what he wanted. He had a look at the selection of meats and salads in front of him and decided on a chicken salad roll with mayonnaise. He marvelled at how she was able to make a sandwich with fingernails more suited for picking at roadside prey. She couldn't have been more than twenty-two or twenty-three, and Delaney could not keep his eyes off her. *What in the world is a gorgeous young woman like you doing serving up sandwiches*? was what Delaney wanted to ask but instead of embarrassing himself he walked over to a massive cooler and took out a cold Diet Coke to go with his roll.

"Will you be having that here or would you like me to wrap it up?" the woman asked.

"I'll have it at one of the tables outside," Delaney said as he reached into his pocket. He pulled out a tenner, got a two-dollar coin back as change and took his lunch to the one empty table that was left.

Backpackers filled most of the other tables. Many looked badly hung-over as they took a stab at their all-day breakfasts. The stifling heat and humidity were not helping. But they'd be back at it again that night, drinking and carrying on just as Delaney did when he was their age.

I'll be getting up before some of them even get to bed, Delaney thought with a tinge of envy.

Delaney averted his eyes from the teens and twenty-somethings and instead gazed at the steady parade of locals and tourists walking by on the wide footpath. An old timer crossing the street with the aid of a walker was noticeably limping. Delaney put the affliction down to old age. He looked to be about a hundred. He then noticed a young mum pushing a pram with a white umbrella over it headed in the other direction. She too was walking with a limp. Across the street a fellow steered a maroon SUV into an empty parking spot, climbed out of the car, carefully looked at a parking sign to make sure he was legally parked and limped to the post office across the street. *This town either has the worst podiatrist in the southern hemisphere or everyone is wearing the wrong-sized shoes*, Delaney thought as he polished off his salad roll and Diet Coke. He adjusted his hat and sunnies, tossed the empty can in a nearby bin and brought the empty plate back inside.

He bought a bottle of water to take with him, handing over the gold coin he had earlier received as change. Taking the same route back home, Delaney was passed by a lad on a bike who had deftly veered onto the street to avoid him.

"Hey, Tim," Delaney yelled to the lad, who was back on the footpath and already a hundred metres ahead of him.

The kid kept going, putting more and more distance between them.

Maybe he didn't hear me. Or maybe it wasn't even him, Delaney thought as he kept walking.

Tim Lake did not show up later that afternoon as Delaney finished painting the fence.

Delaney clapped his hands upon completion of the job and gave it a good long look.

"Not too bad for an old-timer, especially in this heat," he said as he reached into the front pocket of his shorts to have a glance at his watch. It was 3:35. He had just twenty-five minutes to pack up his gear, wash up and get to Judy Seymour's house by 4pm.

He put his gear in his car, drove to his designated parking spot and slowly climbed up the stairs to his unit. Delaney was exhausted. "Did I paint a fence or run a bloody marathon?" he asked as he got to the top of the stairs.

How do tradies work in these conditions? he wondered. *I'd never be able to do this every day.*

Most of the tradies in the area were thirty years his junior, and eventually got used to the heat.

Delaney showered quickly, put on a clean shirt and was out the door at 3:55.

"I'll do this house on McKenzie St – if it is not such a big job –and then I'll go back to playing golf and lounging by the pool," Delaney said as he drove the couple of blocks to Judy Seymour's home. He found it quite easily and parked in the paved driveway behind Seymour's Toyota.

He had a look around before he knocked on the door of the neat ranch-style house. The fence was intact, painted a dark shade of green and stood about waist high. He ran his hands over the wood. It needed a paint job but luckily not much sanding and scraping. There wasn't much room at the back of the fence due to an expansive garden which would have cost a fortune to put together. A very healthy-looking palm tree was its centrepiece. Based on his two-day knowledge of fence painting, Delaney figured Judy Seymour's fence would need two coats of paint.

"If it was twenty degrees and not thirty, I could knock it over in a day," he said as he walked to the front door.

Just as he was about to ring the bell, the door opened, and Judy Seymour appeared. "I heard you drive up. I like a worker who is on time," she said.

"Shall we have a look at the fence?" she asked as she donned a wide-brimmed light blue hat. Dressed in the same sneakers and shorts he had painted in, Delaney felt like a slob next to Seymour, who was wearing a sleeveless summer dress and small heels which matched the colour of her hat.

Is she a fashion consultant or a financial consultant? Delaney asked himself as they walked to the front fence which was separated by a gate.

"What do you think?" Judy Seymour asked as she touched the fence.

Delaney wanted to tell her she looked fantastic. She looked at him as if she was waiting to hear the same thing.

Instead, Delaney swallowed hard and gave her his opinion of the fence.

She nodded. "Okay," she said. "Now let's take a look at the back fence."

"There's a back fence?" Delaney asked, rather disheartened.

"Yup." Seymour smiled. She put her hand on his arm and led the way to the back of the house via the driveway.

Small palms and colourful tropical plants covered the side fences. The back fence was behind a small vegetable garden and was pretty much exposed.

"Quite a spread you have here," Delaney said he gazed around the yard. "Lived here long?" he asked as he walked to the back fence.

"Coming up on twelve years. I lost my husband four years ago. He took care of the fences and did most of the landscaping."

Probably died of heat exhaustion, Delaney thought.

"You and he did a lovely job," Delaney told her.

"Thank you, Gary. I enjoy the gardening and looking at the plants and trees. It brings me a lot of joy. It's not easy living alone once you get to our age."

Judy lowered her head and Delaney wondered if she was thinking of her husband. After several moments Judy wiped a tear from her eye and asked Delaney if he would like to come inside for a cold drink. "We have business to discuss, don't we?"

"I guess we do," Delaney said. He followed her as she opened the sliding back door and walked inside. Delaney closed the door behind him.

Two large ceiling fans, one in the living area and the other over the dining room table, cooled the warm late afternoon air.

"Very nice place you have here," Delaney said as he glanced around. A large and colourful aboriginal painting dominated the main wall of the living area.

Delaney could picture Judy and her husband seated together on the plush sofa with a drink in their hands gazing at it.

"I'm making myself a gin and tonic. Would you like one?" Judy asked from the kitchen.

"I sure would," Delaney answered.

"A bit of lime okay?"

"That's the only way to have one."

Judy motioned for Delaney to take a seat at the glass dining room table. He parked his carcass in one of the six white chairs and let out a sigh of relief.

"Long day?" Judy asked as she handed him a cocktail glass.

"Long, but satisfying," he said as he took the glass. The ice in it was melting faster than the polar ice caps.

"Cheers," they said as their glasses touched.

"Let's get business out of the way first," Judy said, reaching for a pad and pen.

"All right. I reckon we'll need two large cans of paint which should cover two coats on both the front and back fences. That will run you about $100. And since I only need to scrape, sand and paint just the one side, the whole job should take about eight to 10 hours."

"How much would you want for your time?" Judy asked as she sipped her gin and tonic.

"Two hundred and fifty dollars – cash."

"I can manage that," she said with a flirtatious smile. "Do we have a deal?"

"We do," Delaney answered.

"When can you start?"

"As soon as it dips below thirty degrees."

"That might be a couple of months."

"Let me recover from the job at the apartment complex. How about this Monday?" Delaney asked.

"That would be fine. Could you buy the paint though? I would have no idea what brand to get. My husband did all that." She took two fifty-dollar notes from her designer purse and slid them across the table to her newly-hired fence painter. "If it costs any more please let me know."

"I will," Delaney said, as he glanced at his watch.

"Have someplace to go?"

"Not yet."

Judy Seymore smiled. "Since you keep mentioning the heat, would I be right in assuming you're a newcomer to the area?"

"You are. I retired and moved here from Melbourne about eight months ago. This is my first full summer in the tropics, but I'll get used to it, I think."

"You're here with your wife or partner?"

"No. I'm divorced. I came up here by myself to get away from the cold Melbourne winters and for a change of scenery."

"That took a lot of courage, leaving your family and friends."

"I guess, but I wanted an adventure. I spent my whole career sitting in an office. I wanted the exact opposite and that's just what I have here. I play golf, hang out by the pool. So far, so good."

Delaney wondered whether if he should tell Judy about Barbara. After all, they were an item.

"What sort of work did you do, Gary, if you don't mind me asking?"

"I was a sports journalist for over thirty years."

"I'm impressed. Must have been a lot of fun."

"It was Judy. I got paid for doing something most would do for free; going to grand finals, the tennis, the Melbourne Cup."

"Going to the Melbourne Cup is one thing I'd like to do one day."

"I'll see if I can pull a few strings and get you into the members."

Judy laughed. "One for the road, Gary?"

"I better not. I'm going out for dinner and I don't want to show up half sloshed."

"Going with anyone special?"

Delaney pondered his options. He went with the truth.

"A woman from my complex. We go out to dinner a couple of times a week. I occasionally stay the night at her place."

After what seemed like an hour of silence, Judy stood up.

"Well, it's nice to have someone to do things with and thank you for being honest with me. Let me show you out. I wouldn't want you to be late for your date."

Judy opened the front door. "What time will you be here on Monday?" she asked.

"Probably by eight. I'd like to get as much done as I can before the real heat of the day kicks in."

"Eight it is. I'll have a cup of coffee waiting for you."

Judy Seymour gave Delaney a peck on the cheek and watched him walk to his SUV. He got in, carefully backed out of the driveway and honked the horn twice as he drove off.

Judy waved and closed the door. She made herself another drink, stretched out on the sofa and kicked off her shoes.

Nice guy, she thought. *A shame about the girlfriend but I doubt she's in my league. He must have done all right for himself over the years since he retired early. I wonder how much he has tucked away; would have to be at least four or five hundred thousand. Looks like I may have a little bit of homework to do.*

27

THE SKY WAS OVERCAST WHEN DELANEY COLLECTED the *Cairns Examiner* from outside his front door shortly after 7am on Monday morning. He showered, made himself some toast and coffee and had a quick read of the headlines. Tourism was up, yet retail sales remained steady. On the back page there was a big yarn about selectors being in a bind over whom to take to India for Australia's next series of Test matches. "For goodness sake, take another spinner. How hard can it be?"

He turned to the middle of the paper and the weather page. Breaks of sun and a 10 per cent chance of showers was forecast for the greater Cairns area with a high of 32 degrees. "Let's not have too much sunshine," Delaney said as he dropped the paper on his kitchen table and went about gathering his things. His painting gear was packed away in his car so all he had to do was grab his cap and a large bottle of water. He locked his front door, closed it behind him and walked down the stairs to his parking spot. His Honda quickly turned over, as she always did. Delaney zigged and zagged his way through the complex's parking lot where he turned right. It was 7:50am. Two blocks away, Barbara Stevenson was sitting in her Toyota. She wanted to see first-hand what Delaney was up to and had beaten him downstairs by 15 minutes.

She noticed Delaney's Honda head north, turned the ignition key and followed him. Delaney turned left onto McKenzie St and parked on the street outside Judy Seymour's home. As he gathered his things from his car, Delaney didn't notice Barbara Stevenson speed past. "Number 13," she said. "I have a bad feeling about this."

Stevenson didn't see Judy Seymour emerge from her home and it's a good thing she hadn't since Seymour was dressed in a flimsy robe and carried a steaming cup of coffee for her hired hand.

"Good morning Gary. Right on time," Seymour said. "And as promised, a nice cup of coffee to get you going."

"Thanks Judy. If you don't mind, I'm going to get right to work." He handed her the receipt for the paint, which came in two dollars short of the $100 she had given him.

"If you need anything just knock. I'll be heading out shortly. I have a 9am appointment in Palm Cove."

"Not medical, is it?" Delaney asked.

"No, business," Seymour answered. "I have several good clients up that way and check in with them from time to time to see if they want any changes made to their portfolios."

"That's mighty nice of you Judy. These days most communicate through email."

"I've always found that the personal touch works best."

Judy Seymour smiled, turned and walked towards her front door. She looked back, saw Delaney starring at her and winked. *Show them a bit of leg and they're hooked*, she said to herself.

Half an hour later Judy backed her car out of the driveway. "If you're here when I return, we'll have a drink. Otherwise I'll see you tomorrow morning," she said through the passenger side window before shutting it and speeding off.

Delaney nodded and waved and then got back to work. The fence did not need much sanding and scraping so he was able to start painting a lot sooner than expected. It would still need two coats, but he'd be able to get the front fence done by mid-afternoon. Alternating between sitting, kneeling and standing, and working from left to right, the first coat went on so easily he was able to break for lunch just after noon.

Delaney retrieved a cool bag from his Honda and found a shady spot in Judy Seymour's front garden. He planted his plastic $11 Bunnings chair on a nice thick piece of grass and removed the contents of the bag; a roast beef sandwich and a can of Diet Coke, which was still cold. After polishing off his lunch, Delaney leaned back in his chair and admired Judy Seymour's perfectly manicured garden. It was nearly as nice as her shapely legs. *She would have spent a bloody fortune on this,* he thought. His smallish balcony had room for just two plants.

Delaney wasn't looking forward to getting back to work under the hot sun, which was now directly overhead. Most of the morning's clouds had moved off to the west. He took out his phone to check the latest temperature. It was 30 degrees and getting hotter with each passing minute. His plan was to get the second coat on as quick as he could, pack up and cool off in the pool back home.

He went back to where he started and found that the first coat of paint had dried nicely. The fence was looking good and would look even better once the second coat was applied. Just over two hours later he was finished. He picked up the drop cloths and put the lid back on the first can of paint which was nearly empty. He cleaned the brushes with a wet rag, put everything back in his car and wet a hand towel with what was left in his water bottle. He wiped his face and brow and instantly felt better.

Should I wait for Judy or head off? he asked himself. Not knowing when she would return, Delaney decided that the pool was the better option and left. He looked at the fence as he drove off and smiled. "I'm getting pretty good at this, but my fence-painting career ends here. I'm too old to be doing this shit," he said.

28

JUDY SEYMOUR'S TWO MEETINGS IN PALM COVE WENT just as she expected. Retired property developer Sid Fredrickson and his wife Danielle were up first. The aging couple, he was 79, she 77, lived in a two million-dollar plus spread with an ocean view which had graced several magazine covers.

Every morning they ate breakfast on their large bedroom balcony. Neither had to lift a finger. Preparing their pancakes, eggs, toast, coffee and fruit was Rita Nolen, a divorced single mother who was paid $1000 a week by the Fredricksons to make breakfast, clean, do laundry, check the health of a large pool and ferry them to various appointments in the couple's year-old Mercedes.

Fredrickson and his wife were each beginning to show signs of aging. They walked slower, were forgetful at times, took handfuls of pills for various afflictions and were in bed – separate double beds in the same room – with the lights out on most nights before 10pm.

Several years earlier Judy Seymour had set them up with a tax attorney friend of hers who took care of their monthly expenses. Among the expenses that Jim Glickman approved was a $2500 monthly fee to Seymour for her financial services which amounted to a monthly 45-minute visit. Glickman paid himself the same amount. The $5000 monthly expense was a pittance in a financial portfolio which ran well into the $30 million-dollar range.

The Fredrickson's two sons and three grandchildren were raking in so much money from their father's shrewd investments that they had more money than they knew what to do with. They visited several times a year and never once questioned Glickman about their parents' expenses. Glickman made sure they had first class airline tickets and a limo waiting for them on their arrival and had his doctored books ready for inspection if he ever was asked to present them. He never was. In fact, Glickman was toasted by the Fredricksons' children from the bottles of champagne he delivered to their hotel suites. "To Jim Glickman," eldest son Roger Fredrickson said on one occasion. "Long may he keep the money rolling in."

Sid Fredrickson still had enough of his marbles left to make sure Judy Seymour came by on the afternoons his wife was busy with a luncheon. Today's function was something involving the Cairns's arts program, which the Fredricksons gave healthy donations to each year. Next month's luncheon was a Save the Reef campaign, which Danielle had taken a strong interest in. "The reef is dying. Don't you see what's happening?" she asked her husband one morning. "From where I'm sitting, the reef looks fine, but donate as much as you like – within reason of course – sweetheart. Those donations help us come tax time."

"Good, I've sent the campaign a cheque for $50,000."

On hearing the amount Sid Fredrickson choked on a piece of grapefruit. He turned red, stood up and eventually coughed up the offending piece and spit it across the balcony. A bird swooped on it before it even came to a halt.

"Fifty large?" he asked after catching his breath.

"Not enough? Danielle asked wickedly as she wiped her mouth on a linen serviette.

"Sweetheart, Glickman is a whiz but the way you're tossing money around he's going to have to start up a counterfeiting business. Try and keep those donations to no more than $10,000. Okay?"

"Alright honey. I will." She planted a kiss on her husband's bald head as she got up and left the table. *For a few seconds there I thought he was a goner*, she thought. *I'll tell Rita to cut the grapefruit into larger pieces. Maybe next time it will stay lodged in his windpipe.*

She asked Rita to bring her husband a glass of water and told her to plan for an 11:30 departure for their trip into town. Danielle went to her walk-in closet – which was the size of a studio apartment – and started searching for an outfit. "It's 30 degrees outside and it will be 18 in that dining room. I'll speak to someone about that."

Judy Seymour was forced to dodge Sid Fredrickson's wet kisses as soon as he opened the front door, but several found their mark. She kept a bottle of Listerine mouthwash in her car and always took several swigs from it after they said their goodbyes. Judy reluctantly let him feel her sizeable breasts on the visits but being that he was impotent after surgery for prostate cancer five years ago she did not have to worry about things going any further. *The shit I have to put up with for a lousy $2500 a month*, she thought as he squeezed her nipples.

"Danielle never lets me touch her anymore," Fredrickson complained after Judy gave his hands a small slap and told him he had done enough grabbing and kissing for the afternoon. "I might have an out of order sign hanging from my pecker, but I still like a bit of affection Judy."

"I understand Sid. Listen, I know someone who might be able to give you what you need."

"You suggesting I pay for it? Well I ain't never paid for pussy and I never will even with all the money I've got," Sid said angrily as he walked to the bar to fix himself a drink. "You want anything Judy?"

"Whatever you're having is fine." Sid made two vodka and tonics and handed Judy one. After a moment of uncomfortable silence, Sid spoke up.

"You got a picture of this friend of yours?"

"Changing your mind?"

"Maybe. Let's see what she looks like."

Judy took out her phone, called up Vicky Awry's website and handed Sid the phone.

"No offense Judy, but she is hotter than you are."

"She's also about fifteen years younger than me."

Sid Fredrickson laughed.

"I'll text you her number and if you're still interested give her a ring."

"I might. Speaking of numbers," Sid said quickly changing the subject, "how are my numbers looking?"

"They are holding up quite well despite the downturn in the market," Judy said, taking several colourful folders out of her briefcase. "The investments I have made for you and Danielle are still growing – albeit at a slower rate – and show no sign of faltering. Do you want to make any changes?" she asked.

"Nah. You've done well for me and my family Judy. We trust you and Glickman."

"Thank you, Sid. Give my best to Danielle," Judy said as she packed up her briefcase. "I've got another appointment, so I best be heading off. Don't get up. I'll let myself out."

Judy kissed Sid on the cheek and slowly made her way to the front door, adjusting her blouse and bra as she walked.

"Best pair of pins I have ever seen and damn good with money too," Sid said as she closed the door.

Judy drove to the end of the driveway, rolled some Listerine around in her mouth and spit it into the rose bushes that lined the Fredricksons' driveway. She wiped her mouth with a tissue from the glove box, put on some fresh lipstick and drove to her next appointment.

Glickman and she had the same deal with Roger and Janine Healey, who had celebrated their 50th wedding anniversary four months earlier. To mark the occasion, she and Glickman sent the Port Douglas socialites on a week-long cruise to Bali. They had been back just a week and gave Judy a warm welcome, complete with a few gifts from the holiday hotspot.

"We had the most wonderful time Judy. Everything was perfect. There was even a driving range on the ship Roger used every day." Janine Healey said. Her arm was around the waist of her husband as she talked. They were the opposite of the Fredricksons. Even after 50 plus years they were affectionate and preferred each other's company over those of their neighbours who flouted their wealth at every opportunity. The Healeys played everything low-key despite their very comfortable lifestyle.

Roger had been a history professor in Sydney and Janine the office manager of a family medical practice. They too had invested wisely and upon arriving in Port Douglas nearly 10 years ago were given Judy Seymour's details by one of Roger's golfing buddies. "She's one of a kind. I highly recommend her," Rich Osborn said.

The Healeys however did not know that Osborn was granted landing rights on Miss Seymour's smooth fairway in exchange for each wealthy client he sent her way and would have told Healey that the sun shined out of her shapely arse if he had asked.

The Healeys met with Judy at their home over drinks late one afternoon and were so charmed by her that they put their large nest egg of superannuation and savings in Judy's hands. She skimmed a few hundred here and a few hundred there in addition to her regular monthly fee of $2500. Glickman also took his regular fee but thought it was wise to leave it at that since the Healeys were much more on the ball than the Fredricksons.

Over the last 10 years, the Healeys averaged an unheard-of nine percent return on Seymour's shrewd advice. They were so overjoyed with their rising balance sheet that they signed whatever Seymour put in front of them. One document named Judy as one of the beneficiaries in the couple's will. When the day came, she would be a very, very rich woman and still young enough to enjoy the windfall.

Judy Seymour had several other rich clients throughout the Cairns area and lived quite comfortably from the several thousand dollars a month in fees she collected and what she and Glickman skimmed from their accounts.

She had the nice house and the new car, both of which were fully paid off, and a large wardrobe that she added to on a weekly basis. She rarely cooked, preferring to eat lunch and dinner at the fancy cafes and restaurants that lined the Esplanade. Drinks were sent to her table time and time again. When they arrived, Judy picked up her glass and nodded to whomever sent it over. When a fellow got the nerve to approach her table, Judy simply thanked him for the drink and said she was happily married when asked if she wanted some company. Her playmate, which she picked up after her husband Jack died, was a vibrator purchased online.

At 53 Seymour looked 10 years younger and was constantly being asked out. Even before her husband passed away – she never cheated on him – she was constantly being propositioned by men with money and those without. She was even hit on by several women but politely declined their offers. Women were not on her radar but for some reason Gary Delaney was. He reminded her a bit of her late husband. He had Jack's smile and the same sense of humour. He also had what Jack didn't – money – and sensed that he would be an easy touch the way he swooned over her like a lovesick teenager.

Guilt was not part of Judy's make-up. She had no problem inserting herself into Healey's will. If caught, her career as a financial advisor would be over. There was also a chance she could wind up spending a portion of her later years in some minimum-security prison. Swindling Delaney would be her chance at one big score and an opportunity to leave Cairns which she had never really warmed to. It was Jack's idea to retire and leave the Sydney area and head north over a decade ago. A purchasing agent for a large construction company and former club rugby player, he constantly badgered her to make the move. He was beginning to sound like a parrot. "It will be better for my health Judy, it will be better for my health."

Judy finally relented and agreed. Two weeks later Jack was in possession of a nice retirement cheque and they started looking online for properties in the Cairns area. Several caught their eye. They printed them out, rang several real estate agents and flew north for a week to check them out. "The house on McKenzie St has potential," Jack said one evening over dinner. "When I get it fixed up it will be worth at least $100,000 more."

Judy had her sights set on a house in Palm Cove, a trendy well-off suburb about 20 km north of the Cairns CBD. Jack liked the house but said it was "too far out and too much money."

As she had often done over the course of their 22-year childless marriage, Judy caved.

The Seymours put a low-ball offer in for the house on McKenzie St in Holloways Beach, nine kms from the Cairns CBD and two days later it was accepted. Jack wrote out a cheque for $37,000 – 10 percent of the purchase price. The settlement period of 90 days gave them plenty of time to sell their home in Sydney.

With the housing boom in full swing in the Harbour City, it took just three weeks for the Seymour's three-bedroom house to sell. After paying off their mortgage and purchasing the home in Cairns outright, they were ahead more than $280,000.

They said so long to their family and friends over dinner at a local Italian restaurant and picked up the sizeable bill.

A national moving company hauled all their stuff up north two days later and made the arrangements for transporting Judy's Kia. The Seymours piled some of their clothes and everyday belongings into Jack's four-wheel drive and on an overcast and windy Tuesday morning backed out of their driveway for the last time.

"We had a lot of good years in this house," Jack said before slowly driving off.

"We sure did," Judy answered. He planted a kiss on his wife's cheek. "Thank you for doing this Judy. We'll make a good life for ourselves up there."

Once they settled into their new home, Jack kept himself busy by fixing up the house and garden while Judy resumed her career with a local investment firm. The all-male firm of Felder and Flanagan was happy to have her. But after a year of listening to their come-ons and bullshit she resigned. Several of her more well-heeled clients severed their ties with Felder and Flanagan when their contracts were up and put their wealth in Judy Seymour's newly created firm: Seymour Financial.

The steamy tropical air was a tonic for Jack Seymour's aching knees and back. No longer did it take him five minutes to crawl out of bed in the morning. He was also much more limber in bed at night for which Judy was thankful for.

Six years later though Judy Seymour was a widow. Jack had gone out for a run early one Saturday morning and suffered a massive heart attack. He managed to crawl to the curb where he was found by a passing motorist who immediately rang 000. An ambulance arrived within 90 seconds and transported him to Cairns Base Hospital where a team of doctors tried their best to revive him. He was pronounced dead at 8:12am at the age of 58.

Two policemen knocked on the door of 13 McKenzie St just before 9am to give Judy Seymour the awful news. She sank to her knees and cried until there were no more tears to give. After notifying his family and hers, a police officer arrived to take her to the hospital where she identified her husband's body. She kissed him softly on his cheek and forehead. A doctor gave her a sedative while a social worker contacted a local funeral home which came by later in the afternoon to collect Jack Seymour's body.

"Where is he being taken?" Judy Seymour asked.

"To Roberts and Mitchell Funeral home," social worker Joni Cooper said.

For the first time that day, Judy Seymour laughed.

"What's so funny," Joni Cooper asked.

"Roberts and Mitchell? On the highway? The ones with the 'We Know What to Do' sign?

Joni Cooper nodded.

"Every time Jack and I drove by there and saw the sign, he used to say, "THEY BETTER KNOW WHAT TO DO."

The folks at Roberts and Mitchell did in fact know what to do. They made all the arrangements of flying Jack Seymour's body to Sydney where it was met by a hearse from Nash and Elliot Funeral Home. Jack was buried in the Seymour family plot next to his mum and dad. Three days later Judy returned to her home in Cairns and began to figure out what to do with the rest of her life. She was just 53.

29

AFTER 10 YEARS OF HEAT, HUMIDITY, CYCLONE WARN-ings and the loss of her husband, Judy Seymour had had enough of Cairns. She preferred the cooler climes and sophistication of Noosa where she went on holiday every couple of years.

She and Jack usually stayed a week. One year they even drove down, taking the inland route through nearly every small town in Queensland. They stayed at bed and breakfasts, cabins in caravan parks and even a cheap motel or two when it was their only option. A house or an apartment with views of the Noosa River or the ocean, and daily outings to the swank shops that lined Hastings Street were at the top of Judy's wish list.

A few days after her escape from Sid Fredrickson's overeager hands and mouth, Judy took her morning cup of coffee into a spare room she had converted into an office and sat down at her desk, an indestructible beauty made of Tasmanian Huon Pine that she had picked up at a garage sale a few years ago for just $100.

She checked her bank balance, superannuation and a soon to mature term deposit which had just over $100,000 in it. She also had about $25,000 in cash hidden around the house in places where legendary bank robber Willie Sutton wouldn't even have looked. Toss in the nearly $200,000 she got from Jack's life insurance policy and she had about $750,000. She figured to bank about $575,000 from the sale of her house. Good numbers for anyone but not good enough for Judy, who spent more money than the average Australian earned in a year on her wardrobe, which included over 50 pairs of shoes.

The homes in Noosa she was looking at were in the $800,000 to $900,000 range. Apartments were in the half-million-dollar range. According to her calculations she needed about another $350,000 in order to retire and live comfortably. Anything that came her way from the will of the Healeys – unless their family contested the will – would be a bonus.

She placed the sheets of paper where she had scribbled down her assets in the top draw of the desk, and just to be on the safe side locked it. She got up from her luxurious leather chair – ordered specially from Harvey Norman – and walked to a window which looked out over the backyard. Much to her surprise she saw Gary Delaney; hat on his head and water bottle by his side, slapping paint on the yard's back fence.

I wonder how long he's been here, she wondered, glancing at the Rolex she gave herself as a Christmas gift two years ago. *He's a good little worker, good company and kind of cute too.*

She quickly brushed those thoughts from her head. "I wonder how much he has stashed away. I couldn't, could I?" she asked herself. "As those military men say, he would be collateral damage. It's not like he would be destitute. In just eight years he'll have his government pension landing in his account each fortnight. And he has that girlfriend who could help him out."

Judy took a quick shower, fiddled with her shoulder length auburn hair, added a bit of make-up, tossed on a pair of tight white jeans and a blouse, and walked out the back door.

Delaney was so pre-occupied scrapping a knot from the fence he did not hear Judy walking his way. He nearly scraped his left thumb off when she tapped him on the shoulder and said hello. "Geez Judy, you scared the crap out of me."

"Did I? Sorry Gary. Just checking in on my favourite tradie."

"Your favourite tradie's heart nearly stopped."

Delaney stood up, wiped some fence shavings from his shirt and picked up his bottle of water.

"I didn't mean to startle you. Sorry. You did a nice job with the front fence and this one is coming along nicely. When do you think you'll be done with it all?"

Delaney scratched the grey two-day growth on his chin and gave the fence a good long look. "It's going to take another coat, but the paint dries so quickly I just may have it wrapped up by this afternoon."

"Splendid. What do you say we celebrate later with a few drinks and dinner? My treat, and I'll pay you then as well."

"That's very nice of you Judy. A guy would have to be a fool to turn down an offer like that." Delaney took a glance at her blouse, which was misbuttoned, and her firm breasts which were tucked into a lacy black bra.

"In a bit of a hurry?" Delaney asked.

"What do you mean?"

He pointed at her blouse.

"Oh God, how embarrassing."

She turned just a bit, unbuttoned her blouse and rebuttoned it slowly, turning back to face Delaney while she fastened the last couple of buttons.

"I need to be a bit more careful," she said as she smiled. "Did you like what you saw?"

For one of the few times in his life Delaney was speechless. He simply nodded his head up and down.

"Come by and pick me up about six. That okay with you?"

"Sure is. I'll be here."

Judy kissed him softly on the cheek. "Put something nice on. We're going to an upscale place."

She walked back across the yard and closed the sliding back door. *This might be easier than I thought*, she surmised.

Delaney turned back to the fence and carefully adjusted his merchandise.

The last time I had a hard on in the morning like this I was in uni sitting behind Sarah Weiss. At least this time I didn't come in my pants.

30

DELANEY SHAVED, SHOWERED AND PUT ON ONE OF HIS two sport jackets for his big night out. He put a necktie in the navy-blue jacket's left-hand pocket just in case it was needed. Due to the heat and humidity, not too many men in Cairns – except for some lawyers and up-market realtors – wore ties. Even the politicians went around in shirtsleeves. They donned a jacket only when some big shot from Brisbane or Canberra visited.

"Hey, you scrub up nice for a tradie, a jacket and everything" Judy told Delaney when he picked her up. "I'm impressed."

"My paint-stained shorts and sneakers just wouldn't have cut it."

"Do you like Asian food?" Judy asked Delaney as she buckled her seatbelt.

Delaney got a bit distracted by Judy's outfit; a sleeveless dark green dress which rode up a bit as she sat down. She had a light sweater on her lap, just in case the restaurant was on the chilly side and had chosen a pair of tan heels which showed off her nice legs.

"Asian food? Okay with you?"

"Oh, yes. Asian food is fine. Where are we headed?"

"To the Tamarind in the Reef Casino. There's not a bad dish on the menu. And remember, it is my treat."

Delaney drove the ten or so kilometres to Wharf Street and wanting to impress Judy drove right up to the main entrance and handed his keys to one of the valets. Wondering if the young-looking lad had a licence, Delaney was handed his ticket and walked over to the SUV's passenger side to open the door for Judy. "The perfect gentleman. I like that," she said as she stepped out of the car.

"That old-timer is going to have a lot of fun tonight, unless he falls asleep in his soup," the valet said to himself as he watched the pair stroll into the lobby.

Delaney suggested a drink before dinner, if only to calm his nerves. He felt like a high school senior on prom night. They each ordered a gin and tonic. "I'll get this," Delaney said, reaching into his left front pocket for his billfold. He handed the Asian bartender a $20 note only to be told he needed to pony up $5 more.

"You don't get out much, do you Gary?" Judy joked.

"A big night for me is going to the RSL," Delaney quipped.

Judy laughed not knowing he was serious. "How about a toast?" she asked.

They picked up their glasses.

"To fence painters everywhere," Delaney said. "May they all be as lucky as me."

They clinked glasses and engaged in some light conversation before Judy glanced at her Rolex. It was 6:25. "We better get going. Our reservation is for 6:30."

A young Asian woman in a very snappy and colourful outfit – the same worn by the rest of the female staffers – greeted them and led them to their table. The restaurant was busy for a weeknight, but their table was in an area that seemed to be for couples only. The noise from several large parties, with more than a dozen people seated at their tables, barely reached them.

Before a waiter came to their table, Judy reached into her purse and handed Delaney an envelope. "I like to get business out of the way. Count it," she said. "Go on."

Delaney looked in the envelope and saw seven crisp $100 bills. "It's way too much Judy. Much more than we agreed on."

"It is, but you earned it. Not many retirees would work in the hot sun like you did."

"I guess you're right. I never knew fence painting could be so lucrative. Thank you, Judy. Feel free to pass my name around to your friends."

"Not a chance. You're all mine."

The lighting was low, the food exquisite and the bill, which Delaney never saw, had to be well over $250 thanks in part to a $75 bottle of wine they shared. Judy gave the waiter her credit card and a $50 note as a tip when he returned. It was all part of her plan to convince Delaney that money – his money – was the last thing she was after.

After a nightcap at the same bar they had visited several hours earlier, Delaney realised he was in no condition to drive home. Neither was his date. Just as he was about to put forth the idea of sharing a cab home and picking up his car in the morning, Judy took a card out from her purse, put it on the bar and slid it to him. Placing a room key on the bar would have had a greater impact, but room keys had been replaced by cards at most upscale-hotels decades ago. In his somewhat inebriated state, it took Delaney a moment or two to figure out what the card was and to put two and two together. When he did, Judy leaned over and whispered in his ear. "Fancy spending the night with me Gary?" she asked.

"I can't think of a better way to finish off the evening."

Judy tossed two $20 dollar notes on the bar and took Delaney's hand. He wobbled a bit as he stood up but otherwise was fine. Judy took hold of her handyman's arm as they made their way across the crowded gaming floor to the elevators.

"Do any gambling at all Gary?" she asked over the din of the pokie machines.

"Just a couple of dollars here and there on the horses. And when I say a couple of dollars, I really do mean a couple of dollars."

"What do you spend your money on?" she asked as they waited for the elevator.

"Doctors and prescriptions," he joked.

"Do you need any medicinal help in the bedroom, or can you get the job done without the use of those blue pills"?

"You'll soon find out," he said, kissing her playfully on the cheek.

I hope he doesn't have to take Viagra, she thought. *I'd like to get laid but not for four bloody hours.*

Their room featured a magnificent view of the piers and ocean. Judy opened the balcony door to let some warm air into the chilly room, sided up to Delaney and kissed him so long and hard he thought his tonsils had been removed. Judy then pushed Delaney onto the king-sized bed and undressed for him, leaving only her heels on. He was nearly drooling as she took his pants and briefs off. She tossed them on the floor and climbed on top of him.

Delaney did his best to last for as long as he could.

"Looks like my handyman is multi-talented," Judy Seymour said as they lay on their backs catching their breath.

"I'm just getting started," he said.

So am I, Judy Seymour thought. *So am I.*

31

ONCE JUDY FELL ASLEEP, DELANEY TOOK HIS NASAL spray from his jacket pocket and put a couple of spritzes in each nostril

Since it was early days, he was trying to put his best foot forward and it appeared to be working. She seemed to like him – a lot – and he could not help but think she wanted some sort of relationship. Living alone in one's later years as he knew was no picnic. *Wouldn't it be nice to live in her house,* he thought. *All that room, that nice big backyard.*

He looked to his left. Judy was on her side facing him and was fast asleep, a sheet covering just her legs and bum. *How lucky am I to be with her? She's a few years younger than me, absolutely gorgeous, and probably has more cash in her handbag than I have in my savings account.*

By the time Delaney dropped Judy off at her place later that morning and returned to the Coral Reef Apartments it was nearly noon. His jacket was flung over his right shoulder and his sleeves were rolled up to his elbows. It was another scorcher. As he walked to his unit he was unexpectedly confronted by Barbara Stevenson.

"Keeping late hours lover boy?" she asked.

In all the excitement of the past week Delaney had hardly given Barbara a thought. Some quick thinking was needed to keep the peace, but Delaney's hangover had displaced his thinking cap.

"Barbara," he said turning around to face the woman he had all but ignored since he met Judy Seymour. It had been a week since they shared a meal, the same bed or had a meaningful conversation.

"I've been busy I know, and I'm sorry. You wouldn't believe it. I have two fence painting jobs and have been flat out."

"Since when does a fence painter come home from work in a sports jacket?"

"I had a meeting, to see if setting up a business is feasible."

"A business? Yeah right." Barbara moved closer to Delaney, so close that their noses were practically touching. "Tell me the truth Gary. The woman who lives on McKenzie St. Are you fucking her?"

Delaney shifted his weight from one foot to the other and took a step back. *How does she know about Judy*? he wondered. "I'm seeing her if that is what you are asking."

Judy took a moment to process his answer and responded with a sharp knee to Delaney's groin. He quickly crumpled to the pavement in agony. "You bastard. Don't you ever talk to me again, ever."

The commotion drew the attention of several people down by the pool.

"What the fuck are you people looking at?" Barbara yelled before walking back to her unit and slamming the door.

Delaney stayed on the pavement for another few minutes, waiting for the pain to subside. He slowly got to his feet and staggered to his unit. He took a bag of frozen chips from the freezer, took his pants off, sat down and put the bag on his aching balls. "Should have worn a protective cup," he said.

Judy rang Delaney the next morning and invited him to lunch at her place. It was time to get down to business – financial business. She had him hooked. All that was left was to reel him in and drag him aboard. Delaney showed up with a bouquet of flowers to thank her for dinner at the Tamarind and her generosity. If there was to be a return roll in the hay it would have to be a gentle one since he was still a bit sore from Barbara's direct shot to his plums.

"Why aren't you the sweet one," Judy said as she opened the front door and ran her eyes over the colourful flowers. "I'll put them in a vase. Make yourself at home."

Delaney had a look around the living room. He examined a few pieces of bric-a-brac and a few framed photos of Judy and a middle-aged man he guessed was her late husband and took a seat on a couch that was more comfortable than anything he ever owned.

"Quite a place you have here Judy," Delaney said when she brought the flowers in from the kitchen and set them down on the dining room table. "Thanks Gary. My late husband liked to be surrounded by nice things."

"How long has it been since he passed away, if you don't mind me asking."

"Six years," she said, taking a seat next to Delaney on the couch. "We had a good life together and it all ended so abruptly. In the morning I was happily married. That afternoon I was a widow."

"I'm so sorry Judy."

"Hope you've brought your appetite" Judy said after a few moments of silence. She got up and started bringing salads, fruit, meats, bread rolls and condiments from the kitchen to the table.

"Expecting anyone else? We can't eat all of that," Delaney said looking at the spread.

"The secret is to pace yourself sweetie, pace yourself." Judy gave him a short kiss on the lips and told him to sit down and dig in. He did.

Half of his plate was covered with potato salad, pasta salad and cole slaw. He made himself a couple of sandwiches; one ham and the other roast beef, and dug in.

"Fantastic Judy, just fantastic. Make any of this yourself?"

"Just the potato salad. The rest is from a gourmet shop that was recommended to me."

Not having had breakfast, other than a cup of coffee, Delaney sampled everything on offer. If he wasn't chewing, he was drinking from a glass of home-made lemonade.

"If you like it nod," Judy quipped.

Delaney nodded.

"Have as much as you like Gary. We've got to keep your strength up," Judy said with a wink.

"This is top-notch food Judy. If I ate like this every day, I'd weigh 100 kilos in no time."

"It's a good thing I know several ways to keep it off," Judy said. "The first is gardening and there's a lot of it to do around here."

"And the second?"

"I'll show you." Judy slowly got up, sat on Delaney's lap, gave him a long, deep kiss and ran a hand over his crotch. Delaney winced.

"Something wrong hun?"

"Just a little sore."

"I'll take it easy on you, I promise. Come with me, we'll have dessert later." Judy took Delaney by the hand and led him upstairs to her bedroom where they gave the mattress on her four-poster bed a solid 45-minute long workout.

It took a while for Delaney's heart rate to return to normal. A large ceiling fan cooled the sweat on their bodies as they lay on their backs.

"I love a man who can make me laugh and make me cum," Judy said with her head resting on Delaney's chest.

As Delaney stroked her hair and looked up at the whirring ceiling fan feeling completely relaxed, Judy was plotting the start of his financial demise. *First some dessert and then a tour of the house with a stop in my office. A few probing questions and I'll have a pretty rough idea of what he's worth.*

Judy broke the silence. "What do you say lover? Have any room for dessert?"

"I'll make room," Delaney said. He gathered his clothes which were scattered on the floor and bed and got dressed. Judy put on her undies and by design grabbed a rather revealing robe that was hanging on the back of the bedroom door.

"I don't think I'll be eating dinner tonight," Delaney said after two pieces of pie and a dish of ice cream. He rubbed his expanding belly.

"Glad you enjoyed it. I'll make you up a little something to take home in case you get hungry later."

"I can't remember the last time I was treated this nicely. You sure are good to me."

"Could you get used to it?" Judy asked.

"I believe I could."

"How about a tour of the house? I have a feeling you'll be spending plenty of time here."

"Lead the way," Delaney said.

"You've seen the bedroom and ensuite upstairs. There's also a guest bedroom. It hasn't been used in a few years."

Judy put her hand on the sliding door that led to the backyard. "What a difference a little paint has made to the fences? Don't you agree?"

"Someone sure knew what he was doing out there. That's not the work of an amateur."

"There's a lawnmower out in the garage which I can't even get started."

"Let's have a look at it."

"Planning on running this at Bathurst?" Delaney asked as he wheeled the massive mower outside. "Look at the engine on this thing. Better cover your ears."

Delaney flicked a few switches like he had seen some guy do on one of those backyard renovation shows, pulled the starter rope and hoped for a miracle. Nothing. He checked the petrol. It was nearly full. He yanked the rope again and got a bit of a response. Then with one foot on the mower, he pulled the cord with every bit of strength he had, which to be honest was not much. Some brown smoke belched from the back and it turned over. He ran the mower over a small patch of grass and then turned it off.

"I had a feeling you would get it going," Judy said.

"I'd like to say I know what I am doing, but it was just pure luck that it started."

"Nevertheless, maybe now I can dump the mob that I've been paying to mow the lawn. You could do it, couldn't you Gary?"

"I'd be happy to."

"This room is where I come to read and relax. It has a wonderful view of the garden," Judy said continuing the tour.

"Nice," Delaney said. "All the comforts of home. Speaking of comforts, is there a toilet down here?"

"To your left," hun.

Delaney closed the door behind him, had a pee and flushed. He washed his hands with some exotic soap, splashed some water on his face while he was it and grabbed a plush hand towel to dry his hands and face with. He closed the bathroom door behind him and found Judy in her office looking out the window. He quietly knocked on the door.

"I was expecting to find a billiard room," Delaney said.

"Well, we did have a ping pong table set up in the garage, but I sold it. Come in."

"That's one game you can't play by yourself," Delaney said. "I've tried." He joined her at the window.

"What do you do when you're not painting fences?"

"I play a little bit of golf but I'm not very good even with all my trips to the driving range," Delaney said. "It's a good day out though. Have you ever played?"

"I went out on the course once with Jack and was bored silly. I liked driving the cart though."

"Well, I slice my drives so much that when I use a cart I get charged for mileage." Delaney's attempt at humour was met by silence. "You see, I hit the ball all over the place and it takes a while to find it."

"Ah," Judy said.

"What do you think of my office?" Judy asked as she sat down in a massive leather chair which looked like it came off the set of *The Voice*. "A few years ago, I decided to work from home instead of in some stuffy office building."

"You've gotten plenty of awards over the years," Delaney said as he gazed at the many framed certificates and plaques lining the main wall. Healthy yucca plants stood like soldiers on each side of her desk.

"It's a good feeling to be able to give a little something back. I can afford to so why not?"

Fanned out on Judy's desk, by design, were several colourful booklets and pamphlets from well-known investment companies.

Delaney sat in the chair across from Judy's desk and picked one up.

He leafed through the pages. "Guaranteed eight per cent, eh?"

"That firm is having a very good run. It returned nearly 11 per cent last financial year. I have several very happy clients."

"And the others?" Delaney asked.

"Even the more conservative of my clients are still receiving about six percent interest on their savings and super. Plus, I have the best tax attorney in the business. He saves them even more."

"Interesting."

"Mind if I ask who you are with Gary? A man in your profession would have put away a fair bit over the years."

"There wasn't much to put away after my ex-wife stuck her greedy hands into the pile."

Judy leaned back and wondered just how much the former journo had left. *Shit, don't tell me I've been fucking this guy and he's got nothing.*

"A financial advisor at my bank handles my money. From one of the big four." Delaney said. "I have about $400,000 in a pension/retirement plan. I get a decent amount each month from it. Hopefully it lasts as long as I do. I guess that's always the worry."

"It usually is the main worry Gary. What sort of fees are you paying your financial advisor each month Gary?"

"Each month? What do you mean? I paid an upfront fee when I started it."

"Well, Gary. Unless you say you want to opt out of that part of the agreement, you could be paying about $150 a month, or more."

"A hundred and fifty dollars a month? You are kidding."

"I'm not. If you like, bring your latest statement over next time and I'll go over it."

"Thanks for the heads-up Judy. I'll look for it."

When Delaney got home later that afternoon, the first thing he did, even before he turned on ABC24 to get the latest news, was rummage through his paperwork. It took a good twenty minutes to find what he was looking for. He brought the folder containing his pension plan to his kitchen table and started leafing through the pages. Nothing in there about monthly fees. But then he looked at his latest statement and sure enough he was being charged $165 for "advice" by his bank each month. "Son of a bitch. No wonder that bloody bank is making $8 billion a year," he said as he shook his head.

Delaney fired off an email to his financial advisor back in Melbourne, Rodney James Crook, asking him to call him at his earliest convenience.

"I should have known just from his bloody surname."

The next morning, he received a call from Mr Crook.

"Good to talk to you Gary. How are you enjoying life in the tropics?"

"It's bloody hot RJ and to tell you the truth so am I."

"How so Gary? I've got your account up on my screen and the plan we laid out for you is doing quite well."

"It is mate and I have no problem with that. What I am angry about is this $165 dollar a month fee I am being charged."

"It is standard Gary and allows you to pick up the phone and ring me anytime for advice."

"But I haven't asked for advice or changed my plan. I want it left the way it is. Now let's say I choose not to pay the $165 a month, then what?"

"Then you would only be eligible to have your plan altered once a year."

"That's what I want RJ. I want to get rid of that monthly fee immediately. What do I have to do?"

"It's simple Gary. Send me an email stating that you wish to discontinue the monthly $165 fee and it will removed as soon as I receive it."

"I'll do that RJ."

"Anything else I can help you with Gary?"

"No, that's it. I'll send that email off to you now."

"Sure thing Gary. And have yourself a nice day. Bye."

RJ Crook slammed his fist on his desk. "My manager is not going to be happy about this. Damn."

Gary sent the email off to RJ Crook and then rang Judy.

His call went straight to voice mail. "You were right Judy. The bank was charging me $165 a month for nothing. They've agreed to remove the fee, but they should have told me about it when I invested my money with them. I don't know. Maybe they did. I just don't remember. Anyways, it's been taken care of. Talk soon, bye."

32

DELANEY CROSSED PATHS WITH BARBARA STEVENSON later that afternoon down by the pool. He said hello but she ignored him. *Fair enough,* Delaney thought. *Maybe when she cools down a bit, we can at least go back to being friends.*

Judy sent Delaney a text message that night asking him to bring over his pension/retirement plan details and statements the next time he came over. 'I'll look things over for you, make sure you're getting the best bang for your buck."

Two afternoons later Delaney was sitting in Judy's office.

"Let's see what funds your financial advisor has put you in," Judy said. She moved her chair forward, put on a pair of cute glasses – "I just need them for reading" – and started leafing through Delaney's pension/ retirement plan statements and overall financial plan which were strewn across her desk. She took some notes and occasionally punched some numbers into a calculator. She was happy to see that he had close to $400,000 in his pension plan.

"If you want to have a walk around, I'll call you when I'm finished. I'll be about 15 minutes."

Delaney paced back and forth by the sliding back door like an expectant father until he heard Judy call for him.

"Is my guy looking after me alright?" he asked as he sat down across from Judy.

"He is and he isn't. I mean you won't go broke with what he has set up for you, but your plan is not very aggressive and sometimes it's better not to be so conservative. You're laying up and not going for the pin."

"I thought you said you didn't follow golf."

"I must have picked some of the jargon up from Jack."

Delaney leaned back in his chair. "Hmmm. I'm not so sure Judy. When to comes to money I do like to be a bit conservative."

"I understand Gary. I totally do. Let me run some numbers and show you how much better off you'll be if you change plans and go with what I suggest."

"Run the numbers Judy and I'll compare them. I've got nothing to lose."

"Here's all your paperwork back. I've got what I need."

She had everything she needed and more. She had made copies of his statements – which included his signature – while he was in the living room and locked them in her top desk draw.

"What do you say we go out to dinner?" Judy asked. "Up for it? You choose this time. We can swing back here after for your dessert."

Delaney racked his brain for a place to take her. *There's that Chinese place at the night market*, he thought. *We could eat at one of the picnic tables on the Esplanade. Nah. Not her style.* "Do you like Italian food?" he asked. "There's a nice place on Abbott St I've been to a few times. Fantastic lasagne, wood fired pizzas."

"Good choice," Judy said. "For a second I thought you were going to take me to the food court at the night market."

Delaney laughed. "We'll leave that to the tourists."

"Give me 10 minutes. I'm going to freshen up and change. There's some cold beer in the fridge."

"Thanks, I could use one."

Delaney sat down at the dining room table with his bottle of beer. He trusted Judy but just to be on the safe side he took his phone from his front pocket and Googled her. There were plenty of Judy Seymours but not one from Far North Queensland. He typed in the word Cairns next to her name and found what he was looking for. There were two instances of her being given an award by her old financial planning firm and a few paragraphs from the *Cairns Examiner* on the death of her husband. "Jack is survived by his wife Judy. The couple did not have children."

She checks out okay, seems legit, Delaney thought.

What he should have done was call her former firm asking for a recommendation. They would have told him that she had left under somewhat sordid circumstances. A client had come to them with an allegation – which was never proven – that Judy had forged his signature on a couple of documents. It was agreed by all that Judy leave the firm. She got a five-figure payout to walk out the door and keep quiet. The client was pleased that she was booted from the firm, had his account topped up for any "undue stress" he might have suffered and agreed not to take matters any further.

Just as he tucked his phone back into his pocket, Judy Seymour came bounding down the stairs looking like a million dollars in a colourful sundress and heels. Delaney stood up and took a long swig from his bottle of beer. "Wow," he said.

When you have a body like mine it sure is easy to get a man to think with his dick instead of his head, Judy Seymour thought. *There's not a drop of blood left in his noggin. It's all below his waist.*

33

THE NEXT MORNING GARY DELANEY CLEARED HIS kitchen table and sat down with his retirement/pension plan statements and started comparing them to what Judy Seymour and her company were offering. Tedious work indeed, much like doing one's taxes or the form for a Saturday metropolitan race meeting. There were papers to his left, papers to his right, several on the chair next to him and one or two which had fallen on the occasionally swept floor.

Ditching his bank and putting his assets in Judy's seemingly capable hands would give him – if the market held up and his figures were accurate – approximately $730 more each and every month. The extra cash would come in handy, especially if he had any unforeseen medical expenses to take care of.

Delaney also wanted to do some travelling. He had never been to the top end or the Kimberley region and wanted to see Broome and its surrounds before Dina Linehart and her mob dug it all up and left one big hole in the ground. A 12-day cruise of the Kimberley region – from Darwin to Broome – along with several side trips – which he had seen advertised at a local travel agency – was about $5000.

Delaney was not adverse to a flutter every now and then, but changing horses midstream, especially when his horse was well-placed and running as predicted, was a gamble. Maybe too big of a gamble for a man whose 60th birthday was just over three years away. He figured he had, if his health held up, about 15 good years left to truly enjoy himself.

He checked the numbers again and then for a third time to make sure there were no mistakes. There weren't. He then wrote out a list of his monthly expenses and compared them to what he had coming in via the plan set up by Rodney James Crook in addition to his aged pension.

Rent, private health insurance, petrol for the car, mobile phone, internet, newspaper subscription, medicine, clothing, food, the electric bill, household supplies. He added another $350 a month for his golf games and other social outings.

Toss in his once a year car insurance and registration payments and a yearly service bill for the car and he was about $1100 ahead each month. He'd be able to move to a nicer apartment complex with the extra money if he put his nest egg in Judy's basket, maybe to one in Palm Cove or Trinity Beach which were quieter, more modern and more upscale.

"Should I toss a coin and let fate decide?" he asked himself. "Nah. I need to make a rational decision." He got up from the table, looked at the pile of bank statements and paperwork and decided it was time to clear his head; first with a walk and then a swim.

He sat with his coffee at an outdoor table at the corner cafe a couple of blocks away from the Coral Reef Apartment complex and was going over the numbers in his head when he spotted a neatly dressed older couple crossing the street coming towards him. The woman was in front, clearing a path for her husband who was pushing a Woolies' trolley. But there were no bags of groceries in the trolley or anything for that matter that Delaney could see. *The nearest Woolies is about seven or eight km away. What in the world are they doing?* he wondered. It was only when they passed his table that Delaney spotted what looked to be a man's wallet in the trolley. It sat on top of a plastic bag. It was the easiest target a thief could ask for. *Maybe he doesn't realise it's there.*

Delaney got up from his chair and went up to the gentleman, who was moving along at a snail's pace. "Excuse me sir," he said. "I believe you've left your wallet in the trolley."

"What's that? Speak up."

"Your wallet. It's in the trolley. Shouldn't you put it in your pocket to be on the safe side?"

"What for?"

"Well. Anyone could just reach in there, take it and run off with your money, your ID, your credit cards."

At that point the fellow's wife ambled over. "What's the hold-up William? Who's this man you're talking too?"

"He's asking about my wallet."

"You're after his wallet?" she said turning to Delaney. "What kind of person robs an old man? She looked around. "Where's a copper when you need one?" she asked.

"Now hold on," Delaney said. "There's no need to call a cop. I was just concerned that your husband left his wallet in the trolley and someone could just reach in and take it."

"Who is going to take a wallet that has nothing in it?" she said.

"There's nothing in it?"

"No. We just bought it. It's a gift for our grandson Stevie. He turns 12 on Saturday."

"And you need a trolley to take it home?" Delaney asked. "It weighs about as much as a feather. You could put it in your purse."

"William collects them."

"You've lost me," Delaney told the woman.

"He collects trolleys. We have about 30 of them at home."

William then piped up. "I fix them, clean them up."

"Don't you bring them back?" Delaney asked.

"No. Why should I? They're mine."

"Yes, they are," Delaney said. "You look after them now and enjoy Stevie's birthday party."

"Whose Stevie?" the old man asked.

"Your grandson."

"I have a grandson? Ruthie, this fellow says I have a grandson. I want to meet him."

Ruthie took William by the arm. "You will, later. Let's go home sweetheart," she gently said. "Follow me."

William gripped the trolley tightly with both of his bony hands and slowly moved forward as Ruthie led the way.

"That," Delaney said, "is the last time I stick my nose in anyone's business. Unless of course I'm asked."

When he returned home, Delaney had another glance at all the paperwork in front of him and went online to do some research. He looked at the funds Judy wanted him to invest in and found they were all up-market and well diversified. Several were returning twice as much as he was currently getting. He tried but could not find one bad word written about any of the funds Judy was pitching.

He would have liked to discuss his situation with someone before making such a big decision, but his mates from Saltwater Lakes Golf Club had little or no interest in the market. They wouldn't have been able to tell you the current interest rate if they had a nine-iron aimed at their shins. They were more concerned with their handicaps and their current rate of intercourse, which judging by all their bitching of late was close to non-existent. Delaney was the only one of his mates who was getting laid on a regular basis but hadn't told any of them about Judy, at least not yet.

No sense jinxing it until it becomes more official.

He thought for a moment about ringing Warren Mulligan, the only one of the group he spoke to away from Saltwater Lakes. However, the last time he rang Mulligan, a retired city planner from somewhere on the central coast of New South Wales, he and his wife were babysitting three of their grandchildren. "Speak up and speak fast," Mulligan said over a chorus of screaming. "Forget it. It's not important. I'll talk to you next time I see you at the club," Delaney said before hanging up. "Thank goodness the club does not allow anyone under the age of 12 in the dining area and bar because if it did, I would find another one," Delaney said with the screaming still ringing in his ears.

Barbara would have been the perfect person to bounce a few ideas off of, but even a week after he told her about Judy, she still wanted to throttle him. As he had done prior to the dust-up, Delaney continued to leave his copy of the *Cairns Examiner* on her doorstep each morning after he was finished with it. But Barbara returned the paper to its original owner without even opening it up. This afternoon there was a message written in a red marker all over the front page. "I can buy my own fucking paper, thank you. Stop leaving them."

The next morning Delaney made the decision to put his money in Judy's hands. He sent Rodney James Crook an email to advise him of his desire to leave his bank and put his money elsewhere. Crook rang him less than 10 minutes after receiving the email.

"Are you sure you want to leave us?" Crook asked. "We can always take a less conservative approach with your money if you like Mr Delaney. And remember, your money is safe with us.

It is guaranteed up to $250,000. You'll be able to sleep at night if you stay with us."

"I'm aware of that Rodney, but after a lot of thought I am going to switch to another financial advisor. I left you her details. She has yours and will be in touch with you shortly."

"We're sorry to see you go," Mr Delaney. "And, remember, you can always come back to us if you're unhappy."

"I'll keep that in mind Rodney."

He then rang Judy to tell her the news. She answered on the first ring. "You won't regret it Gary. I'll look after you. I promise."

"I know you will Judy. That's why I decided to go with you. I trust you. How could I trust a guy named Crook anyways?"

Judy laughed. "We'll have to fill out a bunch of forms Gary to make it all official. It will take about 10 business days before everything goes through. Come over whenever you can, and we'll get a start on the paperwork. Once we've done that, I'll ring your bank and speak with Mr Crook to tie up the loose ends. He'll have some forms that you'll also need to sign. I'll get him to fax them over."

"I can come by later this afternoon to get the ball rolling if you like," Delaney said.

"Make it around five, okay? I have a three o'clock meeting in Palm Cove."

Judy did a little victory dance after putting down her mobile. *I knew he'd see things my way. Once the paperwork goes through, I can start planning on life after Mr Delaney.*

Judy Seymour figured she would need about six weeks before she started to empty Delaney's accounts. *After he sees that first monthly statement with the higher returns he'll relax. That's when I'll make my move.*

In order not to arouse suspicion, Judy had to keep sleeping with Delaney. *If I cut him off now, he'll wonder if something is up.*

He was five years older than her but there were plenty worse she had gone to bed with before and after her marriage.

Like an advance man working for the prime minister, Judy Seymour had everything planned right down to the last detail. Jim Glickman had put her in touch with someone he knew who would be able to give her a brand-new identity at a fair price. Despite a somewhat shady reputation earned from a couple of trips to the slammer, Glickman told her a fellow he knew named Al Packer who could be trusted. "One hundred per cent Judy. One hundred per cent."

For $25,000 cash – upfront – Packer offered to give her a new name, driver's licence, tax file number, Medicare card and passport before she skipped town. For another 10 grand he was also going to have a new car – recently stolen of course but fitted with new plates – waiting for her in Noosa on the day she arrived.

The car's registration and insurance were in her new name, Diane Bradley.

As a bonus, Packer also found a place for her to stay, a two-bedroom furnished apartment right in town. She was to pay the owner three months of rent in advance, $9000 in cash, which included utilities, the use of a pool and Foxtel – on the day she arrived.

34

DELANEY SIGNED ALL THE NECESSARY PAPERS TO SWITCH his superannuation/retirement accounts on the same afternoon. He first visited the local branch of the bank Rodney James Crook worked for and from an assistant manager's office talked to Crook via Skype. Crook was wearing a shiny shirt and colourful tie under a navy-blue blazer and looked more like a wayward cast member of Guys and Dolls than a financial advisor. He did everything but roll out a red carpet and kiss Delaney's arse to try and get him to change his mind.

"I think you are making a big mistake," Crook told Delaney as he was about to put pen to paper. "It's a chance I'm willing to take," Delaney said as he put his John Hancock on four separate documents.

His bosses downtown did not like losing customers and Crook knew he would hear from them as soon as the paperwork went through.

"If you don't get at least three old-timers to put their money in our retirement plans by the end of the month you'll be out of here quicker than shit through a goose," Tom Morrow told Crook over the phone the following week. "You understand?"

"Yes, sir Mr Morrow. I'll get right on it," Crook said.

Morrow hung up without hearing Crook's meek reply.

"Shit," Crook said after putting down his phone. "He means it. The guy I replaced was barely here long enough to warm up his chair. "Fucking Delaney. I hope the cocksucker loses everything."

Delaney's path to ruin was sealed later that afternoon when he handed Judy Seymour copies of the documents he had signed at the bank. Judy had some additional documents for him to sign and initial lined up on her desk.

Judy put her hand on his shoulder as he sat down and watched him scribble his name five additional times. "Nothing else, is there? I'm getting writer's cramp here," Delaney said as he playfully flexed his right hand.

"That's it," Judy said. "I'll get started on the changeover first thing in the morning. In 10 business days you'll officially be part of my team."

"The last team I was on, an Under 16 footy team, didn't win a game and I hated the head coach."

"Oh? Well what do you think of your new team and your new head coach?" Judy seductively asked.

"Do we have training tonight coach?"

"We sure do. There are a few drills we need to work on away from the main group."

Delaney gathered all the documents from Judy's desk, placed them in a neat pile on her expensive leather chair and lifted his head coach on to her desk. "Time for my favourite drill," Delaney said. He lifted Judy's skirt, pulled her panties down, and using nearly all of the 30-second shot clock, kicked truly with his first possession of the night.

"What do you say coach? Time for a drinks break?" Delaney asked catching his breath.

"We'll have drinks in the lounge" Judy said. "And you know what? I think I've found my full forward. That is if he can handle the workload."

"I'm not a youngster anymore but the body is holding up quite well. Do you agree?"

"I sure do. And mine? Is it holding up well or are you going to be looking for someone younger in the draft?"

"I've found the coach I want to play for. There's no need to look anywhere," Delaney said while buttoning his pants.

"I'm glad to hear you say that Gary." She softly kissed him and followed him into the kitchen.

I hope I can go through with this, Judy thought. *The last thing I wanted to do was fall for him. He treats me as nice as Jack ever did. And he's better in bed than Jack ever was. Damn.*

Channel 12's Rob Banks had been presenting the weather for the greater Cairns area every weeknight for the last seven years. The handsome forty-year-old had done hundreds of remotes over the years. He'd visited area schools, anchored himself to the beach in Innisfail as a cyclone roared overhead, held the Cairns Cup in his gloved hands on cup eve, dodged crocs at a Port Douglas Golf Course and constantly reminded viewers to swim between the flags when they visited the beach.

If only he had listened to his own advice. One Tuesday morning in mid-April he decided to go for a dip in the Coral Sea before work. A strong swimmer, Banks was about 100 metres from shore when he turned around to swim back. As he did, he felt a sharp pain in his left thigh and another in his backside. He had been bitten by a stinger, maybe two. An asthmatic, Banks immediately began to have trouble breathing.

The pain in his leg and arse became worse. He tried to swim back to shore but couldn't. He raised his arm and hollered for help, but the only people on the beach were elderly men and women walking their dogs. Nobody heard his cries or saw him. Since it was just before eight in the morning, the lifeguard station, a few hundred metres to the south, was unmanned. Gasping for breath, Banks tried to keep his head above water but couldn't. Warm ocean water began to fill his lungs and he slipped under the surface.

The current carried his lifeless body out to sea where it was spotted several hours later by two recreational fishermen returning to the marina at Yorkeys Knob.

"Holy shit. There's a fucking body on the port side," Rick Campaneris hollered to his mate.

"Daniel Bateman manoeuvred his 18-footer closer to the body where Campaneris was able to snag it with his large fishing net. It took all the strength they had to get the body in the boat."

"Holy shit. Holy shit. That's Rob fucking Banks," Campaneris screamed.

"The weather guy?" Bateman asked.

"Yup."

"I'd say his weather presenting days are over."

An ambulance and several police met Bateman's boat when it docked at the marina around 11:30am. Paramedics examined the lifeless body of Banks and noticed several areas of purple coloured swelling on his leg and buttocks.

"Looks to me like a couple of stingers got him," Vic Segretti told his partner.

"How long you figure he's been in the water?" Senior Constable William Murray asked.

"Not long, two, three hours tops," Segretti said.

"You know who that is, don't you?" Campaneris said.

Murray and Segretti looked at each other. Neither had a clue.

"That's Rob Banks. The Channel 12 weather presenter. I watch him every night."

"Not tonight," Murray said. "Bag him up and put him in the back of the ambo fellas."

"I'm going to need a statement from both of you," Murray told Campaneris and Bateman. "Ride with me into town. We'll bring you back here when we're done. Catch anything today besides Banks?" Murray asked Campaneris.

"We did alright. It was a good night. A few barras, coral trout."

"Everything on ice?"

"Yeah."

"Good it will keep until you get back."

As the ambulance and squad cars left the Yorkeys Knob Marina, a Channel 12 news van arrived.

"What's happened," Tegan Winterbottom asked a couple of boaters.

"A couple of fishermen found a body on their way in. Some TV presenter I heard. Young bloke too. A shame," Pete Seigel said.

"Do you know who it was"? she asked while cameraman "Handsome" Harry Hirsch filmed it all.

"Didn't get the name," Seigel said.

Hirsch slumped to one knee and put his camera down. He had a feeling it was Banks. The two had often gone out for a swim or a paddle in the morning. *He was a strong swimmer. What happened to him out there? he thought.*

He motioned for Tegan to come over.

"What's wrong Harry? You're as pale as a Tasmanian."

Winterbottom fell to her knees when Hirsch told her what he feared. Tears filled her eyes and dropped onto her blouse.

"Were you and Rob close Tegan?"

"We were seeing each other for the last couple of months. We didn't want anyone to know. And now he's gone," she sobbed.

"You and Rob?"

Tegan nodded and wiped the tears from her eyes.

"You're not serious, are you?"

"What do you mean? Of course I'm serious."

Hirsch looked straight into Tegan's eyes.

"You don't know?" he asked.

"Know what?"

I have to tell her. Better to hear it from me now.

"Rob is married or was. His wife is seven months pregnant with their first child."

Tegan looked at him disbelievingly. "No, that's not true. It's not true."

"I'm afraid it is Tegan."

Hirsh held onto her until her screaming and sobbing subsided and then stopped.

"Don't tell a soul at the station about this, please" she pleaded as they staggered back to the Twelve News van. "You're not going to tell his wife, are you?"

"No Tegan. I'm not going to say a word to anyone. Not a word."

Once Banks's body had been officially identified, it was left to Channel 12 news director Stan Warren to deliver the news to his entire team at a hastily called and rare mid-afternoon meeting.

Producer Veronica Bell put together an emotional two-minute piece on Banks's time with the station which aired after Channel 12 head presenter Darren Jensen opened that night's newscast with the news of Banks's death.

"Our thoughts and prayers go out to Rob's wife Danielle and their families," Jensen said before the screen turned black and Bell's tribute appeared.

Jensen delivered the weather that night.

Down at the Esplanade 17-year-old Robert Fuller and his mates "Big John" Thornton, "Hitman" Hearns and Mitch Weller were sizing up the hundreds of tourists walking past a picnic table they had commandeered from a bunch of young Dutch backpackers. The group looked so intimidating in their basketball jumpers that the backpackers scattered before Thornton even said a word.

Thornton was sporting a green and white Boston Celtics jumper, Hearns a purple and gold Los Angeles Lakers guernsey and Weller a blue and yellow Golden State Warriors singlet. Fuller, who was partial to NHL jumpers due to their long sleeves which he often rolled up to his elbows, was wearing a maroon and gold Cleveland Cavaliers singlet. Thornton, the former rugby league high school star, looked every inch the ballplayer he used to be. The others looked more like badminton players.

"It's your shout tonight Fuller. Go get us some grub," Thornton said.

"I would, but I'm tapped out," Fuller sheepishly said, turning the pockets of his beige-coloured shorts inside out to prove he wasn't carrying any cash.

"Well, you can't eat our grub and not reciprocate. Go pinch someone's wallet or purse. Go on," Thornton said. Fuller turned to Hearns and Weller looking for a bit of sympathy. They put their heads down, their gazes concentrated on a colony of ants that was scurrying from one picnic table to the next looking for scraps of food.

Fuller had stolen plenty of merchandise over the past few months but had never actually robbed anyone. He slowly got off the picnic table and tugged his dark baseball cap with white NY lettering tightly over his head. He approached three Chinese tourists, two girls and a guy, who were sitting on the wall which lined the Esplanade having an ice cream. "Can you spare any change?" Fuller asked. "What you mean, change?" the fellow replied.

"Money," Fuller said. "You have any money?"

Wanting to look like a big shot in front of the two girls, the fellow stood up. He was Fuller's height and no pushover. "No money. Go away," he said, which is just what Fuller did.

He glanced over at Thornton, Hearns and Weller. They were laughing their arses off.

Fuller continued walking down the Esplanade. He was nearly at the corner traffic light where McDonald's was located. It was without a doubt the busiest crosswalk in the city. A seemingly never-ending supply of tourists and backpackers made their way in and out of the air-conditioned building. They either trusted the golden arches or were looking to save a few bucks after their expensive trips to the reef earlier in the day. The cheapest boat to the nearest reef was $90 or in backpacker's terminology – a night's worth of drinks.

They won't be carrying much cash on them, Fuller thought. *I'll try over by the casino. People are always cashed up on their way in. They're just going to toss their money away at the tables or put it in the machines. But how to approach them?*

Fuller gave it some thought. *I could pretend to have lost all my money playing blackjack and ask someone going in if they could spare a few bucks so I could get some dinner.* But Fuller looked a little young to be taken seriously as a gambler and thought of a different tack. He picked up a couple of discarded pamphlets and had an idea. He'd stop the first well-dressed person he saw, someone his size or smaller, tell him he was lost, ask where the nearest backpackers was and then tell him to hand over his wallet. A tap and go debit card was as good as cash.

After a few minutes Fuller spotted a bloke wearing a handsome dark blazer walking towards the casino. He didn't look very big. Fuller guessed he was in his 50s. *Once I take off, he'll never be able to catch me.*

Fuller was as nervous as a first-time starter at Royal Randwick, maybe even more so. But knowing he couldn't go back to his mates empty-handed, he got up and approached his mark. "Excuse me sir. I'm kind of lost. Can you tell me where the backpackers is?" he asked, holding a tourist map of the CBD.

"Which one? There are a few of them."

Fuller racked his brain and spit out the first thing that came into his mind. "The Beach House it is called."

"There's no backpackers here with that name that I know of mate. You sure you're in the right town?" Nick Bellamy asked.

"Of course I am in the right town," Fuller nervously answered.

The two stood there for a moment before Fuller got the nerve to ask the man to hand over his wallet.

"My wallet? You're joking? Aren't you?"

"Does it look like I am fucking joking? Hand it over. Now."

"All right. Just take it easy."

Bellamy reached into his back pocket and before Fuller knew what was happening, Bellamy tackled him to the ground and slapped a pair of handcuffs on him.

"What the fuck?" Fuller asked as he tried to wiggle free.

"You picked the wrong guy to rob kid."

Bellamy took out his wallet, put a knee deep into Fuller's back and shoved his badge in Fuller's face.

"Nick Bellamy, detective, Cairns PD."

A crowd gathered around the pair while Bellamy patted Fuller down.

"You're not carrying, are you son?"

"Carrying? What do you mean?"

"A knife, a gun. Do you have a weapon on you?"

"No sir," Fuller said. He was one step away from bursting out in tears. Bellamy took out his phone and made a call.

"You realise you've screwed up my dinner plans," Bellamy told Fuller before someone came on the line.

"Hey, it's Bellamy. Send a divvy van over to the casino on the double, will you? Some kid tried to rob me. Not a very bright one I'm afraid. Yeah. I'm right out the front."

"What's your name son?"

"Robert Fuller."

"You're a local?"

"Yes sir. North Cairns."

"You have a record Robert?"

"No."

"You've never robbed anyone before? Have you son?"

"No sir."

Bellamy shook his head. "Well, you'll have a story to tell your mates when you get out. Trying to rob an off-duty copper."

"What's going to happen to me?" Fuller asked.

"We'll take you in, fingerprint you, and charge you with attempted robbery."

"You're not going to call my parents, are you?"

"I'm afraid so. Standard procedure if you're a minor."

"Can you do me one favour? Please?"

"What is it son?"

"Can you call my older brother instead? My father will kick me out of the house if he finds out. Please sir? I swear. I'll never do anything like this again. I swear."

Fuller was shaking and by this time large tears were rolling down his sad, youthful face.

Bellamy had heard the same line hundreds of times in his 30 years on the job only to see the same guys get locked up time and time again. But he felt bad for the kid lying face down on the footpath balling his eyes out.

"You don't have to answer Robert. But why?" Bellamy asked.

"I needed money to get my mates and I something to eat."

"To eat? Come on son. Doesn't your mum cook for you?"

"She does, but I am not home much. I hang out with my friends mostly."

"Sounds to me like you need some new friends. You still in school?"

"Year 11. But I don't go often."

"Can I give you some advice son? Find some new friends and get your arse back to school."

Just as Bellamy finished talking, the divvy van, with its lights flashing, pulled up alongside them. Two constables got out, exchanged a few words with Bellamy, lifted Fuller off the ground, put him in the back of the van and closed the doors. A few onlookers applauded. Among those having a look – from a distance – were Thornton, Hearns and Weller. "He better not say a word about us or it's his arse," Thornton said.

"Do me a favour guys," Bellamy told the two young constables. "Take the kid in, fingerprint him, take his mug shot and then toss him in a cell for a couple of hours. Then put the prints in the bin and delete the mug shots. And don't call his parents or his older brother. I'm going to give the kid a break. He's already scared shitless. He'll keep his nose clean."

"How can you be sure Detective?" Constable Don Green asked.

"Thirty-two years of experience. And make sure you give Fuller my card when you release him. Tell him to call me at 8am tomorrow or we'll send a car around to his house to bring his arse back in."

"Okay Detective. We'll take care of it."

"Thanks boys. Appreciate it. And now if you'll excuse me, I have a dinner date with my wife."

Less than five minutes after it arrived, the divvy van left.

35

FULLER'S LEGS WERE SHAKING AS HE WAS LED INTO THE station house. His hands were tightly cuffed behind his back.

Constable Green was on his left side and Constable Simon Hadfield on his right. *I cannot believe this is happening,* he said to himself. *Once mum and dad find out they'll throw me out of the house for sure. What the hell am I going to do?*

Green took Fuller's hat off once they got inside and flung it in the direction of an old wooden coat rack. It landed upside down where it stayed. Green fingerprinted and then photographed Fuller. "I can't find your good side kid. Leave it at home?" Green joked as he took the always unflattering photos; two profile shots and one with Fuller staring straight ahead at the camera.

Green then marched Fuller over to Hadfield's desk. Hadfield took down all his details and entered them into the system. "You don't have any priors Fuller which is good 'cause Judge Carson does not like to see repeat offenders in his courtroom."

"I have to go to court?" Fuller asked.

"Yup. Could be tonight or could be in the morning. Attempted robbery of a police officer is not going to sit well with the Judge."

Hadfield took the cuffs off Fuller and told him to empty his pockets and put everything on his desk. "Your watch too," Hadfield said. He placed every item in an envelope, wrote Fuller's name on it and sealed it.

Hadfield looked at the holding cell behind him which already had eight men in it. "Looks like we can squeeze in one or two more. Come with me Fuller. Hadfield took him by the shoulder and steered him to the cell. "I got some fresh meat for you fellas," Hadfield said to the group in the holding cell. He uncuffed Fuller, unlocked the cell and pushed him into it. "Take a seat Fuller, if you can find one that is. We'll call you when the Judge is ready for you."

Fuller turned around as the cell door closed behind him.

"Well look at who we have here," the largest man in the cell said as he looked Fuller over. The newcomer moved to the one corner of the cell that was unoccupied. "If it ain't Lebron James himself. You're a long way from home, ain't you?" Rick Oakely asked. "And not as big as you look on the TV. Or black. You play ball Lebron or do you just model that there jersey you got on."

Fuller was so frightened he was afraid he'd piss himself.

"I asked if you played any ball," Oakley said louder. Oakley's beer breath reached Fuller before his words did.

Fuller looked at Oakley. He was even bigger than "Big John" Thornton. He was missing several front teeth, his large arms were covered in tattoos and he had a long scar over his right eye.

"I play a bit on the weekends," Fuller said, his voice barely more than a whisper.

"Did Lebron say something?" Oakley asked his cellmates. "I thought I heard something."

Out of the corner of his eye Fuller saw one of the others get down from his perch on one of the bunks and walk towards him. Aaron Woodbridge got so close to Fuller their noses were almost touching. Remnants of Woodbridge's last meal were still wedged between his teeth.

"When Oak asks something, he expects an answer," Woodbridge said.

"I play a bit on the weekends," Fuller said louder.

"That's better. For a second there I thought I lost me hearing," Oakley said to howls of laughter. "You play on the weekends? Well I do believe we is gonna be doing some playing tonight."

"Not if I get out of here," Fuller said, trying to act as tough as he could.

"You think you is getting out of here tonight? You hear that Woody? The motherfucker thinks he's getting out of here tonight."

Oakley laughed. "Look around Lebron. Every one of us has been in here at least one night. What makes you think you're different?"

"One of the constables told me I could be seeing a judge tonight."

"One of the constables? This guy is too much Woody. He's a real comedian, this one, a real entertainer. Now go sit your arse down somewhere."

Fuller looked around the cell but there were no seats to be had so he took a seat where he was standing. "I'll never get out of here," he said, burying his face in his hands.

An hour later Constable Green turned to Constable Hadfield, who was up to his eyeballs in paperwork.

"Think the kid has had enough Simon?"

Hadfield looked over his shoulder. Fuller was in the same spot he was an hour ago. His cellmates were arguing over the night's sleeping arrangements.

"Might as well let him out Greeny. Hopefully he's learned his lesson. If he hasn't, he's as big a schmuck as the others."

Constable Green walked over to the holding cell. "Fuller," he yelled as he unlocked the cell door. Robert Fuller looked up as he heard his name. Green motioned for him to come to the cell door. "Must be your lucky night Fuller. You're first on the judge's docket."

"Thank God," Fuller said. "Thank God."

"Actually, you should thank Detective Bellamy," Green said as he told Fuller to take a seat at his desk. "You're being released."

"After I see the judge?"

"No judge. You're being released. And if I were you, I would go straight home."

"I will. I promise."

"Just one more thing," Green said. He handed Fuller one of Detective Bellamy's business cards. "You are to call Detective Bellamy at 8am in the morning. If he does not hear from you we'll send a car around to get you. Is that clear?"

"Yes sir."

"Now sign this so I can give you your belongings back. And pick that damn cap off the floor on your way out."

"Yes sir. I will. Thank you."

Fuller put his belongings back in his pocket; a few dollars in coins, his phone and his house keys. He picked his cap up and with his legs trembling walked out of the police station and kept walking the dark streets until he was home.

He checked his phone – 9:20pm – took his house keys from his left front pocket and opened the front door. Reginald Fuller was sitting in his favourite chair in front of the TV set which was on but had the sound turned off. He lifted his head from the newspaper he was reading when he heard the door open and was surprised to see his son home so early. He got up out of his chair and was about to say hello to his son when Robert wrapped his arms around his dad and gave him a hug.

Mary Fuller poked her head out of the kitchen and had to do a double take when she saw her son hugging his dad. Reginald looked at her and mouthed the words 'what's going on'?

"Would you like something to eat dear?" Mary asked her son. "I made that chicken casserole you like so much. We had plenty left over."

"That would be nice mum, thank you. I am a bit hungry."

Robert took his seat at the dining room table while his dad, still wearing a surprised look on his face, walked into the kitchen.

"He doesn't smell of beer or cigarettes. And he hugged me. Are you sure that's our boy?" he asked his wife. "I think so. Wait until I tell Peter. He won't believe it either."

Robert polished off two portions of the casserole, thanked his mum, said goodnight to his dad and went to his room. He had several text messages from Thornton and one each from Hearns and Weller. He ignored them. 'Let them think I spent the night in jail', he thought.

Fuller sat down on his bed, took off his runners and Lakers singlet and tried to gather his thoughts. He looked at the card Constable Green had given him, put it on the nightstand by his bed with the rest of his things, turned his lamp off and laid down. He rubbed his wrists which were still a little sore from the handcuffs and stared at the ceiling until he drifted off to sleep.

The next morning Fuller walked to the quieter northern part of the Esplanade which was frequented mostly by local joggers and dog walkers and rang Detective Bellamy at 8am sharp. He answered on the first ring.

"I gave you a break kid. Are you going to straighten your life out or will I be slapping cuffs on you again?" he asked without saying hello.

"I learned my lesson Detective. I really did. I don't ever want to be in a cell again."

"Good to hear son. It's your choice. You can spend your nights at home with your parents or in a cell somewhere with Oak and his mates. I'm not saying don't go out and have fun. I did when I was your age. Just don't do anything stupid, okay?

"Yes sir."

"Because if you do, I'll know about it. You got one free pass. There won't be a second."

"I understand."

"Planning on going to school today son?"

He hadn't. But when Bellamy slapped those handcuffs on him, and he was taken to jail his priorities shifted. He even had his backpack with him, complete with schoolbooks and water bottle.

"I am," Fuller said. "I've missed a few days, but I think I can make up the work and still graduate on time."

"Good. One more thing. As part of our arrangement you're going to be doing what we call it a bit of community service work."

"What do I have to do?"

"It's simple kid, you're going to work at an op shop the Salvos run."

"The Salvation Army?"

"That's the one. You didn't think I was going to let you off scot-free, did you? You tried to fucking rob me."

Aww, shit, Fuller thought.

"Every afternoon after school, for the next two months, you're going to be doing volunteer work for them. They close at 5 and lock up at 5:30. And I'll be getting reports every single week from them. Miss a day, just one day, and you'll go before a judge and be charged with robbery."

Fuller's head slumped to his chest.

"It's not that bad kid. You'll be spending your afternoon with a couple of nice old ladies. Beats spending nights with Oakley and his boys."

"Take down this address Robert. Mr Geoff Duckworth will be expecting you to stop by after school this afternoon. I've arranged your police check to spare you the time and expense. He'll tell you about your non-paying job and what's expected of you. Then tomorrow you'll go to the shop after school and start working. Understood?"

"Yeah."

"Good," Bellamy said.

Silence followed.

"Hello?" Fuller asked.

He looked at his phone. Bellamy had hung up.

A fucking op shop? Shit, it will be like hanging out with my grandmother, only worse, Fuller thought.

36

GARY DELANEY WAS SITTING IN THE SHADE OF A LARGE, somewhat lopsided umbrella at the Coral Reef Apartment complex's pool later that afternoon, leafing through a copy of a woman's magazine someone had left behind when he heard his phone ring. He looked at who was calling and had a feeling that his plans for the evening – dinner with Judy Seymour – were about to change.

"Gary. Glad I caught you. Geoff Duckworth from the Salvos. I'm a bit short-handed mate. Can you help me out?"

"It's kind of late Geoff. What's going on?"

"I need you to take our truck over to Trinity Beach and pick up a shitload of stuff. A couple is donating all of their living and dining room furniture and they won't be home until 5:30."

"I had plans myself Geoff. Can't we do this in the morning?"

"Not really Gary. Delivery guys from Harvey Norman will be there first thing in the morning to drop off new furniture. I'd do it myself but my youngest is in a school play."

"*Death of a Salesman*? I'd like to see an eight-year-old's interpretation of Willy Loman. Are there tickets available at the door?"

"Funny," Duckworth sarcastically said. "Can you do this favour for me Gary?"

"Yeah, I'll be there around 4:30."

"And one more thing. You've got to pick this high school kid up on the way. He's in Cairns North."

"You want me to do his homework for him Geoff?"

"No mate," Duckworth said, laughing. "Robert Fuller is the kid's name. He's in Year 11 and will be with us for the next eight weeks. He's doing community service work."

"You're fucking kidding. You want me to come in on my day off, move a shitload of furniture – and mind you I am 57 years old with a bad back – and pick up some thug along the way?"

"He's a good kid Gary. He was just in the office. And he'll do all the heavy lifting. Just pick him up on the way to Trinity, bring the stuff back here to the warehouse, lock up the truck and you're done. Then drop the kid back home."

Delaney let out an audible sigh and leaned over to look at his watch which was tucked into one of his shoes. It was 3:20. "Yeah, I'll be there. See you at 4:30."

"I owe you one," Duckworth said before he hung up.

Delaney adjusted the cushions on the lounge chair, stretched out and closed his eyes.

When he got back to his apartment, he sent Judy a text message to put back their dinner plans. *Can we reschedule for 7:30pm?* he typed. *Sorry for the late notice but I just found out. The Salvos. Going to Trinity Beach.*

Delaney hopped in the shower, washed the chlorine off his body from his swim in the pool – a whole two laps – and put on a pair of jeans and a blue polo shirt.

He grabbed a bottle of water, turned out the lights and locked the door behind him. His phone pinged as he walked down the stairs. There was a brief message from Judy, very brief. Almost too brief: *We'll reschedule.*

Great, now what do I do for dinner? he thought.

Delaney was not the type who shopped once a week, cooked it all in one go and locked the meals away in plastic containers in the freezer. He liked walking to the shops every day and the added exercise was good for him.

I'll pick up something after I'm done.

Delaney arrived at the Salvos warehouse just after 4:30. Duckworth was waiting outside and handed him the keys to the truck and the warehouse, and a sheet of A4 paper before he even locked his car.

"That's the kid's address – he'll be waiting outside for you – the address in Trinity Beach for the Morrisons, and the security code. You'll need it to get in and out of here. Thanks Gary, you're a lifesaver."

"Remember that when I need a day off."

Delaney stuck the piece of paper in his shirt pocket. He had seen the Salvos truck drop donations off at the op shop where he worked many times but had never been inside the cab. It was littered with fast food and candy wrappings, empty soda cans and water bottles.

"What a fucking mess," Delaney said shaking his head.

He cleaned up the garbage, stuck it in an old Woolies bag he had in his SUV, adjusted the truck's seat and mirrors, turned the key and drove to the front gate. He punched in the code, the gate swung open and off he went. The gate slowly closed and locked behind him.

The truck drove better than it looked. Even the air conditioning worked. He made his way through the downtown area and picked up the kid.

Just as Duckworth said, Robert Fuller was waiting for him outside his family's apartment. He wore baggy grey shorts, a green Boston Celtics T-shirt and a cap with NBA written across it.

"Hop in Robert. I'm Gary," Delaney said extending his hand. "We've got some stuff to pick up in Trinity Beach."

Fuller shook Delaney's hand. "Nice part of town, Trinity," he said.

"Sure is mate. Wish I could afford to live there. Hopefully we can get this done quickly and have you back here in a couple of hours."

Fuller nodded.

"You like the Celtics?" Delaney asked.

Again, Fuller nodded.

"Watch any of their games on Foxtel or that Kayo channel?"

"Nah, parents can't afford Pay TV."

"It's not worth the money. I watch the highlights on YouTube. A two-and-a-half-hour game in nine minutes. Perfect."

"Duckworth tells me you're in Year 11 and have just started volunteering."

"Yup. Year 11 and today is my first day. Was supposed to start tomorrow after school at the same shop you work in, but Duckworth said he needed me to help you pick up a donation."

"What made you – if you don't mind me asking – put your hand up to volunteer at an op shop?"

Fuller shrugged his shoulders. "It wasn't my idea," he said.

"Oh," Delaney said as he steered the truck onto Captain Cook Highway. Peak-hour traffic was starting to build.

Fuller wondered if he should tell Delaney the truth. *Aww, what the heck. Might as well.*

"A detective said I had to do community service work.

"I was with my mates on the Esplanade last night and it was my turn to shout dinner, but I was broke, so I had no choice but to rob someone. I didn't want to do it, but they pressured me."

"How old are you and your mates Robert?" Delaney asked.

"I'm 17 and the others are a year and two older."

"I see. Are you and the others in school?"

"I am in Year 11, the others graduated, or tried to, but don't work. I hang out with them. My brother's busy with his new wife and my dad, well, how many teenagers hang out with their dads?" Fuller asked.

Delaney thought back to when he was a teenager. He didn't exactly hang out with his parents, but they still did things together as a family every now and then.

"Not many," Delaney told Robert. "Not many. Let's go back to last night. Had you ever done anything like that before?"

"Never. Look, I'm no altar boy. I've stolen merch but I've never robbed anyone or hurt anyone. Never," Fuller adamantly said.

"But last night you had to so you wouldn't lose face with your mates. Right?"

"You are. I wish I had just gone home. But they would have started saying shit about me, putting stuff up on Facebook and Snapchat. So, I asked some bloke who was going into the casino to hand over his money, his wallet …"

After a few moments silence, Fuller continued.

"Wouldn't you know it? The guy was an off-duty detective. He had me down on the ground and handcuffed before I even knew what was happening. Then the divvy van came and took me to the cop shop."

"An off-duty detective? Of all the luck. But that might just turn out to be something positive."

"How so?" Fuller asked.

"It was a warning of sorts."

"You should have seen the blokes they tossed me in jail with. Big, ugly types. I was scared shitless."

"How long were you in the lock-up for?"

"A couple of hours. I don't even want to think about what would have happened if I had spent the night in that cell with those blokes."

"Me neither," Delaney said. "Did you see a judge?"

"No. The two constables who brought me in fingerprinted me and took my mug shots and let me go. They gave me the detective's card and told me to ring him in the morning. I did and he told me I was going to be doing community service work for the Salvos."

"Sounds to me like the detective did you one heck of a favour."

"He did. I need to stay away from people who are a bad influence on me and start going to school every day."

Delaney waited a moment and asked the lad about his family.

"To tell you the truth, they should have kicked me out of the house when I started stealing and drinking and coming home late at night. Dad works hard and Mum tried to reach out to me along with my older brother, but I didn't want to talk to anyone about it."

He had a heck of a story to tell if he decided to tell it.

Fuller's problems at school started more than a year earlier when he was finishing up year 10. Several year 12 kids were always on his case and three others he hung out with: Roger Christmas, Randy Elkington and Ted Leishman. The four were top students, rarely missed a day of school, preferred to spend time at the library and always seemed to have a book in their hands. Ninety percent of the other students walked around campus with their heads glued to their phones. With their slim physiques Fuller, Christmas, Elkington and Leishman were hardly the fearsome foursome. The girls on the school's field hockey team looked tougher and were. Fuller and his three schoolmates were the perfect targets for the older and larger kids who teased them every chance they got.

The bookworms merely smiled and walked away until they were asked to do an English assignment by a massive kid named Ian Kulken. Nicknamed "The Hulk", Kulken looked like a heavyweight contender and needed to have several papers handed in over the next four weeks to graduate. Fuller, Christmas, Elkington and Leishman said they would do it in order to be spared a promised beating. Kulken was the sort of guy who could take all four of them on with a hand tied behind his back. If he ran into any trouble, which was doubtful, his tag teammate Ed "Bonecrusher" Sanderson, another Rhodes Scholar, who towered over all of them, would be called upon to finish things off.

At first Fuller refused to give in and do Kulken's assignments. Christmas, Elkington and Leishman told their parents of the threats against them, who in turn marched straight to the school principal demanding action be taken against Kulken and Sanderson. When

Alistar Orr told them nothing could be done since their boys refused to file a formal complaint, the parents threatened to sue Orr and the school. To keep the peace, keep his school out of the courts and the papers, and to save his job, Orr countered with an offer to have the three complete their schooling at St Dominic's, a private school on the outskirts of the city.

"How much is that going to cost us?" Lucy Elkington asked.

"Not a cent. The boys will be given scholarships. Do we have a deal?" Orr asked.

"We do," Lucy Elkington said on behalf of the group.

By the end of the following week Roger Christmas, Randy Elkington and Ted Leishman were enrolled at St Dominic's. Fearful of an over-the-top reaction by his dad, who could be a hothead at times, Fuller had not told his parents what was going on which left him at the mercy of Kulken and Sanderson.

"We'll keep an eye on you," Principal Orr told Fuller at a meeting in his office. "If Kulken and Sanderson threaten you in any way come and tell me and they will be immediately expelled."

They get expelled and it'll be my arse, Fuller said to himself as he walked out of Orr's office.

"Hey, where are your buddies?" Kulken asked Fuller, who was having lunch by himself the next day in the cafeteria. "They ditch you?"

"I'm not sure Ian. I haven't seen them."

Kulken took a seat across from Fuller. "Listen up. I need that English paper done by Monday. You gonna do it for me or what?"

Fuller looked around. Not one teacher came to his aid. *So much for keeping an eye on me,* he thought.

"Here's the assignment," Kulken said, sliding two sheets of paper across the table.

Fuller picked them up and gave them a quick glance.

"I'll do it."

"Smart decision kid. See you on Monday morning. And make it good. I'd like to get at least one A before I get out of here."

"I'll do my best," Fuller said as Kulken walked off.

"Shit. Between this and my own work that's the end of my weekend."

Sick of constantly being picked on and labelled a nerd during school hours just because he studied, Fuller kept company with a less literary crew after 3pm and on weekends; Big John Thornton, "Hitman" Hearns and Weller.

They had met several months earlier on an oppressively hot and humid late February day in the food court at Cairns Central. The place was packed, mostly with locals enjoying the mall's air conditioning which made the building as cool as a winter's day in North West Tasmania. Fuller was having a burger and a shake and had a bright blue NY Knicks cap perched on his head. It covered up much of his light brown hair.

Thornton, Hearns and Weller were sitting nearby munching on fries and frozen Cokes.

"Check that guy out," Weller said to his mates pointing at Fuller. "A Knicks cap. The last time they made the finals Walt Frazier was playing point."

"Hey Clyde," Hearns called out. Clyde was the nickname Frazier went by when he was an NBA all-star in the late 60s and early 70s.

Fuller looked the trio's way. He pointed to his chest and mouthed the word "me?".

"Yeah you Clyde. Why don't you wear a real team's hat like this one here," he said pointing to his Golden State Warriors cap. He exchanged high fives with Thornton and Weller. "You play at all?"

"Play?"

"Yeah, hoops. You play hoops? We can use a fourth."

"A little," Fuller answered. He left out the words when I'm not doing my homework.

"Come join us," Hearns said. He took a bag off the chair next to him to make room for the newcomer. Judging by the shape of the bag it looked to Fuller like it either contained a basketball or a large watermelon.

"I'm Thomas, this is Mitch and this," he said, taking his hat off as if he was in the company of royalty, "is John Thornton."

"Good to meet you all. I'm Robert Fuller."

"Where do you go to school?" Weller asked.

"FNQHS. I'm in Year 11."

"We all went there too. Barely got through it but we all graduated."

"You guys kicking on to uni?"

"We're having a gap year," Thornton said to the laughter of Hearns and Weller.

Fuller finished his burger and looked at Thornton. He knew the face but not the name.

"You're the rugby league player, aren't you?" Fuller asked.

"Was." Thornton answered. "Was."

"You probably get asked this all the time, but how's the hip?"

"I have my good days and bad days Rob. I don't need that walking stick I had been using and the doc says I can start to run soon."

"You're able to play basketball?"

"I just stand under the basket mate, take a few shots here and there. I know my limitations."

"Thanks for livening things up Clyde," Hearns said, giving Fuller a dig in his ribs.

"Sorry John. I didn't mean to ..." Fuller tried to finish the sentence but couldn't find the right words.

"It's alright Rob. Forget about it. I'm just a regular guy now who happens to be 6-4 and 100 kilos."

The four finished their burgers, fries and drinks in silence amongst the din of the food court.

"Let's get out of here," Hearns said. The four stuffed their garbage into an overflowing trash can and took off. They were rocked by the heat and humidity when they stepped outside but some clouds had moved overhead to block out the sun so it wasn't as bad as it could have been.

"Where do you guys usually go to play?" Fuller asked.

"FNQHS."

"Isn't it locked up on weekends?"

"We've got a way in," Hearns said. "Don't we fellas?"

"But there's no nets on the rings there."

"That's why we bring our own," Hearns said. He stopped for a moment, opened up his bag and pulled out two sets of nets. "You can't have a game without hearing the swish of a ball going through a net, can you now?"

37

AFTER A 15-MINUTE TREK FULLER AND HIS NEW MATES arrived at the locked gates of FNQHS. "We spend more time here now than we did when we went to school," Hearns chirped.

"We graduated last year – barely," Hearns told Fuller while he fished for his keys.

"I reckon they just wanted us out of here, but we're back," Weller said as he high-fived Big John Thornton.

Hearns found the key he was looking for, put it in the gate of the fence furthest from the street, rubbed his hands like some sort of jewel thief in an old Humphrey Bogart movie, turned the key and stepped back as the gate opened. "After you gentlemen. One of these days they'll change the lock, but until they do ..." Hearns softly closed the gate behind them and led the charge to the one court which received the most shade from the afternoon sun. It was also partially obscured from the street which meant the odds of being seen were greatly diminished.

"Give me a boost, will you John?" Weller asked as he stood directly under the ring. Weller looked like a young kid on the shoulders of his dad as he attached one of the bright white nets to the 10-foot high ring. He tapped Thornton on the shoulder when he was done, and Thornton lowered him back down.

They each took several shots at the basket; a few rippled the cords of the net on their way through. Fuller and Weller chased down any long rebounds and hoisted up shots from long range. Fuller's first attempt fell short and was met with a chorus of "air ball".

"Just warming up," Fuller meekly said.

Weller banked his first deep shot in. "A little courtesy," he said as he asked for the ball back.

"I'll bet you a buck you don't even hit the ring this time," Thornton called out.

With pride on the line and a gold coin, Weller took his time. He dribbled the ball several times with his right hand, gazed at the basket, then his feet and missed everything. The others cracked up, including Fuller who was enjoying the unplanned outing.

Thornton effortlessly grabbed the wayward shot with one hand. The basketball looked more like a golf ball in his big paw.

"All warmed up?" he shouted at Fuller and Weller. "Half court. Winners out. It's me and Hitman against you two. First team to 11 wins."

Still hobbled a bit by his bad hip, Thornton set up shop in the paint.

Fuller and Weller were outsized but used their quickness to score the first two buckets of the game.

Fuller then missed a short jump shot which Thornton easily snared. He passed to Hearns, who drained the first of three straight buckets. He then fed Thornton underneath, who used his size advantage on Fuller to score the next two baskets.

"Five to two. We've got you covered," Thornton said. He missed his next shot though and Fuller sneaked in to snare the short rebound. He fed Weller, who banked in a shot from beyond the free-throw line.

Fuller was bent over, trying to catch his breath. He wiped the sweat from his face. "How about a drinks break?" he asked.

"After the game," Thornton replied. "You're seventeen not seventy."

Weller and Fuller missed their next four shots which allowed Thornton and Weller to pad their lead. Thornton ended the game with an easy lay-up. He and Hearns exchanged high fives. The four took refuge in the shade and drank from their water bottles. Thornton poured some water on his head to cool himself off. "It's a motherfucker out here today. Damn. But I'm ready for another game. Whose in?"

Fuller looked at his watch. It was nearly four pm. He not only had his own homework to do, more than usual because of upcoming exams, but had that paper to write for Ian Kulken.

"I'm sorry fellas but I need to get going. I've got a lot of homework to do and need to study for exams," he said as he got up.

"There ain't that much homework to do this time of year, is there?" Hearns asked.

"Not usually. But there's some extra stuff I need to do."

"Extra? We all graduated without hardly lifting a finger," Hearns said.

"Yeah, extra," Fuller said lowering his head.

"What's going on mate? You can tell us."

Busting to tell someone, Fuller sat back down on the warm pavement and told the three how he and his mates were being bullied by Kulken and Ed Sanderson, and that Roger Christmas, Randy Elkington and Ted Leishman had transferred to another school leaving him alone to face the "Bash Brothers".

Hearns draped his left arm around Fuller's shoulder. "That shouldn't happen to anyone. The principals know about it?" he softly asked.

"Yeah, but they didn't do a thing. So, if I don't do this paper for Kulken he'll whip the shit out of me."

"Listen up Rob," Thornton said. "From now on you're not doing anybody's schoolwork but your own. Fuck Kulken and Sanderson. Leave it with me mate. I'll take care of it. Those pricks will never bother you again."

"I don't want to get you guys involved."

"Well, we are. Wait till we find those two arseholes."

Thornton turned to Hearns and Weller. "See what you can dig up on those two. Find out where they hang out. They're going to have some company in the next few days."

Fuller spent the rest of Saturday and nearly all of Sunday on his schoolwork. He made a start on the paper Kulken needed; an essay on Tim Winton's award-winning novel *Breath* which met the guideline the essay required. "Explore a relationship in literature which changed a character's life."

His dad had gotten him the book for his last birthday. "It's about kids his age, maybe he'll learn something from it," Reginald Fuller told his wife as he wrapped it the evening before Fuller's 16th birthday.

Fuller had no idea what was under the wrapping when his mum and dad gave him the gift prior to dinner. He feigned interest in it, gave what seemed to be a heart-felt thank you and tossed it on a pile of clothes when he returned to his room and never gave it another thought. That is until a few months later when a massive tropical cyclone skirted Cairns and knocked out most of the city's power for several hours. Unable to charge his mobile phone, housebound and with nothing to do, Fuller looked for the book and found it under his bed.

Fuller knew nothing about surfing, which the story was built around, but was captivated by its depiction of life in a Western Australian country town on the banks of a river. Only an idiot would surf in the waters near Cairns which were full of crocs and stingers.

The relationship that one of the main characters develops with an older woman really piqued his interest. Fuller wondered if something like that could ever happen to him. He was a good-looking boy, smart, with clear skin and a thick head of light-coloured curls thanks to Cairns's relentless sun.

He was a bit quiet with boys his own age, a follower who would never be a leader, and was barely able to put two words together when he was around a girl. He fantasised about girls in his classes and girls who worked at the shops he went to but was unable to find the courage to talk to them. The last time he tried talking to a girl ended in disaster.

He and Jennifer Hughes wound up being the last two students in Mr Gilbert's English class late one morning. Fuller knew the answers to the quiz on Shakespeare's *Romeo and Juliet* but was so distracted by Jennifer, who sat one row in front of him and one seat over to his right, that he barely finished it by the time Gilbert signalled pencils down. Jennifer was wearing white shorts which showed off her long-tanned legs and a blue sleeveless top. Fuller spent half the time allotted to the test staring at the black bra straps under Jennifer's top and the other half trying to hide his hard on.

"I should have studied more," Jennifer said to Fuller as they exited Gilbert's classroom. "I don't think I did very well. How about you?"

Shocked that Jennifer Hughes was actually speaking to him, Fuller had to quickly come up with a response to her query. He searched his mind for the right words, any words. He was two feet away from her, so close that he could smell the cherry scented shampoo from her long brown hair. He looked into Jennifer's brown eyes, lowered his head and said one word, "okay."

Jennifer looked at him, expecting him to continue. But when nothing else came out of Fuller's mouth, she tossed her backpack over her shoulder, said "see you" and walked off to her next class.

Okay? Okay? That's all I'm able to come up with? I am such an arsehole, Fuller said to himself as he walked down a long, nearly empty hallway to the library. *I'm a lock for the Dork of the Year award.*

On Monday morning Ian Kulken rolled out of bed and began to think of new ways to torment FNQHS's underclassman. "What's a Monday without some good old-fashioned extortion?" he asked himself. He had slept well, nearly eight hours, unlike Robert Fuller, who had stayed up until two in the morning writing Kulken's essay. Better to do it in case Thornton was unable to talk to Kulken before Kulken demanded his paper.

Kulken met up with "Bonecrusher" Sanderson a block from school and they walked to their first class together, knocking the books out of the hands of several undersized Year 10 students. As they got to the gates of the school, Kulken's backpack was ripped from his grasp and he was knocked to the ground. Big John Thornton put a knee in his back and pushed his head into the wet grass. Sanderson made a move to come to his mate's rescue, but quickly backed off when Thornton turned to him and told him to move along. "This doesn't concern you mate. If I was you I'd be on my way." Outweighed by some 15 kilograms and aware of Thornton's reputation, Sanderson did as he was told.

"We've got a bit of a problem," Thornton told Kulken, who was on his stomach with one hand behind his back.

"What are you talking about man?" Kulken asked, spitting dirt out of his mouth.

"You're giving a mate of mine a hard time and that is going to stop right now, understand?"

"Who? Who's your mate?"

"Robert Fuller."

"You're mates with that arsehole?"

Upon hearing that Thornton twisted Kulken's arm till it nearly broke in two and shoved his face back into the dirt.

Groups of students walking by gave the two a wide berth but nevertheless stayed around to watch.

"Stop. You're gonna bust my arm," Kulken pleaded.

"You going to leave Fuller and all the others you fuck with alone? It's your choice. And you pass along the same message to that dickhead you hang around with," Thornton said. "Because if you don't, I'll break your arm and shove it up your arse."

"Alight, alright. I'll leave Fuller alone. Just let me go," Kulken yelled.

"It's not just Fuller. It's all the others you fuck with too. Do I make myself clear?"

"Yes, yes. I promise. Let go of my arm, please."

And with that Thornton let go of Kulken's arm and removed his knee from Kulken's back. He extended a hand and helped Kulken up.

Kulken flexed his arm several times to try and get some feeling back into it and brushed bits of grass and mud off his shirt and pants with his good arm.

"You know what?" Thornton asked. "I left home this morning without eating breakfast."

"What, you want me to cook your fucking breakfast for you too?"

Thornton slapped Kulken across the face. The red mark would remain there till well after lunchtime.

"Don't be a wise arse," Thornton said. "How much cash you have on you?"

"I don't know. Fifteen, twenty dollars."

"That'll do. Give it to me."

"You're gonna rob me too?"

"I'm letting you off easy Kulken, too easy if you ask me. Hand it over."

Kulken reached into his pocket and handed Thornton his notes and coins.

"Now get the fuck outta here," Thornton said.

Kulken picked up his backpack and slowly marched through the school's front gate where Sanderson was waiting for him.

"He fucked you over good," Sanderson said, looking at the mark on Kulken's face.

"He'll do the same to you too if we fuck with Fuller or anyone else."

"He said that to you? That he'd do the same to me?"

"Yup."

"Shit. I'm not going near Fuller again," Sanderson said.

"Me neither."

"Hey Sanderson," Kulken said, breaking an awkward silence.

"You got any cash on you."

"Why?"

"'Cause the motherfucker took my money, that's why. I'd like to get some lunch later."

Sanderson reached into his pocket and dug out a fiver. "That's all I can spare mate."

"Thanks," I'll see you at lunchtime," Kulken said.

Fuller saw Kulken walk into Building A and waited for him to come over and collect his essay. Kulken spotted Fuller but walked right past him into Mr Roth's room where he took his usual seat in the back. Fuller noticed the bruise on Kulken's face, put two and two together and realised he had run into Thornton prior to school.

Fuller looked at Kulken's essay, his essay, the one on Winton's *Breath*, that he was holding in his right hand. He could have just walked away and used it himself if he wound up taking that particular class a year later and the same assignment was given out.

Instead Fuller walked into Kulken's classroom and handed the essay to Mr Roth. Kulken was dumbfounded. What is that little shit doing?' he said to himself.

"I found this in the hallway," Fuller told Roth. "It might belong to one of your students."

"Thank you, son." Roth looked at the name on the front page of the essay as Fuller made a hasty retreat out of the room.

"Mr Kulken," Roth said as he addressed the entire class. "Today is your lucky day. A student just found your essay in the hallway."

Realising that Fuller had just saved his arse, Kulken started rummaging through his backpack as if searching for the essay.

"I was just giving it one last read before I handed it in. I must have dropped it and not noticed," he told Roth.

Roth asked the others in his class to pass their essays to the front of the room where he collected them. "I'll have these marked and returned to you by the middle of next week. As for today, we're going to be discussing the decline of good, thorough journalism in Australia and around the world and what can be done to reverse the trend.

"Democracy dies in darkness," Roth said in a strong voice. "Can anyone tell me which publication uses those words as its motto?"

One hand went up.

"Yes, Miss Dutton."

"Facebook?"

Roth put his head in his hands, closed his eyes, rubbed his ample forehead and slumped into his chair. *Are teenagers really this stupid?* he asked himself.

38

WITH HIS BULLYING PROBLEMS SEEMINGLY RESOLVED, he had not been approached by either Ian Kulken or "Bonecrusher" Sanderson in a week, Robert Fuller went back to being a normal high school student. He did his own homework and reports, and no one else's, and was not hounded by a soul. He had "Big John" Thornton to thank.

And Thornton told him just what he wanted in return when they met up the following Saturday at the food court at Cairns Central. "I'd like that new Boston Celtics jumper but am short of cash," Thornton told Fuller over their Whoppers, fries and Cokes. Mitch Weller and Hitman Hearns looked on but did not say a word.

"I've very grateful and all," Fuller said. "I'll see if I can scrape up enough money to get it for you."

Robert had less than $10 on him. The jumper was $89.

"I'd kind of like it today mate so I can wear it when we play at FNQHS."

"I only have about 10 bucks on me. Can you wait a week? I can try and scrape up the money."

"Did I wait a week before telling Kulken and Sanderson to leave you alone?"

Fuller shook his head from side to side.

"It's simple Rob. You're going to have to pinch it."

"You want me to steal it? I've never stolen anything."

"Well, there's a first time for everything. Finish your burger. Then it's showtime."

Fuller looked over at Weller and Hearns for some help but they shrugged their shoulders and stayed silent.

"Second floor mate. You know the store, don't you?"

Fuller nodded.

"You go in first and the three of us will follow a few minutes later. We'll create a diversion and then you pinch it and run like hell. Got it?"

"Yes."

"Just be sure you snag me an extra-large." Thornton said. He laughed. Weller and Hearns followed suit. "We'll meet you later this afternoon on the Esplanade near Maccas. Bring the jumper."

Fuller ate each and every one of his fries and sipped his Coke slowly in a bid to gain some time. *Maybe he'll change his mind.*

"Geez. My 95-year-old great-grandma eats faster than you. Get moving Rob."

Fuller went to toss his trash into a nearby bin, but Thornton told him he would take care of it.

"Put this on mate so them cameras don't get a good look at you," Thornton told Fuller as he handed him a black baseball cap.

"Cameras?"

"Like I said. It's showtime at Cairns Central."

Fuller reluctantly put the cap on his head, pulled it down so it nearly covered his eyes and left the food court. Weller cleaned up the mess. Thornton held onto his drink.

There were three customers in Gene's Sporting Goods when Fuller entered with his head held low. Owner Gene Bennett was behind the register, finalising a sale. A girl about Fuller's age with long blonde hair was folding T-shirts. Fuller looked around and spotted the NBA jumpers near the front of the store. A Cleveland jumper was on a mannequin which had a Cavaliers cap perched on its oval-shaped plastic head. Other jumpers were on hangers on the near sidewall. Fuller walked to the jumpers and then looked at the door. It was barely 10 metres away.

"Can I help you with anything?" the blonde sales assistant asked.

Fuller jumped back and nearly fell onto a rack of track pants.

"Sorry to startle you," Amy McNamara said. "You look a little lost. Looking for anything special?"

Fuller caught his breath. "Just having a look at the jumpers, for a birthday present for my little brother," he said.

"Okay. If you need anything just ask, okay?"

"I will. Thanks."

"Say, don't you go to FNQHS?"

"Yeah, I do. I'm in Year 11."

"I thought you looked familiar. You look older for someone in Year 11. I'm in Year 12. Hi." She pointed to her name tag. "I'm Amy."

Fuller was not used to talking to girls and it showed.

"I'm Rob," he finally said, stumbling over his own name.

Amy stuck out her hand. Her nails were painted a bright red. She lifted the cap off his head so she could get a better look at his eyes. "You're kinda cute."

"Me? You're the cute one."

"You think?"

They were interrupted by a shout from the back of the store.

"Amy. I'm not paying you to talk to boys. Get back to work for Christ's sake," Gene Bennett yelled from behind the register. "The place is a mess. Put everything where it belongs. Please."

Amy picked up several caps from the floor and turned to Fuller. She winked at him. "See you in school, eh?"

What just happened here? Fuller asked himself. *She couldn't be interested in me. Could she?*

Fuller's daydreaming was interrupted by the entrance of Thornton, Weller and Hearns. There was one other customer in the store; an older fellow who was trying on North Queensland Cowboys NRL caps.

Thornton had his drink with him and was sitting down trying on a pair of size 13 sneakers when Gene Bennett came over to have a word. "Excuse me son, but there is no food or drink allowed in the store. We have a sign posted up front."

"I didn't see any sign," Thornton said. He pointed to Weller and Hearns. "You fellas seen a sign?"

"Nope," answered Weller and Hearns.

"Can you please take the drink outside?" Bennett asked.

Thornton handed his half full cup to Weller. "Take this outside, will ya? Don't want to be breaking any rules"

Weller took the cup, took several steps and intentionally caught his shoe in a clothing rack and went down. What was left of the drink spilled onto the cheap beige carpet. That was Fuller's cue to get going. "That's why there are no drinks allowed in the store," Bennett screamed. He turned to Amy. "Go get some rags from out back. Quick."

As Bennett carried on, Fuller grabbed an extra-large Celtics jumper off the rack and ran out of the store. The security tag sounded but by the time Bennett made his way to the front of the shop and looked down the crowded corridors, Fuller was long gone. With his cap tucked down the back of his pants and the jumper down his shirt he ran from the shop and squeezed into a crowded elevator headed to the ground floor. He was on the street in less than a minute.

"The fellow who took the jumper, was that the boy you were talking to?" Bennett asked Amy, who was mopping up the mess left by Weller.

"I'm not sure."

"Do you know him?"

"No. Don't even know his name."

"Damn. Bloody shoplifters. It ain't even worth reporting it to mall management. Let's get back to work. We've got customers here."

Bennett approached Thornton and Hearns. Weller had already left.

"How are those sneakers? Fit alright?" he asked Thornton.

"They're a little tight. You got these in a size 14?"

"Fourteen? No. They only go up to size 13."

"That's a shame. I really liked these." Thornton stood up. "Thanks anyways and sorry about the drink mate."

As agreed, Fuller and his shoplifting cohorts gathered later that afternoon on the Esplanade which was teeming with tourists and locals. Fuller pulled the jumper he stole out of a Woolies bag and sheepishly handed it to Thornton. "It's an extra-large, just like you asked for."

A large smile came over Thornton's face as he unfolded it.

"Try it on mate," Weller said.

Thornton took off his T-shirt and tossed it in the direction of Fuller who grabbed it before it hit the grass. He pulled the green and white jumper over his head and let it hang over his white shorts. "Looking good John," Hearns said, giving Thornton a fist bump.

"Whaddya think Fuller? Think I could pass for one of them Bostonians?"

"Absolutely."

"League was always what I wanted to play but if I hadn't fucked my hip up I'd at least be playing for the Taipans. I'm unstoppable in the paint, ain't I guys?"

His three mates nodded their heads in unison.

Thornton turned to Fuller and put an arm on his shoulder. "You done well. You're part of our family now mate."

How do I get out of the family? Fuller asked himself. *I can't afford to get into any more trouble, but then again I don't want Kulken and Sanderson to start busting my balls again. Shit.*

39

DELANEY AND FULLER ARRIVED AT TRENDY TRINITY
Beach just as the sun was going down. A cool breeze coming off the
ocean knocked the temperature down a few degrees, so it was just a
lazy 28.

"Now let's see if we can find this place," Delaney said looking at the
paper he took out of his shirt pocket. "Sunset Drive, number 367 is what
we are looking for. Here's Sunrise Crescent. I'll go out on a limb here and
say Sunset Drive is the next street."

It was. Delaney quickly found the house, a beauty with a view of the
beach. "How much you think this goes for Robert? Six, seven hundred
thousand?"

"At least."

Delaney backed the truck into the driveway, being careful not to
scrape the BMW to his left. He got as close to the garage as he could,
stopped, put the truck in park, put on the hand break and shut her down.

A massive palm tree took up most of the front yard. As Delaney
and Fuller had a good look around the plush property, Betty and James
Allenson walked out of the front door and greeted them.

"Thanks for coming by after hours," James Allenson said. "We
got a call from Harvey Norman this afternoon saying they'd deliver
everything tomorrow. We thought it would be early next week. You can
come in through the garage, it will be much easier that way."

The garage was cleaner than a hospital operating room. Tools and tins
of paint lined the shelves. Delaney moved an electric lawn mower out of
harm's way. It was one of the newest on the market and didn't need a

long extension cord which limited its reach. This model had a battery which could run the mower for an hour before it needed to be recharged. He didn't spot the obligatory suburban leaf blower which merely blew leaves and dirt from one spot to another and always seemed to be used on weekends before 9am.

Delaney introduced himself and Fuller, opened the back door of the truck, grabbed the hand trolley and followed the Allensons inside.

Shit, this is even nicer than Judy's place, Delaney thought as he had a look around. *It's like walking into a museum.*

Expensive paintings covered the walls, and the furniture which the Allensons were getting rid of, looked like it came out of a magazine.

Even Fuller was gobsmacked at the opulence of the place. *So, this is what it's like to be rich. Our whole fucking apartment could fit in the living room.*

"Everything in the living and dining areas?" Delaney asked.

"Anything that isn't nailed down," Betty Allenson said. "Would either of you like some water? Or some lemonade? I made it myself."

Delaney looked over at Fuller, who nodded. "Two lemonades would be nice, thank you Betty."

"What do you say Robert, the bigger pieces first, eh?"

"Yup. Let's get started."

In order, they grabbed two couches, a very large bookcase, two recliners and a coffee table and then the dining room table and chairs, and a massive fridge. Without the truck's hydraulic lift Delaney and Fuller would have needed another hand or two. Having seen movers in the past work, Delaney covered all the items with large blankets and tied them down the best he could. It was hard work though and time consuming. It took the two amateur removalists more than an hour to load and tie all the pieces down. Everything was top quality and would fetch a fortune for the Salvos.

Emptying the truck would be a lot easier. By the time Delaney and Fuller put all of the Allensons' furniture in the Salvos storeroom, it was close to 7:30. He locked the truck, put the keys in the mail slot and heard them plop down on the office carpet. "Job done," Delaney said to Fuller. "And a bloody big one too. I won't be doing this again. I'm aching."

Twenty minutes later Delaney dropped Fuller off at home.

"See you next week at the shop," Delaney said.

"I'll be there, but only because I have to," Fuller answered.

It had been several days since Delaney had heard from Judy Seymour and he was getting a little worried. *Who knows? Maybe she went away for the weekend. But it's unlike her not to answer a text message. I'll go over there tomorrow,* he thought.

Delaney was sitting at home that Monday night, the television remote in one hand, a cold glass of water in the other and a mint in his mouth. He had just finished dinner, an awful one at that, one he had reluctantly picked up at Woolies and tossed in the microwave. 'These damn frozen things never look like what's pictured on the box. Why do I even bother?' he asked himself. The mint helped remove the taste of the rubbery Salisbury steak from his mouth.

The balcony door was open, letting a pleasing evening breeze drift inside Delaney's apartment which could get a bit stuffy during the heat of the day. The screen door kept the mozzies where they belonged – outside. The ceiling fan in the living room was set on low. Its breeze slightly ruffled the pages of that morning's *Cairns Examiner* which was on the coffee table and opened to the sports pages. He tilted his head a bit to get a better view of a headline. Broncos primed for Cowboys it read. By default, that was to be his night's entertainment; a rugby league game for the former Melburnian and AFL fan, who when back home only watched league when it was State of Origin and grand final time.

While Delaney watched the Cowboys score the first try against the hosts at Suncorp Stadium, Judy Seymour was sealing the last of several boxes she had packed over the weekend.

It was 8:12. *Time to ring Packer,* she noted. Packer's phone vibrated several times before he picked it up. "Al, it's Judy. I'm ready to go. When can you get here?"

Al Packer and his associates, a mountain of a man who went by the name of Sloane and a smaller stocky fellow named Pederson, showed up just before 9pm in an unmarked dark-coloured truck which they backed into her driveway and parked just in front of her Toyota. Packer had disconnected the reversing beeper so not one of Seymour's neighbours on McKenzie Street heard a thing. The truck was well hidden by the tall hedges which separated Seymour's home from her closest neighbour.

"As quickly and as quietly as you can boys, just as we discussed, take everything out of the house and put it in the truck. Save those boxes in the living room for last. Understand?" Packer asked. Sloane answered for himself and Pederson. "We'll get everything in the truck in 30 minutes."

"Good. Let's get to it."

Sloane and Pederson emptied the two bedrooms and study in less than 20 minutes. Only the carpet and light fixtures remained. Every item in the closets had already been packed away. They'd be the last boxes tossed on the truck.

Picking up the living room furniture like it was made out of balsa wood, Sloane and Pederson then went to work on the dining room table and chairs and the outside furniture, including the large barbecue which had cooked many tasty meals over the years. Everything was going to be dropped off at a second-hand furniture place in Earlville owned by a bloke named Klotz, who Packer had met at the casino. Packer used the

$1500 he got from Stan Klotz to pay Sloane and Pederson and for the use of the truck. Packer kept Judy's TV entertainment unit for himself. It was nicer by a country mile than anything he owned.

Thanks to Judy's good taste Klotz got top dollar for everything. He wound up getting over four times as much as he gave Packer selling her furniture over the next few months. The king-sized bed and mattress along with the two bedside tables went for $700. Judy's things wound up in houses and apartments throughout the Cairns area. One young couple, she an artist and he a writer, liked her dining room table and chairs so much they lugged it up the mountain to Kuranda. With its legs removed the table just fit in the back of their Kombi van.

Sloane and Pederson next attacked the boxes in the garage which contained tools, paint cans and assorted odds and ends Judy's late husband had accumulated. The last thing to leave the garage was the lawn mower which was just a couple of years old. Judy took one last glance at the garage's bare shelves. She wiped a tear from her eye, pressed a button on the remote and watched the garage door come down for the last time.

This is not the time to get sentimental Judy, keep it together. We've still got a lot to do. There'll be plenty of time for tears later, she told herself.

The sound of Packer's voice ended her daydreaming.

"We're nearly ready to go Judy. The boys are putting those last few boxes in the truck."

"Oh, okay," she said. "Those are going in the car to Noosa, right?"

"Just as you asked. Sloane is driving your stuff to Noosa tonight. He'll be there in a couple of days. The boxes will stay in the boot of your new car and the keys tossed in your letterbox. The guy who shows you your new apartment will bring the boxes upstairs."

Judy nodded her head. "And everything else?"

"Right here," Packer said.

He took a cream-coloured envelope from his back pocket and opened it. Inside was her new driver's licence, passport, Medicare card, bank details, a debit card, credit card and tax file number.

"The car's registration and insurance forms, in your new name, will be in the glovebox."

Judy took the envelope from Packer, put it in her handbag and took one out in return.

"As you requested Al, here's the $35,000. Twenty-five for the new paperwork and $10,000 for the car."

"It's a pleasure doing business with you Mrs Seymour," Packer said as he folded the envelope and put it in his front left pants pocket.

Packer glanced at the now empty house. "Just your suitcase? Is that it Judy?"

"Yes."

"You have the keys for the Toyota Judy? Pederson will get rid of it tonight."

Judy handed Packer the keys.

"Can you give me a minute Al? I'll meet you in the truck."

"Sure thing Judy."

There was not even a place for Judy Seymour to sit down. She leaned against the wall by the door, her handbag at her feet, a tissue in her hand.

"I'm sorry Jack. I am so sorry. I know how much you loved this house and if you were still here, I would never get rid of it. I miss you everyday sweetheart."

She paused, dabbed at her eyes, picked up her handbag and tossed the moist tissue in it.

"And I'm sorry Gary. But business is business. If you meet another pretty woman remember to think with your head and not your dick."

Judy Seymour turned out the lights in the living room and front hallway, locked the front door, closed it behind her and walked to the truck where Sloane and Packer were waiting.

Packer drove. Sloan took her hand and helped her into the front seat of the truck. She closed the passenger side door and placed her handbag on her lap. There was just enough room for the three of them. Without saying a word Packer started the truck and with the lights off turned left onto McKenzie St and slowly drove off. He glanced in his rear-view mirror. Sloan was following in the Toyota, also with its lights off.

Sloan turned on his headlights when he approached a roundabout leading to Captain Cook Highway and turned right. Packer turned on the truck's headlights and turned left towards the airport. He stopped about a kilometre down the road at a hotel which was just three kilometres from the airport. Judy had a 9am flight to Sunshine Coast Airport and then a cab ride to Noosa.

Judy got out of the truck and waited for Packer to bring her suitcase around to the hotel's entrance. "Take care of yourself Diane," Packer said, setting the suitcase at her feet.

"What?"

"From now on, you are Diane Bradley. Don't forget it."

"Right, right. Sorry, just a little overcome by it all. And Al, do me a favour," she said taking her iPhone out of her handbag. "Get rid of this for me. Feed it to the crocs."

Packer nodded, walked to the driver's side of the truck, turned the key and drove off.

Diane Bradley wheeled her luggage into the hotel's empty lobby. She walked to the front counter and rang the bell.

A middle-aged man dressed in a smart jacket with a pair of reading glasses in his hand came out of the adjacent office and approached the counter. "Good evening," he said.

"Good evening. I'd like a room for the night."

"Is that just for yourself?"

"It is."

"I have several single rooms and a junior suite. Which would you like?"

"I'll take the junior suite."

"That's fine. Just fill this out please. Paying by cash or card?

"Cash."

Diane Bradley wrote the name Susan Davis on the standard hotel form. She drew a line through the space reserved for a car's make and rego number.

"Thank you Miss Davis. That's $169 even."

Diane Bradley handed him four $50 bills. She was handed her change and asked for a wake-up call for 6:30am.

"Heading home are you?" the hotel clerk asked.

"Sure am. Back to Melbourne."

"Enjoy your stay up here?"

"I sure did, thank you."

"You're in suite 412. Here's your room card. I can help you to your suite if you like."

"Thanks, but no. I'll be fine."

Diane Bradley smiled and walked to the elevator with her suitcase which did not make a sound as it rolled along the carpeted lobby. Rodney Wynne leaned over the counter to look. He watched until the elevator door closed. Diane Bradley had that sort of effect on men.

The power at Judy Seymour's house was turned off automatically at midnight.

After not getting an answer to his call and texts earlier in the morning, Gary Delaney showed up at 13 McKenzie St just after 9am.

He parked in the street. Judy's Toyota was not in the driveway. "I guess she must be at an appointment," Delaney said.

He sat in the car for a few moments and decided he would leave a note.

Delaney found a pen and a sheet of paper in the glove box and scribbled out a few lines.

"Worried about you. Can you give me a ring or a text? Gary."

Delaney waited for a car to pass, opened the car door and walked to the front door. There was just enough room for him to slide the sheet of paper inside.

But instead of walking back to his car, curiosity got the better of him. He peaked in the living room window and was stunned by what he saw – or didn't see. Every piece of furniture was gone, including the paintings on the walls and the throw rugs. The dining room area was also completely empty. No table, no chairs. Even the crystal cabinet which housed her finest silver and wine glasses was gone.

What the fuck is going on? Delaney wondered.

He opened the fence to the backyard, the same fence he had painted just several weeks ago and walked into the backyard. All the outdoor furniture was gone, even the barbecue.

A robbery? he wondered. *Couldn't be.* He peered in the garage windows. It too was empty. The lawnmower, the gardening tools, all gone. The shelves? Bare.

"I don't believe it. She's left. Just like that. She said she owned the place."

Delaney did not remember seeing a For Sale sign on the lawn. "Was she renting it? This doesn't make any sense."

Delaney thought back. "Okay, today is Monday. That much I know. The last time I saw her was last Tuesday. Right? I think it was. So that's why she didn't answer my calls or texts. She just took off. I don't understand. What's happened here?"

He sat down on the front step of the house and tried to figure things out.

"MY MONEY," he screamed. "I handed everything over to her and her company. SHIT."

Suddenly Delaney felt sick. His breakfast was rising into his throat. He forced it back down and took a deep breath. "Let's not jump to conclusions here. There's got to be an explanation to all of this. Even if she has left, my savings could be safe. It's insured, isn't it?"

What Delaney didn't know was that three weeks earlier, with the help of Jim Glickman, Seymour had sold the house without it ever being listed, to a Chinese couple. Judy asked for $610,000. The couple countered with an offer of $608,888, the number eight being a lucky number for the Chinese. Judy and Glickman took it without a moment's hesitation.

Glickman took $25,000 off the top for brokering the deal and gave Judy a cashier's check for the rest. It was made out in the name of Diane Bradley. Judy deposited it in her new account on her first afternoon in Noosa, parking $500,000 in a six-month term deposit and leaving the rest in a savings account. Pocket money for her, a year's salary for many. Two weeks later she had second thoughts, withdrew the $500,000 and told Glickman to stash it along with the rest of her assets in one of her business accounts in the Cayman Islands so no one would be able to access it except her. "Good thinking Judy. I'll have it all sorted within 48 hours."

"Keep 10k for your troubles and put the paperwork in that safe deposit box of mine."

Glickman did as instructed and then called his travel agent. "I've had a good month Karen. Book a cruise for me and my wife if you would. At least seven days and for no more than $10,000."

Karen Romney rang Glickman 90 minutes later. "You're in luck Jim. There's a cruise departing from Cairns in three weeks bound for Darwin by way of Bali. You've got a balcony suite, a three-night stay in Darwin and business class seats from Darwin back home."

"Perfect Karen. Perfect. And whatever your commission is, double it."

The Chinese couple, Herbert and Sue Li, who were still in their 40s, had made a killing in the Shanghai real estate market and needed a place to park their money. They closed the deal just weeks before the Chinese government clamped down on large amounts of money being sent overseas. Cairns was the perfect place for Mr and Mrs Li. They loved the climate and the casino where they tossed a seemingly endless supply of hundred-dollar bills at the gaming tables.

They quickly became favourites with the pit bosses who comped them dinners and drinks in exchange for their business. However, Herbert Li was bad for their business. He had a photographic mind and each night at the blackjack tables wound up with piles of hundred-dollar chips in front of him. The pit bosses soon limited his bets and watched him like a hawk to see if he was cheating. He always tossed the dealer a few chips when he had had enough, bowed to the pit bosses and carried his chips to the cashier's booth where they were replaced with stacks of hundred-dollar bills which barely fit into his jacket and pants pockets.

"How the fuck does he do it?" pit boss Dean Donovan asked the dealer who was the recipient of a $300 tip. "There are six decks of cards here for crying out loud plus we've got cameras from all angles looking down on him."

"I'm not sure," Rob Lindsey said. "Maybe he's just on a winning streak."

"For two fucking weeks? The law of averages has to catch up with him. It has too."

Each evening Herbert and Sue Li dined at the casino's finest restaurant and drank bottles of its finest wines. All of it was on the house and after every meal Herbert Li tipped their waiter and sommelier $100 each.

Sue Li preferred playing keno and the pokies. Every evening after dinner she waited until precisely 8:08pm to place her first bet. Her biggest haul was a $12,000 win on Keno. Mrs Li did not possess the photographic mind that her husband had and instead randomly stuffed dollar coins into two pokie machines which became her favourites. Like 99.5 percent of those who played the machines, she went home a loser most evenings. Herbert Li gave his wife a bundle of $100 bills on the ride home to raise her spirits and promised her another bundle if she dressed up like one of the casino's cocktail waitresses when they went to bed.

A limousine took them home each night. Two armed bodyguards, both of Chinese descent, and a $100,000 security system kept them safe at 13 McKenzie St.

Not even three weeks into their two-month stay, an excavator and several workmen showed up at the house. The excavator was directed into the backyard where it started digging the hole for Herbert and Sue Li's in-ground swimming pool.

A shattered Gary Delaney took a large gulp of water from the bottle he carried in his SUV and sat in the vehicle with the air conditioning on high until he regained his composure and was able to think straight.

Maybe it's not so bad. Everything was in order with the first statement I got from Judy's company. Just because she left it doesn't mean my money left with her. But why wouldn't she tell me? Did she want to spare me the pain of breaking up? I'm a big boy. I could have handled that.

When Delaney arrived home, he turned on his laptop and researched the funds Judy had him put his money in. Everything checked out. In fact, most of the funds had gone up since he last checked.

A few days later though his worst fears were realised when he received his second statement from Far North Queensland Financial Services in the post. He brought the envelope upstairs, sat down, took a deep breath and gingerly opened it. His balance was zero. His money had all been withdrawn. Three hundred and seventy-five thousand dollars. All gone.

"Fuck, fuck. fuck," he yelled. Delaney put his head in his hands and cried. "It's all gone. All of it. What am I going to do? Rely on the old age pension? That will barely cover the rent."

The only smart thing Delaney did before transferring his retirement savings to Judy's mob, was to take $25,000 from it and put it in his everyday bank account. He would not be destitute but his dream of moving to a nicer complex and a long holiday to WA was gone.

Delaney picked up his phone and rang Judy. Again, there was no answer. He sent her several text messages. There was no reply.

He rang the office number of Far North Queensland Financial Services which was on the statement he received. After two rings, he heard a recording. "I'm sorry, but the number you rang has been disconnected."

"Motherfucker! How could I have been so stupid?" he asked himself. "If only I had listened to that fucker at the bank. The first $250,000 was insured for Christ's sake. What was I thinking? I'll never be able to replace $375,000. Where could I go to make a complaint? The cops? They'd laugh at me."

"You were swindled mate," the copper would say. "I could make out a report but from what you said your financial advisor has left the building. The odds of you or us tracking her down and getting your money back are about 1000-1."

Delaney went to his bedroom closet, found a folder marked bank details, sat on his bed and opened it.

As of three weeks ago he had $36,675 in his everyday bank account. He rifled through the top draw of his bedside table where he tossed his ATM receipts and found the latest one. It was three days old. He had $36,250 to his name. He would have to live off that for now and any winnings from his share in Too Hard Wrong Spot.

"Fuck. I'm going to have to get a part-time job of some sort. The last thing I wanted to do was go back to work. Who's going to hire an old-timer like me anyways? I am fucked, completely fucked."

40

"I NEED SOME AIR. I'VE GOT TO GET OUT OF HERE AND think," Delaney said.

He grabbed his keys and water bottle and slowly walked to the parking lot.

He opened his car's door, got in and put his hands on the warm steering wheel. His hands shook and his chest was tight. "I can't drive like this," he said.

He got out of the car, the same one which transported him from Melbourne to Cairns not even a year ago; when he had money, hope; when he was embarking on a new life.

"How soon will it be before I start eating cat food? With my luck a cyclone will pass right over this fucking complex, reduce my rental to rubble and leave the others untouched."

Delaney grabbed a baseball cap from the passenger seat of the car; no sense adding a case of skin cancer into the mix, locked it and walked to the pool. He loudly closed the gate behind him and dragged one of the wooden chairs into the shade. Being that it was 11am on a work and school day it was no surprise he was the only one there.

"Who's making that racket down there?" Barbara Stevenson asked herself. She put down her magazine of crossword puzzles, got out of her comfortable chair, walked over to her front window and pushed back the blinds.

"That's Gary. I wonder what's going on with him. He looks like he's crying. Not my concern anymore," she said closing the blinds. She went

"

back to her chair and picked up her magazine but couldn't come up with another word to the puzzle she was working on.

Delaney kicked the chair he was sitting in as he got up, walked into the pool area's small kitchen and filled his water bottle from the tap. He stuck his hat on his head and started to walk towards a nearby bus stop. A bus pulled up a few minutes later. He looked at the destination – Palm Cove.

"Why not?" Delaney thought. "One return for Palm Cove please," he told the bus driver. Delaney reached into his pocket, pulled out a $10 note and handed it to the driver who gave him $3 change along with a paper ticket.

The driver looked at his watch, checked his side mirror for any latecomers, put the bus in gear and took off for the 35-minute trip north. The drive by car usually took about 20 minutes. The bus took a more circuitous route, exiting and then re-entering the Captain Cook Highway several times before it reached Palm Cove which was the end of the line.

The air conditioning kept the bus as chilly as the frozen food aisle at Woolies and felt good on Delaney's skin. There were about a dozen people aboard, mostly older folk since it was the middle of the day. They kept to themselves, sitting apart from each other. Each had a bag or two of shopping next to them, mostly groceries. One older fellow held his fishing rod in front of him. It was in two pieces. He joined them together when he got to his favourite spot and took it apart when boarding the bus. He had numerous age spots and several band aids on his ruddy hands. A strong smell of fish came from his direction, most likely from the bait he had earlier cut up since the bucket he had with him was turned upside down. Delaney wondered if the driver would let someone on with a bucket full of fish. *I would. The guy goes to a lot of trouble just to throw a line in the water. How could you say no?*

Fishing was a dangerous hobby in these parts if you were not aboard a boat or on a pier, safe from the crocs which lurked in just about every creek and waterway.

Delaney took a seat towards the back of the bus. The seat was raised, which gave him a better view of the landscape, which featured palm trees and sugar cane fields. The Macalister Mountain Range was on his left. Shadows from the passing clouds moved across the range from right to left. Delaney took his phone from his pocket and took a couple of snaps but the glare off the window ruined the shots and he deleted them.

He was more relaxed than he had been 20 minutes ago. A coffee followed by a walk on the Palm Cove pier would clear his head.

About 10 minutes into the journey, the bus pulled over to the side of Captain Cook Highway where an old wooden bus shelter stood. Four teenagers flagged the bus down and boarded.

Smithfield Shopping Centre, their likely destination, was two stops away. The bus fare would be peanuts. Big John Thornton did the talking when the bus driver politely asked each of the four to pay $1.60 so he could continue his route.

"We don't pay mate," Thornton said to the bus driver. He told his travelling companions – Fuller, Weller and Hearns – to find themselves seats while he took care of things.

"I don't want any trouble sir. I'm just asking you to pay your fare just like everyone else on this bus has done," the driver said in a calm voice.

"Well, you'll have yourself some trouble if you don't take us to Smithfield," Thornton replied.

Ordinarily Alex McGuiness would have steered the bus back on to the highway and forgotten about the fares.

But the bus company was clamping down on fare evaders and expected its drivers to enforce its "no pay, no travel rule. "A small video camera, no bigger than a pen, was attached to the rear-view mirror of each bus and recorded each transaction as passengers boarded. Four non-paying passengers would not look good on McGuinness's record.

Alex McGuinness was just an average-sized bloke with nearly 10 years on the job. Big Joe Thornton had about six inches, 30 kilograms and 25 years on him. But McGuiness did not back down.

"If you do not pay your fare, I am going to have to ask you and your friends to leave the bus."

"Leave the bus? If anyone is going to be leaving this bus it is you. Drive this fucking bus to Smithfield. Understand?"

McGuinness hesitated. "And if I don't?"

Thornton took a switchblade from his front pocket and opened it. "Then I'll fucking drive it."

McGuinness felt his colon tighten. *Losing a few fares is one thing, but to lose a bloody bus? I'll be out on my arse,* he said to himself. He pondered his options while Thornton held the knife just a few inches from his neck.

Several passengers in the front of the bus screamed when they saw Thornton reach for his knife. Delaney poked his head into the aisle to see just what was going on. *Why am I not surprised by all of this?* he asked himself. *There'll be no reasoning with that guy.*

"I don't like this," Robert Fuller said to Weller and Hearns, who were seated together to his left. Fuller had caved when Weller called him earlier in the day. "C'mon man, we're getting the band back together."

"I'm done with all this," Fuller told Weller.

"Big John is going to be very disappointed to hear that," Weller told Fuller.

Shit, Fuller thought. *He did save my arse from Kulken and Sanderson.*

"One last time Mitch, one last time."

When Fuller saw Thornton produce a knife, a chill past through him, "Has he ever taken out a knife before?" he asked Weller.

"Never. That driver must have really pissed him off."

"You think he'll use it?" Fuller asked Weller.

"I don't know. Maybe."

"This is fucked. We've got to stop him. He'll wind up in jail or worse," Hearns added. "Fuller. See if you can talk him out of this. He respects you man."

"Me?"

"Yeah, you. Stop wasting time."

Fuller stood up, glanced at Hearns and Weller and yelled to Thornton at the front of the bus.

"John. John," he said walking into the aisle. "It's not worth it mate. Let's just get off this bus and forget about Smithfield."

As Thornton turned at the sound of his name, Alex McGuinness took the keys out of the ignition, dashed from his seat and scampered out of the bus. He locked the doors and yelled back at the bus. "You won't be going anywhere without these."

Dangling the keys over his head so Thornton and the others could see, McGuinness dropped the keys into a storm drain and ran down the side of Captain Cook Highway. Madly flailing his arms at passing traffic, McGuiness managed to get a vehicle to pull over and stop. "I'm the driver of that bus," McGuinness told the tradie who stopped his ute. He pointed to his light blue shirt and name tag to prove who he was.

"Some guy with a knife hijacked the bus. Drive me out of here. Please. I'll call for help."

The tradie opened his passenger door and told McGuinness to get in. "Thank you, thank you," McGuinness said. He took the mobile phone the company gave to its drivers at the start of each shift – they had to leave their personal mobiles in their lockers – and called dispatch.

"McGuinness here. A gang of kids has taken over my bus. Yes, that's right. They took over the bus. One of them is armed with a knife. I got out of there with the keys. There's about a dozen passengers aboard. The bus is on the northbound side of Captain Cook Highway. Yeah. Northbound, two stops before Smithfield."

Thornton was bewildered by the sudden turn of events. He charged at the front door and tried opening it. It wouldn't budge. "Try the back door, Fuller," he yelled. "We've got to get out of here. That fucking driver has probably called the cops."

"They're locked," Fuller said. Weller and Hearns got up and tried the door themselves. "Shit, we're locked in," they screamed.

Gary Delaney's ears perked up when he heard Thornton yell the name Fuller.

Fuller, Fuller. Isn't that the name of the kid who is working with me at the Salvos? The one who was arrested for trying to rob a cop? Don't tell me this is the same kid. So much for that promise of turning his life around.

Nick Bellamy was finishing up some paperwork at his desk when a constable approached him. "You better take this call detective. We might have a hostage situation on the highway."

"Hostage situation?"

"Yup. Line 2. Some guy named Baker from Cairns Links, the bus company."

"Detective Bellamy here. What's going on?"

"I'm the head of operations at Cairns Links. One of our drivers just called in to say that his bus has been hijacked on Captain Cook Highway near Smithfield."

"Who am I talking to?" Bellamy asked.

"Ramon Baker."

"Okay Ramon. Tell me exactly what the driver told you. And don't leave anything out."

"The driver is Alex McGuiness. He's been with us nearly 10 years. Spotless record. He stopped to pick up four teenagers two stops before Smithfield. They didn't want to pay their fares. McGuiness told them they'd have to leave the bus if they did not pay their fares. One of them pulled a knife on him. Somehow McGuinness got out of the bus and locked it. No one on the bus can get out. There are about 12 passengers on the bus."

"You say there are four of them?"

"Yes."

"Did your driver say if any of the other three are armed?"

"He said he couldn't be sure. But he thinks it's only the one guy, the guy with the knife."

"Shit. When did this all happen?"

"Not even 10 minutes ago detective. The bus was travelling north bound on the highway to Smithfield. McGuinness stopped for the kids at that old bus shelter on the highway."

"I know the one," Bellamy said. "We'll get over there right away."

Bellamy quickly walked across the office and knocked on the open door of Senior Sergeant Lou Mendelson. "Lou, we've got ourselves a potential hostage situation. Four kids, one of them armed with a knife, are on a bus near Smithfield on the highway. The driver took off and locked the doors of the bus. No one can get out."

Mendelson took off his reading glasses which he needed for his computer work and laid them on his desk. "Why the hell did he lock the doors?"

"I guess he panicked when one of the four pulled a knife."

"Why did he pull a knife on the driver. Was it a robbery?"

"Not from what the head of operations at the bus company told me. The four refused to pay their fares and got into an altercation with the driver."

"So you mean we've got this mess because some kid didn't want to pay a $2 fare? Unfuckingbelievable."

"Yup. How do you want to handle this?"

"Let's keep this quiet for now. We'll go over there and see if we can defuse the situation. Get a car. I'll meet you out front."

41

BELLAMY GOT BEHIND THE WHEEL OF THE UNMARKED car. As required, whenever a car was taken out, the officer first had to check in with dispatch. Mendelson picked up the radio as soon as he jumped into the passenger seat. "Mendelson here. Bellamy and I are on our way to Captain Cook Highway. There's a city bus parked on the northbound side just before Smithfield. The driver got out and hasn't come back. We're looking into it."

"Roger that," the dispatcher said.

"No need to mention the words hostage or knife, at least not yet," Mendelson said to Bellamy who nodded.

Bellamy swerved in and out of traffic and floored the car when he found an empty stretch of road.

"Who are you? Daniel Fucking Ricciardo?" Mendelson asked. "I lost a kidney a mile back."

Bellamy smiled and eased off the gas. He was doing about 100 when he spotted the bus. It was right where the dispatcher said it was, parked right in front of the old wooden bus shelter. "How the heck is that thing still standing? It's bloody older than I am," Mendelson cracked.

Bellamy parked the car about 50 metres behind the school bus. Mendelson put a pair of field glasses to his eyes and zoomed in on the bus.

"From what I can see there doesn't seem to be any sort of hostage situation. The passengers are scattered about. Let's go have a gander, see if we can talk some sense into the one with the knife."

Bellamy and Mendelson put on their vests and slowly approached the back of the bus.

At just that moment, Channel 12 reporter Tegan Winterbottom and her cameraman, "Handsome" Harry Hirsch, passed by on their way to Smithfield where they were scheduled to do a piece on a lottery winner who had purchased his ticket at the shopping centre's newsagent. "Don't use my name," Ron Griggs told the newsagent. "I don't want my wife to find out," the newest member of Australia's millionaire club said.

"What are you going to do? Wear a disguise when you are on camera?" the newsagent asked.

"Maybe they can pixilate my face," Griggs said.

Hirsch slowed down when he noticed Bellamy and Mendelson. "Those two are coppers," Hirsch said. "I have a hunch something is going on. I'm going to pull over."

With his rugged good looks Hirsch was better suited to be in front of the camera but he was the best cameraman at the station and opted to stay with Channel 12 after it gave him a $10,000 raise and added an extra year on to his contract with the promise of an on-camera reporting job to follow. Hirsch made sure he got that bit in writing.

Hirsch brought the Channel 12 van to a stop about 100 metres in front of the bus.

"Looks like we've got some company John. Take a look at this," Hearns told Thornton, who had given up trying to open the back door.

With his knife back in his pocket, Thornton walked to the front of the bus and saw the Channel 12 van. A woman holding a microphone and a guy with a camera were getting out of it.

"What the fuck?"

He wheeled around and looked at the passengers. "Did any of you motherfuckers use your phones to call the TV people?"

Those that weren't paralysed by fright collectively mumbled "no".

"Then what the fuck are they doing here?"

Hearns and Heller walked to the front of the bus to find out what all the commotion was about. Fuller stayed where he was as Bellamy and Mendelson neared the back of the bus. Bellamy put out his hand and gave the less-heavier Mendelson a boost so he could see in through the back window. He lightly tapped on the window to draw the attention of a male passenger who was wearing a light-coloured baseball cap.

Delaney slowly turned around and saw Mendelson, who put his left index finger to his mouth and flashed his badge. Delaney managed to move to the very back of the bus without anyone noticing. "In one minute," Mendelson mouthed as he looked at Delaney, "open the emergency exit and stand clear. One minute," Mendelson said, holding up one finger and pointing to his watch.

"Okay. One minute," Delaney mouthed back to Mendelson.

With all attention focused on the front of the bus, Delaney moved to the emergency exit. How Thornton and his pals did not see the red "Emergency" writing on the window astounded him. If they had they would have been long gone. Instead, two cops were about to board the bus. Delaney was worried about the safety of the other passengers but decided that as soon as the cops got through the window he would climb out. *Let someone else be the hero*, he thought.

He looked as the second hand of his watch slowly moved. Twenty-five seconds had passed. Bellamy and Mendelson silently walked to the emergency exit. They drew their guns when they got there.

Exactly after a minute, Delaney quietly lifted the handle of the emergency exit, stepped back and pushed the window out.

Mendelson climbed in first. Bellamy followed. Their guns were drawn. "Everybody get down. Get down," they yelled. Screaming filled the air as the passengers looked towards the back of the bus and saw the two-armed officers.

Delaney grabbed Fuller by the arm and pushed him down in a seat. He put his hand over Fuller's mouth. "Not a sound Robert, not a sound."

Fuller nodded.

"Does Thornton or the two others have a gun?"

"No. We didn't even know Thornton had a knife," Fuller whispered.

"Stay down."

"Officers," Delaney yelled. "There's no gun. Just the one knife. The big fellow has it."

Mendelson and Bellamy slowly made their way to the front of the bus.

Just then Hirsch leaped onto the top of the bus's bonnet. Winterbottom handed him his camera and he starting filming.

"Put that fucking camera down," Thornton yelled.

Hirsch kept shooting.

The passengers were all safely behind Mendelson and Bellamy. Delaney tapped all of them on the shoulder and whispered "follow me."

Every passenger, except one, elderly pensioner Sadie Bernbaum, escaped out the window. Ninety-year-old Bernbaum refused to leave her groceries behind. She cradled them like a mother nestling a newborn.

The last two to escape through the window were Fuller and Delaney.

On Delaney's urging all the passengers gathered behind the bus until the all clear was given.

"Well, if I wasn't fucked before I am now," Fuller told Delaney.

"Join the club," Delaney responded.

"What do you mean?"

"I'll tell you when this nightmare is over. In the meantime, let me think of a way to keep you out of this."

"Thornton," Mendelson called out. "Get down, now. And you two as well," Mendelson barked, looking at Weller and Hearns. "All of you get down on the floor now."

With Bellamy and Mendelson's guns trained on them, Thornton, Weller and Hearns got down and stretched out on their stomachs. "Hands up over your heads," Mendelson hollered.

Mendelson put his weapon in its holster and handcuffed Thornton. Mendelson reached into his front left pocket, pulled out the switchblade and opened it. The blade was about eight inches long. Bellamy tossed his partner two more pairs of cuffs and he slapped them on Weller and Hearns. Bellamy used his radio to call for a divvy van and back-up. The area would soon be swarming with detectives.

"Was anyone else with you Thornton?"

"No," he answered.

"Just you three?"

"Yeah but these two had nothing to do with it. You should let them go."

"Not until we question the witnesses, and that includes the bus driver who is still wiping the shit from his pants."

"I didn't do a thing to him."

"That's not what he says."

"You'll get nothing more out of me. I'm done talking."

"Suit yourself."

Hirsch got everything on tape but wanted more. He reached under the driver's side of the bus and pushed a hidden lever. The front doors of the bus swung open "I've seen drivers do that when they go get a coffee or take a leak," he told Winterbottom.

Holding her microphone which had a large number 12 in red stamped on it, Winterbottom climbed the few steps to the bus and was ushered right back out by Bellamy. "You should know better Tegan. It's a crime scene in there. After we question the passengers you can have a talk with them. But for now, you and pretty boy keep back."

Four squad cars with their lights blazing soon appeared and pulled off the road. One officer laid witches' hats around the bus which effectively blocked a lane of northbound traffic.

By this time traffic in each direction had slowed to 10kph as people slowed to have a look at what was going on. Detectives and uniformed officers marched Thornton, Hearns and Weller off the bus and placed them into a divvy van.

"Do you have anything to say?" Winterbottom asked Thornton.

"Yeah. You are much cuter in person."

Not wanting to be recognised, Weller and Hearns kept their heads down.

Bellamy and Mendelson did a sweep of the bus, looking for weapons and evidence.

All they found was Sadie Bernbaum tucked down in her seat.

"Why didn't you get off the bus with the others?" Bellamy asked.

"And leave my groceries? I'm on a fixed income," she said.

42

AS THE ESCAPED PASSENGERS MILLED BEHIND THE BUS, Delaney put his hands on Fuller's shoulders and looked him right in the eye.

"The way I see it is you have once chance," Delaney told him. "You need to get the hell out of here, now. I won't say a word. If they ask I'll just tell them that someone took off. It's not my job to chase down crooks. One more thing Robert. This is strike two. One more and I or anyone else won't be able to step in and help you out." Fuller looked at Delaney, mouthed the words 'thank you', walked into the clearing by the side of the road, looked out from behind a few trees to make sure that no one was following him and started running towards a nearby housing development. He stopped only when he could no longer stand upright. Ten minutes later he got back to his feet and continued running. When he got to within a kilometre or two of his North Cairns home, he slowed to a walk. He stopped by a drinking fountain and drank the warmish water until he couldn't down another drop.

Bellamy and Mendelson went to the back of the bus where Delaney and the other passengers were waiting quietly. Two elderly gentlemen had taken seats on the splintered bench at the bus shelter to get out of the sun.

"There'll be another bus coming by shortly to take you folks where you need to go. We'll give you back your personal belongings in a few minutes," Bellamy said. "We're going to take down all your details and in the next couple of days ask you to come in and give statements. Is that okay with everyone?"

The passengers all nodded their heads.

"Nick Bellamy," the detective said formerly introducing himself to Delaney.

The two shook hands.

"Thanks for the help earlier. If it wasn't for you this could have ended up a lot worse."

"Gary Delaney. Don't mention it. Happy to help out. I'm just glad this all ended peacefully and nobody was hurt."

"Where were you headed?"

"Palm Cove."

"Is that home?"

"No. I live in Holloways. I was just getting away for the day."

"I'll take you there. You can tell me what happened along the way, okay?"

Delaney agreed but told himself he would not mention Robert Fuller's name unless Bellamy brought it up first.

Fuller's name did not come up.

After being heavily promoted all afternoon, Winterbottom's exclusive report ran at the top of Channel 12's 6pm news that night. Two other news crews arrived at the scene well after Thornton, Weller, Hearns and the passengers had been taken away. They had to be content with shots of the empty bus. Hirsch had the money shots. Winterbottom had also gotten the name of the bus driver from Bellamy, but a very embarrassed Alex McGuiness slammed his front door on Winterbottom and Hirsch 90 minutes before she reported live from the scene of the crime.

"We'll come back in the morning, see if we can get a shot of him leaving the house," Winterbottom told Hirsch.

Snappily dressed presenter Ron Snyder stood in front of the Channel 12 news desk holding a mini iPad – the latest directive from the suits in Sydney for big, breaking stories – and adjusted his bright red tie as a stage manager counted down the seconds until he went live.

"Three young men have been arrested and are being held without bond after allegedly holding a busload of passengers hostage this afternoon on Captain Cook Highway," he told tens of thousands of viewers. "We switch live to Tegan Winterbottom at the scene. Tegan, what exactly happened out there?"

Winterbottom stood in the stairwell of the bus. Her right hand held her earpiece in place while she peered into Hirsch's camera.

"More than a dozen passengers received the fright of their lives late this morning Ron when three teenagers held them hostage on this very bus on the Captain Cook Highway. The incident is thought to have begun when an argument broke out over the payment of a fare. The driver is said to have fled from the bus when a knife was allegedly waved in his face. Channel 12 news understands that a male passenger helped police enter the bus from an emergency exit. Our cameraman Henry Hirsch caught the exact moment when the three thugs were surprised by two armed police officers and arrested."

In the station's control room, Ryan Nolan, the newscast's director for the last 12 years, gave a hand signal to his assistant who rolled the footage. Hirsch's pictures through the front window of the bus won him a Walkley Award later in the year. Producer Sid Kerkfeld earlier told Nolan to leave in the bit where a handcuffed Thornton told Winterbottom that she was cute. "It's just too good to leave out."

"And back to Tegan," Nolan yelled after Thornton's remark aired.

"Police reportedly recovered a large knife used by one of the attackers. After being interviewed by police, the passengers were put aboard another bus, provided by Cairns Links, operator of the area's bus services, which took the passengers to their destinations."

"Roll tape," Nolan barked.

"How do you feel after your harrowing ordeal?" Winterbottom asked passenger Sadie Bernbaum. "It was all very exciting, but my dinner is worthless," the barely five-foot 90-year-old said as she held a TV dinner to the camera. Gravy from the once frozen roast beef and vegetable meal was leaking from its saturated carton. "Somebody owes me a dinner damn it. I'm on a fixed income."

"And back to Tegan," Nolan said.

"I've been told that just a few minutes before we went on the air, Cairns Links delivered a full roast beef dinner – and dessert – to Mrs Bernbaum's home."

"I can't eat all of this by myself. I'll get sick," she told Cairns Links head of operations Ramon Baker, who brought along a company photographer to document what should have been a touching moment. "Are you guys trying to kill me?"

"No, no Mrs Bernbaum," Baker said. "We can stay and have dinner with you if you like."

"Stay? I'm not having strange men in my apartment," she said, covering herself up with her favourite sweater. "What will the neighbours say?"

"We'll get going then," Baker said taking a step towards the front door. "Enjoy your dinner Mrs Bernbaum. Oh, I almost forgot. Here is a lifetime pass for you. A gift from Cairns Links."

Mrs Bernbaum looked at the pass for a moment, which was on a colourful lanyard, and then draped it over her neck. It hung down past her waist and nearly touched her knees. "Thank you," she said.

"You're very welcome," Baker replied. Bernie Bunning snapped a few shots before they left. They were earmarked for the company's monthly magazine.

"What's this?" they heard Mrs Bernbaum say after they closed her front door. "Pumpkin pie? I hate pumpkin. Bloody arseholes."

Baker laughed. "What a character, what a character."

"A nice ending to what was a horrific day," Snyder added when Nolan cut back to the studio. "Thank you, Tegan. Also making news in Far North Queensland tonight ..."

"Horrific?" Nolan said shaking his head. "It wasn't 9-11. Where did we find this arsehole again? Oh yeah, the station owner's nephew."

"Fuck she is good," Dixie Moore told Anna Nimmity as they watched the broadcast in the newsroom. "She's got all the contacts too. And what did I cover today? Someone's 100th birthday. It won't even air until the weekend, if she lives that long."

"She won't be here too much longer," Anna whispered to Dixie.

"What do you mean?" Moore asked.

"Johnny made a couple of phone calls for me."

"Pastrami? Your boyfriend in Melbourne?"

"That's him. Tegan is going to be taking a job in Brisbane which leaves a spot for you – and me – when I'm not doing the weather. Hot and sunny with the chance of a shower, hot and sunny with the chance of a shower. That's all I fucking say. I'm like a fucking parrot."

"That's fantastic," Dixie told her colleague and roommate. She gave her a huge hug. "Johnny sure looks after you."

Too be honest Pastrami was looking after himself. Now that he was dating a dark-haired stunner named Jenny Hunt, he didn't want Anna around to cause trouble.

"She could be the one Fingers," Johnny told his mate Frankie Tannenbaum over the phone the day after Jenny spent the night at his place for the first time.

"And get this, she's a prosecutor for the Victorian Attorney General's office."

Fingers laughed. "You're joking."

"Nope. And she is so bloody smart. If she was ever on that *Chase Australia* show she'd wind up owning the network. I'm spending more time reading *The New York Times* than I am doing form. Not that I need to place another bet with all I won on Sun-Up."

"I'm happy for you mate. Bring her up here to Airlie Beach the next long weekend. Jacquie and I would love to meet her.

"And Johnny, I've got news too. Jacquie is pregnant."

"Holy shit. You finally put one past the goalie. Congratulations mate. How far along is she?"

"Three months. And, get this. We're going to get married too."

"No? Really?"

"Yup. It's all happening. Meeting Jacquie was the best thing that ever happened to me. If you hadn't put me on that Melbourne Cup winner, I never would have had the cash to move up here, get a house, settle down."

"It took the two of us to pull off that coup Frankie. Just one thing mate, when it comes time to choose the wedding invitations, don't skimp. Pick something from the front of the book."

Tannenbaum laughed. "I can't believe it. I'm going to be a dad."

"And a damn good one mate, a damn good one. Pass along my congratulations to Jacquie."

Pastrami said goodbye to Frankie, hung up and placed his phone on his kitchen table. The scent of Jenny's perfume hung in the air while he washed the dishes and coffee cups from breakfast.

Good for Frankie. He deserves a girl like Jacquie.

Johnny flicked on his iPad and Googled Electoral College.

Jenny had been talking about it over dinner last night at a swank Southbank restaurant and Johnny had just nodded and went along with everything she said.

"It is antiquated," he said not knowing what the hell he was talking about.

"What a dumb fucking system the Americans have," he said as he read about the Electoral College. "You can win the popular vote and lose an election? It's first past the post. Always."

He then logged onto the websites of *The New York Times* and the *Sydney Morning Herald*.

"I'm in Jenny's league financially and looks wise, but if this gets serious, I'm going to have to know my shit, and, keep Anna at a distance.

At present, that distance was nearly 3000 kilometres. Just as Johnny planned, Anna got more airtime on Ch.12 once Winterbottom departed and she was so happy with being on television five or six times a week that her texts and phone calls started dwindling from a couple a day to a couple a week.

When Anna hooked up with "Handsome" Harry Hirsch, she dumped Pastrami by text. "Best text message I've ever gotten," he told Frankie.

Also watching Channel 12's 6pm bulletin on the day of the bus drama was Barbara Stevenson. Straight away she noticed Delaney in the pack of passengers as Hirsch's camera swung across them.

"Leave it to him to get mixed up in something like this."

As the camera panned the group of passengers, Stevenson noticed that Delaney was the only middle-aged man among them. "The others wouldn't have been able to lift their arms over their heads let alone open an emergency exit. If took a lot of guts to do what Gary did. Maybe I'll ask him about it in a few days."

Delaney made sure to tell Bellamy on their drive to Palm Cove that since he was seated near the back of the bus he hadn't seen or heard much of the commotion which led to Thornton producing the knife and McGuinness fleeing the bus with the keys.

"If we need you to come in for questioning, I'll be in contact with you. Thanks again for your help," Bellamy said as he pulled into a parking space. The two shook hands when Delaney exited Bellamy's unmarked car near the Palm Cove pier.

Delaney walked along Palm Cove's main drag. Its many cafes were buzzing. Remembering that he had to keep a lid on what he spent, he bypassed many of the expensive eateries which had their fancy menus posted outside. "Twenty-two dollars for a bloody chicken sandwich? That's insane," he said out loud.

Delaney walked about another hundred metres until he found a regular family takeaway place and ordered a roast beef roll. The cost for it and a can of Diet Coke was $9.

Delaney crossed the street and found a shady spot on the beach. He unwrapped his lunch and took a bite. "This isn't half-bad. In fact, it's damn good."

He devoured it, wiped his gravy stained hands with a napkin he found in the bottom of the bag and stretched out on the warm sand. He adjusted his hat until it blocked out much of the afternoon light and closed his eyes.

Well, that was an interesting morning, he thought. *That Fuller lad better find himself a better crowd to pal around with. Come to think of it so should I. Look what hanging out with Judy did to me. She was playing me right from the start and I was too blind to see it. Wouldn't be the first time a man succumbed to the charms of a gorgeous woman. Damn. It has cost me a fucking bundle though, a fucking bundle.*

Delaney closed his eyes and was awakened nearly two hours later when a beach ball being kicked around by a couple of kids landed square on his chest.

He looked up and saw a kid about nine years old dressed in blue board shorts that came down past his knees staring down at him.

"Sorry mate, didn't mean to bother you," he said.

Delaney checked his watch. It was after 4pm.

"It's okay son. I'm glad you did. It was time to get up."

Delaney tossed the ball back to the lad, dusted the sand off his shirt and shorts, picked up the paper bag and empty can from lunch and tossed it in the nearest waste bin. He walked back towards the pier and the bus stop. A small group of tourists were waiting. Delaney checked the bus schedule tacked onto a pole and glanced at his watch. There was six minutes till the next bus back to Cairns.

43

AFTER BEING QUESTIONED BY DETECTIVES, BIG JOHN Thornton was charged with theft of services, weapon possession and intimidation. After a lengthy deliberation with prosecutors and Thornton's court-appointed attorney, Judge Clarence Eagleton decided to release Thornton on $10,000 bond and urged both sides to work out a plea bargain arrangement to avoid a trial. Eagleton knew of Thornton's troubles through his son William, who was manager of the FNQHS rugby league team when Thornton suffered his career-ending hip injury. He remembered how distressed William was afterwards. "I hope I never see anything like that again Dad. It's six hours later and I can still hear him screaming."

Judge Eagleton was also aware of Thornton's addiction to pills and alcohol, and according to police, who had interviewed him at length, hadn't touched either or gotten into any sort of trouble until his injury.

"Sending him to jail would be of no help to anyone and could make things even worse. Let him serve a couple of hundred hours doing community service. Maybe with that and some counselling he can get his life back together," Eagleton told prosecutors.

After several lengthy discussions – head prosecutor Tina Radansky had her doubts – the two sides agreed to abide by Eagleton's request. Four weeks later, wearing a shirt and tie, a contrite Thornton appeared in Eagleton's courtroom.

"Ordinarily son, with charges this severe, I would commit you to stand trial. We preferred seeing you on the back pages of the newspaper rather than the front and I for one have sympathy what you have gone through with your unfortunate injury. I believe in second chances and hereby sentence you to 300 hours of community service and weekly therapy with a counsellor of the court's choosing. Failure to comply with the plea-bargain agreement will result in its termination and the revoking of your bond. Do you understand Mr Thornton?"

"Yes sir I do," Thornton said.

Eagleton closed the folder in front of him, put it in a growing pile to his right and called for the next case. Thornton was quickly ushered out of the courtroom by Carl Stanton – his court-appointed attorney. "Thank you for keeping me out of jail," Thornton said shaking his hand.

Stanton set his battered briefcase down on a table in the wide corridor and opened it. "You're welcome. Now if you'll excuse me, I have another case before the judge in a few minutes."

Thornton walked out of the courthouse leaving Stanton to review the paperwork on a 19-year-old driver who blew a 0.75 two days after she got off her P Plates. *This one won't be as easy*, he thought. He scanned the busy corridor but could not find Louise Denton, who he had met just once. *I hope she's not having a few cold ones before her appearance.*

After many hours of questioning, Hearns and Weller were not charged over the incident on the bus and were released. "If I was in either one of your shoes, I'd get my arse back to school or find some employment mighty quick," Nick Bellamy told the pair.

Hearns and Weller took Bellamy's advice. Hearns enrolled in a nearby TAFE and took classes to become a mechanic while Weller got a job at Woolies stocking shelves. "Why does it have to be so fucking cold in here? I can't stand it," Weller told Vern Watson, his supervisor of three hours.

"You're cold? Awww. I'm sorry. Why didn't you say so sooner? I'll turn the heat on for ya," Watson sarcastically told the newest member of his team. Watson was well protected from the chill by 40 kilos of excess blubber and would have worked shirtless if the choice was his. The buttons on his extra-large green-coloured Woolies shirt were in eminent danger of popping due to his girth. He had no sympathy for a beanpole like Weller.

"You have two options," Watson told Weller. "You can either wear a shirt under your Woolies shirt with a matching pair of mittens and scarf or get the heck off my team. Now open all these damn boxes and start stocking the damn shelves for goodness sake."

Weller felt like sticking a two-litre bottle of Coke up Watson's arse – he was sure it would fit – but had to do as he was told. His old man had gotten wind of his part in the bus debacle and threatened to toss him on the street unless he found a job within a week. "I'll wear another shirt tomorrow, but where the hell am I going to get some gloves in Cairns?" he wondered as he filled shelf after shelf with bottles of Coke, Diet Coke, Coke Zero, Coke Vanilla, Coke Orange, Caffeine Free Diet Coke, Pepsi Free and Pepsi Max. "Hey mate," Rudy Orr said in a near whisper to Weller after Watson went into the storeroom to bring out more pallets of soft drinks. Orr, a first-year student at James Cook University, should have been studying for finals, but instead was down at the end of the same aisle restocking near-empty shelves of bottled water. He held up his glove-covered hands. "I got these in the gardening aisle. They help." With his bank balance hovering near zero, Orr was forced to study during the day and work at night.

Weller nodded his head and gave Orr the thumbs-up sign.

On his next break Weller went to the deserted gardening aisle and took a $3 pair of one-size-fits-all gloves off the shelf. He walked to the do-it-yourself checkout machine at the front of the store, scanned the gloves and dropped three one-dollar coins into it. He bought the thinner ones, figuring they would be better for grasping boxes and bottles and they were. His shift finished at 2am and he was happier than a lifeguard at a nude beach when he strode out into the balmy 26-degree evening. The cheap gloves were stuffed into the back pocket of his jeans.

A few nights later Weller was filling the ice cream freezers with his near numb hands when he overheard a conversation between a couple of locals. Their polo shirts had a catamaran pictured on the front and back along with the words "To the Reef and Back, $109 passingwind.com.au."

"Guys can't quit without giving notice," the taller of the two said as he scooped two cartons of ice cream from the freezer. We'll have to bust our arses for the next few days until the boss finds a replacement for that arsehole. And I hear we are booked solid tomorrow."

Early the next morning Weller went down to the marina and the offices of *Passing Wind* and enquired about a deckhand job. A gal at the ticket desk about his age told him to take a seat and the next thing he knew he was being interviewed by Charlie Wilson, *Passing Wind*'s captain.

"I had a bloke quit on me yesterday. It's your lucky day if you know anything about diving and snorkelling." Like many kids who had grown up in Cairns, Weller had spent hours scuba diving and snorkelling on the reef.

"I've been diving since I was about 10 and know my way around a boat too," Weller told Wilson who was seated behind an old desk.

"You're not going to quit on me in a month or two if I take you on, are you? We can't afford to train someone for a week and then have them walk."

"I give you my word Captain Wilson. Hire me and I'll be here every morning for the next year."

Wilson took a quick look at the application Weller had filled in earlier and nodded his head. He liked the fact that Weller had put on a pair of pants and shirt and not walked in wearing flip flops, shorts and a T-shirt.

"You have any referees?"

"Not really. I just started working at Woolies 10 days ago," Weller answered. "My boss was giving me a hard time. Vern Watson is his name."

"You had to work for that arsehole?"

"You know him?"

"Went to school with the bloke. I wouldn't hire him to sweep the floors here."

"It would be great to give him my notice at the end of my shift tonight."

"What time do you finish?"

"2am."

Wilson glanced at his watch. It read 8:10.

"You finished work just six hours ago and you came here looking for work?"

"Yup."

"If you want the job Weller it is yours. Can you be here at 7am tomorrow to start training?"

"I can."

"Tell Vern at the start of your shift. He'll get so pissed he'll tell you to take a hike then and there. That way you can get a good night's sleep before you start."

"I'll do that."

Wilson got up from his chair and shook Weller's hand.

"Good to have you join the team. I've got to get going Weller. We sail at 9am and are short-handed today. Amy at the desk will give you some paperwork and an operational booklet. I've got to get on board."

Weller followed Wilson at the door.

"Amy," he hollered. "Fix our newest employee up, will you?"

"Great day for a trip to the reef," Wilson said to no one in particular. He put his captain's hat on, walked outside and down the pier where *Passing Wind* was docked and being fuelled up.

As Wilson suggested, Weller told Watson at the start of his shift that it would be his last.

"Oh no it ain't," Watson said." Your last shift was last night. Get the fuck out of my sight."

Weller did just as he was asked. He stopped at the front of the store to hand in his work shirt and left. From then on, he vowed only to shop at Coles.

After a week of paid training, which included having to pass scuba diving and lifesaving tests, Weller joined the team of *Passing Wind* as a deckhand.

Passing Wind was one of the many catamarans which ferried tourists out to the Great Barrier Reef. Most boats docked at two reefs during the day, some three.

Weller helped dispense wetsuits, scuba and snorkelling gear when *Passing Wind* arrived at the first of the two reefs it visited each day.

He helped serve lunch in between and was in charge of putting the gear away at the end of the afternoon. He helped numerous passengers who were having a go at scuba diving and snorkelling for the first time. Many were bikini-clad young women who often spoke limited English. They flirted with him, Weller flirted back and more often than not he found himself spending the night with one of them at a crowded backpackers hostel in town. Weller could not believe his luck. "How many nights did I lay awake dreaming of something like this? This is unbelievable."

When there was more than one invitation, and many afternoons there was, Weller spent his evenings with cashed-up Asian girls who threw Australian notes around like they were confetti. There was plenty of food, the booze flowed freely and later, in the dorms, the girls, many wearing just their bras and panties, willingly posed for photos. Weller took a photo of every woman he slept with and kept them in a special folder on his laptop. The girls took photos of him – he made sure he was always wearing at least a pair of shorts – and immediately posted them on Facebook and Instagram.

The only downside was the massive hangovers he had to deal with the next morning. Weller quickly learned to cut down on the booze since he had to be back at the marina no later than eight the next morning. His phone alarm pinged at 7:15 and after a quick trip to the bathroom he gathered his clothes and quietly left the dorm rooms before any of the girls woke.

He occasionally caught up with Hearns and bragged about all the girls he was shagging. "Have any photos?" Hearns asked the first time Weller brought it up. "Take a look," Weller said, handing him his phone. "Jesus," Hearns said as he flipped through them. "They're all gorgeous. I'm in a garage and classroom all day and here you are banging starlets. I'm a little jealous."

"Tell you what. Next time I have two lovelies at my side I'll give you a ring," Weller said.

Weller and Hearns avoided any contact with Big John Thornton, who was spending his days doing community service work with Cairns Council's Community, Sport and Cultural Services Department. Weller saw Thornton early one morning on his way to the Marina. Thornton was cleaning the lagoon pool, sweeping a long pole across the surface, snaring any leaves and debris in the pole's net and dumping it in a clear trash bag by his feet. Thornton sensed someone was looking at him and lifted his head. Weller waved his baseball cap and Thornton waved back, a wave which acknowledged their past and left little doubt about their future. They had grown up and moved on.

After his 300 hours of community service were up, Thornton was offered a full-time job with the small team which looked after the department's many sports grounds and facilities. Thornton's tasks included the watering and marking of rugby league and AFL grounds and cleaning up after games and events. The pay was good, the job was for the long term if he wanted it and not once did the blokes he worked with ever mention his past. His trophies, medals and newspaper clippings – both good and bad – were stuffed inside two cardboard boxes and tucked away in the bedroom closet of his one-room flat in North Cairns. His one vice was the six pack of beer he guzzled down every Friday night while he watched the NRL game on Channel 9. If I hadn't wrecked my hip that would be me up there, he thought.

He was right.

After the fiasco on the bus, Robert Fuller steered well clear of Thornton, Hearns and Weller. Working at the Salvos wasn't all that bad but once his two months were up, he said his goodbyes and never returned. He spent his afternoons studying and his nights thinking about Amy McNamara of Gene's Sporting Goods.

After replaying the conversation he had with Amy dozens of times prior to running out of Gene's with the jersey for Thornton, and exchanging very brief hellos with her twice at school, Fuller found the courage to go to the mall late one Saturday afternoon and wait for her to finish her shift.

She was closing the shop and reaching for the rolling shutter door to pull down and lock when Fuller reached up and grabbed it for her.

"Come back to the scene of the crime, eh?" she asked with a hint of a smile.

Easy now, don't blow this, Fuller told himself.

"Taking that jersey was just a prank. I came back and paid for it, but you weren't here. Ask your boss, he'll tell you," Fuller said.

She looked at him for a long time, wondering whether to believe him.

"Look, I don't hang around with those guys anymore. I'm studying and put in an application to work at Coles."

"The Coles here in the mall?"

"That's the one."

"I don't suppose you have a car, do you?"

"Not yet, but as soon as I start to put some money away ..."

Fuller was half-expecting Amy to say something like, 'well once you get a car maybe you can take me home'.

Instead, she looped her arm inside his and said, "How about walking me to the bus stop? Unless you have somewhere you need to be."

"Just home."

"Which is where?"

"North Cairns. It's not too far."

"Where's home for you Amy?"

"Earlville. Too far to walk. My dad usually picks me up but he's working tonight, so I'm taking the bus."

Who works on a Saturday night? Fuller thought.

"What does your dad do if you don't mind me asking?"

"He's a detective with the Cairns PD."

Oh shit. If her dad is Nick Bellamy and she tells him about me I could get a six-figure job with Facebook and she'd still never come near me again.

Fuller was tempted to ask but came to his senses. *I'll cross that bridge when we come to it, if we ever get there.*

44

GARY DELANEY WAS TOO EMBARRASSED TO TELL ANYONE about his misfortune. He stayed away from Saltwater Lakes and his golfing buddies and didn't even set foot on the complex's putting green. He spent days moping around his unit, not shaving and ordering in pizzas and Chinese food. He didn't bother checking the form guide, and just glanced at the emails from City Winners Syndication informing him that Too Hard Wrong Spot was enjoying his time in the paddock and would begin his spring campaign in Melbourne with the goal of running in his third straight Melbourne Cup. "We're going to win it this year," Big John McGraw wrote. "The horse has never been better."

Delaney's latest bank statements and pension fund papers from Far North Queensland Financial Services were fanned across his dining table. Geoff Duckworth from the Salvos rang several times asking if he was available to do his usual shifts, but Delaney's heart wasn't in it. He told Duckworth he had the flu and would get back to him when he felt better.

The only time Delaney stepped outside was to collect the *Cairns Examiner* which was left outside his door early each morning. He scanned each edition from front to back and then again from back to front looking for news of Judy Seymour. He checked the missing person notices, the obituaries, every news story but there was nothing. He went online and Googled her name and then the name of Far North Queensland Financial Services only once again to come up empty.

"I was duped. Pure and simple. There's no getting around it," he moaned after his latest failed search.

Late one afternoon he drove over to Seymour's house to see if anything was in her post box. Perhaps there'd be a clue. He had left Melbourne 16 months earlier but was still getting mail delivered to his former address down south even though he had his mail redirected and left his new address with everyone he had dealings with. The couple which moved into his flat just two weeks after he left had asked a neighbour if they had Delaney's new address and once a month the Steins sent him an envelope with his mail. After the first one arrived Delaney sent a parcel with a dozen self-addressed stamped envelopes to the Steins thanking them and asking them to put any mail in them and send them off to spare them the cost. He was always a bit startled when he opened the post box and found an envelope addressed to himself with his handwriting on it.

When Delaney rocked up to 13 McKenzie St he was surprised to find a removalist's truck in the driveway. He checked the post box when the movers were inside and found nothing except a couple of spiders. He slammed the lid shut and walked up the driveway.

"Excuse me mate," he said to a young bearded removalist whose shirt and shorts were covered in sweat. "I live down the street and am curious. Someone moving in or out?" Roderick Holmes wiped his forehead with a rag from his back pocket, opened the passenger side of the cab and removed a bottle of water from a cooler. Whatever ice was in it had melted but the water was still cold.

"They're moving in. An Asian couple is what I hear. They've got a shitload of stuff which was shipped over from China. They're expected in this weekend."

"China? No kidding. Hope you don't mind me prying, but did your company move the people who used to live here?"

"Nope. This area is my territory and I would have known about it,"

Holmes answered. "Now if you don't mind, I've got to get this truck emptied."

"Sorry to keep you. Thanks for your help."

"Meeting the neighbours Rod?" a voice coming from the garage asked.

"This fellow is wondering whose moving in. It's an Asian couple, right?"

"It is," Tom Rowland confirmed. Rowland was in charge and walked to the back of the truck. He hopped in, stacked several, well-sealed boxers on the hydraulic lift and pressed a button to send it to street level where Holmes slid a hand cart underneath the load, balanced it and wheeled it inside.

"You wouldn't know which company moved the previous owners out, would you?" Delaney asked Rowland. "I haven't a clue mate, haven't a clue."

Delaney thanked Rowland for his time and slowly walked down the driveway to his Honda parked on the street. He had another look at the house, got in, started the car up, did a U-turn and began to head home. "Might as well go to Woolies and get some shopping done and also go to the ATM and make sure that savings account of mine hasn't been touched."

Delaney parked and quickly walked to his bank branch's ATM. He tapped his card, punched in his four-digit password, withdrew $100 and waited for his cash and receipt. He pocketed the two $50 dollar notes and then gingerly removed his receipt. He took a deep breath, closed his eyes for a moment and took a peek at his balance: $36,812.50. *Thank goodness. It's all there. If I had given Judy my statement she would have cleaned out this account too*, he thought. Delaney tucked the receipt in his shirt pocket and stepped away from the ATM. He turned to the young couple waiting and apologised for taking so long.

"That's alright mate. Have a good night."

"You too."

Fresh bread and milk were at the top of Delaney's shopping list along with coffee, fruit and meat for the barbecue downstairs. *Might as well return to the land of the living*, Delaney said to himself as he waited in line at a register with a trolley full of supplies.

It took Delaney two trips to bring his groceries up the stairs to his unit. It was nearly 6pm by the time he unpacked everything. He took a bottle of beer from the fridge and sat down on his balcony.

After 10 minutes in the freezer the beer was just cold enough to enjoy. He looked at the barbecue area, saw that it was empty, got up, quickly made two burgers from the package of mince he bought and peeled an onion. "I can get down there, cook these up and hopefully not run into anybody," Delaney said. "I'll shave and shower tomorrow morning and get on with things. There's not much else I can do."

While Delaney was cooking his burgers and onions and finishing the rest of his beer, he realised he had one hope left in his bid to locate Judy Seymour and his missing money. That hope was Detective Nick Bellamy. *I figure he owes me one. I'll go down there tomorrow and speak with him. Maybe he can put out a few feelers and find out what happened.*

The smell of the burgers and onions on the barbie wafted up and through the screen door of Barbara Stevenson's unit. Curious to see who was barbecuing, she got up from her plate of stir-fry – she always made enough for two nights – pulled the curtains back and saw Delaney cleaning the grill. She hadn't seen him in a week. *Maybe he's been sick or staying with that woman. At least he's okay. My stir-fry would be better for him than those burgers but ...*

Stevenson's anger had eased a bit but not enough for her to ring him or knock on his door. Delaney did not have the courage to face her. At least not yet.

Delaney rose early the next morning and tossed a load of clothes from his overflowing laundry hamper into the small washing machine adjacent to his bathroom. In the hour it took to finish, Delaney shaved, showered, scarfed down breakfast and glanced through the *Cairns Examiner*.

When the machine started beeping, he quickly emptied it, set up the small airer on the balcony and hung his washing out to dry. The morning breeze and warming temperature had everything dry by the time he returned from the cop shop.

Delaney didn't have to wait long to see the detective, who greeted him with a strong handshake and a couple of taps on the shoulder.

"Good to see you again Gary. Staying off buses?"

"As a matter of fact, I haven't been on one since I saw you last."

"What can I do for you today?" Bellamy asked as he led him into his office. "You're not in any sort of trouble, are you?"

At Bellamy's urging Delaney sat down in one of two chairs facing the detective's desk while Bellamy got comfortable in his high-backed leather seat.

"I am but I'm afraid it's my own fault," Delaney said as he shook his head from side to side.

Bellamy put his reading glasses on his desk and leaned back in his chair.

"Start from the beginning and don't leave anything out."

For the next 15 minutes Delaney filled him in on his relationship with Judy Seymour, her disappearance and the loss of his superannuation and pension money invested with Far North Queensland Financial Services.

"I'm sorry Gary. That's a lot of money. People get taken more often than you think. This woman really thought things out."

"Can anything be done to find her?"

"People don't just disappear Gary and eventually they slip up. You said she told you she was originally from Sydney?"

"Yes, she and her late husband."

Bellamy picked up his glasses, turned to a fresh page on a yellow legal pad and started taking notes.

"Did she ever go on holiday and tell you where? People become very set in their ways as they get older. I don't think a woman in her mid-fifties is going to be flying off to Rio."

Delaney racked his brain for a moment and remembered a trip to the Sunshine Coast she and her husband took the year before he died. "She went to the Sunshine Coast, or maybe it was the Gold Coast."

"That's a start. What I'll do is get in touch with detectives on the Sunshine and Gold Coasts and in Sydney and fill them in. You might not be the only person looking for her."

"I never thought there could be others," Delaney said.

"Do you have a photo of her Gary? If she's smart she has probably changed her appearance, but it would help."

Delaney removed his phone from his pants pocket and found several photos of Judy. He handed the phone to Bellamy.

"She's quite a looker Gary. She would have been hard to resist."

"Yeah. If only I had thought with my head and not my pecker."

Bellamy chuckled. "Email those pics to me will you?"

Delaney went to his Gmail account, opened a new email and attached two photos of Judy.

"What's the email addy?"

"Nick.Bellamy@Cairnspd."

Ten seconds later Delaney's email landed on Bellamy's desktop. Bellamy opened it to make sure everything was in order and stood up from his chair.

"We'll do what we can Gary. I can't make any promises, but we'll give it a shot. I'll get in touch when I have some news."

Delaney stood up, shook Bellamy's hand and thanked him. "You're not going to the press with this, are you?" he asked.

"No Gary. Only if we make an arrest. And if we do, we'll keep your name out of it if that is what you want."

"I do. I don't want to see my name in the papers or my face on the telly."

"I understand Gary. You take care. I'll be in touch."

Delaney walked out of the Cairns PD building with a glimmer of hope which was more than he had before he walked in.

Later in the afternoon Delaney rang Duckworth at the Salvos and said he was feeling better and was available to do a shift or two.

Delaney worked a few more shifts in the coming days and found that the work was a lifesaver. It took his mind off Judy Seymour which is just what he needed.

After a couple of weeks, he caught up with a few mates at Saltwater Lakes. "I had a case of the flu I couldn't get rid of," he told them. "It sure felt good being out on the course again even if it was just nine holes."

Warren Mulligan, the retired city planner from New South Wales, kept everyone at the table entertained with a yarn his social-worker sister-in-law told him a few years ago.

"True story. One of her co-workers, aww shit I forget her name now, I'll call Pamela, gets a call at home one night from a client of hers. It's from a near-hysterical mother with a young child.

"'My ex-husband just called. He's been drinking and said he was coming over to kill me and take our baby,' she cried. 'I have a restraining order but don't know what to do. Where are we going to go?'

"Pamela got the woman to calm down and advised her to call triple zero immediately. But just in case she didn't, she asked for her address instead of opening her laptop and finding her case. 'Yes I have it, 1222 Coast Road,' Pamela said as she wrote the address down. Coast Rd was in one of Cairns's poorer suburbs, which saw more than its share of domestic violence.

"Pamela rang triple zero and gave the dispatcher the details. 'He's probably bluffing,' the dispatcher said. 'They rarely go through with it.' She sounded bored by it all. 'And if he isn't?' Pamela asked. 'Are you going to send an officer over there or not?'

"'It's not a high priority, we have several medical emergencies we're attending to at the moment.'

"'If someone isn't sent to this woman's home immediately, she'll become one of your medical emergencies. You want that on your conscience?'

"'Mam, in my experience ...'

"Pamela interrupted her. 'Do you know the mayor?' she hollered. 'I do. I met with him earlier this week and we discussed this very issue.'

"'Are you going to send a car around to 12 Coast Rd now or not? If you don't, I'll have a chat with Mayor Lindsey first thing on Monday morning. And I'm guessing you'll be having a chat about your employment soon after with your boss.'

"'Are you threatening me mam?'

"'No. I'm asking you to do the right thing and send someone over to 12 Coast Rd immediately.'

"Fifty-five-year-old Regina Pratt adjusted her headset and examined her options. She was 10 months away from 20 years on the job and retirement. The last thing she needed was trouble with her boss.

"'I'll send an officer to that address immediately mam. Thank you for your call.'

"'Thank you,' Pamela said. She hung up the phone. 'Jesus Christ. Why does everything have to be so damn difficult?' she asked."

"Three minutes later officers Rick Cartwright and Brett Keating arrived at Coast Rd and parked their marked car across the street from number 12. It was just after 7pm. The sun had set an hour earlier. The streetlights had come on although several were not working. No other cars were parked in the street. They were all in their respective driveways or front lawns, some without registration plates or tyres. Cartwright and Keating got out of their car and walked across the street. 'It's pretty quiet,' Cartwright told his younger partner. 'I reckon we got here before the women's ex.'

"A neighbour's dog barked at them from an adjoining yard as they approached the front door. Just as Cartwright was about to knock, there was a screech of car tyres. Cartwright and Keating turned around just in time to see a battered old Holden Commodore smash into the front end of their new Kia Stinger. 'Son of a bitch,' Keating yelled. 'We've only had the car for three weeks.'

"Cartwright ran to the Commodore to check on the condition of the driver. Walter Schmucker was bleeding from a large cut on his forehead. Empty beer bottles were strewn across the front seats. Cartwright tried to open the driver's side door but couldn't and motioned for Schmucker to try the passenger side door.

"Schmucker slid out of the Commodore and steadied himself with his left hand. A bottle of XXXX beer, Queensland's finest, was in his right hand. The stench coming off Schmucker was worse than the anti-freeze and burning oil pouring out of both vehicles. The airbags had deployed in the Kia. The ancient Commodore had come off the assembly line well before airbags had been made mandatory.

"Cartwright grabbed the bottle out of Schmucker's hand and put it on the curb. 'Do you realise you were driving on the wrong side of the road and that you are drunk?' Cartwright asked.

"Schmucker tried to steady himself and started walking across the street to No. 12. Gloria Schmucker poked her head through her living room curtains and saw her ex staggering across the road. 'Where is that bitch? I'm going to kill her,' he screamed.

"Cartwright took him by the arm and spun him around. 'Who are you going to kill?'

"'My fucking wife, that's who. Now get your hands off me,' Schmucker yelled.

"That was all Cartwright needed to hear. He tossed Schmucker onto his stomach and pushed his face against the pavement while Keating handcuffed him. 'Well, we better not put him into the car. The thing could catch on fire. On the other hand ... Set him on the curb,' Cartwright said. 'I'll call it in.'

"'Car 3624 here on Coast Rd. We're going to need a replacement car, two tow trucks and the fire department.'

"'Yup. That's right. A replacement car. Some drunken arsehole rammed into us. Keating and I are okay. The bloody car is ruined though. A complete write-off I'd say.'

"People started pouring out of their homes to see what was going on just as a fire truck came racing down the street. Three firemen hosed both vehicles down and sprayed foam on the leaking oil and anti-freeze.

"The only person to stay inside her home was Gloria Schmucker. She was holding two-year-old Sam close to her chest with her right arm when Cartwright knocked on her door. Her blonde hair was pulled back from her face. Her eyes were red and damp with tears.

"'Mrs Schmucker? Is that your ex-husband we have handcuffed?' Cartwright asked.

"She took a look. 'It is. Thank goodness you are here. He said he was coming over to kill me and take little Sam.'

"'You don't have to worry. Your first name is?'

"'Gloria.'

"'You don't have to worry about him anymore Gloria. He'll be going away for a while. He's about four times over the legal limit and I'm guessing this is not the first time he's been caught drinking and driving.'

"'You mean we are safe?'

"'For now, yes. Does your ex-husband have any family or friends you know of who might want to harm you and your boy? Sam is his name?'

"'Yes, Sam is his name.'

"*Sam Schmucker. Oh boy. This poor kid is not going to have it easy,* Cartwright thought. Cartwright ruffled the lad's hair. He was busy sucking on his thumb. His Spiderman T-shirt had chocolate stains which he picked at with his free hand.

"'I don't think anyone will come after us,' Gloria Schmucker said. 'His family, and even the few drunks he hangs around with keep him at arm's length.'

"'Someone from social services will be here within the hour to see if you need anything, okay? For now, just stay inside until this mess is cleaned up.'

"'I will. He didn't say anything about me or Sam, did he?'

"'No mam. He was rambling on about his car and his broken bottles of beer.'"

"Several minutes later a squad car came and took Walter Schmucker to the station. He first tossed his cookies in the street and then refused to get in. It took three officers to throw him into the backseat. He was later charged with harassment, violation of a restraining order, drink driving, several road violations and driving with an expired license and registration. Bail was denied and he was remanded until his trial.

"Cartwright and Keating stayed at the scene until the two damaged cars were towed away and the whole mess was cleaned up. A squad car arrived soon after and picked the pair up. They still had four hours left on their shift.

"Six weeks later Schmucker was convicted on all counts.

"Judge Michael Webber asked Schmucker if he had anything to say before he passed sentence.

"'Nope,' Schmucker answered.

"The no-nonsense judge then sentenced him to 60 months in jail. 'Consider yourself lucky Mr Schmucker. You've got a record as long as my pecker. If it was up to me I'd lock you up for twice as long.' He motioned to one of the court officers. 'Take this piece of human garbage out of my courtroom,' he yelled."

The blokes around the table laughed.

"Imagine having a job dealing with shit like that and for shit wages too," Mulligan said. He got up, walked to the bar and ordered another pitcher of beer.

Delaney joined him, if only to stretch his legs.

"Did all that really happen?" Delaney asked.

"Most of it. I embellished it a bit."

"Geez. I guess no matter how bad you think you have it, there's always someone worse off."

Delaney then told him about how he lost his retirement money and Judy Seymour's disappearance.

"That's bloody awful Gary. If there's anything I can do mate, if you need a few grand, anything, let me know, okay? I've got plenty stashed away. I won't even miss it."

Delaney thanked Warren for his offer. "I'm okay for now as long as that horse of mine keeps finishing in the money. But down the track I'll have to go on Newstart until the pension kicks in."

"Too Hard being prepared for another run in the Melbourne Cup?"

"That's the target. Third time lucky, eh?"

No matter how hard Delaney tried to put thieving Judy Seymour out of his mind, she just wouldn't go away. Since he hadn't heard a word from Detective Bellamy, Delaney decided to take things into his own hands.

He rang Duckworth and told him he was taking a holiday and would be unavailable for about 10 days. When you're a volunteer, and a good one at that, you're always welcomed back. And that's what would happen when he returned.

"Where you headed?" Duckworth asked.

"The Sunshine Coast. I've got some business to attend to down there. I'll ring you when I get back."

Later that afternoon Delaney softly knocked on Barbara Stevenson's door. "I'm over here Gary," she said from her balcony. Delaney looked up and moved a few steps to his right. "Sorry to bother you Barbara but I just wanted to tell you I'll be going away for a week or so. Would you mind picking up the paper each morning and emptying my mailbox of any circulars? They pile up quickly."

It was the first time they had spoken in close to eight weeks.

Delaney could have rung the local newsagent and told them not to deliver his paper for a week, but he didn't want anyone to know his unit would be unoccupied for a week and free to be burgled.

"I'll do that for you Gary. Where are you going if you don't mind me asking?"

"To the Sunshine Coast. I've got some business to attend to."

"I see. Does it involve that women you've been keeping company with?"

"It does."

"You still seeing her?"

"No. She took off without saying a word."

"Sorry to hear that Gary," Barbara said although she was as pleased as punch the woman was out of the picture.

Delaney took a few moments to respond.

"It's a long story."

Barbara's curiosity got the better of her and she asked Gary to come in and have a seat on the balcony next to her.

Over the next 30 minutes Delaney told Barbara every sordid detail.

"I'm so sorry Gary. Really, I am. I wouldn't wish that on anybody. But at least you still have some money and the government pension in a few years time. It's not like you'll be forced out onto the street."

Delaney filled his former lover in on his travel plans and told her he would be leaving the next morning.

"Do you want some company? I'd be happy to go with you and help you find her. Separate beds though," she said.

Delaney laughed. "Thanks for the offer Barb but this is something I need to do on my own. I'll send you a message now and then to let you know how I'm going."

"Are you driving or flying?"

"I'm going to drive. The cost of airline tickets and a rental car are about the same on what I'll spend on petrol and overnight accommodation on the way down and back."

"Makes sense. Just be careful, okay?"

"I will," Delaney said as he got up. "I'll show myself out."

45

THAT NIGHT DELANEY PACKED A BAG WITH ENOUGH clothing to last for 10 days. He filled a much smaller bag the next morning with his meds, toiletries and all-important nasal spray.

He was out the door just after 7am. He took the *Cairns Examiner* with him so he had something to read when he stopped for lunch. He filled the SUV with petrol at the first service station he saw and took off, following the signs to Townsville.

On his second night on the road, Delaney bought a road map of Queensland at a small petrol station and circled several places he thought Judy Seymour may have fled to. He felt like a fisherman searching for a bite on a massive lake without a fish finder. Finding Judy would be like trying to land the one fish tagged by the organisers of a bass fishing tournament. But time was on his side. There was no countdown clock to worry about.

He plotted a path to the Gold Coast, avoiding Brisbane entirely.

It's too busy for her in Brisbane. One of those fancy apartment buildings on Broadbeach with a view of the ocean; that would be a good place to start, he thought. *There's plenty of shopping and lord knows she loves to shop.*

On a clear, sparkling winter afternoon two days later he pulled into Broadbeach. He found an older style motel for $110 a night just a mere two blocks from the ocean. It boasted that it had a three-star rating. It was basic but clean. On Friday and Saturday nights the same room went for $175. He unpacked and started his search at a nearby Officeworks. He needed help since he had no idea how to print photos from his phone.

An Officeworks employee came to his rescue. Within two minutes several crystal-clear images of Judy popped out of a printer. Delaney then handed a uni-aged sales assistant a business card that Detective Bellamy had given him and asked if he could print off 500 of them.

"Wouldn't you know it I forgot to have the station print these out for me and I'm down to just half a dozen." The kid looked at the card and nodded his head. "I can do that for you Detective."

Delaney had a peak at the kid's name tag which was pinned to the left pocket of his blue Officeworks polo shirt

"Much appreciate it Jake, and if you could, replace the mobile number on it with this one. I got another phone last month, one I use for the job only. I don't want anyone calling me on my personal mobile anymore." Delaney wrote down the number on the back of one of the cards and handed it to Jake.

"Give me 15 minutes and I'll get it sorted for you."

Delaney had a look around the massive store while he waited. *A new laptop would be nice, but there's no sense throwing away another $450,* he thought.

Fifteen minutes later he spotted Jake out of the corner of his eye motioning for him to come to the printing area.

"All done Detective. How do they look?"

Delaney looked at the card Jake handed him. A perfect job.

"Outstanding Jake. Terrific work. Thanks."

"Anything else I can help you with?"

"Nope. That will do it. Ring me up."

Delaney tapped his debit card on the bank-issued machine by the register, took his box of cards and photos of Judy and stepped away from the register before turning back. "One last thing Jake."

The blood quickly rushed from Jake Newlin's face. Before starting his shift he had bought several joints from a mate on the beach. They were in his front pocket. *If he busts me I'm fucked,* Newlin thought.

Delaney held up one of the photos of Judy. "Has this woman been in this store?"

Newlin looked at it carefully. "She doesn't look familiar. Want me to ask any of the others?"

"Good idea. How about that greeter at the front door? The bloke in the tie. He sees everyone come in and out."

"His name is Donald Lansdown and he works here full time," Newlin said.

Delaney sidled over to him. "Excuse me Donald. Have you seen this woman come into the store?" Delaney asked.

He handed Lansdown a photo. "Take your time. Look it over carefully."

"Someone like her I would notice. She's gorgeous. But I'm sorry, I haven't seen her. Is she in trouble?"

"Something like that. If you see her, give me a call will you?"

Delaney handed Lansdown one of his freshly printed cards and walked out into the blazing sunshine. *Impersonating a detective. Couldn't be more than a misdemeanour, could it?* he wondered.

Delaney drove down Broadbeach Blvd with the windows open. Unlike Cairns there was hardly any humidity. He parked at the dazzling Broadbeach Surf Lifesaving Club, put on his blue and orange New York Mets baseball cap and had a brief walk on the massive beach before having a late lunch. A few surfers tackled the small waves while kids played in the sand, their heads covered by large white hats, their faces covered in sunscreen.

With its stunning view of the beach, the dining area of the surf lifesaving club was packed. Many were done eating and were finishing off their meals with wines and coffees. Delaney ordered a burger, chips and a beer at the bar and waited for an older couple to leave their table before he pounced on it. A cheerful waitress brought him his meal. He took his time eating it.

The Gold Coast has its detractors, but I've got to say, so far I'm impressed, Delaney thought as he looked at the blue-green waters of the Coral Sea through the ceiling to floor, spotlessly clean glass window.

Judy could do a lot worse. With all the tourists coming and going this would be a good place to start a new life. I doubt the folks working here would see customers more than once.

Remembering why he was there Delaney got a wriggle on and began checking out the massive skyscrapers along the beach. Apartments in the better towers went for a minimum of half a million dollars. Top floor penthouses were more than a million. He ducked into several towers and asked a few people waiting for elevators in the luxurious lobbies and by the meticulously landscaped pools if they had seen the woman in the photo he held. None had. Strike one.

It was closing in on 4pm when Delaney pulled into the huge and upscale Pacific Fair Shopping Centre. He started walking down the long corridors which were full of perfectly coiffed women carrying bags from the centre's high-end shops. Heels and heavy make-up were the norm. He glanced twice at several women who were about the same height and weight as Judy but on closer look they had different features. As some stores started closing their front shudders at 5pm, Delaney made his way back to the parking lot. It took him a while to find his car. It reminded him of trying to locate his old Holden after an AFL game at Waverley Park, but without the mud.

He drove back to his motel, showered and watched the TV news from Brisbane while he dressed and got ready for dinner.

His last stop for the day was the Star Gold Coast Casino. According to a pamphlet he got at the motel office, the casino offered world-class dining along with gaming and five-star accommodation. Delaney put on his navy-blue sports jacket, his best pair of pants and a recently laundered long sleeved shirt and drove to the casino. Valet parking was out of his price range and with no one to impress, he parked in one of the casino's many lots which surprisingly were nearly full on a weeknight.

Seymour was not a gambler, although she took a risk absconding with his funds, so Delaney walked right past the noisy pokie machines and table games on his way to the restaurants. He ducked past the young hostess at the upscale Italian restaurant, telling her he was late for a dinner engagement. Delaney looked around the elegant dining room but again did not find anyone who resembled Judy.

Next stop was a fancy Japanese restaurant. Delaney waited in a long line and latched onto a large party which had a reservation for 12 people. He walked with the group and glanced at every table. When they sat down, he kept walking. He eventually was stopped by an older waiter.

"Can I help you sir?"

"You sure can. Which way are the toilets?"

"Over in the right-hand corner sir."

Delaney thanked the waiter and slowly walked to the toilets. He spun his head to the left, then to the right and nearly collided with another waiter. On his way back from the toilets he took a different route to the exit but again none of the women at any of the many tables or at the bar looked familiar.

Damn. I knew this was a long shot at best, but it's getting a little discouraging. Might as well get something to eat while I'm here.

Delaney splurged for a meal at the casino's buffet. "One please," he told the cashier after the long line he was in started to move.

"That's $32.50 sir," the cashier said.

"Seniors card make a difference in the price?"

"Maybe somewhere else, but not here," she said.

A buffet was not the sort of place that Judy would frequent but Delaney had a look around anyway as he filled his plate, not once but twice. Unlike others who packed their plates with something from every hot and cold tray and left half of it which had to be thrown out, Delaney ate everything he took.

He ordered a beer, which set him back an even $40 for the night. "Oh well, got to treat myself every so often." Delaney had two pieces of strawberry shortcake topped with ice cream for dessert. "It was worth every cent," he said. He loosened his belt a notch, left his table and walked to the exit. Again, after a good look around, there was no sign of Judy Seymour.

Delaney took out his Queensland road map when he returned to his motel room. He figured out the distance to stop number two – Bribie Island – and noted that even if he checked out at 10am he'd still arrive there before lunch.

Before getting on the M1 and travelling north, Delaney filled up his trusty Honda with petrol, setting him back another $55. Traffic was on the moderate side as he passed Brisbane. Half an hour later, just before Caboolture, he took the exit for Bribie Island and headed east.

Home to more than 20,000 people, Bribie Island is a popular holiday spot for Brisbanites and tourists. Nearly a third of the island is a national park but the Island's amenities are so spread out that one hardly ever feels crowded. With bush camping and walking, boating, fishing, a gorgeous golf course and some of the most amazing beaches in Australia, there is plenty to do. Delaney figured he'd stay one night and tried the local caravan park first. Luck was on his side. One cabin was left, for $155, and he took it. The park's manager was nice enough to let him check in well before the standard time of 2pm. He unpacked his lone suitcase, put his toiletries in the bathroom and drove to the island's main shopping centre. Looking to save some coin, especially after shelling out $40 on dinner the night before, Delaney went to Woolies for lunch. He bought a few slices of ham, a long white roll and a can of Diet Coke. The damage was $6. He took a seat on a bench outside and as he ate he tallied up how much he had already spent. Between petrol, accommodation and food, it was north of $1000.

An expensive fishing expedition, but Delaney knew he wouldn't catch anything if he didn't toss a line or two in the water. He spent the afternoon slowly driving through the Island's nicer areas looking for a nibble. Several women were tending to their front gardens but again none resembled Judy. He stopped at the post office, showed Judy's photo to one of the locals who worked behind the counter and asked if she had seen her. The answer was no. He browsed around the shops and looked at the homes advertised in the windows of four real estate offices. He went into all of them, showed Judy's photo, and asked if anyone had shown her a home. Again, the answer was no. He left his card with the receptionist at each office and asked them to get in touch with him immediately if someone fitting her description showed up.

They promised they would, but Delaney figured his card would wind up in the nearest bin before the end of the day. He pulled into the local medical centre and then the local dentist. He went through the same drill and again came up empty. Running out of options, Delaney pulled into the parking lot of Target which was the island's most upscale store. He had a look around and felt like a perv as he went up and down each isle of the women's section. Jokingly, he asked a mannequin if it had seen the woman in the photo he held up to it. "Nothing? You sure? Take another look."

Delaney went back to Woolies, bought a six-pack of Corona, a pre-cooked chook, a tub of potato salad, the local paper and went back to his cabin. He took one bottle out, put the remaining five in the fridge, and sat in one of the two green plastic chairs on the balcony which was shaded by several large and sturdy gum trees. It was nice and quiet, just as he liked it. He read the paper until dinner time. The chook was still warm when he tucked into it. *Not on a par with last night's meal but good enough,* he thought. He washed it down with another beer, watched a bit of ABC24, unfurled his road map and planned the next part of his trip.

At his property near Kerang, trainer Vern Baker feared the worst as veterinarian Hugo Z Hackenbush examined Sun-Up's swollen right foreleg.

"I'm pretty sure he's bowed a tendon, but let's give him a scan just to make sure."

Baker kicked the dry dirt outside Sun-Up's stall. "I was afraid of that. The best horse I've ever trained, and he'll never run again," Baker said. "Fuck. Why didn't I take the money from those two yahoos who wanted to take him to Hong Kong?"

Baker and his wife owned the majority share in Sun-Up. Kerang businessmen Nick Marino and Dale Mullins owned 45 per cent of the galloper and wanted to accept the $250,000 offer but was knocked back by Baker just two weeks earlier.

"I've raised this fella since he was a day old. He's like a son to me. I can't sell him. We'll make plenty more than $250,000 once he starts racing in the city," Baker promised.

But one morning on the same grass covered course he had jogged hundreds of time, Sun-Up took a bad step while being exercised by regular jockey and track rider Leonard Hawley and slowed to a crawl. Hawley jumped off Sun-Up's back, checked the front foreleg which the horse was favouring and slowly walked him back to his stall.

Baker put the injured foot in a bucket of ice to try and reduce the swelling, gave the horse a dose of an anti-inflammatory and got Hackenbush on the phone.

A scan at a nearby equine hospital confirmed Hackenbush's diagnosis. "I've seen worse," he told Baker. "He'll need at least six to nine months rest before we can even think of putting him back in work."

"What would you do if you owned him?" Baker asked.

"I'd find a couple of nice broodmares and see if he can pass on that speed of his. If he can get himself a few winners from his first crop, he could develop into a valuable stallion."

"I suppose so," Baker answered. "I don't want to take the chance of racing him again and having him break down on me. You'll send me the bill?"

"I will. You can pay in instalments if you have to Vern."

"No need."

Hackenbush drove off to his next appointment leaving Baker alone with his three-year-old colt. He stroked Sun-Up's neck and fed him a couple of carrots. "A stallion's life is a pretty-good one pal. You rest up now and let those meds do their job, okay?"

Hawley was mucking out a nearby stall when Baker gave him the bad news on the end of Sun-Up's racing days. "Go keep an eye on him, would you please? I've got to talk to my misses and then have a word with Marino and Mullin."

Maybe I can buy them out, Baker thought. *Toss 'em five or 10 grand each. They might jump at that.*

Delaney left Bribie Island before eight the next morning. He started his Honda and was about to leave when he remembered the three bottles of beers in the fridge. He retrieved them, put them into a cool bag he kept in the back seat and dropped his key off at reception. The SUV was just one of a handful of vehicles going over the bridge back to the mainland. Traffic the other way was rather heavy with families going away for the weekend and buses full of overseas tourists coming over for the day. He got back on the M1, having missed the Friday morning rush and headed north to the Sunshine Coast. The nice seaside town of Caloundra would be his first stop. The surf was much rougher than it was at Bribie Island. Numerous apartment buildings, most no more than six or eight stories high, dotted the shore and gave its occupants magnificent views of waves crashing onto the rocks and beaches from their balconies.

Delaney found a place to park and walked up and down Caloundra's main drag. He stopped at the post office, the largest chemist and a cafe where he had a coffee and a blueberry muffin and again showed Judy's picture. No one had seen her. *It's not all bad,* he said in a bid to cheer himself up. *I'm having a bit of a holiday and there are still places to look.*

He checked out the apartment buildings on the four main beaches: Kings, Shelly, Moffat and Dicky, and asked several people heading in and out of them if they had seen the woman in the photo he handed them. A couple of men commented on her good looks, but no one thought she looked familiar.

Back in his SUV, Delaney picked up Route 6 and headed north, hugging the coast until he arrived in Noosa two hours later.

"This is my last roll of the dice. She's got money and Noosa is where the money is," he said. With accommodation in Noosa well out of his price range, he pulled into a nice caravan park in the small town of Tewantin which had its vacancy sign turned on. It was just a five-minute drive from Hastings St and the heart of Noosa.

"I'm looking for a cabin for two nights," he told the woman at the reception desk. The collared polo shirt she was wearing had the name of the park on it.

Delaney learned the next day that the woman, who he guessed was in her early 50s, ran the place with her second husband and lived on the premises. Earl Sloane could fix anything and saved the couple hundreds of dollars each month that otherwise would have wound up in the pockets of plumbers, electricians and handymen. She put on a pair of reading glances, sat down and glanced at her computer screen.

"Today's your lucky day. Usually we're full up on weekends but we had a cancellation via email first thing this morning."

"I'll take it," Delaney said.

He parted with \$350 – weekend rates – filled out a card with his details and was handed the key to cabin 9 and a map of the park.

"You're welcome to check in now if you like Mr Delaney. "The cabin was cleaned earlier."

"Thank you so much. I'm sorry. I didn't catch your name."

The woman pointed to her name tag which somehow Delaney forgot to notice.

Georgia it read.

How the fuck am I ever going to find Judy if I can't even see the woman's damn name badge? he thought. Delaney carefully backed into the spot next to cabin 9. Small, but full, palm trees were on either side of the cabin. *Old man Sloane is one hell of a gardener,* he thought.

He put his three remaining bottles of beer in the fridge, unpacked, aired out the cabin and had a walk around the park. According to the park map he was given by Georgia Sloane, the Noosa River was a short walk away. Near reception was a good-sized, heated pool. He checked his watch. It was 1:30. He drove into town for a bite to eat, had a look around and stopped at the local bakery where he bought a chicken and vegetable pie and a Diet Coke. He ate it at one of the tables outside and gave it a pass mark.

He noticed a hotel across Poinciana Ave and pencilled it in for that night's meal. A Woolies anchored the shopping area. *I'll go in there and get a few things after dinner. The only thing I'm doing this afternoon is unwinding at the pool.*

Back at his cabin, Delaney put on the one pair of bathers he packed, a short-sleeved shirt, plunked a hat on his head and grabbed a towel off the double bed in the main bedroom.

He opened the gate to the pool and the first thing he noticed was how crystal clear the pool water was. He nodded to several mums and dads who were watching over their kids.

He found an empty lounge chair on the far side of the pool, removed his runners and dipped his toes in the water. It was nice and warm. He placed his towel on the chair and like the older man he was, used the steps in the shallow end to get in. His days of cannonballs and diving were well behind him. Delaney swam a couple of easy laps in the deeper end away from the young kids who stayed in the shallow end of the pool. When he was through, he dried himself off, adjusted the wooden chair to his liking, picked up its cushion which was on the ground, and stretched out under an umbrella to enjoy the perfect 26-degree afternoon. He took a selfie with his phone and sent the image and a note to Barbara back in Cairns. *Poolside in Noosa. No luck locating Judy on the Gold Coast. Staying here two nights then heading home. See you in a few.*

Towards the end of the afternoon Delaney was the only one left at the pool. He checked his watch which he had tucked in his runners while he swam. It was 4:45. He collected his things and dodged several kids on their bikes on the way back to his cabin. An older fellow in the cabin across the small road from Delaney waved from his chair.

"How long you staying?" he asked.

"Two nights. And you?"

"A week. Visiting the grandkids. Better to stay here on me own than with my daughter and her husband."

The parking space by the fellow's cabin was empty. The old-timer saw Delaney looking around for a car.

"I don't drive any more," he said. "My daughter picked me up from the airport and she's coming to get me soon for dinner. They live in Noosa."

"Where are you from?" Delaney asked.

"What'd ya say?" the man said cupping his right ear.

"I asked where you're from?"

"Ah. Western Sydney. The same place where that football team nobody gives a rat's arse about is."

"The Giants."

"That's them."

"You been to a game?"

"Nah. Too hard for me to get to and they play at night. Too bloody cold at night. I watch 'em on the TV."

"Well, we can't complain about the weather today. It is perfect."

"That it is."

Delaney wanted to wrap things up without hurting the old man's feelings, so he walked over to him and put his hand out.

"Gary," he said. Good to meet you."

"Clement. Same here."

"You'll have to excuse me. I have a few calls to make and need to take a shower. Have a good night with the grandkids."

"Thanks mate. See you in the morning," Clement said.

By the time Delaney showered, dressed and watched a bit of the news on ABC24, Clement was no longer sitting outside. The lights in his cabin were off. His daughter must have come and picked him up.

Delaney went to the local pub for dinner. He ordered a parma with chips and salad, a beer, and ate in the near-empty bar area instead of the dining room. Harness and dog races were being shown on two wide screen TVs. He hadn't bet on a dog or harness race in years and when a $1.10 shot failed to run a place despite breaking from the inside box at The Meadows in Melbourne, he thought of all the money he had saved over the journey. Delaney bought a loaf of bread, a tub of butter and a jar of jam at the near-empty Woolies for toast the next two mornings and went back to his cabin.

The next morning, after a breakfast of coffee and toast, Delaney ambled over to the Noosa River. There were several anglers along the shore, some with two and three rods in the water. Delaney looked into the buckets at their feet; no fish, just river water.

He walked about another 30 metres to where a middle-aged fellow and a young lad about nine or 10 were sitting in beach chairs trying their luck. Before he even had a chance to say hello the rod the man had in the water suddenly bent in half. He rose from his chair and grabbed it tight. "We've got something son. Have a go at bringing her in."

The man reeled in some line and handed the rod to the boy, who was jumping out of his skin.

He struggled with whatever was on the other end of the line and handed the rod back to his dad. "How big do you think it is dad?"

"I'd say at least four or five kilos. Grab the net."

The two were in the water up to their knees. After a good fight the fish eventually tired and was visible on the surface. As it was reeled in closer to shore, the boy put a good-sized net under the fish but couldn't lift it out of the water. In fact he could barely budge it. The man handed the rod to his son, took the net and scooped the fish from the water and onto the sand. It was a massive flathead. Delaney could not believe the size of it and neither could the young lad. "Wow, wow," he yelled. "That's the biggest fish I've ever seen."

"We're going to need a bigger barbecue," the man joked as he took the hook out of the monster's mouth.

"How much do you think it weighs?" Delaney asked.

"I'd say close to eight or nine kilos. We'll be eating this for lunch and dinner for the next week."

"Ever catch anything this big before?"

"Not in this river."

Delaney watched the man rebait the rod. He handed it to his son who made a nice cast. The line plopped into the river about 10 metres out. The lad kept his hand on the rod as he stood ankle-deep in the river. Much too big for the buckets he and his dad brought, the flathead needed to be put on ice until they called it a day.

"Would you mind watching my boy for a few minutes while I run and get some ice?" the lad's dad asked Delaney.

"You stay here mate," Delaney said. "I'll get it for you. The caravan park has bags of ice and bait in their freezer. I noticed it yesterday when I checked in."

"That's nice of you," Bob Tomlinson said. He reached for his wallet, but Delaney waved him off. "Don't worry about it. I'll be right back."

Delaney bought two bags of ice and instead of lugging them back to the river, a melting bag in each hand, he put them in the SUV's back seat and drove the 300 or so metres to the end of the street and the river's edge.

He put the ice in a Woolies shopping bag and carried it to where the Tomlinsons were fishing.

"How much they charge you?" Bob Tomlinson asked.

"Five bucks per bag but don't worry about it. It was worth the $10 just to see you land the thing."

Delaney wished the two continued good luck and trekked back to his car. He was gobsmacked the next morning when he turned on the local news and heard that a large bull shark had been spotted in the Noosa River the previous afternoon. *Geez, they were in there up to their knees.*

It was near noon when Delaney drove into Noosa. He parked close to the beach so that if by chance Judy was there, she wouldn't recognise his car. He put on a pair of sunnies and his New York Mets baseball cap and strode to Hastings St and its wall-to-wall cafes and fancy gift shops clad in a pair of beige loafers, tan chinos and a pale blue, long-sleeved shirt.

He ordered a coffee at a cafe in the centre of town and after paying took Judy's photo from his pocket and asked the young lady manning the till if she recognised the woman.

"I was supposed to meet her half an hour ago but got side-tracked. Has she been here?"

The cashier took a good look at the photo. "I'm pretty good with faces but I haven't seen her this morning."

"Thanks anyways," Delaney said. He took a seat outside and watched the parade of the well-off walk past. Not one woman looked like Judy although he remembered that Detective Bellamy said Judy would likely have changed her appearance. After polishing off his coffee, Delaney had a long walk up and down Hastings St. He browsed in several shops and asked another four shopkeepers if they recognised Judy from the photo he showed them. All said they hadn't. "Give me your number," one woman said "and if I see her I'll ring you straight away." Delaney handed her his card but wasn't expecting a call.

With walking paths cutting through native vegetation surrounding the town, a big, wide beautiful beach and the finest restaurants, hotels and gift shops, Noosa is a playground for the rich, not for a Newstart recipient staying at the local caravan park. Delaney tossed away $18 for lunch an hour or two later and took a stroll on the beach before he decided to call it a day.

While he was having a swim back at the caravan park, Diane Bradley was catching the late afternoon TV news in her luxury apartment just eight kilometres away. It was just what she had expected, with a view of the ocean from her living room and the Noosa River from one of the bedrooms. She was leafing through a magazine when she noticed the time: 5:18. It left her an hour to get ready for her dinner engagement with Sue Paice, a woman from her building she had met at the pool a few days after she moved in. They had a reservation at popular Italian restaurant Locale for 6:45pm.

Diane hopped in the shower, shampooed her recently cut, coloured and styled hair and marvelled at her size 10 figure in the large mirror over the twin basins as she dried herself off with a soft towel the size of a bedspread. "Looking good Diane," she said.

She sent Sue a text since she was running late. *I'll meet you at Locale. Grab our table, will you please? We don't want to lose our reservation and be forced to wait.*

Diane Bradley hated being late but knew Sue would understand.

Delaney showered after his dip in the pool and relaxed with a beer on the balcony of his cabin. He had the urge for a wood-fired pizza with the lot and liked the look and menu of Locale from his walk earlier in the day. He put a sports jacket over the same shirt and pants he wore earlier in the day. "Who is going to know?" he asked.

As he slowly drove down Hastings St looking for a place to park, Delaney took notice of a woman in a tight-fitting, cream-coloured dress and a low pair of heels walking past an ice cream shop on the opposite side of the street. It had a line of people waiting to get in.

That sure looks a lot like Judy, he thought. Much to his surprise someone was pulling out of a parking spot on Hastings St. Delaney put on his indicator, waited and gently eased his SUV into the spot. Locale was a couple of blocks away. He put on his baseball cap and followed the woman from the opposite side of the street. She was walking briskly and Delaney had to hustle to catch up. She crossed the street at the next light and Delaney hid behind a massive black limo in order not to be seen and to get a look at the women's face. *Holy shit. I don't believe it. That's her. She dyed her hair blonde but that is definitely her. What are the odds?* he thought.

Delaney stayed well behind the woman, who strode though the open front door to Locale. *This is unfuckingbelievable.*

Delaney whipped out his phone and rang Detective Bellamy.

"I think I've found her," Delaney said excitedly.

"Is that you Gary? Where the heck are you?"

"In Noosa. Judy dyed her hair, but I am pretty sure it's her. She just went into a restaurant named Locale on Hastings St."

"No shit. You're a better detective than the guys I've got looking for her."

"What should I do? Go in and confront her?"

"Not yet mate. Let me ring the locals, explain things to them and see if they can get a car over there. If she just walked in she'll be there for a while even if she is just having a drink."

Delaney paced outside and kept checking his cheap watch. Five minutes passed, then 10. Fifteen minutes later Bellamy rang back.

"They should be there in a minute."

"I see them."

"Good. Have a word with them and ring me back after they have her in custody."

"Will do."

Two officers got out of the squad car they double parked and approached Delaney.

"You Delaney?" the older of the two asked.

"I am. Thanks for getting over here so quickly."

"Detective Bellamy filled us in," Constable Patrick Stockton said.

"I'm actually shocked that I've found her. But it's definitely her. Would you mind if I went in first and approached her? I've been waiting two months for this moment."

Stockton thought it over. "All right. But be careful. Who knows how she'll react."

Stockton glanced at Constable Ryan Malone. "You guard the back entrance. I'll go in two minutes after Mr Delaney and put the cuffs on her. I'll radio you when she's in custody."

Malone nodded, walked to the end of the block and made his way to the back entrance near the kitchen. He sniffed the air. *It sure smells good. I'll have to bring Patty here one night.*

Delaney took off his baseball cap, tucked it in his back pocket, took a deep breath and walked inside. He was met near the front door by the maitre'd.

"Do you have a reservation sir? We are nearly fully booked tonight," Antonio Scaramucchi asked.

"I'm meeting friends."

Delaney looked around and spotted Judy and her dining companion. "There they are," Delaney told Scaramucchi. "I'll go join them."

Before Scaramucchi could get out another word, Delaney was gone. He approached Judy and Sue Paice's table. Judy's back was turned to him. Delaney got to the table, walked past it and then approached it again. He looked Seymour right in the eyes. "Judy? Judy Seymour? Is that you. Been a long time. How the hell are you?"

Delaney gave her a peck on the cheek. "Mind if I join you two?" He took a chair from an adjoining table and sat down.

Judy Seymour nearly chocked on her gin and tonic when Delaney sat down.

"Who's Judy?" Sue Paice asked.

Delaney looked up, saw Constable Stockton standing by the bar and continued.

"New hairdo, eh? And a blonde too? You nearly had me fooled."

"What are you going on about?" Sue Paice asked.

"And a new identity. You really went all out Judy."

Seymour was so stunned she couldn't get a word out.

"Is it Miss, or is it Mrs?" Delaney asked Seymour's dining companion, a petite brunette with a fine figure for a woman in her mid-50s.

"Miss. Miss Sue Paice. Who are you?"

"Tell her Judy. Tell her who I am."

Judy reached into her purse and took out her phone which Delaney grabbed out of her hands.

"Not a good idea Judy. We have company."

He looked over at the bar where Constable Stockton was standing and motioned for him to come to the table.

"Constable, this is Judy Seymour. She's wanted on how many counts?"

"At least half a dozen I'm aware of," Stockton said.

He politely told Judy to get up and then handcuffed her. Judy was shaking as the cuffs went on her wrists.

"What's going on?" Paice asked. "This is Diane Bradley. Not this Judy person you are after."

By this time every eye in the restaurant was on Constable Stockton as he led Seymour from the restaurant in handcuffs. She had her head down and was crying. She hadn't cried this much since the day they lowered her husband into the ground.

Stockton radioed Malone to tell him that the subject was in custody. Malone came into the restaurant from the kitchen and followed Stockton and Seymour to the squad car.

"You're arresting one of my customers?" Antonio Scaramucchi loudly protested. You can't do that. She already ordered. Who's going to pay her bill?"

"Put the bill in the linguini," Stockton said.

"No sense letting all this good food go to waste Miss Paice," Delaney said as the main dishes arrived at Seymour and Paice's table. "It's so hard to get a reservation here."

"I'm not eating dinner with you. Get out of here immediately or I shall call the manager."

"Miss Paice. I suggest you first check your bank accounts and see how much money you have left. Miss Bradley, as you call her, is a shifty one and might have cleaned you out just as she did to me."

Panic filled Paice's face and all but ripped out the sutures from her latest facelift.

Delaney meanwhile tucked into Judy's main course.

"This linguini is fucking fantastic Sue. You going to have any of that lasagne?"

46

THE LINGUINI AND LASAGNE WERE SO GOOD THAT Delaney didn't get around to ringing Detective Bellamy in Cairns until he put away the desserts that came with the meals that Judy Seymour and Sue Paice ordered.

Paice kept peppering Delaney with questions about her friend Diane Bradley which Delaney did his best to answer in between bites of tiramisu and gelato. Paice had not eaten a thing and eventually told Delaney she had close to $250,000 locked away in a term deposit.

"Consider yourself lucky Sue, she could have taken it all. Make sure you check your savings or checking account. She's pretty good at forgery," Delaney said. He picked up his cloth serviette from his lap, dipped an edge into his water glass and carefully wiped his mouth. "I got a legitimate statement from her firm the first month after I turned my money over to her. The next statement four weeks later had a line of zeroes listed next to my balance."

Paice's face nearly fell onto the table. "Oh, my goodness. That's awful."

"I'm guessing my money is in an account in the Cayman Islands or somewhere else in the Caribbean. Those accounts are just about impossible to locate even with the best attorneys and tax men. A word of advice Sue, keep your money in the bank. Don't get involved in any scheme offering a nine or 10 percent return on your money. If you do, you'll wind up in a long line of suckers like yours truly."

"You think there are others she stole from?"

"I'm not sure. I hope it is just a handful."

"Why is that?"

"Because if she is convicted, any assets she has will likely be split amongst those she stole from. Of course, any attorneys or tax accountants we hire will get a slice of the loot too. Probably about a third."

Paice nodded as if she understood, but Delaney had the feeling that everything he told her went in one ear and out the other.

"Do you own your own place here in Noosa Sue?"

"It's in my name, yes."

"Then you are in a lot better shape than I am. I rent a place in Cairns and put just about everything I had in her hands. All I've got to live on is the cash in a savings account I wisely held on to."

"Geez. She really cleaned you out."

"She sure did. It was my fault. I let my dick do my thinking for me."

Paice blushed at the mention of the word dick.

"Sorry about the colourful language."

There was a pause in the conversation. Finally, Sue spoke up.

"You really fell for her? Didn't you?"

"I did. It was all part of her plan Sue, all part of her plan."

Delaney knocked back the rest of Seymour's second gin and tonic which was brought to the table after she was frog-marched out of the restaurant.

"You've known her for how long? Six weeks, eight?" he asked.

"About that."

"I'm curious Sue. Did she ever mention my name? Even in passing?"

"She said she had been seeing someone before she moved here but said there had been a falling out."

"That's a kind way of putting it," Delaney said. "What she did was take off one night without telling a soul, changed her name and started a new life for herself. I was an idiot to think I could have been a part of her life. I should have seen through her. But ..."

Delaney shifted in his chair and was about to get up and walk out. But he had one more question.

"You live in the same building with her?" Delaney asked.

"Yes. We met in the lobby one morning and became friends. We both like to shop and eat out."

"If you don't mind me asking what's your apartment worth?"

"About $625,000."

"Is it similar to Judy's?"

"Just about. The only difference is the better view. Her apartment is two stories above mine."

And worth another $35,000 or so Delaney thought.

Delaney checked his jacket pocket but couldn't find the pen he thought he had put there.

"Do you have a pen on your Sue? I could keep you informed on Judy's case if you like."

Sue Paice searched her handbag and found one. Delaney handed her one of his cards. She jotted her number and address on the back of it and handed it back to Delaney. He tucked the card in his wallet and got up from his chair.

"Thanks for dinner Sue. I'm quite destitute so you'll have to pick up the cheque. I'll be in touch. Cheers."

Delaney scampered out of the restaurant, dodged the crowd of diners still waiting in line to get in and walked the couple of blocks to where he had parked. Hastings St was buzzing, but Delaney was mentally exhausted. He slumped into the driver's seat, took out his phone and rang Detective Bellamy in Cairns.

"She's in the hands of the Noosa police," he said.

JUDY SEYMOUR WAS SENT BACK TO FAR NORTH QUEENS-
land to stand trial on 10 counts with the most serious being embezzle-
ment, grand larceny and fraud. After a two-week jury trial in which
Delaney and one other victim testified, Seymour was found guilty on all
counts and sentenced to serve eight to 12 years at a minimum-security
prison.

Delaney kept Sue Paice informed every step of the way. "Did she
show any remorse at all, make an attempt to talk to you?"

"No on both counts Sue. I thought maybe when she saw me she would
show some emotion, but there was nothing, nothing at all."

"I'm sorry Gary. It must hurt."

"It does, but I'll have to move on and try and forget about it."

"If I can be of any help, let me know, okay? You've got an open
invitation to come to Noosa and visit. Not every woman out there is
after a bloke's money."

Judy Seymour was released from prison after five and a half years by
an all-male parole board for good behaviour.

One afternoon two weeks after her release, Mary Hackett, the
wife of parole board head Dennis Hackett, came home and found
her 52-year-old husband in their bed being ridden and whipped by a
naked Judy Seymour. During the commotion, Seymour absconded
with Hackett's wallet and Mrs Hackett's purse. Hours later, after the
Hacketts finally stopped screaming and threatening each other with
lawyers, they realised they had been robbed. They cancelled their credit
and debit cards but not before Seymour had racked up thousands of

dollars of bills at several shops at Cairns Central. She was asked time and time again if she wanted any cash out and ended up with nearly $3000 in $50 notes and a one-way airline ticket to the Gold Coast where she used her considerable charm, long legs and cleavage to secure a job in the money room at the casino.

A court ordered that proceeds from the sale of Seymour's Noosa apartment, its furnishings, her luxury car and two wardrobes full of high-priced clothing – just over $725,000 in total – be distributed to the three parties who Seymour had deceived and robbed: Mr Gary Delaney of Cairns, retiree Charles Blackmore of Port Douglas and an old-timer named Herman Melton of Palm Cove. Melton, 82, was the scheme's guinea pig and had lost too many marbles to be an effective witness. A conniving lawyer did all his talking for him. None of the money the three invested was able to be located and recovered. Delaney lost close to $400,000, Blackmore half of his $250,000 investment and Melton nearly $175,000. After the lawyers took their hefty cut, Delaney was given a cheque for $195,000 and Blackmore a cheque for $100,000. Melton's cut was $75,000, which went directly into a local nursing home's account where he spent the rest of his days asking staff members when Judy was coming to visit him.

Happy to see any money come his way, let alone $195,000, Delaney and Barbara Stevenson eventually found a nice ground-floor rental in a gated apartment complex in Trinity Beach and moved in together. Two months later Stevenson tossed Delaney out after she found explicit text messages and nude pictures of Sue Paice on his phone. At the bequest of Ms Paice, he moved down to Noosa and took up residence in her apartment.

He became a member of Noosa Golf Club where he carded a hole-in-one on the 131-metre-long 12th hole in just his fourth time playing the picturesque and crocodile-free course.

Later in the clubhouse after buying a round of drinks as tradition dictates, Delaney was asked by 70-year-old Chuck O'Rourke, one of the members of his foursome, why he moved to Noosa.

He took his phone out, fiddled with it for a few seconds and handed it to O'Rourke.

"Damn," O'Rourke shouted as he looked at photo of a topless Sue Paice.

"Sometimes it pays to listen to your pecker," Delaney joked before turning serious. "Just watch where you put your money."

ACKNOWLEDGEMENTS

Special thanks to Kerry Russell, Simon McEvoy, David Turner, Brad Beitzel, Professor Quincy Adams Wagstaff, Dr Hugo Z Hackenbush and the Forty South team of Lucinda Sharp, Kent Whitmore and Rayne Allinson for their support, suggestions and encouragement.

—Marty Shevelove
Cairns, July 2022